MW00472811

"A chilling tale that k
dering its truths. *The*
Blumer's bibliography, ... o. thrillers with spiritual
depth will find much to enjoy."

—C. J. DARLINGTON
author of *Thicker than Blood* and *Bound by Guilt*

"Suspense of biblical proportions! Adam Blumer does a masterful job transforming the biblical plagues to a modern-day scenario full of twists and turns that will keep you riveted until the very end."

—BONNIE S. CALHOUN
publisher of *Christian Fiction Online Magazine*,
author of the Stone Braide Chronicles

"Adam Blumer writes a suspenseful story with a passion for God not often seen in today's marketplace."

—CRESTON MAPES
bestselling Christian fiction thriller author of
Fear Has a Name, *Dark Star*, and *Full Tilt*

"*The Tenth Plague* delivers a compelling premise of a Bible/Qur'an hybrid sparking controversy and murder that will thrill readers of clean Christian fiction!"

—BRYN JONES
author of *The Next Chapter*

"An intriguing premise with suspense that will keep you on the edge of your seat. Blumer's crafted a great thriller in *The Tenth Plague*."

—GRAHAM GARRISON
author of *Hero's Tribute* and *Legacy Road*

9/24/2016
R.L.S.

"Adam Blumer's *The Tenth Plague* sweeps an ordinary couple into a current of extraordinary events—all with a mentally deranged man calling the shots. Here's a novel that will keep you wondering what can possibly go wrong next!"

—RICK BARRY
author of *The Methuselah Project*

"An almost-forgotten mine disaster, a misguided conference on Bible translation, a twisted take on the book of Revelation, a botched ATF-FBI operation, a gifted autistic child—Adam Blumer has woven these strands and more into a page-turning tapestry of a mystery. You won't want to lay this one aside till the author has tied up all the loose ends."

—RICHARD C. LEONARD
coauthor of *Heart of the Highriders*

"Adam Blumer weaves an unlikely combination of characters with a plot that will keep you guessing in an intriguing novel that speaks to the heart. I appreciate Adam's distinctively Christian viewpoint that challenges the characters to live in an ethical way that honors Christ. "

—DEB BRAMMER
author of *Edges of Truth* and *Broken Windows*

"From the first riveting scene until my satisfied sigh at the conclusion, I could not put *The Tenth Plague* down. Memorable characters, endless twists and turns, and a message of hope woven into the fabric of the story make Adam's Blumer's novel unforgettable suspense."

—SUSAN LAWRENCE
author of *Atonement for Emily Adams*,
winner of the Grace Award for
Women's Fiction/General Fiction

THE TENTH PLAGUE

ADAM BLUMER

THE TENTH PLAGUE

ADAM BLUMER

KIRKDALE PRESS

The Tenth Plague

Kirkdale Press, 1313 Commercial St., Bellingham, WA 98225
Visit us at KirkdalePress.com or follow us on Twitter at @KirkdalePress

Print ISBN 9781577996880
Digital ISBN 9781577997146

Kirkdale Editorial: Elizabeth Vince, Abigail Stocker
Cover Design: Jim LePage
Back Cover Design: Liz Donovan
Typesetting: ProjectLuz.com

For my father,
Larry Dean Blumer
June 7, 1940–August 17, 2011

Greatly loved, sorely missed
Finally at peace

*"Each morning puts a man on trial
and each evening passes judgment."*
—Roy L. Smith

*"There is therefore now no condemnation
to those who are in Christ Jesus."*
—Romans 8:1

PROLOGUE

—*November 3, 1926*
Near Ishpeming, Michigan

On the morning from his worst nightmares, 22-year-old Rutherford Wills woke early, the frigid world outside his window still dark, and slipped noiselessly out of bed to avoid waking Bruna, his wife of only two months. He hated to leave her side, her warm body close to his, but he was a married man now with obligations to fulfill and bills to pay.

God granted no clues that this day would be different from any other.

Wills reported for the day shift at the Barnes-Hecker Mine and entered the crowded electric elevator or "cage" for the ride down the 1,060-foot shaft to the second level. It was 7:20 a.m. on a Wednesday.

As Wills descended into the earth, he wondered what life on the surface would be like today. Now that Halloween was past, the weather had turned cold. Were the early snow predictions true? Would he later rise to a world of white?

At 800 feet, the elevator jerked to a halt, and Wills followed a dozen trammers, stemmers, timbermen, and pumpmen into the second of three levels. His hard hat's carbide lamp chased away subterranean shadows, and the ever-present aroma of damp earth filled his nostrils. In the distance echoed the staccato blows of pneumatic drills, the hiss of compressed air, and the rumble of explosives.

He followed the pebbly corridor toward the electric locomotive that pulled cars loaded with iron ore down the 3,000-foot tunnel to the main shaft. There they were emptied through chutes into a "skip" or cable car that raised the ore to the surface.

Wills took his seat at what everyone referred to as the "motor" and glanced at Jack Hanna, his 23-year-old brakeman. "Ready?"

"As ready as I'll ever be." The work garb, baggy on Hanna's skinny body, was stained ore red.

"What's it been now—four weeks?"

"Nope. Three."

"Well, for only bein' on the job three weeks, I'd say you're catchin' on pretty fast."

Hanna ducked his head with a shy grin and glanced away.

Wills started the engine, and the motor jerked forward. Electric lights strung along the tunnel's ceiling at regular intervals illumined their way like glimmers of hope in an otherwise dismal world. No one had any idea their hope was about to run out.

Wills checked his watch as a light swept past. 11:20 a.m. He yelled to Hanna over the locomotive's roar. "How about one more trip before we break for lunch?"

Hanna nodded, his face grimy from the ever-present dust permeating every crack and crevice of the place. Soon their 50 coworkers would ride the elevator to the surface for lunch. Perhaps if they hustled, they could beat the noon rush.

From somewhere deep in the tunnel above them, the muffled blast of explosives rumbled. Wills assumed his fellow miners were blasting one last time before lunch. When they returned later, the next load of ore would be ready and waiting for them.

Wills engaged the motor, and the locomotive lurched forward. During each interval between the lights, shadows swung over them like drapes of perpetual night.

A minute later, Hanna raised his hand and braked hard. The locomotive lurched to a halt. Hanna clambered off and dashed to the closest car, which was almost overflowing with large, reddish chunks of iron ore.

Wills dismounted and strode toward his friend, wondering what could be so important that it would interrupt their trip. "What's wrong, Jack?"

Hanna searched the pieces of ore. "I noticed something strange when they loaded the cars. I thought I saw—"

A sudden gust of air swept through the tunnel and blasted them like the rush of wind in the wake of a storm. The two men exchanged puzzled glances. The look in Hanna's brown eyes was unmistakable.

What was that?

Seconds later, another blast of air—this one stronger than the first—knocked them to their knees on the damp, rocky floor and extinguished the carbide lamps on their helmets. Thankfully the ceiling lights still glowed.

Wills scrambled to his feet and groped for the tunnel wall, heart drumming in his chest. "Come on! Let's get out of here!"

Distant thunder rumbled. It drew closer and increased in intensity until it was suddenly upon them. The tunnel bucked under their feet.

Wills gasped and huddled against the craggy wall with Hanna, dread clawing like a live thing in his belly. He recalled the recent muffle of explosives. Had the first level caved in?

The underground thunder faded in the distance, the tunnel still intact. A sudden change in air pressure plugged Wills' ears, and he swallowed hard to clear them. Then something from his worst nightmares came true.

The ceiling lights flickered, brightened, then died. A total eclipse swallowed them whole.

"Rutherford!" Hanna's panicked voice sliced the darkness. "W—what's happening? Where are you?"

Wills gripped his friend's arm. He tried to sound brave, though his legs were trembling. "I'm right in front of you."

Another growl, this one deafening, pealed through their world. Wills pressed his hands over his ears and imagined a freight train bearing down on their heads. How long did they have before the tunnel caved in and crushed them like bugs underfoot?

"God help us!" Hanna cried.

Wills' skin prickled in a cold sweat. Without electricity, they couldn't escape on the locomotive. "Come on, follow me."

Wills stumbled forward, arms outstretched like a blind man, in the direction of the main shaft. He managed to discern the right direction by the feel of the narrow-gauge track against his rubber-toed boots. He debated taking the ladder down to the third level and seeking refuge in the concrete pump house, but the voice in his gut rebelled.

Climb to the surface. Get out. Now!

He neared the main shaft opening, where an avalanche of water, mud, and rock streamed down from above. A prick of fear touched his nerves. Could they even escape through the main shaft? How long before the rising tide of water and mud filled the tunnels and then the shaft?

Wills yelled to Joseph Mankee, the second-level cage operator, who'd been the best man at his wedding. "Joe, are you there?"

"I'm here!" came the anxious shout.

"Come on, we gotta get out of here!"

Without electricity, the elevator wouldn't budge. Wills reached the manhole and clambered onto the emergency ladder, peering upward. Amazingly, he saw it—a tiny light marked the four-by-four surface opening 800 feet above. As long as the light remained, they had a way out. But how much time did they have? He shoved the question aside and began to climb.

The thunder petered off to a relentless growl. More muck rained down from above and slid down Wills' helmet, cascading down his arms. His gloves became slick with mud, and the ladder rungs grew slippery.

Once, he lost his grip, but he regained his hold just in time. He jerked his gloves off with his teeth and flung them into the void before pressing on. His thighs burned, and air burst from his lungs in explosive gasps.

Two hundred feet higher, still 600 feet from the surface, he reached the first-level tunnel.

"Kirby, get out!" he shouted to the level's cage and bell-signal operator.

He had no idea whether Thomas Kirby even heard him, but he pressed on, gritting his teeth against the burning in his legs. With the steady rumble came a new sound. The rush of water, mud, and debris was filling the shaft. How long before the rising tide reached him?

Something massive plummeted toward Wills out of the dark. Its blast of air buffeted him, its mass missing him by mere inches. The unseen rock slammed into the ladder somewhere below his feet with an earsplitting crash. The impact almost tore him from the rungs.

Hanna, Mankee, and Kirby shrieked. Their cries were suddenly cut off, as if they'd been crushed by the rock or overtaken by the rising flood.

Wills gasped, his body trembling. He yelled their names, but his friends didn't answer. He knew he'd share their fate if he didn't press on.

A torrential flood rose and drew ever closer. Wills recalled the muffled explosion before his race with Hanna to the ladder. Had the blast ripped open an underground lake?

A raging whirlpool swirled around his boots and hungrily licked up his legs. Icy muck rose to his waist.

Wills pressed on in a panic and worked his arms and legs like pistons. The level rose almost as quickly as he could climb.

He was panting so hard he thought his heart might explode. His thighs and calves screamed at him to stop, but he couldn't stop. There wasn't time—he had to keep moving.

He tried not to think about the pain. Tried to focus on Bruna and on the years they would share together. If only he could reach the top alive.

The flood pulled back, and the rumble of thunder faded away. Gasping, Wills smeared mud from his face and peered up the ladder. His heart galloped.

Edward Hillman and Albert Tippett, his stepbrother, peered down at him from the ladder above. *Almost to the top!*

"What happened?" Albert called. "Is anyone else behind you?"

Wills raised a hand to shield his eyes from their blinding headlamps. He could barely speak through his panting. "Hanna, Mankee, and Kirby—they might be below me." But even as he spoke the words, he doubted they were true.

Hillman shone his light into the darkness beyond Wills and shouted the miners' names. The only reply was the distant rush of water.

At 11:30 a.m., Wills climbed out of the mine opening with Albert's assistance and collapsed onto the frozen ground. Immediately his arms and legs began to spasm and cramp. He wept from pain and exhaustion.

"It's okay, Wills. You're gonna be okay." Albert rubbed Wills' twitching legs in a vain attempt to comfort him. He yelled to Hillman to get a blanket and call an ambulance.

"The o—o—others." Wills' teeth chattered; he was suddenly freezing. Was he going into shock? "W—w—where are the o—others?" Bruna's father, Sam Phillippi, and his other stepbrothers, Walter and Captain William Tippett—they had gotten out ahead of him, right?

"Others?" Albert shook his head, his eyes heavy with shock and despair. "There haven't been any others. Only you."

Wills' brain cramped as his muscles had. No, it wasn't possible. Out of 52 miners, he was the sole survivor?

He rolled painfully to his side, his spent legs like dead things, and stared at the mine opening and prayed for others to come out. Surely there was still time for some of them to escape. But then he remembered the freezing muck lapping at his waist. The rising tide had filled the tunnels and had nowhere else to go except up the main shaft.

As the minutes ticked by, so grew the truth he didn't want to accept. For the rest of his life, until his death at age 69, he relived their deaths in his dreams. Night after night, all 51 died somewhere in the heart of the earth, their last cries drowned out by icy muck rising above their heads, their mouths upturned like fish nibbling bugs at the surface of a pond. Dying alone in the merciless, cold tomb of the earth.

Nobody should ever die like that.

Later, 10 bodies were pulled from the debris, including those of Hanna, Mankee, and Kirby. Months later, further recovery efforts to find more bodies and reclaim the mine were abandoned. A concrete slab was poured to seal off the main shaft, and everyone—including Wills—left in pursuit of other work.

But Wills never forgot that day. Over the years, he often puzzled over his last moments with Hanna, before their desperate escape. What exactly had Hanna seen in the ore car?

Wills didn't know, but it hardly mattered now. The mine had been sealed closed. No one would ever explore those tunnels again.

A discovery of significance? No one would ever know.

PART ONE

THE WRITING ON THE WALL

*"Faithful indeed is the spirit that remembers
After such years of change and suffering!"*
—Emily Brontë, "Remembrance"

"A fierce vindictive scribble of red."
—Robert Browning, "Easter-Day"

Even before the child was in her arms, Gillian Thayer knew with certain dread that someone would try to take him away from her. She tried to shrug off the irrational fear, tried not to think about the children who'd been taken away from her, victims of her inadequate body. She tried to focus on the fact that this was supposed to be a happy occasion—that her elusive dream of having a son was finally coming true.

The judge said she loved adoption cases because they made the courtroom a happy place, at least for a while. A rare event indeed. She was a kind, matronly type, if not full figured. Certainly not the type you'd expect to wear the title of "judge" and wield a gavel. But when she spoke, her official facial expression matched the inflection in her voice, underlining in Gillian's mind that this was serious business.

"Once this adoption is final," Judge Alisyn Newton said from her bench at the front of the small courtroom in Seattle, "there's no turning back. Do you understand?"

No turning back.

Her eyes seemed to bore into Gillian, who met her gaze with a strength beyond her own. From her place in the third row on the left side, Gillian felt herself nodding while microscope eyes bore into her soul as if seeking her fear and identifying it:

Insecurity. Weakness. Doubt that she would ever be a mother good or deserving enough.

"This child will be yours as if you'd given him birth."

Gillian rejected nagging voices of self-doubt that whispered at the edges of her consciousness. *Are you really ready to do this—to be a mother again, at 44? What are you thinking? He doesn't even belong to you. What if he has genetic problems you don't even know about?*

Judge Newton turned to Paige and asked her to verify whether the Thayers were fit to be parents. The willowy, fresh-faced social worker—who didn't even look old enough to be passing such judgment—rose to her feet and agreed in a child-like voice that this was indeed true.

Gillian took a deep breath and let it out slowly, measuring her exhalations, trying to relax. *It's okay. Everything's going to be okay.* What other roadblocks could possibly stand in their way after the countless interviews, the never-ending bills, the reams of paperwork, and the maddening months of waiting?

She flexed the fingers of her free hand. She hadn't done any calligraphy in weeks, and her fingers ached to script something as a way to combat her stress. If set loose, she knew what they would say. They would echo Thoreau's sentiment that "nothing is so much to be feared as fear."

By any standards, the open adoption had moved forward without a hitch, its speed and lack of hurdles a surprise to everyone. Janna, a 17-year-old, had become pregnant out of wedlock, and her parents had encouraged her to give the baby away. Out of dozens of applicants, she'd chosen the Thayers to be her son's parents.

Gillian broke her perspiring hand away from her tall husband's and blotted it against her skirt, embarrassed by her nerves. Marc glanced down at her, a smile on his lips, and reached for her hand as if he didn't care. They were beyond cooties, after all.

How can he be so calm? They were about to bring a baby boy home with them—a living, breathing son to call their own. Was she the only one experiencing butterflies right now?

But Marc's confident blue eyes seemed to repeat what he'd told her the night before when she'd been unable to sleep, certain that something was going to go wrong.

We've prayed about this adoption and given the matter to God. It's time, Gill. Time to take the step. Sure, it's scary, but God knows, and He's here with us all the way. Remember, God will never lead us where His grace cannot keep us. Relax. Rest in Him.

Judge Alisyn Newton declared, "Today, May 13, Marc and Gillian Thayer are declared the parents of their son, Chase Henry, by the power vested in me by the state of Washington."

Marc turned to Gillian with a broad smile and pulled her into an embrace. Gillian peered over his shoulder at the ceiling, which rippled through her tears. A prayer of gratitude breathed through her lips. They'd finally come to the end of the grueling, exhausting process. She'd always wanted to give Marc a son so he could pass on the basketball tradition. Now God had given them the son they'd always wanted.

She should have felt relieved, and she did to a point. But later, when Janna, the birth mother, said good-bye to the infant so the social worker could transfer the baby to her arms, uneasiness gnawed away inside her—doubts she didn't want to admit, not even to Marc.

Though this baby boy was legally theirs, the dread was back, the conviction that someone, sometime, somewhere would try to take this baby away from her.

She shook her head, steeling herself against her fear.

Over my dead body.

2

Long before the first rays of the sun flickered over the ridge, Cyrus woke from dreams of revenge on the massive complex he inhabited alone on the outskirts of San Antonio. He lit 10 candles in a circle around him and sat, legs crossed, on the cool hardwood floor of the bedroom. He feared fire more than anything else, but candles were a contained sort of fear that ushered him into a deeper spiritual dimension. Sometimes a little fear was a good thing.

And the number 10. Ah yes. Of all numbers, 10 was his favorite.

As he did every day when important decisions needed to be made, he untied the leather band and opened the camel-skin pouch, casting the Urim and Thummim across the floor. He intoned a sanctifying prayer before murmuring the question in his mind.

Should I visit my son today?

During Old Testament times, high priests had used the Urim and Thummim to discern God's will. He used them now for a similar purpose. Like dice, the two small, polished stones—one side white, one side black—tumbled, spun, and settled, shiny and glistening in the flicker of candlelight.

Deciphering their message was simple enough. Black meant no, but white meant yes. If both sides were black, his answer was a definitive no. If both were white, his answer was an unequivocal yes. But if one was black and one was white, his direction was unclear, and he must pray, wait, and hope for a clear answer at another time.

This morning's reply offered no ambiguity.

He reverently collected the stones and returned them to the pouch, thanking the spirits for another clear manifestation of their will. For some time he'd been preparing for what he knew he must do, but waiting had taken longer than expected, leaving his patience frayed. Now, at last, the time for action was drawing near. In fact, he was practically at the door. Exhilaration rushed through his body. His scalp tightened.

He listened to the glass, drywall, and wood of the complex creak in the mournful howl of the desert wind. He detected no trace of a presence other than his own. Not even Linus, his sable ferret, who slept up to 14 hours a day, stirred in his multi-level cage.

Cyrus peered out the large bay windows and scanned the far reaches of his 150 acres of barbed-wired private property. He wondered if somebody was out there, watching him with high-powered binoculars.

Some might call him paranoid, but he didn't consider himself so. Just realistic. If only they had experienced what he had. His mind ambled down long-dusty corridors of recall, and for an instant he slipped into another world. He remembered: *Nights of trying to sleep with his friends, who were trapped with him in a three-story structure slapped together out of salvaged lumber, thin drywall, and cheap siding. Outside wailed a cacophony of hellish sounds as a means of psychological warfare: bagpipes, howling coyotes, buzzing dental drills, crying babies, strangling rabbits. Then Nancy Sinatra's infernal song "These Boots Were Made for Walking" froze his blood with two prophetic lines he would never forget:*

> *And you keep thinking that you'll never get burnt (Ha!)*
> *Well, I've just found me a brand new box of matches*
> *(Yeah!)*

He jerked out of the mental snapshot, gasping, and wished he could forget. But the memories invaded his days and haunted his dreams, sometimes waking him in the dead of night, drenched in sweat. Sometimes they kept him up to the wee hours, and all he could do was quote verses from various sacred scriptures to chase the memories away and give him a solid footing of sanity to stand on.

He reminded himself of the fifth seal—that many saints would be massacred in the last days. That he must be willing to die as well for the cause. But not yet. No, not yet.

Others needed to die first.

C omfy in a hotel suite with Chase sleeping peacefully in her arms, Gillian couldn't take her eyes off his beautiful face as she shared the happy news with her mom over the phone. Tomorrow they would fly home with their son—she could hardly believe it!

"Hungry?" Marc asked after she finished her call.

"Famished."

He pressed a hand to her face, fingers lingering on the curve of her jaw. "That Chinese place across the street looks pretty good. How about I get us some take-out?"

"That sounds terrific."

"Okay, be right back." He kissed her. "You keep my son safe while I'm gone."

She watched his retreating back, brows knit. What an odd thing for him to say, considering her lingering fears.

After he left, she turned the dead bolt and remembered the hundreds of folks back home who'd prayed for this moment and would want to know how the hearing went. What better way to let them know than to post some photos to her Facebook page and the Facebook group a friend had created to solicit prayers on their behalf?

She laid Chase on his back in the middle of the bed, where there was no fear of his toppling off, and grabbed Marc's laptop. She skimmed through the photos on the digital camera, chose a dozen, and posted them to a Facebook album titled "Chase, Our Son."

There. Now all she needed to do was sit back and wait for the congratulatory remarks to start pouring in. She was just about to close the browser when she remembered it was Sally Lamonte's birthday. She should probably wish her a special day. When Gillian saw the most recent happy birthday wish, her pulse quickened. "Hope your day's as special as you are. Remember spitballs during study hall? LOL."

She stared at the tiny photo of his profile, hands trembling. There was no mistaking that face, even after all these years. How long had it been?

Her hand hesitated on the mouse. Temptation begged her to click on his photo, to see if he was still as knock-out gorgeous as she remembered. But no. How could she even entertain the thought after what he'd done to her?

Gillian closed the browser, slammed the laptop shut—harder than she intended—and rose on weak legs. She crossed to the window and peered out, her right index finger tracing calligraphy letters on the glass.

Her mouth hardened, her thoughts rebuking her. Hadn't she forgiven him in her heart years ago? Hadn't she once let go of this hurt?

He'd been so caring at one time, so affectionate. What if things between them had worked out?

Through binoculars in her mind, she looked past the sunset and the tall oaks lining the newly paved parking lot. She peered through the years and saw a teen reflection of herself doing exactly what she was doing now.

Standing at a picture window. Peering out. Waiting.

Waiting for the man who said he loved her.

But tears clogged her girlish eyes because he'd turned his back and driven away. And even to this day, he'd never told her why.

4

Cyrus planted his cowboy-booted feet beside the grave and pocketed his hands. He was amazed that he hadn't worn a path here yet—he certainly visited frequently enough. His eyes lingered on the American flag, and he couldn't help thinking of the 1990–1991 Persian Gulf War.

If only the missiles had done their job then. The more recent Iraq War could have been averted altogether. So many families could have been spared the pain he was suffering now—of boys leaving home and never coming back.

Never, ever coming back.

He stood somberly, hands clasped behind him, and allowed himself to weep. It was the only time he, who masterfully internalized his angst, allowed emotion to overflow to his face. But this was the closest he could come to the dearest person he'd ever known, and it was here that he bared his soul. At any other time he sealed himself in his stoic shell because emotion was weakness, and he never allowed weakness after his time of grieving.

He must be strong—especially considering what he knew he must do.

He peered past the Stella de Oro lilies, his son's favorite flowers, which he'd recently planted around the headstone, and let his eyes crawl over various mementos: a silver track-and-field medal on a faded blue ribbon; a weatherworn, brown teddy bear his son had slept with as a child; a wooden cross his son had whittled out of two sticks.

The wind picked up, tugging at what remained of his balding pate. He absently rubbed his hand along his patchy crew cut, hair like sharp, gray bristles against his hand.

"I miss you so much," he said through his tears. "More than words can possibly say."

The grave replied with silence, the white-veined slab of gray marble unmoved. The name etched across the face, Alexander Turrow, seemed to dare time to try wiping it away. The years—1983–2005—and the engraved drawing of Alex's face were grim testament to a young, innocent life that had been cruelly, unjustly snatched away.

"I know who they are, the men responsible for your death. It took quite a bit of digging, but you know me—I couldn't give up. Your mother says I'm relentless." *Guess that's what drove her away.*

On the Internet, he'd enjoyed a satellite tour of their neighborhoods and studied their houses, imagining endless ways to kill them. "As sure as you're lying there," he continued speaking to the grave, "you can be sure your father is making plans so they pay for what they did."

Cyrus regretted he couldn't do more—couldn't claw his way into the earth and drag his son's corpse back into the sunlight and somehow force decay to reverse itself like some scene in a cheap horror flick. But only God could do something like that, and he certainly wasn't God, though he could play god and fix God's mistakes. But no matter how hard or how much he prayed, he knew God would never reverse the natural order of things he'd set up long ago.

Not for one solitary, grieving father like him.

The father drew another breath, fueled by fury, and cleared his throat. "They're going to pay—every last one of them. Do you hear me? You and the children will not be forgotten."

Perhaps it was his imagination, but his son's smile seemed to deepen a scintilla. It was the affirmation he'd long been seeking, the approval that his plans were ordained by fate. He drew in a deep, ragged breath and let it out. Knew he must go. Time waited for no man, especially a holy assassin.

"I may not be back for a long time, if ever. As you know, sometimes a soldier must be willing to give his life for the greater good. But do people care? For Pete's sake, do they even know your name?"

His chin trembled, and he grappled with the injustice of it all, with the anger. After his escape from the flames, his son had joined the Marine Corps against his advice and become allies with the very government Cyrus so vehemently distrusted and opposed. He'd begged his son not to go, but Alex had made up his mind, said it was the right thing to do. Even if that meant walking away from his father's counsel.

Cyrus had been quick to forgive. After all, Alex had been full of youth and false bravado, determined to choose his own path. He hadn't been thinking clearly, and his decision had led to his ultimate undoing, proving that his father had been right all along. But at what a price!

He checked his watch. "I gotta go. Never forget that I love you and that I'm doing this for you." *And for justice. And for the children.*

He turned on his heel. Just as quickly as he'd opened the floodgates of emotion, he closed them again and sealed them off, perhaps for all of time. He strode to his black Lexus, clenching his fists.

Oh yes, they'll pay. Every last one of them.

5

—Two months later

In the future, Brianne Hyde would never look at the simple act of turning on a faucet the same way again.

At the antique-replica pedestal sink, one of several lined up like sentries in the posh bathroom, she peered at herself in the mirror and cringed at her 36-year-old reflection. Her bloodshot brown eyes made her look even more tired than she felt. If only the pounding headache would go away. She dug into her purse, found a couple of ibuprofen, and splashed them down with a paper cup of cold water.

She glanced at the fogged window and imagined the woods encroaching just beyond the perimeter of the resort and conference center. How she longed for a walk amid the trees minus the stilettos that pinched her aching feet. She'd been sitting too long and taking notes at one of the most boring meetings in recent memory. Besides, she hated being stuck indoors on such a fine summer day, and the resort offered so many more enjoyable diversions: horseback riding, golf, swimming, and hiking. These meetings were a waste of a good resort.

"Don't you wonder if those guys are ever going to stop talking?"

The voice from the nearest stall made Brianne jump. A toilet flushed, and Tessa McCormack—certainly the prettiest among the secretarial pool—emerged. She sauntered toward her with a wan smile, purse dangling from a strap over her shoulder.

Hand pressed to her chest, Brianne felt the familiar thumping start to slow down. "Wow, you scared me! I didn't realize anybody else was in here."

As usual, Tessa was impeccably attired: A purple dress expertly contoured the youthful curves of her slim, trim body. She glided to one of the other sinks and began washing her hands. "You agree with me, don't you? You've never heard bigger windbags in all your life. Admit it."

"Okay, you don't have to twist my arm or anything." Brianne grabbed another paper cup from the dispenser and filled it. She'd been extra thirsty since the lasagna at lunch.

"I didn't know there could be so much hot air on one planet." As if to illustrate a pun, Tessa blew out a blast of air. "Somebody ought to call Al Gore. 'Hey buddy, you lookin' for evidence of global warming? You just get your sorry little self up here to the north woods. Mama knows where it's comin' from—smack dab in Michigan's Upper Peninsula.' "

Brianne couldn't help chuckling, though Tessa's irreverent talk made her uneasy. After all, the 30 men Tessa referred to staffed one of the most prestigious Bible translation committees in the country. Didn't they deserve a little more respect?

Brianne wasn't so sure about hot air. Brains certainly. The heated discussions were sometimes way over her head—not that she really needed to understand. Still, she was beginning to comprehend what all the fuss was about, and the truth of what many of these men proposed unnerved her.

She drank the water down, shivered, and tossed the crumpled paper cup into the trash, wondering what was wrong with her today. Maybe it was just being in a strange place. It didn't help that the biannual meeting was being held at one of the most remote corners of the planet. Sabbath Resort and

Conference Center, though beautiful and upscale, was located too deep in the woods for her.

Well, in a couple of days, the meeting would be over, and she'd return to her seminary-student husband and her two sons. Back to her routine in Detroit—just the way she liked it.

The chant of the protestors with their placards and messages of gloom and doom blaring over loudspeakers seeped through the window.

"Listen to those fools." Tessa studied her ebony face in the mirror and began applying more eyeliner. "You'd think we were nailing Jesus to the cross all over again."

"Well, I suppose everybody has the right to free speech. There's nothing illegal about holding a sign and saying what you believe."

Tessa shot her a look sharper than daggers. "Oh, come on. What's the big deal? It's just another parallel Bible, for crying out loud. What's so unusual about that? It's like—like a pretty piece of music. Some people like Beethoven." She wrinkled her nose to show what she thought of classical music. "Others, like me, prefer jazz. People just want the Bible to sound the way they like it."

Sound Islamic, you mean. Wasn't that what all the fuss was about—the other sacred writings included in the parallel Bible? Hadn't Islamic jihadists sent their sons flying into the twin towers of the World Trade Center and the Pentagon while shouting "Allah Akbar!" and "Death to the infidels!"? On the other hand, maybe some of the committee members were right. Maybe the parallel Bible would have evangelistic merit.

Tessa snapped her coordinating purse closed, flung the strap over her shoulder, and sauntered toward the door like art in motion. She swiveled on one heel. "You comin', girl?"

"In a minute."

The door swooshed closed behind Tessa. Brianne turned on the faucet to wash her hands and held her fingers in the warm water, waiting for it to turn hot. How wonderful a hot bath would feel right now. Maybe tonight.

She pushed the mental image away when the water didn't turn hot. In fact, it turned ice cold.

Brianne frowned at the faucet as the water sputtered, choked, stopped altogether. Then, as if with hydraulic force, the water gushed forth in a crimson deluge. Ricocheted off the porcelain. Splashed every direction.

On the sink. On the mirror. Across the floor. On her clothes.

Brianne leaped back in dismay, trying to avoid getting sprayed. But she was too late.

It looks like ... Her breath hitched in her throat.

It smells like ... Her stomach roiled at the coppery aroma.

But it couldn't be blood, could it? How could this be happening?

Brianne twisted the faucet off, but blood kept pouring out. Something was wrong with the drain, too. The sink was filling. In fact, it was cresting and overflowing onto the tile floor. Had someone plugged the drain?

She dashed to another sink and twisted the faucet. More blood.

She tried closing the valve, but again the blast refused to stop. The apparent crimson blood gushed forth as if the waters of the deep, tainted by the transgressions of mankind, longed for release. As if nothing could hold them back.

As if in harmony, the chanting voices of protestors mingled with the gushing of blood as if intoning a blessing over a sacrifice. They proclaimed that God would judge them all with plagues for meddling with his Word. Wasn't that what the book of Revelation said?

Brianne sprang back helplessly and struggled not to slip on the blood-slicked floor. She dashed to the door and reached for the handle, heading to call someone from maintenance. But the handle held fast—it didn't budge. Had Tessa locked the door?

Brianne pounded on the door. "Hey! Somebody let me out!"

There was no reply.

The coppery aroma made her stomach tighten. Brianne glanced at the window. Could she get out that way? She wasn't one for acrobatics, especially not in her dress and high heels.

Blood had pooled under the sinks, and a crimson stream snaked across the tile floor toward her deviously.

She pounded on the door with one hand while pressing the back of the other to her mouth. "Let me out! Please! *Somebody!*"

Finally, a voice. A man told her not to worry, said he'd get her out in a jiffy. A key turned in the lock.

Somebody really had locked the door? Had Tessa pulled a prank?

The door swung open, and a goateed man in a blue maintenance outfit reached for her. She was going to be okay.

His disbelieving look made her glance back for proof. The bloody room confirmed that she hadn't made any of this up. His jaw slackened at the sight.

She pushed past him and found the way blocked by a crowd gathered outside the door. At the sight of her blood-spattered dress, they drew back, eyes accusing—as if Brianne were somehow to blame.

Questions about what had happened flew at her from every direction. She opened her mouth to explain and heard somebody say that the entire water supply had been affected.

So it's not just this bathroom. I'm not losing my mind.

She leaned against the wall for support, more shaken and spent than she realized, yet relieved that she hadn't been the only target. Then Tessa pulled her into her arms, her serious black eyes proof that a prank had been the farthest thing from her mind.

How could someone have rigged a prank like this?

6

The rope was tight around her neck, closing off her windpipe, and she couldn't breathe. Couldn't break the killer's hold on the rope, no matter how hard she tried.

Starved for oxygen, Gillian Thayer realized she was going to die. Instinct pushed her into panic mode. Frenzied by the lust to live, she pounded her fists against his hands, but they didn't budge. Wouldn't budge.

Help me. Somebody. Please!

It was a silent plea—the rope prevented the use of her vocal cords. Then Gillian jerked awake, clammy with sweat.

She was sitting in the Tahoe with Marc on a Thursday morning, and he was driving them to Ishpeming for an extended weekend getaway. She inhaled a deep breath to clear her head, her heart starting to slow down. She stole a sheepish glance at her husband.

Concern flashed in Marc's eyes. "Hey, you okay?"

She forced a chuckle. "I'm fine. Just another silly nightmare."

"Let me guess—Haydon Owens?"

She nodded. Would she ever completely forget the attempt on her life a year and a half ago? The Magician Murderer, the strangler of five women, had gone after their daughter, Crystal, before going after her. God had been merciful, and they'd both survived the ordeal, but she wondered if she'd ever get over that gut-wrenching feeling of being at the mercy of some sick killer.

In an attempt to allay her fears, Marc had taken her target shooting with his 9mm Glock. At least now she knew the basics of how to handle a gun—an ability she doubted she'd ever use. But at least the experience made her feel not quite so powerless.

July sunlight splashed through the window and caressed Gillian's denim capris. She focused on the gray ribbon of highway unraveling before them. The gentle cadence of rubber kissing cement lulled her.

She closed Jane Austen's *Persuasion*, which still lay facedown on her lap, and flexed stiff fingers. She realized how much she missed her calligraphy pens, the steady stream of projects, and the business she'd temporarily set aside for motherhood. Oh, well. Motherhood came at a price, and Chase was well worth it.

Gillian glanced at the backseat, where Chase was clearly in la-la land. She still couldn't get over the wonder of having the son she'd always wanted to give Marc but never could. She faced forward and leaned her head back against the headrest, letting her neck muscles relax. The drive *was* relaxing, but she'd be more relaxed if she could stop worrying about Crystal.

Be anxious for nothing...

What did she have to be worried about anyway? Four hours away, Crystal, the singer in the family, was serving as a summer counselor at music camp, giving little tykes voice lessons and tips on proper singing posture. Perhaps her anxiety sprang from the fact that other than Chase, Crystal was the only baby she had left. Though Crystal was 18 and planned to attend Bible college this fall, Gillian still couldn't suppress her overprotective side.

God, please break me of this. I've gotta let go of her so she can start making decisions on her own.

Gillian grabbed her bottle of spring water from the middle console and took a swig. "Want more music?" she asked. She had listened to some soothing solo piano music, but Marc hadn't even played his Sons of the San Joaquin music yet, and

drive times were usually prime times for him to enjoy his classic cowboy music.

"No, that's okay."

"You've been awfully quiet."

He kept his eyes on the road. "Have I?"

"Uh-huh. Something on your mind?" *Probably his dad*.
Perhaps Marc didn't want to talk about the relationship that
seemed broken beyond repair.

Marc blew air out of ballooned cheeks. "I thought for sure
the baby pictures I sent him would soften his heart just a little.
After all, he *does* have a new grandchild. I just thought—"

"—that he'd want to come for a visit or something?"

"Or something." He steered his cornflower-blue eyes to her
face for a split second before focusing back on the road. "Is he
ever going to forgive me and move on?"

Gillian reached over and ruffled the gray-flecked blond hair
that curled boyishly around the backs of Marc's ears. "Only God
knows, Marc. What else can we do but love your dad, speak the
truth, and ask God to work in his heart? God can, you know,
but His timing may not be ours."

"I know, but it's so hard to wait. The years are speeding by,
and I don't feel like I'm making any progress." He glanced toward her with moist eyes. "I just want to resolve our differences
and see him turn to God before it's too late."

"I know." She rubbed his shoulder.

They lapsed into silence, both knowing there was little more
to say. They could only love Marc's dad the best they could.
They needed to trust God for the rest—and He was enough.

She decided to change the subject. "It sure was nice of Jared
to invite us on this weekend getaway. I guess it *is* a good idea."

"What? You had doubts?"

They should have discussed this earlier; she hated to sound
like a complainer now that they'd almost reached their destination. But going on the weekend getaway had been a rather

hasty decision. "Well, I wasn't sure that taking Chase to a different place would have the greatest effect on his routine."

Marc's jaw pulled to one side. "Oh, sorry. I didn't think of that."

"It's okay. He should sleep fine wherever he is as long as we stick to our schedule."

"That's good to hear. I guess I thought the getaway would do us both good. The last few months have been pretty hectic for both of us. You need some rest."

Do I look that worn out? Gillian smoothed back wavy, reddish locks she'd trimmed due to the summer heat. "Well, you need some time off, too. Your schedule's been pretty crazy this summer."

On top of pastoring Faith Bible Church in Newberry, he'd spoken to youth at a Christian camp in Wisconsin just last week, and a few more speaking engagements were scheduled in August. Not to mention basketball clinics he'd been conducting for neighborhood youth as a means of outreach.

She couldn't help wondering if the rat race they'd left in Chicago before their move north was slowly creeping back on them. She'd once blamed the craziness on Chicago's hectic pace, but she suspected the real reason was sitting in the seat beside her. Marc wasn't one to rest, perhaps even when he should.

He reached for her hand and caressed her knuckles with his fingertips. "Well then, it's unanimous. You're beat, and I'm too busy. Maybe some time away is exactly what the doctor ordered. Think of it as a second honeymoon."

"A second honeymoon, huh?" She raised an eyebrow. "You're forgetting one little detail. We've got a baby in the backseat."

He chuckled. "Oh, yeah. Well, then, a second honeymoon—with a baby."

She detected the faintest flirtation in his eyes. "I like the sound of that."

"And free food without any prep."

"Sounds glorious."

"Top-notch accommodations with our own gas fireplace and whirlpool."

"Sounds heavenly."

"Time to just relax, swim in the pool, go for a walk."

Gillian stretched and wiggled her sandaled toes. "Sounds like we'll be absolutely spoiled."

"And my phone will be turned off."

She searched his face. "You really mean it?"

He flashed startled eyes. "Of course!"

She enjoyed teasing him about his addiction to his electronic gadgets. If the devices could someday be surgically implanted, she suspected Marc would be the first in line. To his credit, he'd left his laptop at home.

"Come on, Marc. I know you."

He flushed. "Okay, then this is what we'll do. When we get there, I'll give you my toy—as you like to call it—"

"—and I'll hold it hostage until it's time to go home."

He held up a finger. "One exception. We check messages in case Crystal calls ..."

She pressed hands to her face. Of course, she needed to keep tabs on her daughter's music camp experience.

His twinkling gaze caught hers. "... because I know you."

7

From the kitchen window across North Lake, Lacey Caruthers frowned at the protestors clogging the lodge entrance at the Sabbath Resort and Conference Center. The sight only added fuel to her already-sizzling flame of annoyance.

She stood at the marble counter in the mansion-sized, plantation-style house her family shared with her father, who owned the resort but left it to others to run. After an early lunch, her husband, Quinn, head of maintenance, had stormed off to do more errands for her father, muttering under his breath that he was sick and tired of being at her dad's beck and call at all hours.

Like a common slave. His words.

Not a good sign as to how the rest of the weekend would play out. And right now, they needed to stay on their toes with those protestors drawing unwanted media attention and polluting the typically serene ambiance. Much of their business came from city slickers, who arrived in shiny Lexuses and wanted to take in the peaceful amenities the north woods resort offered. These chanting voices might make those city slickers turn around and head back to the city.

Uneasiness sank like a rock in her stomach. Who was behind the weird incident with the blood, and why? So far nobody knew. Whatever was going on would adversely affect their lives until somebody put a stop to it.

Ever since the incident, Quinn had seemed particularly stressed—and for good reason. A troublemaker was lurking somewhere on the grounds and getting into things he or she shouldn't have access to, and Quinn didn't like it. Not one bit.

Lacey reached for the coffeepot and filled her mug with the hazelnut brew for the third time that day. She hated to become a coffee addict, but the chronic sleep disorder that woke her frequently during the night left her feeling exhausted most of the day. Without her coffee fix, she'd stumble through each day like the walking dead.

Lacey stepped into the living room, which echoed with the chirp of her prized canaries. Ten-year-old Sammy sat beside the coffee table, head bent over his latest drawing. Right now, most kids his age would have been glued to the latest Pixar movie on the big-screen TV, but not Sammy. He preferred to draw, his arm moving in a frenzy, forehead furrowed in concentration.

What made the little guy so passionate about drawing? It wasn't that she had anything against his drawing—or the weather, his other fixation. She'd rather he draw than zap brain cells by watching too much TV, but something was unnatural about his drawing compulsion. Then again, little about Sammy had seemed natural since he'd been diagnosed with autism at age three.

She stepped closer so she could peer over his shoulder without disturbing him, coffee mug in hand. With admirable intensity, he was drawing blotches of green that were apparently floating on a sea of blue.

"Hey, Sammy."

He turned in a rare response to his spoken name and swiveled dreamy blue eyes that didn't seem to focus. "H—h—high 82, l—l—low 63. Sunny." Then he made the odd sounds she was used to by now: unintelligible words muttered under his breath and clicking sounds with his tongue.

"Yep, I already know the forecast, buddy." She crouched and pointed at his drawing. "Hey, what are those green things?"

In an instant he was back to his drawing again as if shutting out the rest of the world, including her. Of course, he wasn't going to answer her question. That was simply too much to ask.

Come on, kid, let me into your world. I'm talking to you here. "Lily pads, Sammy? Is that what you're drawing?"

He ignored her. His head swung from side to side as if matching the rhythm of a song playing in his head—probably one of those Swiffer commercials they'd recorded, which he played over and over again.

Lacey bit her lip. Sammy rarely spoke, and when he did, he usually parroted her words back at her. When he spoke his own words, he almost never spoke in complete sentences. He also didn't seem to hear her most of the time, even when she called his name. No, it wasn't that he didn't hear, she reminded herself; for whatever reason, his little brain didn't always know how to process the information and respond. Communication, therefore, was always a challenge.

They'd undergone special training through various thera-pists, whose bills had made her dad's invitation to remain living with him harder to refuse. But so far, little seemed to be helping Sammy become the boy she knew him to be deep down inside. She'd come to the conclusion that she just needed to accept her son as God's good gift—developmental problems and all.

She rested a hand on his arm. Sometimes he didn't like to be touched, but he didn't flinch or jerk away this time as he had on other occasions. She took a shot in the dark. "Little green men from Mars?"

Sammy sighed, as if to say, "Puh-lease." Then he opened his mouth, and something came out. *Leaping* or *reaping*? She wasn't exactly sure which. She chose *reaping*. Maybe those green things were supposed to be apples in an orchard, and somebody was picking them.

"Green apples?"

More stonewalling.

She grabbed his Picture Exchange Communication book—a little book filled with pictures of basic lifestyle activities—and slid it toward him. A plate with utensils meant he wanted to eat. Because he didn't like to talk, he sometimes used the pictures to provide an answer. But this time, he ignored the book, and she didn't want to cause a tantrum by pushing him further.

She was turning to leave when she saw it. Mud caking the bottoms of Sammy's white shoes had crumbled onto the beige carpet.

She frowned. Hours ago, he'd gone into the backyard to play, while she'd sat on the patio lounge chair with a paperback, watching from a distance. Unfortunately, she'd fallen asleep. When she awoke a few hours later, Sammy was playing in the backyard just as she'd left him. She assumed that he'd remained in the fenced-in backyard, but now she wondered whether he'd climbed the fence and gone somewhere else.

It wasn't unusual for him to wander off from time to time, but she tried to avoid such episodes for his own safety. In Toledo, he'd sometimes bolted down the street into traffic before she could reach him, heart in her throat. At least here he had space to run without as many dangers, and he feared water, so the lake and pools weren't threats.

But where had the mud come from? They hadn't had rain in days, if not weeks. In fact, Quinn had complained that if they didn't get more rain soon, his lawn crew would be using sprinklers 24-7.

On her way to fetch the broom and dustpan, she couldn't help wondering: *Where had Sammy gone to get mud on his shoes like that?*

8

They paused at a rest stop so Marc could stretch his legs—his right knee in particular. Injuries from a car accident years ago refused to heal, at least not completely, and the knee especially bothered him if he sat too long without stretching.

After they hit the highway again, Gillian asked, "So this resort's pretty popular, huh?"

"Not *this* popular." He gestured to the unusually heavy traffic.

"Didn't the founder used to be some Hollywood big shot?"

"Yep, before he turned to Christ he was producer of some of the biggest-budget flicks of yesteryear. But then he walked away from the industry—decided to pour some of his excess cash into a place that would make a difference in people's lives."

The Tahoe rounded a curve, and the parting trees revealed a green, idyllic valley below. Over the last half hour, the road had become strangely crowded with traffic. Little traffic was heading away from the resort, but a whole caravan seemed to be bearing down on it.

Gillian eyed the TV-station van lumbering down the road in front of them. "Did we miss something? Is the president making an appearance?"

Marc snorted. "Hardly. I wonder what's up."

"Tell me more about Jared Russo. I'm having trouble matching his name with his face."

"You remember Jared. He was the one who filled my bed with popcorn."

She remembered now. One night while working campus security in college, Marc had come home to his dark dorm room around 2:00 a.m. with plans to slip into bed and avoid disturbing his roommates. He hadn't expected what was hiding under the covers.

Gillian chuckled. "Jared, the class clown. He had a terrible crush on my roommate once, if I remember right. Will his family be here, too?"

"No, he's just here for some kind of meeting. Since he's in the area, he thought he'd be a jerk if he didn't try to reconnect."

"Sure is generous of him to invite us here just to catch up on old times."

"An all-expense-paid weekend getaway on Jared's dime? Uh, yeah. You know we rarely have money or time for such things. How could I have said no?"

The traffic meandered past a fenced-in horse pasture, flowed through a stone gate, and snaked down a hill. In the valley below lay a sprawling complex dominated by large, rustic buildings built in log cabin style. Gillian glimpsed the sparkling blue waters of a small lake and the greens of a golf course in the distance.

They crept past a sign with the words "Sabbath Resort and Conference Center" painted in fancy, white cursive on a dark wood background. The road merged into a crowded parking lot, and Marc pulled into one of the only remaining slots. When he shut off the engine, the rise and fall of a man's impassioned voice seeped through the windows, echoing as if broadcast over loudspeakers.

Memories of childhood summer camp swept over Gillian, a man's voice echoing across the grounds. *Okay, campers, it's time to rise and shine. We've got a big day planned for you today. So open those eyes and jump out of bed! We're burnin' daylight.*

The difference was that anger echoed from this man's voice.

Gillian glanced at Marc. "What's going on here?" She reached for her door handle and got out. She glanced at Chase through his side window; he was still asleep and should be fine.

Fifty feet away, just outside the lodge entryway, a crowd of several hundred had gathered around the rear of a red pickup truck. Two large speakers beside the truck amplified the deafening tirade, while protestors held multicolored placards with messages Gillian could just make out.

Some slogans appeared to be professionally printed, while others looked as if a sixth-grader had scrawled them with a marker: "Prepare for God's Wrath," "Don't Meddle with My Bible," "Prepare for the Plagues," "God's Judgment Is Coming," "Veterans for Bible Preservation," "Pharaoh Didn't Like It, and Neither Will You," and "This Bible Is an Abomination."

A bank of cameramen occupied a stretch of sidewalk only yards from the protestors, no doubt shooting video for the six o'clock news. Several reporters were interviewing protestors on camera.

Marc walked around the front of the SUV and reached Gillian's side, lacing his fingers into hers. Uneasiness squeezed her gut and didn't want to let go. Their expectation of a peaceful weekend getaway now seemed in peril.

A husky, bald-headed man stood in the back of the truck and spoke into a microphone, the sleeves of his white dress shirt rolled up to his elbows. He balanced a black Bible in one hand while his red tie flapped in the breeze.

"You folks know what God says in the Bible about those who meddle with His holy Word. Why, if the men inside this building carry out their diabolical plans, the plagues described in the book of Revelation will fall on this place. Do you believe it?"

The crowd responded with a weak, "Yes."

The man repeated, this time with more spirit, "Do you believe it?"

More passion erupted this time. "*Yes!*"

"Now hear me. That's not Brother Micah Coombs saying this—always remember that. Who promised to unleash plagues of holy judgment on truth meddlers?"

The crowd was waking up now. "God did!"

"Who?"

"GOD DID!"

"Uh-oh," Marc said.

Micah Coombs stepped down from the truck, and a wiry teen hopped up with a guitar in hand. He strummed a spirited intro to the hymn "The Bible Stands," and the crowd joined in with gusto.

Gillian raised her voice to be heard. "Jared's here for some kind of meeting, right?"

"Yeah, he's on some kind of Bible translation committee."

"Maybe that has something to do with what's going on here."

"Let's leave our stuff here for now and check in at the front desk. Maybe somebody there can tell us what's going on."

Marc opened the rear passenger door, and Gillian reached in to unclasp Chase's carrier. She swung it low by its handle, thankful he was still out cold. But she wondered how much more sleep he'd get with the clamor blaring from the protestors.

Sure enough, Chase sprang awake, his little hands jerking up in a startled gesture she'd seen countless times before. His blue eyes popped open, and his face clouded over in that look that always preceded the storm.

Oh no! Gillian skirted the mob and rushed toward the glass entrance doors, desperate to get Chase inside and away from the noise. A step ahead, Marc held a door open for her.

In the quieter lobby, Chase settled down, and relief washed over her—he wasn't going to cry after all. Miracles never ceased.

The place was classier than she'd expected for the north woods, offering plush burgundy carpet, glass, and chrome. A freestanding stone fireplace stood to their left. Beyond that lay a free coffee station and a cozy conversation area furnished with overstuffed chairs and couches. Framed paintings of mallard ducks and deer leaping through sun-dappled forests hung on the walls. A Smoky Mountain–style bluegrass rendition of "Amazing Grace" drifted from pinhole ceiling speakers.

At the mahogany counter, on which stood various brochure displays, a woman in a conservative navy business suit turned from one of the computers with a smile and asked if she could help them. Her gold name tag identified her as Janice.

Marc gave her their names and explained the reason for their stay. She nodded as if their stay on Jared's dime was the most common thing in the world and looked them up in the computer. Satisfied, she gave Marc some paperwork to fill out along with two electronic key cards, an informational brochure, a map of the grounds, and directions to their room, in an adjacent building.

"Great," Marc said. "Thanks for your help."

"No problem."

"Janice, do you mind telling us something?"

"If I can."

"The protestors outside. Do you mind telling us what's going on?"

She waved a dismissive hand. "Oh, that. A Bible translation committee is here for their biannual meeting, and the group outside doesn't like the Bible they're producing—or something or other." She shrugged. "I'm not exactly sure what the fuss is all about, to be honest, but it sure is attracting a lot of attention. All I know is that those folks sure can make a lot of racket."

"Well, what kind of Bible is it?"

Her hazel eyes flickered as if she knew more than she was willing to say. "Well, Mr. Russo's on the committee, right? Maybe when you see your friend, you can ask him."

9

When exactly had the stomach cramps begun?

Jared Russo didn't know the answer as he shuffled away from the resort restaurant with a weak wave at his buddies. He headed—or rather staggered—toward his suite. The stabbing pains in his gut grew more intense by the moment, but he did his best to hide the pain. His jaunt in the armed forces years ago had taught him at least one important lesson: Never show the pain. Grin and bear it.

He broke out in a cold sweat, and dizziness made him grope for the wall to steady himself. A passing secretary eyed him with concern and probably would have offered to help if he hadn't flashed one of his charming smiles and insisted he was fine.

It wasn't true. Something *was* wrong, but a quick lie-down would probably do the trick.

A swipe of his key card, and he was back in his suite just in time, legs shaking. He hustled to the bathroom, the stomach-churning weakness a prelude to undesirable things to come.

He vomited once. Twice. Three times.

Along with his stomach's contents, he expelled any remaining energy reserved for the rest of the day. He wiped his mouth on a hand towel and slumped on the bathroom floor, as weak as a newborn colt. Could he even stand? His navy polo was drenched in sweat, yet he was freezing.

Good grief! He hated getting sick while on a trip away from his family. If his wife, Melissa, were here, she'd probably tell him not to be such a wuss. *Until you've had a baby, you don't even know the meaning of pain.*

He didn't have time for this. He had more meetings later—important meetings if there was any hope of halting the project.

He rubbed his eyes. Something was wrong with his vision, too—the room was turning fuzzy and going out of focus. What on earth had he eaten?

He reviewed his lunch menu. A BLT. A salad. An iced tea. Nothing fancy. Perhaps something had been wrong with the bacon.

Where was his cell? He needed to call the front desk for help.

He tried to get up, but another spasm knifed through his gut. He decided to stay put and rest until he could muster more strength.

A masculine figure loomed in the bathroom doorway. Somebody was there, but how had he gotten in?

"Feeling sick, Jared?"

The voice was familiar, but Jared couldn't place the face. How considerate! He'd exited the cafeteria rather abruptly, after all. Thankfully, someone had come to check on him.

Jared dragged his tongue across dry lips. "I don't know what's wrong with me. I feel terrible."

"Well, of course you do. Anybody who got as much of the drug I gave you would be feeling pretty sick right about now."

Perhaps his hearing was going along with his eyesight. He had pulled plenty of pranks in his time and knew when the tables were being turned. Perhaps this was payback time.

At lunch, someone had jostled him from behind, and he'd spilled his drink. A courteous server had offered him a fresh cup. Jared played along. "So what was it—the iced tea? I know it wasn't Ex-Lax in the brownies. So what did you give me?"

A dry laugh rustled like autumn leaves. "Definitely some-thing stronger than Ex-Lax, my friend."

Jared felt colder than he had moments before. What odd timing for somebody to pull a prank when he had important meetings to attend.

"What is this? Some kind of joke?"

"No, Jared, this is no joke. This is justice."

Justice? "I don't understand. What did you do to me?"

Another husky laugh. "Come on, Jared, you disappoint me. I poisoned your body, not your mind. Use the brain God gave you."

He poisoned me?

"Think, Jared. It's important that you remember."

Jared felt himself start to panic. A hot flash washed over him. "Remember ... remember what?"

"Remember how we met long ago. Remember someone who died—someone who shouldn't have."

Jared realized who this man was and began to shake. What was he doing here? He'd met the man once before, but he didn't think the others had. They would never see him coming.

The shadow slid from the doorway, slithered across the floor. It rose like a snake, a cobra as big as a man, ready to strike. "Remember, Jared? Remember what I told you?"

His memory was clear though his body seemed to be incre-mentally shutting down. He gasped for breath. "You said you'd forgiven me, that everything was buried in the past."

"Ah, so you *do* remember. But guess what, Jared? I lied." The playfulness in his voice morphed into rage. "In fact, every day I've relived *what you took away from me*."

Jared groped for the toilet, tried to pull himself up. But his arms trembled with uncharacteristic weakness, and he slumped down, deflated.

His poisoner chuckled. "What are you trying to do, Jared—get away? Do you really think you can escape justice?"

Justice? Justice for what? Jared again raked his tongue across fear-dried lips, his mind racing. He hadn't done anything wrong.

"What does that verse in your Bible say? 'Be sure your sins will find you out'? Your sins *have* found you out, Jared. And sins must be punished. You know the punishment for murder, don't you?"

The man was delusional. Jared's eyes flicked frantically from left to right, left to right. Vernon Brannon, one of his colleagues, knew about as much as he did; surely he would put two and two together. And the Thayers were coming for a weekend getaway. They'd start asking questions, and when they did—

"Of course you do because you know your Bible like a good little boy in Sunday school. Okay, little boy, time for a little quiz before class is over. So what's the punishment for murder, hmm?"

The spasms were gone, but paralysis seemed to have taken its place. Could he even lift a finger? Jared tried. Nothing.

Raw anger exploded out of the shadow. "Come on, Jared. For Pete's sake, grow a brain! What's the punishment for murder?"

"Death," Jared whispered.

"I can't hear you, little boy. Speak up!"

A little stronger this time. "Death."

"That's right. Your own words condemn you—you realize that, don't you?"

Jared's breath exploded out of him in panicky gasps. He realized he was trapped—trapped in his body. Maybe somebody would check on his condition—perhaps the secretary he'd passed in the hallway.

The shadow loomed closer, a mass of malevolent blackness. "Oh, yes, Jared. I know your Bible too, enough to know that God punishes sinners."

Jared burned with sudden fury. This man was an impostor, a heretic, a wolf among the sheep. If only he could warn them—

"And that's what you are, Jared. A sinner who must be punished!"

"But *my* God extends mercy."

"I'm not your God, Jared, nor do I care to be. He leaves messes for others to mop up. And for some sins, there is no mercy." A pause and then a grunt of irritation. "Enough of this."

The shadow rose and towered over him in obvious dominance. "Jared Russo, I find you guilty of murder in the first degree. Your sentence"—the voice paused, the inevitable poised on the edge of a cliff and edging toward a certain plunge—"is death."

Jared trembled—whether from cold or fear, he couldn't say. Color had vanished from his sight, and he could see only vague shapes now. If he could have distinguished color, he would have seen something golden. Something yellow, writhing, and wet being pressed to the sensitive skin on his forearm.

If he could have pulled away, he would have. But he didn't. Couldn't.

A cold tingling. He didn't know what it was, but his mind did a good job filling in the blanks. It felt cool and wet with a burning that slowly became more intense, like a cold stove burner set on high. Whatever it was, he had only moments left.

The icy grip of paralysis shut down his organs one by one, like a janitor flicking off the lights on his way out of a building.

So this is how a condemned man on death row must feel. God, help me!

10

M arc whistled. "Wow, this place is much nicer than I expected."

"And Jared paid for all this just for us?" Gillian knew she sounded doubtful.

The log cabin–style exteriors had tempted her to misjudge their accommodations. The suite wasn't rustic at all. On the contrary, it was beautiful, spacious, and surprisingly state of the art, offering a kitchenette just beyond the entryway to her right. To her left lay a roomy living area with overstuffed, hunter-green couches and polished oak end tables. Furnishings included plush carpet, tasteful draperies, a gas fireplace in the corner, and an enormous bedroom with a hot tub—everything accented in a classy outdoorsman theme with framed fish and fishing lures.

Somebody had paid top dollar to furnish the place. The widescreen plasma TV facing the living room couch looked almost too large for the wall bearing it.

Gillian moved to a window and brushed aside the coordinating curtains, taking in the sights: a manicured lawn, a swimming pool surrounded by lounge chairs, a basketball court, and a wide sidewalk flanked by antique-looking streetlamps. On the opposite side of the distant lake, a big, white, plantation-style house with pillars piqued her interest. Who lived there?

She turned from the window, admiring Jared Russo's thoughtfulness. He and Marc had been close once. If she remembered correctly, Marc had invited Jared to be a grooms-man in their wedding, but Jared had been serving in the military somewhere and couldn't come home. Perhaps he'd been fighting in the Gulf War. The memories were fuzzy.

Marc had said something about meeting Jared for coffee that afternoon. Maybe when she saw Jared again, she would remember.

Marc went to get their luggage and returned five minutes later. Gillian left Chase sleeping in his baby carrier in the living room while she unpacked. When she was done, she glanced at her watch, realized it was well past noon, and went in search of the map to find the resort restaurant. She glanced around, wondering where she had put the map. Maybe it was in—

Somewhere nearby, a woman screamed.

Gillian whirled toward the door. More screams, short and high pitched, came next. They sounded like they were coming from the hallway outside their suite.

Gillian hovered over Chase protectively as Marc darted into the room from the bedroom and stared at her with wide eyes. He darted toward the door and glanced back. "I'm going to see what's wrong. Lock the door behind me."

Gillian nodded.

Marc flung the door open and charged into the hallway.

Gillian rushed to the door and closed it behind him, turning the bolt. She pressed a hand to her chest. Her heart wouldn't slow down.

God, whatever's wrong, let it be okay.

A drenaline rushed through Marc's bloodstream like espresso. He jogged down the hallway and searched for the source of the screams, which had now ceased. He rounded a corner and almost collided into a wheeled cart loaded with towels and cleaning supplies.

Beside the cart, a cleaning lady leaned against the wall, one hand pressed to the rise and fall of her uniformed chest. With the other hand she pointed to the open suite doorway to their left.

Her voice shook. "In there. A man. I think he's dead."

Marc glanced quickly at the hallway beyond, then back at the way he'd come.

There was no one.

If the man was dead, there wasn't anything he could do—they needed to call the police. But what if the woman was wrong? He'd taken CPR training and could help if somebody needed medical attention. There was only one way to tell.

He inched toward the lit doorway and peered in, gasping. *What on earth?*

At first Marc didn't notice the man lying on the carpeted floor because of the writhing mass of green. The mass was moving. It was breathing. Then he realized what he was seeing, blinked, and looked again. It was simply too weird.

Frogs. Dozens of them.

They were everywhere. Crawling across the bedspread. Leaping off the shade of the bedside lamp and onto the nightstand. Massing on the back of the man who lay facedown and unmoving in the bathroom, his face turned toward the opposite wall away from Marc.

Fine hairs rose on the back of Marc's neck. A sickening pang churned in his stomach. Was the man dead?

Marc reminded himself not to touch anything and crept into the room, careful not to step on any of the leaping amphibians. He wanted to see if the man needed help, but so many frogs were blocking him from accessing the body.

Something out the corner of his eye drew his gaze to writing on the wall. Somebody had scrawled "Revelation 22:18" in jagged, blood-red capitals that dripped down like something from a horror movie. The body bore no obvious wounds. Where had the blood come from—that is, if the blood was real?

Closer to the body now, Marc crouched on the only vacant spot he could find and studied everything, eyes wide, trying not to miss anything important. Fear hummed along his nerves.

The scene would have felt like a prank—clearly somebody's idea of a joke—if not for the man's eyes, which were open and fixed, staring in a death grimace of shock or pain.

Mind-numbing shock froze Marc in place when he recognized the face.

His college classmate Jared Russo stared at him with lifeless brown eyes.

12

One down. Several to go.

Cyrus knew the corridors well by now—certainly well enough to make his way to the resort security office without missing a beat. It wasn't a large office by anyone's definition. After all, why would a big-shot security force be needed in a place filled with God-fearing men and women, like Jared Russo, who did no wrong?

He smiled at his own sarcasm and replayed Jared's declarations of innocence. *We're all guilty, Jared—all of us. And we all pay in our own way. You just paid earlier than you expected.*

What did God-fearing people need to fear in a safe haven like Sabbath Resort and Conference Center, where framed Bible quotes hung on the walls and ethereal—in his opinion, nauseating—music drifted through ceiling speakers? He'd much prefer some heavy metal. Yes, that would wake them up, wouldn't it?

Well, he'd show them that even in their utopian microcosm, there *was* reason to fear. They could quote their lofty-sounding platitudes and pretend they were holy all they wanted, but he knew human nature better than most. He knew that even the most whited sepulcher hid a deep, dark secret, and there was plenty of guilt to spread around.

And now you've paid for yours, haven't you, Jared? Paid just like the others will pay.

He absently fingered the rubbery, stringy scars contouring the right side of his face and trailing down to his neck, like tree roots seeking sustenance below. After five skin grafts, he didn't resemble a Halloween mask anymore. At least kids who noticed him at the grocery store no longer ran away, howling, to their mothers.

But I'm not about to win any beauty pageants either.

He'd accepted the scars from the fire as a sort of badge of honor he took with him wherever he went. They reminded him—lest he should forget—that out of 76 people, he was one of the few who had made it out alive.

Near the security office, he pulled what resembled a typical department-store credit card from his pocket. But looks could be deceiving. The analytic scanner he'd used to enter Jared's suite and was about to use again could detect and repeat the release code securing any electronic lock system.

He found the security office door locked and checked the empty corridor before using the scanner to gain entry. Not a soul was in sight—maybe the staff were on break. Well, that would soon change. Not long now, and this office would be one of the busiest places at the resort.

He eased past a bank of computers, their amber lights blinking like eyes probing the dark. He paused at a counter where several TV monitors lined up in a row were broadcasting live feeds from various security cameras. Most monitored interior hallways. One watched the parking lot.

The sight of the monitors pushed his mind back to another place—in some ways, a place similar to this one, though not nearly as grand. If only they'd had surveillance cameras telling them what the feds had been up to. Later, he'd learned that fiber-optic microphones and cameras had been inserted into the walls and air vents, allowing the feds to tape their conversations and see inside their rooms. Infrared devices had pinpointed everyone's location in the center based on his or her body heat. They'd been sitting ducks—especially the children.

He again marveled that he'd somehow escaped. Perhaps he'd done so for this very moment—to ensure that his comrades weren't forgotten.

One steady, red light stared at him like a probing eye. He pushed a button, and the red button went off. He pressed another button, and the machine—a dinosaur in the world of technology—spat out a small video cartridge.

He'd expected digital backup on DVD at the least. If this antique was any indication of the high-tech nature of the resort, his plans would be even easier to execute than he'd expected.

He pocketed the surveillance video on his way to other corridors and darker deeds.

He smiled. The fun was only getting started.

13

The sunny world outside the suite windows had turned slate gray, the sky overcast and foreboding. *The change in weather seems indicative of our stay here*, Gillian mused as she looked out the window. *Not all it was cracked up to be.* Her notion of a romantic weekend getaway had apparently died with the man lying under a pile of frogs down the hallway.

Jared Russo was a classic joker and prankster. Was it only coincidental that his death scene looked like a joke, as if Jared had somehow staged it himself? Of course, the notion of Jared committing suicide was absurd, but who would have intentionally placed Jared's lifeless body under a pile of frogs like that? And why?

Was someone trying to make a statement of some kind? If so, what was he trying to say other than what the Bible reference, scrawled on the wall in apparent blood, suggested—that Jared's death was judgment of some kind for whatever the protestors were all fired up about? Which was what, exactly? If Jared had meant to explain what was going on, he'd unfortunately missed his opportunity. Bewildered, she hoped they would get some answers soon.

Gillian held Marc's icy hand and cradled Chase close with the other as they sat on the suite couch.

"I already told you. I didn't touch anything," Marc told Sheriff Miles Griswold, a lean man in his mid-40s with a military haircut and an odd patch of white over his left ear. Wiry and athletic, he was probably a runner, the type who ran marathons rain or shine and seemed barely winded afterward.

Gillian had offered the sheriff a seat, but he'd declined, saying that he concentrated better on his feet. He now paced restlessly like a caged lion, as if the movement of his feet somehow connected something in his brain he might not otherwise engage.

"Okay, but why'd you enter the room?" Griswold wrote everything down on a small, black notepad. "Why didn't you call for help?"

"The maid said she thought the man inside was dead," Marc said, "but she could have made a mistake. He could have been seriously hurt. I know CPR and didn't want to waste my time or his."

"But you could have used the hall telephone and waited for help to arrive."

"Again, I didn't want to waste precious time. If the man was injured and needed help, I didn't want to just stand there. It seemed best to see if he was okay and offer help if he needed it."

Griswold shot Marc a stern look, as if reproaching a disobedient child. "Even if you didn't know what you were steppin' into? The assailant could have been waitin' inside with a gun. It was a big risk."

Marc appeared unflustered. "It was a risk I was willing to take. The cleaning lady made the initial survey of the scene and didn't say anything about a gunman. She just thought a man was dead. Look, sheriff, I was part of a criminal investigation once before. I know what you guys look for, so I did my best to be careful."

"I'm well aware of that, Mr. Thayer, but you could have contaminated the scene."

"I already told you—I didn't touch anything. Your techs will confirm that."

The sheriff changed the subject. "Okay, now how exactly do you know this Jared Russo fellow?"

Marc rubbed his forehead. Gillian knew the telltale signs and bit her lip. *Please God, not a migraine. Not now. Let us at least salvage part of our weekend.*

Marc shared some background. "Jared just said he wanted to catch up on old times. We hadn't seen each other in years. After college we both moved away, got married, lost touch— you know how it is. We exchanged Christmas cards each year and e-mailed occasionally, but that was about it."

"Do you know anyone who might have had a reason to harm Mr. Russo?"

"No, but like I said, we weren't in touch until only recently. He could have had enemies I didn't know about. You think this is murder?"

The sheriff cleared his throat. "I'm not exactly sure what to think just yet. I've never seen anything quite like this before. It's bizarre." He passed a hand over his face and sniffed, eyes bewildered. "All I can say so far is that I see a healthy man who shouldn't be dead and a death scene that looks anything but natural to me."

"What do you think it means?"

"The frogs?" He shrugged. "Oh, I really can't say. Not in 23 years have I ever seen anything so weird. Right now, your guess is as good as mine. Maybe he had a heart attack. Beats me. But that still doesn't explain why frogs were crawlin' all over him. Maybe the CSI will shed some light on what's goin' on here."

"Let's hope so. I'd like to know what happened to my friend."

Griswold sniffed again. "Since you're a Bible scholar, I wanted to know your thoughts about the writin' on the wall."

Marc stared at him blankly. "It's a Bible reference."

"I know that, but what does it mean?"

Marc grabbed his Bible from the end table and looked up the verse: "For I testify to everyone who hears the words of the prophecy of this book: If anyone adds to these things, God will add to him the plagues that are written in this book."

Griswold scratched his head. "Well, that sort of makes sense, then. Aren't these guys workin' on some type of newfangled Bible or somethin'? That's what's got everybody outside hollerin', right?"

"Actually, I don't exactly know myself. I was hoping Jared would fill me in."

The sheriff spread his hands. "Well, *I* don't even know, and I'm the sheriff, so join the club. If the writin' on the wall means what you say it does, then we've got a clear connection between your friend's death and whatever this controversial project's all about. Smells a little fishy to me." He paused to rub his forehead, as if Marc's headache were contagious. "Man, and here I thought the incident with the blood was an isolated incident."

"Pardon me?"

Gillian stared at the sheriff. *"Incident with the blood"? What was he talking about?*

"Oh, nothin'." The sheriff forced a smile as if he'd said too much. Apparently satisfied, he thanked Marc and said he'd contact him later if he had more questions. After the door closed behind him, Marc leaned forward, elbows on his knees, and clasped his hands.

"I can't believe this is happening." His thick voice swam in emotions. "I haven't seen Jared in years. I didn't even get to say hello, and now he's dead—and in such a weird way, too. Like he's part of somebody's sick game."

Marc cradled his head in his hands. "Why does time have to create such distance between people? I mean, it seems like only yesterday Jared was quizzing me on my Hebrew verbs and bringing me leftovers when I couldn't make it to the cafeteria."

He looked at her. "You may recall that those were particularly tough times for me, but Jared was a real friend, Gill.

He was one of the most real friends I've ever had, but for some reason I didn't stay in touch."

Gillian rubbed his back in a circular motion. "Time and distance separate all of us from those we love." She thought of her own father, separated by more than time and distance. He'd gambled away his life savings in a casino, and though he'd turned to Christ for help, he seemed incapable of making any real life changes and tearing down the wall he'd erected between himself and those he loved.

"Now I can't tell Jared how much he meant to me. I won't be able to say the thank you I should have said a long time ago. And now, some stranger will call his wife and kids with news nobody should ever hear. It just seems so senseless." He threw up his hands and then paused. "Yet I know God's in control."

"I don't know what to say. I didn't know Jared like you did, but I'm very sorry about what happened."

"But what exactly *did* happen? That's what I want to know."

"It doesn't make a whole lot of sense, does it?"

Someone knocked on their suite door. Marc looked spent, so Gillian pushed to her feet to see who it was and glanced at the visitor through the peephole. She expected to see the sheriff with more questions, but on the other side of the door stood a man she'd never met before. He didn't look like a murderer, but what were they supposed to look like?

She opened the door a crack but kept the chain engaged. "Who is it?"

"My name's Vernon Brannon. I'd like to talk to your husband, Marc."

Gillian unfastened the chain and opened the door wide.

The man was burly and blue eyed, with thick black hair that was trimmed short. A distinctive widow's peak disrupted the straight, clean line of his forehead. Black chest hair peeked from the open collar of his green polo shirt. His bare arms were equally hairy, reminding her of a gorilla. She guessed he was in his mid-forties.

"You must be Gillian Thayer," he said in a deep voice.

"That's right." Gillian wondered how he knew who she was. She sensed Marc at her back and stepped aside so the two men could face each other.

The man's gaze swiveled to Marc. "Are you Marc Thayer?"

"Yes."

"We need to talk."

"What about?"

"About what you saw in that room."

14

With his errands for Lacey's dad complete, Quinn Caruthers was just checking Travis' progress on mowing the 10 acres of the main grounds when his cell phone rang. He covered one ear with one hand to block the roar of the riding mower and listened with the other.

He responded with a few words, said good-bye, and clicked off. He passed the other hand over his face and swore.

How could this be happening? How could a man be dead? The incident with the blood had been one thing, but this was something else.

He reached for his brown-but-turning-silver goatee and smoothed it down. It wasn't supposed to happen this way. All his hopes and dreams of severing ties with his controlling father-in-law and finding his own means of support were in jeopardy.

He longed to take Lacey and Sammy away from this god-forsaken place. What hope did Sammy have here? He deserved therapy from the best doctors to unlock the mysteries of his autism—and Quinn was determined to find the means to pay for them out of his own pocket.

His plans were in jeopardy, but not destroyed—at least not yet.

Inside flared the realization that he'd been used. Used for another agenda.

His mind sorted through possibilities and chose the right path. One word tasted like sour milk on his lips.

Cyrus.

He hit speed dial and waited for the husky voice to pick up.

"Quinn, my friend. Having fun with your lawn buddies?"

Quinn made fists. Cyrus had stationed hidden cameras everywhere and apparently knew his whereabouts at all times. "A man's dead. We need to talk."

15

Marc opened the suite door wide and stepped aside to let Vernon pass. As the stranger moved toward the couch, Gillian and Marc exchanged puzzled looks. After they took seats across from Vernon, Gillian tuned her ear to the bedroom. Not a sound. Chase was still asleep.

Vernon rested his right ankle across his left leg, revealing expensive brown suede shoes. Gillian noticed the tattoo of a fanged green snake coiled up his right arm. *He's been in the military.*

After an awkward moment, in which the two men locked eyes but nobody began the conversation, Marc asked, "So what's this all about?"

"Like I said," Vernon said in an accent that reminded Gillian of New York City, "I need to talk to you."

"But I don't know you."

"No, but Jared did. That's why I'm here. He said I could trust you."

So some people can't be trusted. Gillian decided to remain silent and let Marc do the talking.

"Okay, why don't you start by telling us exactly who you are," Marc said. "You already seem to know us."

"Fair enough." Vernon pressed his fingertips together, forming a tent. "Jared Russo and I are—or were—both members of the Generation Life Publishers Bible translation committee. Maybe you've heard of Generation Life?"

Marc cocked his head. "Nope, can't say that I have."

"We're a small publisher of Bibles and inspirational nonfic-tion. If you haven't heard of Generation Life before, you will soon. About 30 other men are here for our biannual translation committee meeting. If you noticed the protestors out front, you've probably gathered that we're not a very popular bunch."

"So why all the fuss?" Marc asked. "What are you working on that's making people so riled? A Bible in baby speak?"

The faintest of smiles tugged at Vernon's lips. "You're the one who found Jared's body, right? Do me a favor and don't tell anybody except the police and your wife here"—he cut his eyes toward Gillian—"what you saw in that room."

"Why all the secrecy?"

"Let's just say that whoever staged Jared's death is looking for notoriety. He clearly wants the world to know what you saw, and there are a bunch of journalists outside who'd love to spill the beans."

Marc shrugged. "I'm not exactly sure *what* I saw. It didn't make much sense."

"The frogs, you mean."

"That's not exactly something you see every day."

"Actually, the frogs make sense once you understand their context." Vernon pressed his index finger to where his lips came together in a pucker. "Let me back up a bit so you get a clearer picture. Something odd happened here a couple days ago that scared one of our secretaries silly." He described the plague of blood in matter-of-fact terms. "Every water faucet on the grounds was affected."

Marc leaned forward, poised on the edge of his seat. "You're kidding me!"

"Wish I were. In case you didn't know, blood stinks. Half of us were sick to our stomachs just from the stench. We had to shut the whole place down for a thorough cleaning."

"I can only imagine."

"Now that you know about the blood, maybe the frogs make more sense. Jared told me he knew you in Bible college, so I'm assuming you know something about the good book."

An "aha!" moment crossed Marc's face. "Oh, I get it. First a plague of blood, and now a plague of frogs, like the plagues of Egypt in the book of Exodus."

"You catch on quick."

"Well, I'd be pretty blind not to notice the obvious. So somebody's recreating the Egyptian plagues."

"That's what it looks like."

"Can you tell me more about the plague of blood?"

Vernon nodded and described Brianne Hyde's scare in the bathroom. "Focus centered on the secretary because somebody had locked the bathroom door, and she couldn't get out. Of course, her yelling probably helped, too. She's got a powerful set of lungs."

"Any idea how she got locked in?

"Not yet. Somebody must have rigged the plumbing beforehand. The drain was oddly clogged, so the blood overflowed the sink and went everywhere. Somebody had also written 'Revelation 22:18' on the wall, just like in Jared's room. So the two incidents are definitely connected."

Marc shook his head. "Wow. Rigging blood like that must have taken careful planning."

"The sheriff made an important discovery a few hours after the plague began. Somebody hooked one of those big tanker trucks, used for hauling gas or milk, to the water tower through the access hatch—except the tank wasn't filled with gas or milk. In fact, it wasn't filled with blood, either."

"You mean, it wasn't real blood?"

"Nope. From what we can tell right now, it was water with fancy food coloring—not the type you use to color Easter eggs—and something else to create the smell. Somebody went to an awful lot of trouble to make it look and smell like real blood."

"What about the blood on the wall near Jared's body? Was that the same stuff?"

"The substance will need to be analyzed before we know for sure, but so far the sheriff's pretty sure it is."

Marc shook his head. "This is bizarre."

"Actually, it makes the investigation easier. CSI might be able to track down where the substance came from."

"Any suspects?"

"How many protestors are out front polluting the air waves as we speak?"

"You think the protestors are responsible?"

Vernon's look clearly indicated he was questioning Marc's intelligence. "Who else would do something like this but a bunch of translation fanatics? You should read some of their hate mail. Some of them would do almost anything to halt our project."

Gillian's mind drifted to the protestors out front. They certainly seemed passionate in their disapproval of the project.

"These folks believe we're meddling with God's Word, that God will literally judge us with his plagues," he continued. "But they only show their ignorance. You're familiar with what Revelation 22:18 says, right? The context there's pretty clear. The verse refers to the 'plagues that are written in this book.' The words 'this book' are probably referring to the plagues described in the book of Revelation, not to the Egyptian plagues in the book of Exodus."

"Whether the person responsible is interpreting those verses correctly is irrelevant," Marc said. "What's important is what they mean to him or her."

"I guess it isn't so unusual. Some cults are renowned for taking certain verses out of context and twisting them to meet their own agenda."

Or cutting them out altogether. Even Thomas Jefferson had taken a razor to his Bible, slicing out the parts he didn't like.

On the other hand, the Mormons had added their own writings to Scripture.

"Maybe the protestors think they're here to give God a helping hand." Vernon uncrossed his legs. "Maybe they see themselves as his instruments of divine judgment."

Marc shrugged. "If you know the protestors are doing this, tell the sheriff to go arrest them."

"He can't arrest anybody without physical evidence."

"What about the tanker truck? Certainly somebody left evidence of some kind."

"Nope. The license plate was stolen. No fingerprints—the place was wiped down. No fiber evidence either. Very professional—very clean. The police tracked the vehicle registration number. The truck was stolen from some trucking company down near Saginaw. No clue yet who was behind it."

"Okay, so how did the perpetrator get in Jared's room?"

"There wasn't any evidence of forced entry. Either somebody obtained an extra key card and got in that way, or Jared let the assailant in."

"Jared may have known the person well and trusted him. I saw no signs of a struggle."

Vernon nodded. "We'll need to check on the key cards and see if somebody could have obtained an extra one to gain access to Jared's room."

"What about surveillance cameras? Any video footage of someone coming and going from Jared's suite?"

"The police contacted resort security, but the video appears to be missing."

"Missing?"

"Somebody must have taken it."

Marc scrubbed a hand across his face. "So tell me—how do you know so much about this investigation?"

"I'm sort of the unofficial liaison between the committee and the police."

Gillian studied his face. How convenient if Vernon was somehow involved. But why sabotage his own project and murder his best friend?

Vernon inhaled deeply through his nose. "Jared mentioned that he'd invited you here for a getaway and a reunion of sorts. I hate to say it, but since you found Jared's body, you're involved now whether you want to be or not. The police probably won't let you leave town until they finish their investigation. While you're here, we might as well work together and help the sheriff figure out who's responsible."

Gillian didn't like the idea of being trapped here. "Why not just let the police handle it? Why should any of us get involved?"

Vernon's smirk spoke volumes. "No offense to local enforcement, but in case you haven't noticed, we're about as deep in the north woods as you can get. I'm sure Sheriff Griswold is a fine man, but, frankly, I'm not confident he knows how to investigate something as complex as this."

He sighed. "Besides, Jared was a good friend, so I have a personal stake in this. And, as you can imagine, the committee wants to continue their business without distraction. It's a little tough making important decisions while some wacko is reenacting a small-scale version of the plagues of Egypt."

Marc rubbed his bemused face. "A friend of mine is a retired homicide detective. Mind if I contact him for advice?"

"Sure, if you think he can help. You saw the crime scene, so you're already a step ahead of most people."

Marc raised his eyebrow. "Crime scene? We don't even know how Jared died yet."

"Granted, we won't know for sure until the medical examiner does his thing. But isn't that what it looks like—like Jared was murdered in his room? If Jared died naturally—of a heart attack or something—why stage his body with the frogs?"

Marc's voice dripped with sarcasm. "So I take it you don't think these plagues are divine acts of God's judgment?"

Vernon snickered. "Hardly. We all know God isn't going to do something like this."

Gillian chewed the inside of her cheek, wondering why Vernon felt he could read God's mind. She wasn't so quick to dismiss God's outright warnings in Scripture.

"My advice is to take a look at the protestors first," Marc said. "Find out who the ringleader is and talk to him."

"The sheriff's already taking a hard look at the main coordinator, Micah Coombs, a religious activist from lower Michigan. Of course, he denies any involvement, has an alibi, and the police haven't discovered any evidence linking him to the plagues or Jared's death—at least not yet. They certainly don't have enough for an arrest warrant. If they did, then we could finish our meeting in peace and move forward with our work."

Assuming Micah's responsible. Gillian folded her arms.

"So what exactly *are* you working on?" Marc asked.

Vernon rolled his head, cracking his neck. "A new Bible translation. Actually, it isn't just a new English translation—it's a parallel Bible."

"A parallel Bible," Marc repeated. He paused. "Parallel with what?"

The corners of Vernon's lips tightened. "Before I tell you, keep in mind that we're only in the preliminary stages of this project. The committee is evenly split between moving forward and nixing the project altogether due to certain ... uh ... disagreements. Actually, now that Jared's dead, the balance has shifted in favor of moving forward."

"Hmm. If Jared was an obstacle to the project, there's another reason why someone might have wanted him out of the way. I take it the project's pretty controversial."

Vernon smirked. "Just for the record, Jared and I have been against the project from day one."

"So what's causing all the fuss?"

"I know this is going to sound crazy." Vernon sucked in a breath and seemed to hold it. "The plan is to merge a new English translation with the Qur'an."

16

Diapers, baby powder, onesies. Gillian grabbed everything she'd arranged in the bedroom drawer only hours earlier and stuffed it back into the bag. She blew out her cheeks.

A second honeymoon? Whatever. How could this be happening?

She asked Marc without looking at him, "You really think we could be in danger here?"

"Gill, Jared's dead, and it looks like murder. Until we find out what's going on, wouldn't you say this is a dangerous place?" He sighed. "Until we know more, I'd just feel better if you stayed at a hotel for your own safety."

He had a point. She looked at him with a slow nod, fearing for his safety and wishing he would come too. "How long?"

"Hopefully just for tonight until I figure out what's going on."

She faced him. "But what if it's more than tonight? What if you and Vernon can't figure this thing out?"

He stepped toward her and planted his hands on her shoulders, massaging them. "If not me, somebody will. Somebody has to. Until we know otherwise, the protestors *are* the most likely culprits."

"I don't know. They seem like a pretty dedicated bunch to leave their jobs and spend vacation time up here in the north woods to exercise their first amendment rights."

"But there could be a rotten apple in the barrel."

Marc turned and sank onto the edge of the bed Gillian had been looking forward to sharing with him. Her eyes lingered on the hot tub in the corner, taunting her with expectations of a romantic weekend. She glanced away bitterly.

He shook his head. "Can you believe it? A parallel Bible with the Qur'an. What was the committee thinking? Of course they're going to attract attention."

She tucked strands of hair behind her ear. "It sounds to me like they were looking for attention. Maybe this is just a marketing ploy, the type of controversy to boost book sales. Remember the craze over *The Da Vinci Code*?"

"Well, I don't want to question the committee's motives until I know otherwise. You heard Vernon. He says the motives are more evangelistic than anything else."

She shook her head. "Just because it's evangelistic doesn't make it right. So by putting the Qur'an and the Bible together under one cover, more people are likely to see the truth and turn to Christ? Come on!"

He shrugged. "It's possible. A lot would depend on the study notes. Perhaps they'll point out the contradictions between the two books and refute the Qur'an."

Gillian shook her head. "But doesn't putting the Qur'an with our Bible under the same cover appear to give it some validity? I can see why some folks would feel uncomfortable with the idea."

"And don't forget the devout Muslims. Imagine how they'd feel to see their sacred Qur'an merged with what they believe is our corrupt Bible. You're bound to make enemies on both sides."

"Who knows? Maybe Islamic jihadists are behind this."

"Terrorists in the north woods?" Marc chuckled. "Then again, maybe I shouldn't laugh."

He rose, pulled her into a hug, and kissed her. "Look, I'll carry your luggage to the Tahoe. Then you better go before I change my mind."

"So what's your plan?"

He looked like a little boy lost in a supermarket. "I'm no in-vestigator, but I need to start snooping around this place and see what I can find out."

"What about Chuck Riley?"

"I plan to call him, but I have no idea where he is. He's retired and has nothing to do, right? Pray he can drop whatever he's doing and get up here as quickly as possible."

17

M arc carried Gillian's luggage to the Tahoe and returned
to the suite. She grabbed the baby carrier, brushed a kiss
against his cheek, and headed out the door with a promise to
call him later.

She sighed. *God, why does this have to happen now? Why can't
we just get away once without some major catastrophe disrupting
our lives?*

She knew Marc's desire to help Vernon went beyond just being a good Samaritan. Jared had once been Marc's best friend;
it was only logical that Marc would feel some responsibility to
do what he could to catch his friend's killer. She understood his
feelings—to a point. They'd come here for a romantic getaway,
not to catch a murderer.

Perhaps he was overreacting by sending her away for her
safety, but didn't he have a right to? Ever since the Magician
Murderer had almost strangled her, he'd been oversensitive
about her safety, and his thoughtfulness touched her. It showed
that he truly cared, and isn't that what every woman wanted
from her man? To feel prized?

She exited the lodge entrance and pushed through the
tangle of bodies, hoisting the baby carrier in front of her
and muttering apologies. Over the protesters' loudspeakers, a
woman with a pretty voice was singing a song she didn't recognize—something about obeying God's Word for every area
of life. Now that she knew more about the Bible project, she

couldn't help feeling more sympathetic toward the protestors. Apparently Jared had been protesting in his own way by trying to keep the project from seeing the light of day. She had to give him credit for that.

She'd almost reached the Tahoe when something—she wasn't sure what—prompted her to steal one more glance at the crowd. A man stood slightly apart from the group, watching her.

Recognition pricked her memory, and air emptied out of her lungs like a dying breath.

Stunned to weakness, she almost dropped the baby carrier. Then she was striding, almost running, to the Tahoe. Her breaths burst out of her in explosive gasps.

Did he call my name? That was the funny thing about people and time—even after all these years, his baritone voice sounded the same. She ignored the voice that threatened to hurtle her back more than 20 years to a maelstrom of tears and hurt.

She made a beeline for the Tahoe and set the baby carrier down. She thrust her shaking hand into her pocket and grabbed her keys. Dropped them. Snatched them off the pavement and rose.

"Gillian!"

Approaching footsteps pounded the pavement.

God, please get me out of here. I can't do this!

She hit the unlock button and heard the locks respond. She opened the backseat passenger door and swung Chase inside. She snapped him into place in record time, closed his door, and turned—

Gabriel Jacobi. Concerned brown eyes. His unforgettable cleft chin.

"Gillian?"

One quick glance was enough. He was as handsome as she remembered—perhaps even more so. Funny how some people grew more attractive as the years passed, while others shriveled into ugly shells of their former selves.

Indeed, the years had been kind. But her emotions told her he was someone who had been dead to her for a long time. Why now, and why here after all these years? Seeing him online had been one thing. But now to see him face-to-face—

No, God. I ended that chapter in my life long ago. Please don't make me go back.

He was blocking her way. She turned and headed to the driver's-side door by going the long way around.

"Gillian, don't be mad at me. I'm sorry."

She reached her door and paused to glare at him over the Tahoe's hood. She didn't know why she even gave him a hearing.

"It was a long time ago," he said. "I hoped—"

"—that I'd forgotten you abandoned me when I was pregnant with your child?"

She hadn't meant to speak, but there—she'd said it. Her chest and hands were quaking. She hated herself for her reaction. She should have been stronger than this, should have exhibited more control. It wasn't fair. No one should have that kind of power over anyone.

"I'm sorry," he said again. "Please forgive me."

The foul stench of long-concealed resentment filled her nostrils. "Go away! I don't want to talk to you." The coldness in her voice came as a surprise. Was that really *her* talking?

She got into the Tahoe and slammed the door so hard the whole SUV rocked. Air shuttled through her lungs so hard she wondered if she might hyperventilate.

She thrust the key into the ignition, started the engine, and mashed the gas pedal to the floor. The engine roared, but the vehicle went nowhere. She'd forgotten to put it into gear. But even when she realized her mistake, she didn't move.

A wail erupted from the backseat. Chase was like a gauge on her emotions, always knowing the storms in her life and verbalizing them when she was more prone to hold things inside—like now.

She stared at the speedometer, wishing she was speeding far away from this place. More inconsolable sobs arose. She ignored them.

Out of the corner of her eye, she spotted Gabriel Jacobi's khakis lingering just beyond the passenger-side window. She shielded her face with a trembling hand.

Come on, Gabriel. Please. Just go.

She reached for the automatic door locks and hit the button. The thudding response was like a key turning in her heart. At least she was safe for now. Even if he pounded on the window, it wouldn't change anything—she wasn't letting him in.

She left the SUV in park and decided that she needed to calm down before driving away. She stole another glance.

He'd finally taken the hint.

Blessed relief swept over her, but it was quickly replaced by an intense ache that broke somewhere in her throat. Hot tears bit her eyes. She gripped the steering wheel with both arms, couching her head in between.

God, how can this be happening? And why now?

18

The sky's good-bye kiss to another day of gorgeous weather faded over the distant ridge as they followed paths they knew well from countless seasons of going after the big buck. Hunting season was how they'd met, and they'd chosen to meet at the most familiar place of all: the old but surprisingly high-tech hunting cabin nestled deep in the woods. It was where Cyrus had set up headquarters while working on maintenance staff, though they both knew he was here for another agenda.

Quinn paced the one-room cabin in front of the friend he both loved and feared. The man's past was layered with events and deeds that would have made anyone nervous. *But perhaps that's what had made the friendship inviting to begin with*, Quinn mused. It represented something daring, adventurous, and not altogether expected. He liked that—the clear departure from the humdrum of life.

But sometimes departures came at a price.

Now he marveled that his friend could just sit in the rocking chair, so relaxed and carefree, considering their situation. A pouch sat beside his feet, and on the floor lay the two stones Cyrus had tossed like dice to confirm the timing of their meeting. It seemed like an odd way to communicate with God, but Quinn wasn't one to question Cyrus.

"For Pete's sake, Quinn, sit down." Cyrus' voice bore the deep, husky timbre of a chain smoker. "Your pacing is annoying me." He reached up and casually scratched Linus. The ferret clambered playfully on his right shoulder and made gentle clucking sounds. The little nose thrust into the air as if seeking new smells.

Quinn loathed the odd pet but had learned to make concessions for his special friend. "How am I supposed to sit down? The sheriff has interviewed me twice. This wasn't supposed to happen."

Cyrus, always composed and in control, nailed him with his piercing, blue-gray eyes. "You knew there'd be publicity and that people would ask questions. So what's the problem? Did you tell the sheriff anything beyond what we discussed?"

"Of course not."

"Then your alibi's rock solid."

"I guess so."

Annoyance bubbled. "What do you mean—you guess so? How many times have we gone over the details? Just do as I say, and you'll be fine."

Quinn nodded, unsure but compliant. "But nobody was supposed to die."

Those enigmatic eyes flared. "I don't know anything about that."

"You don't know anything about who killed this man?"

"That's exactly what I'm telling you."

Quinn stilled. When had Cyrus ever been clueless about anything? Hadn't he meticulously planned every detail months ago? "Then somebody else is involved—that's what you're saying."

"Well, if it wasn't me and it wasn't you, somebody else must be involved, right?"

Quinn's mind spun. *Someone is using the plagues for their own agenda. But who? The protestors? Who else could have gotten a key card to Jared's room? Who else would have had access?*

Cyrus rose and ambled toward the door, cowboy boots clattering on the hardwood floor. He turned and faced Quinn. "I'm the detail man, remember? Everything will be fine if you just keep your head and do what I say. Now I really need to go. No rest for the wicked."

Quinn mustered some courage—or perhaps stupidity, he realized later. "You wouldn't be lying to me, now, would you?"

Cyrus spun on his heel, eyes hard, fists clenched. "Have I ever lied to you?"

Quinn saw his mistake and hung his head, gaze dropping to the floor. "No."

"I can't hear you."

Louder this time. "No."

Though older than Quinn by a good 20 years, Cyrus was fitter than most men his age, his physique wiry and strong. He certainly knew how to use his fists.

Cyrus took two steps toward Quinn, stopping when they were practically nose to nose. "We've been friends for a long time, haven't we?"

Quinn couldn't meet Cyrus' eyes, so he stared at his scar from the fire and felt himself sweating. Cyrus' wrath was like a sleeping lion, not something to be roused if he could avoid it, and right now his friend was dangerously close to the edge.

Cyrus thrust a finger at Quinn's face, the scar on his face and neck pulsing red. "I expect more from you—do you understand?"

"I'm sorry." In Cyrus' presence he felt like a passive child who did what he was told and didn't ask any questions.

Cyrus sighed. "The next time you go flinging accusations around, stop and remember how many years we've known each other. Think about how our plans are going to benefit both of us. Then ask yourself if you really want to throw them all away."

19

After a long, hot bath, Gillian sat in one of the functional chairs beside her bed, hands cold, emotions numb. But then an idea dawned on her. Maybe she had a way to take her mind off her troubles. She'd providentially brought along some parchment paper and a few calligraphy pens—just in case she got bored or the urge came, as it did now.

Something about pressing the nib of her Osmiroid pen to paper and feeling the gentle glide as she shaped the first letter in old English always felt right, as if this was what God had destined her to do. At least this hobby, which had become a means of financial gain, gave her some sense of control over her life. Perhaps that's why she ran to it whenever life seemed like such a tangle.

A favorite quote from Emily Dickinson manifested itself on the page at the small desk.

> *Hope is the thing with feathers—*
> *That perches in the soul—*
> *And sings the tunes without the words—*
> *And never stops—at all—*

Finished, she sat back and frowned. A little rusty but not bad. And she had hope, didn't she? Hope that God would somehow work Gabriel's horrible reappearance for good.

Her cheeks flamed at the memory of her response in the parking lot. A bitter woman had been living under her skin all these years, hidden away and just waiting to come out, even after she'd decided to forgive Gabriel and let it go. How could old hurts return fresh and raw in an instant, just like that?

She glanced at Chase, who slept as if nothing unusual had taken place in their lives. But what could he know of such things? Let the veil of childlike ignorance drape over his understanding as long as God willed. Sometimes ignorance truly was bliss.

Her cell phone blurted Beethoven's "Fur Elise." Gillian set the pen down on tissue paper and checked her caller ID. It was Crystal, calling from music camp. She was probably worried because they hadn't called her after arriving at the resort as they'd agreed.

Gillian rubbed her forehead, sensing the beginnings of a headache that always accompanied a good cry. Her mind groped like a hand in the dark. What could she say? Certainly nothing about Gabriel. So she told her about Marc finding Jared Russo's body instead.

"Your father was concerned about my safety, so he sent Chase and me off to a hotel. He's doing some detective work at the resort now, but he said he'd join us here later."

"Wow. Some weekend getaway, huh?"

"Well, you know us. Whenever we travel to a new place, something strange always seems to happen." *Like we're homing pigeons to trouble.*

"Sorry, Mom. I know how badly the two of you wanted a break. So how's my baby brother? Put him on the phone so he can tell me about his day."

Gillian glanced at Chase, one hand pressed to her aching neck. "I think I can interpret. Ten diaper changes, eight feedings, and plenty of bonding with the sandman."

"Oh, I wish I could see him. I love the way he curls his fingers over his face when he's sleeping. Is he doing that now?"

"Yep. So how are you doing?" Gillian felt herself relax. Talking to her daughter on the phone was always cathartic.

Crystal told her about some of the more challenging students and described her new voice teacher, who was much tougher than her old one. Crystal had sung the national anthem at the Fourth of July church picnic. Gillian thought she'd done a terrific job—so poised and confident as she'd sung her heart out. Thanks to those many years of voice lessons, she'd even won a college scholarship. The sudden thought of college this fall reminded Gillian that she would have to let go of her daughter sooner than later.

Girlish laughter pealed in the background.

"Are you with some of your friends?" Gillian asked.

"Yep, we thought we'd crash with a pizza and a movie."

Gillian heard the ding of a doorbell.

"Gotta go, Mom. The pizza guy's here."

"Don't stay up too late, and don't watch any scary movies, okay?"

"You know I don't watch scary movies anymore."

True. Ever since the Magician Murderer had almost strangled Crystal, she'd avoided anything scary. Movies about serial killers hunting down young, defenseless girls were especially off her list for all of time.

"Well, I don't want your pizza getting cold," Gillian said. "Take care."

"Stay in touch, Mom. Love you."

"Love you, too."

Gillian clicked off and settled back into her chair, longing for Marc's presence. Certainly he'd received her tearful voice mail by now. Ten minutes later, her wish was granted when he knocked on the door.

He kissed her and held her for a long moment before leading her to the bed. There he held her some more, just letting her cry with her face against his chest, the faint scent of his woodsy aftershave mingling in the air around them.

"I got your voice mail and came as soon as I could."

"Any news on who killed Jared?"

"Not yet. The sheriff's waiting on toxicology reports, which always take longer than you see on TV. Hey, I also reached Chuck Riley. He and his wife, Emily, are flying here tomorrow."

"Good. I've always wanted to meet Emily." She peered into his eyes and felt relieved. His eyes looked fine. There was no sign of the migraine she'd feared was coming.

He studied her face. "How are *you* doing? I can only imagine how shell-shocked you must feel right now. Tell me what happened."

So she did. "What I can't figure out is what Gabriel's doing here, of all places."

"I did a little research. The protest organizer, Micah Coombs, is an activist representing some religious, current-event-awareness ministry downstate. Gabriel Jacobi is his assistant."

So Gabriel hadn't become the businessman his dad had always wanted him to be. What a blow that must have been. "His assistant? When Gabriel and I ran off together years ago, he'd pretty much had it with anything religious. Of course, at the time, so had I."

"But that was a long time ago, Gill. Long before we even met."

But it doesn't feel like that long ago. It feels like only yesterday.

In the dusty corridors of recollection, a lonely girl was still standing at an apartment picture window, staring down at the street below. Waiting, hoping, but never finding. In her emotional sphere, it was as if time had stopped like a wind-up toy, waiting for somebody to wind it up again.

They'd had a terrible fight. Hours had passed since Gabriel stormed out after their argument, saying he was going to pick up supper at Pizza Hut and be right back. She'd waited for him like the naïve person she was, knowing all along he'd driven away and wouldn't be back. Knowing that he'd abandoned her to her loneliness—and her morning sickness.

"Maybe God has worked in his heart liked he worked in yours," Marc suggested.

"But what he did to me—"

"It must have hurt."

"You have no idea, Marc. He said he loved me. Said we'd get married and grow old together, but then … he just drove off." *Like he didn't care at all. Like I was a piece of trash to be thrown away.* Pain pushed more tears out of her puffy eyes. She grabbed another tissue from the bedside table and dabbed them away.

"He never made contact, not even to say he was sorry?"

She fiddled with the tissue with restless hands. "No. I waited for him for days. I even called the police and filled out a missing persons report. I wondered if he'd been killed in an accident."

She sighed, weary of telling the story over again. "Later, after my parents took me back home and I had the miscarriage, I thought Gabriel would at least call to make sure I was okay. After all, the baby was his too."

"But he never called?"

"Nope. Never said a word."

"Is it possible he didn't know about the miscarriage when it happened?"

"It's possible. His parents didn't even know where he was—at least that's what they said. It was like he'd disappeared off the face of the earth."

Marc shook his head, pursed his lips.

"But Marc, he *knew* I was pregnant. If he was alive, certainly he would have wanted to know that his baby was okay, right?"

"That would be the natural reaction."

"I mean, who would do something like that? I began to think it was me—that he really hated me that much."

Marc's mouth twisted to one side. "No, I don't think so. Maybe he felt too guilty to show his face. I mean, what set him off? The news of your pregnancy, right?"

She nodded.

"Maybe the guilt of what he'd done was simply too much for him to handle. He didn't want to face the music. Everybody in your immediate circle would find out what he did, so maybe he ran. Like a criminal. Ran away like Jonah instead of doing what God wanted him to do."

More like a fool. Though they'd attended separate churches on the opposite side of town, they'd gone to the same Christian school. It wasn't long after she returned home that tongues began to wag.

"Maybe God used the guilt to turn Gabriel around, but maybe not right away," Marc suggested. "Maybe it just took some time."

"You sound like you're defending him." Gillian regretted the edge in her voice.

"No, not defending him. I'm just saying that sometimes people change. *You* changed, Gill. Remember?"

She eyed the textured ceiling. *Me, yes. But no, not him. Not Gabriel. Impossible.*

"I need to ask you a hard question."

She steered her gaze back to Marc's face.

"Are you really sure you've forgiven him? I'm hearing resentment in your voice."

She gritted her teeth. "I forgave him in my heart long ago, Marc—really. But seeing him today ... it was like having an old wound ripped open. I can forgive him in my mind, but letting go of the hurt isn't that simple."

She hooked a lock of hair behind her ear. "I'm not going to lie to you. Even though I've forgiven him, the pain and anger don't want to go away. In fact, today they're as fresh as ever. It's like I'm still 17 and sitting in that apartment, sick and pregnant, waiting for him to come back and knowing he never will."

Marc repositioned himself behind her, his nimble fingers probing her stiff neck and shoulders, massaging every knot away. "I'm sorry for how he hurt you. I don't know what else to say other than what you've heard before. Forgiveness isn't an emotion—it's a choice. You can let go of the hurt in your will even though your emotions want to hang on. You know what the Bible says about forgiveness."

"We're supposed to forgive others as God has forgiven us," she recited in monotone. It was amazing how his fingers always found the right places, as if he'd been trained as a masseur.

"If a brother or sister has hurt us, we're not even supposed to worship until we've gone to that person first and made things right."

She hated to state the obvious. "So you're saying I need to confront Gabriel about this."

His warm hands rested on her neck. "I'm saying you need to search your heart and ask yourself if you need to. Only you can decide that. If you can't let go of the hurt and release Gabriel from what he did, then yes. You need to confront him about how he hurt you and forgive him, even if he doesn't seem sorry. The Bible says that's the next step to take, and now that I see how upset you are, I think that's what you need to do."

"He already said he's sorry."

His hands began working again. "Then the next step is up to you. It's your choice. Will you let go of what he did to you?"

She pondered his words over the next hour as they lounged, snacked on salted peanuts and Coke, and cuddled with the TV turned off. She lingered in his embrace, so glad to have him close right now. His presence meant she was safe, that everything was going to be okay. Besides, now that Marc was involved in this murder investigation, maybe this was all the weekend they would enjoy together. Might as well make the most of it.

He rose as if to go.

"Where are you going?"

"I need to do more snooping around at the resort, and frankly the nighttime is the best time to do that."

He checked his phone for messages. Because of the investigation, she'd given his "toy" back, but now she regretted it. Strange how an electronic gadget felt like competition.

She reached for his hand. "Please, Marc, don't go. Stay with me. Remember what you said? This is supposed to be our second honeymoon."

He turned, and the sight of her did to his eyes what the sun does to butter. He turned off the phone and set it on the TV stand. Then he returned to bed and put his arm around her, pulling her close.

"Well, since you put it that way..."

20

A sliver of light gleaming through the folds of the curtain hit Marc square across the face. He rolled to his side, trying not to wake Gillian, and everything came back. The weekend getaway. Jared's bizarre murder.

His eyes stung. Jared was really gone—he could hardly believe it. The world seemed like a much emptier place now.

As he crept out of bed and headed to the bathroom for a shower, he hoped Gillian had slept well. *God, would you please give her soul peace today? Would you teach her how to let go of this hurt?*

Marc stretched his tall frame under the hot shower, glad to be away from his office chair for a few days. He had a tendency to hunch, and his chiropractor had warned him about worse back pain if he didn't improve his posture. *Chest high, shoulders back. Yada, yada.*

Marc turned his head and let hot needles of water pound against his shoulders and chest. He allowed his thoughts to drift back to Gillian's encounter with Gabriel.

All of us make mistakes. Certainly I have. Should Gabriel's mistake haunt him for the rest of his life?

Verses flooded his mind then, reminders that God had separated Gillian's sins as far as the east is from the west. Gabriel's sins, too. That is, if Gabriel was a true believer. If he was covered by the blood of Jesus.

Marc needed to know if the guy was sincere or just toying with Gillian. If Gabriel was just playing games, Marc would be more than happy to connect his fist to the guy's nose.

Easy, Marc. What he did happened a long time ago. Remember what you told Gill. You need to practice what you preach, buddy. Forgive him and let go.

Marc shaved, got dressed, read some encouraging verses in 1 John, and checked his phone. He found a message from Vernon, but still no reply from his dad. The non-response was like a slap across the face. He loved his dad and hated to see his estrangement linger. What could he do to patch things up? Then again, maybe it wasn't up to him. Sometimes following Christ meant making enemies.

He found Gillian standing in front of the vanity, pulling a comb through her short, wavy red hair. He crept up and embraced her from behind, nuzzling his nose against her neck. Gazing at their reflections in the mirror, he deemed they looked rather nice together.

"You're up early," she said.

"I'm getting old and can't sleep in anymore. Besides, I need to go."

She turned, her amazing green eyes tinged with concern. "Go where? What's so urgent?"

"Vernon Brannon wants to meet me for breakfast at the resort in half an hour. Says he's got important news. Why don't you join us?"

Gillian glanced at Chase in his crib and considered. "I hate to wake him. They're serving a continental breakfast downstairs. We'll be fine."

"I'll call you later then, okay?"

She nodded, bit her lip. "I know Chase and I are here for our safety, but you weren't really thinking we'd spend the whole weekend cooped up in this hotel room, were you?"

"Sorry. I'm not sure what I was thinking. I just wanted you safe."

"The Rileys are arriving sometime around eleven. If I hang out with them, I should be safe enough, right?"

He realized he was being overprotective, but he couldn't stand the thought of losing her. "You're right. That should be fine."

"Stay in touch, and we'll catch up with you later. Sound good?"

He kissed her and pulled her into a tight, lingering hug. He wished he could just stay with her and not head to this meeting with Vernon. Wished he could send Gabriel Jacobi, this sudden distraction in their lives, somewhere far away—maybe Siberia.

While driving to the resort, he hoped the night there had passed uneventfully. But something in his gut told him that wasn't the case.

21

Tiny animal shapes had been woven into the hotel room's drapes. Threads of blue and tan crisscrossed and mingled in a grand design only machines could perfect. Camels or ostriches? Gabriel Jacobi wasn't sure. He decided they were more likely ostriches, those animals inaccurately known for hiding their heads in the sand.

Cell phone to his ear, he brushed the drapes aside and peered out at the brightening world beyond, wishing he could be one of those ostriches—but hiding more than his head.

Hiding the past he didn't want to remember.

Just back from the five-mile run he took every other day, he dabbed at the sweat still streaming down his face and neck. His damp red T-shirt was beginning to chill his cooling body. He had intended to hop into the shower, but then the phone rang, his wife, Celia, at the other end. She had a habit of calling at odd times, especially when he was on business trips. It was as if she didn't fully trust him.

"I'm doing fine," he said. "Why wouldn't I be?"

Celia laughed girlishly and said in her honey-dripping Georgia accent, "Oh, Gabriel. Don't you think I know you better than that by now? I can tell when somethin's wrong. I can hear it in your voice."

Certainly Celia knew he'd been no saint during a certain period of his life before they met. He'd of course told her all about his past entanglement with Gillian Canfield Thayer. Since they'd agreed never to keep secrets from each other, he decided right then to tell her everything, his slick hand tightening around the phone.

"What's *she* doin' there?" Suspicion oozed from Celia's voice.

"I don't know, maybe she's here on vacation. Like I said, we didn't really get to talk. I can tell she's still pretty mad at me about what happened."

He half expected Celia to say, "Well, she's got every right to be," but thankfully she didn't. Instead, she said, "Well, you better keep your distance from that woman."

"I will—as much as I can. But some things in our past were never resolved, so I think I better seek her out and have a talk." *And say I'm sorry—that is, if she'll even give me a hearing.*

A long pause passed. "Is she pretty?"

"Celia, it was a long time ago. I'm committed to you—you know that."

"Is she pretty?" she repeated.

"Okay, yes, she's pretty, but not as pretty as you are. Not by a long shot."

She giggled. "You're just a flatterer. That's what you are."

He relaxed. "I thought you liked flattery."

"Oh, just stop."

"Now don't worry, everything will be fine." The words seemed like wasted effort because she was such a worrywart, though her spunkiness did a good job of hiding it. In fact, right after their call she would probably run to his mom with the news, seeking to be consoled.

He said, "What happened with Gillian was a long time ago. You're my wife—I love you."

"Oh, Gabriel. That's sweet." She paused. "Well, why don't you tell me more about yesterday. Anything exciting happen?"

He reluctantly told her about the bizarre incident with the frogs and Jared Russo's murder.

"Oh, mercy! First the blood and now this? Have the police found whoever killed that man?"

"Not yet, but I'm afraid they've got their sights on Micah."

"You don't think they'll arrest him, do you?"

Actually, getting arrested and spending time in jail weren't that unusual for Micah. An ardent and sometimes belligerent activist, Micah didn't mind crossing the line of legality from time to time when he believed his cause was just.

He switched the phone to his other ear. "No, I don't think they'll arrest him, unless they find some evidence I don't know about. Look, I really need to hop in the shower. I need to meet Micah in a half hour."

"Good grief, you poor dear. Didn't you have a meeting with him last night? How much sleep did you get anyhow?"

"Oh, I don't know. Maybe four hours."

"*Four hours!* Gabriel James Jacobi, you tell Micah he can just cool his jets while you go back to bed and get some proper rest."

Her mothering ways made him grin. He shook his head at her childish, simplistic solution. "Celia, you know I can't do that. He hired me to be his assistant, remember?"

Silence lingered on the other end as Celia thought hard to counter his reply with something clever. But Celia wasn't clever—just loving, simple, and loyal. And that's just the way he loved her.

"Look, I'm a big boy. I'll be fine. I'll just take a nap this afternoon and catch up."

"Promise?"

"Promise. Now I've really gotta go."

"Well, all right, but I'll call you tonight, okay?"

"Okay."

"Just wanted to check on you. You know how I hate it when you're gone."

"I know, and it's nice to be checked on. Keeps me out of trouble."

She giggled. "You sly devil."

"Give our babies kisses for me."

"Will do."

"I love you."

"Love you too. And you be careful with Gillian, Gabriel."

"I promise. Bye."

After he clicked off, his mind slid back to Gillian's bitter re-action in the parking lot. What was she doing here? And why now of all times?

Even after all these years, he couldn't dismiss the fact that he still had feelings for her. After all, she'd conceived their child, though the baby had died not long afterward. He'd hoped that the distance of years meant she would face him more as a for-getful acquaintance than an offended party.

What did you expect, you moron? You drove away and left her there. Why would she be happy to see you again after you treated her like scum?

In the shower he reached for the soap and lathered one arm, wishing the painful memories and Gillian's hurt could mingle with his sweat and wash down the drain together. Out of sight, out of mind. He aimed a feeble prayer heavenward. God knew, didn't he? He would help him sort through this mess, right?

All things work together for good, he reminded himself. *But that doesn't mean they're always easy.*

One thing was certain: A future meeting with Gillian Canfield Thayer was inevitable. The broken bone caused by his hurtful choices would never be reset until they talked. Between now and then, he needed to decide what he was willing to say.

The question was, when Gillian heard the truth, would she even believe him?

22

Unlike the day before, Marc had no problem finding a parking spot. It was apparently too early for even the newshounds and protestors. Too bad. He would have to check out Gabriel Jacobi another time. But even if they met, what would he say? *You had her first, but she's mine now, so keep your paws off?*

He strolled into the Backwoods Grille, the resort restaurant, right on time, purchased the breakfast buffet, and filled his plate with biscuits and gravy, scrambled eggs, bacon, and grapes. He surveyed the milling group of maybe a hundred people, both young and old, but he didn't see Vernon anywhere. He was probably running late.

Several men, casual in khakis or dress jeans with polo shirts, crowded around one person in particular. The potbellied man was in his late 50s or early 60s, his thick, wavy hair more white than gray. Scholarly, black-framed glasses perched on his aquiline nose.

After Marc had gotten settled at a table in an isolated corner that offered some privacy, Vernon strolled up with a plate even more heaped than Marc's. "Sleep well?" he asked.

"Nothing ever keeps me awake." Marc sprinkled pepper on his scrambled eggs. "You?"

Vernon unloaded himself across from Marc. "Not so good. I kept thinking about Jared and who might have killed him."

"Yeah, I've been thinking about that too and wish I had some answers." Marc aimed his chin toward the white-haired man, who was still the magnet for attention. "Hey, who's the rock star?"

Vernon twisted his neck to look. "Oh, that's Dr. Matthew Colbert, chairman of the translation committee. He's the top dog, you might say. I'll have to introduce him to you sometime."

They bowed heads, and Marc asked God to bless the food. He also prayed for Jared's family during this difficult time and asked God to lead them to the killer so they could stop him before he hurt anybody else.

Afterward, Vernon asked, "Where's your wife and the baby? They were welcome to join us."

Marc explained about the hotel and his safety concerns.

"Can't say I blame you. If my family was here, I would have done the same thing."

Marc tasted his scrambled eggs. Yep, they were homemade. "So what's the news?"

Vernon bit into a sausage link and chewed it thoughtfully. "A lot happened after you left last night. First, I received news that Jared was probably poisoned."

"Probably?"

"The initial exam didn't show any obvious causes of death. No bruises, no blunt force trauma. But something investigators found at the scene makes poisoning a logical bet."

Marc raised his eyebrows.

"When you found Jared's body, did you notice anything unusual?"

"Other than the frogs crawling all over his back? No, I don't think so."

"Maybe one frog was unusual? Stood apart from the rest?"

"Now that you mention it, yeah. One was a little odd—yellow, I think. A little guy."

"Investigators have identified it as a golden poison frog. Ever heard of it?"

"Nope."

Vernon spread strawberry jam on an English muffin. "Specimens like this one apparently only come from Colombia. You know what they say—'Good things come in little packages.' No kidding with this little guy. One milligram of his poison is enough to kill 10 to 20 men."

Marc whistled. "I sort of gathered we weren't talking about Kermit the Frog here. So you're saying the killer poisoned Jared with a frog?"

"That's what it looks like—until we find out otherwise. I did some research last night you may find interesting. Apparently, when the Chocó Indians bake those frogs over an open fire, the frogs sweat the deadliest toxin known to man. The Indians soak their arrow tips and darts in the poison, making them lethal for more than a year."

"That's amazing."

"Unfortunately, toxicology reports could take some time, so we may need to wait a while until we know for sure. But the sheriff's pretty sure we found our smoking gun."

Marc mulled on this stunning news. "So what do we know about Jared's last movements?"

"He ate lunch with his colleagues here, said he wasn't feeling well, and retired to his suite to rest."

"Maybe somebody slipped something into his food. Just enough to make him sick and isolate him in his room."

"Maybe. But why kill somebody in such an unusual way?"

Elbows on the table, Marc cradled his coffee mug between his hands, the rich, dark-roast brew warming his fingers. "To link his death with the plague of frogs, I guess."

Vernon's eyes flickered. "The murder *is* linked to the plagues for the simple reason that nobody keeps a golden poison frog in his pocket just in case somebody ticks him off."

Marc smirked. "Well, I don't, but maybe you do."

A light smile touched Vernon's lips, then he twitched as if stung by the inappropriateness of humor in light of his friend's death. "Whoever planted the poison frog must have known that the plague of frogs was going to take place. That tells us the killer and whoever is doing the plagues are probably the same person."

"Or perhaps a few people are working together." Marc thought about the protestors he'd seen yesterday. They'd looked like law-abiding, God-fearing people, but perhaps their benign appearance was only an illusion.

Then another possibility dawned. *Was an evil imposter using them as a shield?*

23

It was funny how his mom fell asleep on a backyard lounge chair at roughly the same time each day. A book lay face-down on her lap. Her head leaned to one side, and brown hair fell across one shoulder, partly covering her face.

Sammy knew she would be out for hours. Now it was time for his fun little game.

Find Daddy. Find Daddy.

That morning before leaving his bedroom, he'd grabbed his crank flashlight and stuffed it into the pocket of his baggy shorts. Now he faced the loose section of fencing and took a deep breath, remembering what one of his therapists had told his mom. Yes, he heard and understood more than anybody realized.

Sammy gets easily overwhelmed by choices. If he just takes things one at a time, he should be able to do just about anything. And repetitive actions are best of all.

He focused on the fencing and pushed the loose section outward like a gate while making clicking sounds with his tongue. *One thing at a time. One thing at a time.* The fence opened to another world. The exhilaration of success washed over him.

He followed the usual trails in the woods and found Daddy and his pickup on the resort's north side. He flapped his hands excitedly and squinted into the sunlight.

Found Daddy! Found Daddy! Fun game for Sammy.

He paused behind some wild honeysuckle, hands on his knees, to catch his breath. His shirt stuck to his sweaty chest. He squinted around in amazement, grunting. The colors in the woods were so much more alive than his crayons.

The scent of pine trees mingled with the morning breeze that caressed his face. It reminded him of the music in a TV commercial—the one with the woman standing by the window and breathing deeply while the wind blew the curtains. He liked that song and bobbed his head at the memory.

His dad was checking on Joey and Travis, who were riding around on those wide, red things that did a complete circle in seconds. Around and around and around. He'd excitedly pointed to those red things one day, but his mom had done what she always did, babying him like a three-year-old who couldn't even button his own shirt. His mom and dad had talked with loud voices after that. He couldn't stand it when they talked about him as if he wasn't standing there. As if he didn't even exist.

Maybe someday he would get to ride one of those red things, but not today. Today he needed to move quickly before Daddy drove off and left him behind. The back of the pickup was right in front of him. If he moved quickly, he could hide under that tarp in the back as he'd done before.

Truck. Truck.

He froze. His dad was crossing the lawn toward the pickup. Sammy cowered in the brush, heart sinking, and realized he was too late.

Wait. One of the guys, Travis, called his dad's name. Daddy turned, walked back, and crouched on the lawn with Travis to check something under the big, red thing.

Now Sammy had his chance, but he needed to move quickly before Daddy returned.

Run. Run.

Sammy sprinted toward the truck. He climbed into the back and lay on his side, pulling the tarp over himself. It was dark under here, and sometimes the dark made him scared. But he had no choice if he was going to ride along with Daddy. He flicked fingers in front of his face to calm himself.

Just in time. Daddy's work boots thudded against the ground—he was coming back. His familiar voice intruded on the thick, humid air. "Okay, thanks for letting me know." A sigh. "We'll have to order a new part, I guess. Can't believe it. That mower's only two years old."

Sammy wanted to giggle but kept quiet.

Daddy doesn't see me. Daddy doesn't know.

Sounds and sensations rushed over him. The opening of the driver's side door. The rocking of the truck as his dad got in. The slamming of the door. The cranking of the engine.

The truck lurched forward and rocked over uneven ground in a motion that made him want to dance and twirl. An open fold near Sammy's face framed another world. Trees and brush rushed past in a brown-green blur. Two brown wheel ruts hemmed in by green trailed away and curved around the bend. The tarp stank of gasoline and mold.

His pulse accelerated. Was Daddy going to the special, hidden place?

24

Vernon enjoyed two bites of his English muffin before say-ing, "To me it's obvious that somebody has some pretty strong feelings about the Bible project and is doing all he can to sabotage it. You probably don't like the idea of the project either. It's okay—you can be frank with me."

Am I that transparent? People had always told Marc he wasn't very good at hiding his emotions. "It doesn't really matter whether I agree with the project or not. I just want to find out who killed Jared. I just want to know the truth."

"The truth?" Vernon raised his eyebrows. "It might be a while before we know what that is. In the meantime, what's your best guess so far?"

"I can see someone rigging the plague of blood. There must be suppliers for all that fake blood in those spook houses that pop up every Halloween. I can even see someone simulating the plague of frogs. Frogs probably aren't too hard to obtain if you have access to some biological supply company. But mur-der—that seems to go beyond opposition to the project, don't you think? It seems more—I don't know—personal."

Vernon drank down the last of his coffee. "Not necessarily. How much do you know about Islam?"

"Just the basics, I guess. Why?"

"Ever since the *700 Club* ran a story about our project a few months ago, Generation Life has been swamped with hate mail—a lot of it from Muslims living in the US. It's an understatement to say that devout Muslims are opposed to the Bible project too. While they cling to their sacred Qur'an, they despise the English Bible and say it's corrupt. To merge a supposedly corrupt Bible with the Qur'an—"

"—would be an insult to their faith. And everybody knows how seriously they take their faith." Funny that he and Gillian had just discussed this. He glanced at several Middle Eastern-looking men chatting at a far table, probably translators of some kind. Could Islamic jihadists be to blame?

"Of course, not all Muslims are jihadists ready to strap a bomb to their waists and blow themselves to kingdom come for Allah," Vernon said. "Most are peaceful, law-abiding citizens like you and me, but I think many underestimate the radical fringe and how far they're willing to go. Consider how many suicide bombers have given their lives for the cause."

Marc shook his head. "Just look at their dedication—being willing to fly planes into the World Trade Center and the Pentagon due to their hatred of the United States."

"By the way, to jihadists Israel is the 'Little Satan,' but the United States is the 'Great Satan.' If you think they hate Israel, consider how much they must hate us."

And now infidels are meddling with their sacred Qur'an. Vernon had a good point. Anyone who studied the Qur'an knew what it said about infidels. They were to be converted to Islam or beheaded—end of story. Thankfully, not all Muslims interpreted the Qur'an the same way or applied it to the same degree, but those verses were certainly the engine that drove the extremists.

"So there are other reasons why somebody might want to halt the project or perhaps even commit murder," Vernon said. "Jared Russo was one of our lead Hebrew scholars. His death puts a roadblock in our path, at least for the Old Testament text. We'll have to find somebody else to take his place, and that'll take some time. Hebrew scholars of Jared's caliber aren't exactly a dime a dozen."

Marc's mind skipped like a rock across a pond of college memories—of Jared quizzing him on his Greek, of Jared praying with him when he was ready to throw in the towel. He mentally shook himself and sipped his juice, realizing he didn't have time to dwell on the past. He owed Jared the favor of hunting down his killer—and the clock was ticking.

Retired homicide detective Chuck Riley, who preferred to be called "Riley," had told him that the first 48 hours of any murder investigation were always the most critical. If they didn't catch the killer soon, the trail could turn cold.

Marc cleared his throat. "Okay, we've had two plagues so far. Let's break it down. What's the main difference between the two as far as outcome?"

Vernon thought a minute. "During the plague of blood, the secretary was traumatized, but nobody was murdered. Maybe the guy was just getting warmed up."

That's what I'm afraid of. "Then during the plague of frogs, Jared was murdered. So far whoever's doing this is following the biblical order. So what comes next on the list, if the plagues continue?"

"Gnats, mosquitoes, or both. But we have no idea who the killer's next target could be."

Just the thought of the little varmints crawling all over his skin and biting him made Marc itch. "At least we know what to expect. Any way to prevent them?"

"Well, sure. Pesticides would do the trick, except we don't know where the next plague will occur—if there'll even be one. Will the bugs be isolated to one room like the frogs? Or will they be more widespread like the plague of blood?"

"How widespread was the blood?"

"You mean, did it affect the lake on the property? Nope, but the fake blood *did* affect the whole water supply for at least several hours. We don't know how precise our assailant intends to be. Perhaps he's only targeting those he believes need to be judged."

The word "judged" darted around in Marc's mind like a pesky fly, and he couldn't swat it away. Perhaps the killer saw himself or herself as an instrument of God's justice.

But who exactly is the killer judging? All the mind-bending scenarios made Marc's head throb. *Maybe I'm just thinking too hard and making this case a lot more complex than it needs to be. Boy, I sure wish Riley would hurry up and get here.*

"Okay, let's say whoever's responsible is playing God and meting out judgment," he said. "Based on what we've seen so far, who would he be judging?"

"For the first plague, my guess is the translation committee or maybe the secretary locked in the bathroom, though she seems unlikely."

Marc rubbed his forehead. Too broad. How could they possibly check out all those people?

"For the second plague, it's pretty obvious Jared was his target."

Marc nodded. Somebody had wanted him dead, but why? Maybe Micah or one of the other protestors *was* responsible. Perhaps what seemed simple and obvious was the most likely solution after all.

Marc let his eyes wander around the massive room. He took in the high pine beams, the mounted deer heads, and the massive windows overlooking the picturesque lakeside tableau. Vital clues as to who was behind the plagues could be hidden anywhere on the premises. The resort was sprawling, but he needed to search as much of it as possible.

After breakfast, Marc spent an hour searching the grounds, a small groomed section of 2500 acres of wilderness. Since he'd grown up working for his dad's landscaping business, he couldn't help casting an appreciative eye on the choice of flowering shrubs and mulch. Whoever had done the landscaping had known what they were doing. During his search he called Gillian and filled her in on his breakfast conversation. She sounded stunned to hear about the poison frog. She agreed to call him after the Rileys checked in.

He continued his search but found little of interest, though he wasn't sure what he was looking for. At the suite he decided to wait for Gillian's call. He'd switched on the giant TV and was checking the latest headlines when the blurt of his ringtone startled him. It was an electronic version of "Ghost Riders in the Sky," a favorite cowboy song.

He pulled out his phone and checked his caller ID. "Hey, Vernon."

"Hey, I'm calling you quick between meetings. Thought you'd like to know that the police just picked up Micah Coombs for questioning."

Marc clutched the phone tighter. "Why? What happened?"

"During a routine police search of Micah's room, Sheriff Griswold found a sales receipt with Micah's name on it. Get this—the receipt was for a golden poison frog. Micah allegedly ordered one from an exotic pet website."

25

The pickup rolled to a stop, and Sammy froze, sudden panic pouncing on him. Heat washed over him, and his muscles tightened. He felt trapped and flicked fingers before his face, trying to calm down.

Remember, Sammy. Remember.

He could deal with this change, but only if he relaxed, stayed focused, and took one step at a time.

He sucked in several deep breaths. The first step was dealing with whatever happened next. If his dad came to the truck's bed and grabbed the tarp, he was dead meat.

No, Daddy. No.

Sweat trickled down his face, dripped on the truck bed. Wow, was it hot under the tarp! He longed for fresh air, but not yet.

Wait. Wait.

Daddy got out of the truck and slammed the door. Then, to Sammy's relief, his footfalls moved away and got quieter until Sammy could hear only the birds and the wind in the trees. Daddy must have gone tromping off into the brush like last time.

Sammy waited a full minute before acting. Certain Daddy was gone, he flung off the tarp and crawled out of the truck, flapping his hands excitedly. Fresh air washed over his sweaty body.

He glanced around and saw only the truck and lots of trees. Crushed weeds marked his dad's path into the woods.

Follow Daddy. Follow Daddy.

Where was Daddy going? Was he looking for monkeys, too? Sammy had seen pictures of monkeys in some of the books his mom read to him. He wanted to see monkeys, but how come he never saw them here? Didn't monkeys like trees? Maybe he would bring bananas next time. Then the monkeys would come out for sure.

Sammy felt a bug on his arm and slapped it. He tried to wipe off the yucky red stuff it left smeared on his arm. Sunlight streamed down through leaves and branches above, burning the back of his neck and making him squint in the light. It was going to be another "sizzler," just like the nice man on TV had said.

He approached each bend cautiously and giggled into the hand covering his mouth. Part of the fun was following Daddy without Daddy knowing. If Daddy decided to return to the truck for some reason, though, he would need to dart into the trees and hide. Thankfully, he saw no sign of Daddy as he followed the crushed weeds deeper into the woods.

Trees gave way to a small, sunny clearing and what appeared to be a brush pile. From the pile a dirt road wound up a hill and meandered out of sight. Sammy grunted excitedly and flapped his hands. He was so close to the secret place now.

He looked down at the dirt and saw Daddy's footprints there. They headed straight toward the brush pile and then seemed to disappear, but they weren't gone.

No, no. Sammy knows where they went.

Sammy felt something in his chest pound harder, faster. He left the trees and stepped into the clearing, feeling suddenly naked and exposed. Had Adam and Eve felt the same way when they realized they were naked before God? In fact, couldn't God see him right now like his mom had told him? Did God see him as a naughty boy for sneaking away from his mom?

Sammy didn't have any answers, just an urge to go around the brush pile and follow Daddy. He made clicking sounds with his mouth.

Thick pieces of wood framed the tunnel opening. He eyed his dad's footprints in the dirt. Footprints leading into darkness.

He reached into his pocket, grabbed his crank flashlight, and turned it on. His skin prickled with expectancy as he stepped into the tunnel, ready for another grand adventure.

26

In the hotel lobby, where some old Beatles song styled with Mantovani-esque strings emanated from ceiling speakers, Gillian paced beside Chase's carrier, impatient for the Rileys to arrive. She ended the call and slid her hot pink cell phone back into her purse, stunned by what Marc had learned during his breakfast meeting with Vernon Brannon.

It was simply too unbelievable. A poisonous frog? Who would have done something so bizarre?

She decided not to answer the phone again if she didn't recognize the caller ID. Gabriel Jacobi might get her phone number somehow and try calling her. He'd left a message at the front desk for her to call him, but she didn't plan to talk to him—at least not yet, though she supposed another meeting was inevitable. Memories of their awkward encounter in the parking lot yesterday still left her head reeling with emotions.

Why, God, did he have to walk into my life now? I thought the whole painful situation was in the past where it needed to stay.

A tan rental car pulled into an empty parking space. She took a deep breath and tried to relax. What would Emily Riley be like? To be married to Chuck, she must be a special person.

A year and a half ago, after Marc had been arrested for a crime he couldn't have committed, Chuck had graciously stepped out of retirement, booked a plane to Michigan, and helped clear him of wrongdoing. She and Marc owed him a debt of gratitude they could never hope to repay.

The grandfatherly man with the shiny, balding head and the Friar Tuck fringe of white hair got out of the car and circled around to open the door for Emily. He was such a gentleman. Hand in hand, he and his wife strolled toward the glass lobby doors like newlyweds who hadn't outgrown the honeymoon, regardless of how many years had passed since.

Inside, Riley pulled Gillian into a hug. "Wow, it's great to see you again. When was the last time?"

"Two years ago this fall," she answered. The overwhelming aroma of Chaps aftershave burned her nose.

"Gillian, this is my wife, Emily."

The short, thin woman with the thick head of white, wavy hair offered Gillian a bony hand, fingers knobby and bent with arthritis. Her hand seemed so fragile that Gillian shook it gingerly, as if afraid it might break. Stunning blue eyes that looked like they might glow in the dark swept over her—not in a critical, scrutinizing way, but in one that seemed to admire everything she saw. Emily's head was tilted oddly to one side. Perhaps her neck was stiff after the flight and the drive from the airport.

"It's great to finally meet you," Gillian said. "I bet you've never been this far north before, have you?"

"Nope, never." Emily adjusted the strap of her purse, a bulky black thing that looked like it could knock a burglar to his knees if swung at his head. She smiled at the baby carrier and bent for a closer look. "And this must be Chase. Such a beautiful baby boy. His face reminds me of yours."

Gillian thanked her and decided not to go into the whole adoption story right now. Certainly Riley already knew about their adopting Chase, but maybe he'd failed to tell Emily. Or perhaps she'd simply forgotten. While Riley checked them in and went to get their luggage, Gillian and Emily exchanged small talk.

"Well, it sure is nice to be here for an investigation this time," Emily said. "During the Magician Murderer investigation, if you recall, I had to stay in Florida and wait for Chuck to come back. It was torture."

"It's too bad he had to leave you behind. You two had just started your retirement, right?"

Emily nodded and abruptly changed the subject. "Chuck's told me all about your calligraphy. I can hardly wait to see a sample of your work. He said you know so many poems and famous quotations that people call you 'The Quote Lady.'"

Gillian's cheeks warmed. "Well, some do—mostly the folks I do projects for."

Emily pulled out snapshots of her twin granddaughters and, brimming with stories to tell, didn't seem to know when to stop. In fact, she was mid-sentence when Riley came along, grabbed her elbow with an obvious eye roll, and began pulling her away.

"No waiting for this man!" Emily said with a laugh. "I guess it's time to find our room."

"I'll follow you up," Gillian said.

The Rileys found their room, which was just around the corner and down the hallway from Gillian's. Everyone agreed to meet in the lobby in 15 minutes before heading to the resort.

With the baby carrier in hand, Gillian strolled down the corridor toward her room and froze. A man had crouched at her door and was slipping something beneath it.

She darted into the alcove holding the ice and soda machines. She peeked around the corner just in time to see the man heading down the hallway away from her, his stride and physique unmistakable. He reached the stairs and disappeared. Thankfully, he hadn't seen her.

Gillian slipped into the room with Chase and closed the door behind her with a relieved sigh. She retrieved the piece of hotel stationery lying on the floor. A phone number was written at the top. Below it was a note in familiar cursive that made her mouth turn dry.

> *We need to talk. Call me.*
> *—Gabriel*

She sucked in a breath. Was Gabriel staying at the same hotel? How odd that he'd tracked down where they were staying.

She pressed her back to the door. *God, please. Couldn't you just make this all go away?*

She flipped her phone open to let Marc know about the Rileys' arrival. While the call went to voice mail, she eyed Gabriel's note again. She couldn't put off this meeting forever—could she?

27

"No way!" Marc said into his cell phone. "Micah Coombs ordered the poison frog?"

"I know—it sounds too good to be true," Vernon said.

"Maybe that's because it is. If Micah was guilty, wouldn't he have hidden the receipt?"

"Anybody with half a brain would have, and Micah's no dummy. I agree—the receipt seems a little too convenient. Micah, of course, says the receipt was planted and insists he had nothing to do with Jared's death."

Marc paced the suite. "Maybe he's right. Somebody could have created the receipt, or perhaps credit card fraud was involved."

"I'm sure the sheriff will check into that. He plans to subpoena the records from the online store. That'll tell him the date and time when the frog was purchased. He may even get the IP address, which he can use to track down the physical address of the computer used."

"What would that prove?"

"It would help determine whether Micah has an alibi for the purchase."

"But what if he doesn't?"

"Then the sheriff may not arrest him. He'll want to make sure his case against Micah is rock solid before making an arrest. There's also the problem of motive. I know what you're thinking—Micah organized the protestors—but that's not a motive for murder. So far there's no evidence that Micah and Jared ever met, though Micah says he knew Jared by reputation."

Marc paused at the window, peered out at the lush lawn. "Okay, but what about his alibi yesterday?"

"Micah was outside with the protestors all day. He never went anywhere near Jared's suite."

"Hmm. Then somebody else must have killed Jared. Any idea how far in advance this committee meeting was scheduled at the resort?"

"I think the event went in my calendar, oh, about a year ago, but I'd have to double check to be sure."

Plenty of time for an organized psycho to stage this whole thing. Marc rolled his shoulders. "One other question. That woman trapped in the bathroom during the plague of blood. What's her name?"

"Brianne Hyde. She's one of Dr. Colbert's secretaries. Want to talk to her?"

"I do."

"She might be in some meetings right now, but you can always try calling her."

So the meetings were continuing as planned, even though a committee member had been murdered. Marc shook his head in surprise. Could anyone be so calloused?

Vernon gave him Brianne's room number and extension. "So why do you want to talk to Brianne?"

"The plague of blood isn't adding up. The bathroom door was locked as if Brianne wasn't supposed to escape, but there was no real threat to her life. So what was the point?"

"Maybe it was just a scare tactic to start things off. Perhaps she was just a good pawn." He chuckled. "Definitely a good yeller—I'll tell you that."

"But why her? The same goes for Jared. There must be a reason those two were singled out."

"I've been mulling over that question too. So far, I haven't a clue. Everybody liked Jared. He didn't have any enemies as far as I know."

Someone knocked on Marc's door. Marc crossed the suite, phone to his ear, and glanced through the peep hole. His spirits lifted.

"Hold on a second, Vernon. That retired homicide detective I told you about just showed up." Marc opened the door wide to let in Gillian, Chase, and the Rileys.

"Well, I better go," Vernon said. "You've got company, and I've gotta run to a meeting. Oh wait—almost forgot. Some of the guys heard you used to play basketball for the Chicago Bulls."

"Uh-huh." Marc knew this topic would come up eventually.

"Between sessions a few of us play hoops on the outdoor court. Care to join us around two?"

Why not? The opportunity would give him an opportunity to scope out the committee members, not all of whom were in favor of the project. Could one of their own be the saboteur? "Sounds good, but I'll try to talk to Brianne first. If I'm not there by two, go ahead without me."

"Okay, talk to you later."

Marc hung up, kissed Gillian, and crouched to rub Chase's soft head. He turned to Riley. "Boy, am I glad you're here."

Riley gave Marc a bear hug. "Have you grown since the last time I saw you?"

"I don't think so." Riley's white hair seemed thinner, his face more haggard, than Marc remembered.

Riley cocked his head. "Must be my terrible memory then. You seem taller than I remember."

"No, he hasn't grown," Gillian said with a smirk, arm around Marc's waist. "If he did, believe me, I'd be the first to know. It takes a lot to feed this man."

Marc offered Riley a soda from the fridge, but Riley declined. Instead, the retired detective pulled out a family-size pack of Juicy Fruit gum and offered Marc a stick.

Marc chuckled at Riley's sole addiction and accepted. Did the man ever change?

While Gillian gave Emily a grand tour of the suite, Marc said, "I can't thank you enough for cutting your trip to Ohio short and joining us."

Riley had strolled to the window and peered out. "Not a problem. Besides, this is beautiful country. Emily and I enjoy seeing new places, and now that I'm retired, I have the freedom to do so."

Marc rubbed his hands together. "So where do we start?"

Riley turned and sank onto the couch, crossed his legs. "Maybe over lunch you could fill me in on what's happened since the last time we talked. Later, I'd like to interview Micah Coombs."

"That might be a problem. The police are holding him for questioning, but they might release him later."

"The most logical culprit of the plagues is one of the protestors—or perhaps several of them working together. Micah would know the identities of his more radical members, the ones who wouldn't think twice about taking justice into their own hands."

With the finger of suspicion pointed at the protestors as primary suspects, Marc mused, plans for further protest were probably up in the air, if not dead entirely. He turned to his phone. "Before we head to lunch, I need to schedule an interview."

"Mind if I come along?"

"Actually I was hoping you'd conduct it."

Marc called Brianne's room, and her pretty voice picked up. *The plagues began with her. Maybe they'll end with her, too.*

28

Sammy walked into a tomb without realizing it.

One hundred feet into the twisty tunnel supported by wooden beams, he inhaled the musty aroma of earthy dampness and sampled the sensation of being closed in, of being forgotten in this great underworld he never would have guessed existed a month ago. Water trickled somewhere in the distance.

The shadowy tunnels would have left anyone confused. But not him, he thought with a giggle. He knew he wasn't like everyone else; he had an unusual talent for sensing the right direction and finding his way.

Where was his dad? What was he doing down here?

Find Daddy. Find Daddy.

Sammy made clicking sounds with his tongue and almost called out his father's name. But he closed his lips tightly, realizing his foolishness. He wasn't even supposed to be away from his mom. Certainly his dad wouldn't be pleased if he knew Sammy was down here spying on him. But wasn't that part of the game?

Daddy doesn't see me. Daddy doesn't know.

When his flashlight dimmed, Sammy cranked it for 40 full revolutions until the light was bright and steady again. Then he pushed on, head swiveling from side to side, the TV commercial song playing in his head. He searched dark corners with his bright beam, wondering if monkeys might be down here. He didn't see any.

Shadows embraced him as if he were a permanent resident like the bats darting and squeaking above his head. The first time he'd heard their squeaks, he'd nearly messed his pants. Now their chirps were like music, a reminder that he was never completely alone.

But unlike those who'd been trapped down here long ago, he could leave whenever he wanted to. Delicious delight washed over him to be visiting his secret place, away from people who stared at him and didn't understand. Away from his parents' angry voices. To the quiet, dark place where he could be alone.

At least here he was understood because he had only himself to understand.

His mom had told him that long ago, children had worked in the mine with donkeys to haul the ore and caged canaries to test the air. Surely the birds must have been afraid in the dark, wondering why it was night all the time. Not understanding why anyone would bring them here. Terrified about what was going to happen to them next.

After his mom had told him the story, he'd cried into his pillow for the canaries. Nothing was worse than not understanding or not being understood.

The air could still be dangerous. That's why he brought canaries if he explored new tunnels; poisonous gases could linger in dark, secret places underground—clever gases you couldn't even see. And he dreaded that the most—the thought of breathing invisible fumes—because things he couldn't see perplexed him.

So the canaries saw for him with their tiny lungs. They could tell if nameless death lingered for anyone who might breathe the poison. But no birds had died as yet, and he was glad for that. He would have hated the thought of a living, breathing creature dying on his account. He didn't believe death was ever justified, and that's why he returned to the cold and the dampness.

Because he wanted to know.

Were any of the 41 men, lost down here long ago, still alive? Were they still digging at the damp earth with their fingernails, trying to claw their way out? As if someone had accidentally buried them in a grave, thinking they were dead when they were still alive?

He shuddered at the thought.

To be buried alive—he couldn't imagine knowing you were going to die and being unable to do anything to stop it. So sometimes he just sat in the dark with Roberta, his caged canary, and cried for those 41 men who'd been buried alive and would never see daylight again.

But maybe they weren't as gone as everyone said. Perhaps if he found them, he could help them escape. Wouldn't his dad be proud of him then?

Find them. Find them.

But then again, weren't the men dead? Weren't they beyond saving?

Sometimes he hugged his head because so often things didn't make sense, and just when clear understanding seemed within reach, something happened to thrust it farther away. Like Gertrude, the canary who'd gotten away. For a split second the bird had hovered close to his hand, but then it had fluttered farther from his grasp. No matter how hard he'd tried, he couldn't reach it—feathery wings just beyond his reach, wing on fingertip, and then gone.

But wasn't so much of life like that for him? Wasn't clear understanding so often just beyond his reach? He tried so hard to understand and to communicate, but no one understood.

Especially his dad.

But his dad assumed he didn't know anything; in reality, he understood much more than his dad realized. If only his dad would look closer, then he would see. But perhaps his dad didn't *want* to see. Perhaps Sammy was more useful, more bendable to his wishes, as long as he remained a dunce.

See, Sammy understands a lot more than they think.

In fact, wasn't that why he came back day after day? The tunnels were proof that he could find the old mine when his dad thought he was a baby who couldn't even escape his mother's watchful eye.

So sure of himself, wasn't he? So certain no one else could be right but him.

Maybe someday his father's eyes would open, and he would realize that his son wasn't the complete idiot people thought him to be.

Maybe.

Until then, Sammy would just keep searching for those buried in hopelessness as much as he was. Until the day when they would all be set free.

The nearby crunch of gravel underfoot made Sammy start. His head whirled toward the sound, heart hammering. He flapped his hands, made anxious grunting sounds.

Someone was coming. His dad?

He glanced left and right, wondering where he could hide. Before he could decide, a man emerged from the shadows, his familiar face and the ugly scar half shadowed by lantern light.

"Sammy. How nice to see you here."

Sammy relaxed. It was Uncle Austin, a friend of his dad's who often came to the house, especially lately, and spent extra time with him.

But Sammy wasn't supposed to be in the mine. Uncle Austin would tell his dad. He would be in big trouble now.

Uncle Austin stepped closer and mussed his hair. "Why do you look so surprised? You thought I didn't know you were here? You forget that Uncle Austin knows all."

Sammy flicked his fingers in front of his face.

"Now don't you worry. Your dad's busy in another part of the mine and doesn't even know you're here." He lowered his voice to a conspiratorial whisper. "I won't tell him, okay? This'll be our little secret as long as you keep doing little errands for me. How's that?"

Sammy made relaxed grunting sounds.

"You like helping me, don't you, Sammy?"

At least Uncle Austin understood that he could be useful. Uncle Austin beckoned with an outstretched hand. "Come here. There's something I want to show you. Do you like bugs?"

29

After lunch, Marc and Riley left for their interview, and Gillian and Emily headed outdoors with Chase to do some exploring on their own. They followed the zigzag of crowded sidewalks, the wheels of Chase's stroller humming against the concrete. Along with regular vacationers, who lingered in spite of the protestors, teens and teen workers were milling everywhere. Apparently equestrian camp and a few other events were on the schedule for the weekend as well.

Remnants of morning clouds had drifted away, and the sun beat down with intense heat. Gillian paused to gain her bearings and studied the map. "They have quite a few walking trails here. I see they have a couple of outdoor pools too." Riley had once told her that Emily had won an Olympic bronze medal in swimming years ago. She apparently still loved to swim every chance she got. "Did you bring your swimsuit?"

Emily's eyes twinkled mischievously. "I never leave home without it."

"Technically Marc and I are staying here, and you're our guest. I'm sure we could fit in a swim. In fact, I might even join you."

The grounds were more sprawling then Gillian had expected. The lodge included the visitor's center; the Backwoods Grille, with seating for up to 300; and 70 hotel-style rooms. Two additional buildings offered 60 luxury suites, one of which was hers to share with Marc, though she doubted it would get much use this weekend.

At the center of the grounds, encircled by the lodge and the two additional housing wings, stood an old, white chapel used for church-style services and meetings. To the south of the chapel stood a water tower, an outdoor basketball court, and a building that housed a gymnasium and a large auditorium all under one roof. Weaving between the buildings lay a plush, green lawn divided by meandering sidewalks, picnic tables, park-style benches, and gas grills. Two outdoor swimming pools stood adjacent to the two housing wings.

Gillian eyed the pools, where several children frolicked under the watchful gaze of their mothers. She did an about-face and studied North Lake, which shimmered in the distance.

"I don't see any signs of a public beach at the lake," Gillian said. "I wonder why nobody swims there."

"Maybe it has a bacteria problem," Emily suggested. "Or maybe campers just prefer to swim in the pools."

They followed a sidewalk down the hill toward the lake. Eventually, the paved sidewalk and manicured lawn ended, replaced by quack grass and a pathway of newly replenished wood chips. The terrain was rougher on the stroller, but Gillian persevered.

The path meandered along the lake's edge, where ducks skimmed across the surface. At the water's edge, where a gentle breeze tousled their hair, Gillian stood tall and pocketed her hands. The water was amazingly clear, the lake bottom visible even at a depth of five or six feet. So if the lake was clean, why was there no beach here for swimming?

The sun slipped from behind a cloud, and the heat ticked up several notches.

The path meandered toward a line of trees before plunging into the woods. They followed it and soon found themselves among sun-dappled maples, birches, and pines. Just as Gillian wondered where the path was taking them, the trees gave way to a small, grassy clearing to their left. There, a chain-link fence enclosed a pyramid-shaped monument resting on a concrete slab amid thigh-high ferns and nameless brush and weeds.

"What do you think that monument's for?" Emily asked.

"I have no idea. Let's see."

They left the trail, and Gillian struggled to reach the monument with the stroller. They wedged fingertips between the fence wires. Raised copper-colored lettering covered the black plate dominating the monument's face.

SITE OF
BARNES-HECKER MINE DISASTER
NOVEMBER 3, 1926
IN MEMORY OF THE 51 MEN WHO DIED
DIGGING RED ORE DEEP IN THE EARTH
41 REMAIN HERE TO DIG ORE FOR ETERNITY

Below this text was a listing of 51 names. Asterisks beside 41 names indicated those still underground, the ones digging ore forever. Apparently only 10 bodies had been recovered after the disaster.

"How sad," Gillian said.

"I wonder what happened?"

What kind of disaster could have snuffed out so many lives? Gillian made an educated guess. "Probably a cave-in or fires fed by toxic underground gases."

"Maybe somebody at the lodge could tell us more."

The thought of so many men dying together underground, presumably at this spot, both saddened and fascinated Gillian. A hushed, sacred quality seemed to embrace the disaster site— it was a tomb, after all. She shivered in spite of the heat.

She wondered how the families must have felt, know-ing that the means of their livelihood, the place where their husbands and fathers went to work every day, had become a tomb. How many people go to work and never leave, trapped there as permanent residents?

Gillian imagined being buried under tons of rock. Marc had hated closed-in spaces ever since he'd been trapped in wreckage after a car accident years ago, needing the Jaws of Life to free him. Just the thought of being trapped underground would probably make him break out in a cold sweat. Mining was definitely not his line of work.

"There's another monument, a stone really," said a woman's whispery voice.

Gillian glanced to her right, not realizing someone was standing there only feet away. She wondered where the overweight woman in the blue jeans and purple blouse had come from so suddenly.

"The memorial stone"—the woman fixed sad eyes on the monument—"is located at the Michigan Iron Industry Museum near Negaunee. In fact, there's a lot more information about the disaster there, too." She must have noticed their startled expressions. "Oh, sorry. Didn't mean to surprise you."

"No problem," Gillian said. "I guess we were more surprised to find this monument here."

"It's easily missed, isn't it? Most folks who come to the resort don't even have a clue the monument's here. Isn't it pathetic—the way people live and die and are so easily forgotten with the passing of time?"

The woman studied them with hazel eyes. Limp, shoulder-length brown hair that could have used more style framed an oval face with sculpted cheekbones and a high forehead. A faint scar interrupted the horizontal line of her right eyebrow.

"So this is where the disaster happened, huh?" Gillian asked.

"Yep, the exact spot." The woman gestured to the monument. "The cement slab at the base there was placed over the main shaft to seal it off for all of time."

"So what happened, exactly?" Emily asked.

The stranger tilted her head to one side as if reciting a poem from memory. "The men were blasting with dynamite and accidentally opened up an underground lake or river or an old swamp—nobody really knows for sure. The mine filled with water, sand, and rock too quickly for everybody to get out. There was one survivor, though. They say the guy actually climbed 800 feet of ladder in 10 minutes. Can you imagine?"

Gilliam couldn't. *She knows her local history pretty well. She ought to be a tour guide.*

Gillian wondered why the woman didn't put more effort into her appearance. Most women at least tried to look pretty, unless they had no one to impress. But she *was* wearing a wedding ring. Perhaps she'd been rushed for some reason and hadn't had time to fix herself up.

The woman motioned toward the trees, and only then did Gillian recognize the blue of North Lake glinting through the leaves. "When the mine caved in, the ground sank 60 feet in a space the size of two city blocks, creating this lake."

"So it's not a natural lake," Emily said.

"I guess that depends on how you define 'natural,' " the woman said.

Gillian nodded. "That explains it then."

The woman studied her. "Explains what?"

"Why there's no beach. Why nobody swims there."

The woman's voice hardened as if the idea were offensive. "The lake is as much a tomb as this monument is. Swim in there? I don't think so. Let the lake be a reminder of what happens when people go after what they want and rape the earth in their drive to do so."

Oh, great. Now I'm going to get a lecture from an environmentalist. Gillian felt like a reproved child.

The woman seemed to realize her diatribe. "Oh, sorry. Here I am babbling away when I'm actually trying to find my son."

She searched their faces. "He's 10 years old. Blond hair. Name's Sammy. Have you seen him?"

Gillian shook her head. "Sorry, we haven't seen anybody around here except you."

"Well, he must be around here somewhere." The woman glanced around as if lost. She turned to return to the path, then stopped and glanced back. "Sorry. Where on earth are my manners? I should have introduced myself. I'm Lacey Caruthers. My father owns the resort and lives in that that big white house with my family on the other side of the lake. Maybe you've noticed it?"

Gillian nodded. "I wondered who lived there. It's beautiful."

Lacey chuckled. "Actually, it's quite the monstrosity. I should know—I get to help clean it. My husband, Quinn, is in charge of maintenance here. Maybe you've met him?"

Gillian shook her head. "Sorry, I've only been here since yesterday." She went on to introduce herself and Emily.

"Well, it's nice to meet you," Lacey said.

"Likewise."

"Enjoy your stay while you're here. Well, I need to find my son. Maybe I'll see you again sometime." Lacey turned, headed around a bend in the path, and vanished into the greenery.

Gillian watched her go. *So that explains who lives in that big, white house across the lake. Does Lacey give tours of the place?*

30

The Urim and Thummim said yes, so he knew it was the perfect time for the next step in his master plan. The man was in meetings all day, and his room was empty, quiet, and inviting. The analytic converter did its job, and the door opened with a gentle click.

Inside, Cyrus waited in the dark for his eyes to adjust and pulled on the face mask and rubber gloves that felt like second skin. His gaze probed the room, partly lit by the sunny world beyond the windows, and fixed on the suitcase in the corner.

The man hadn't even bothered to unpack.

Cyrus opened the unzipped, navy suitcase, pulled the bottle from his pocket, and unscrewed the lid. He gingerly sprinkled so little of the white powder onto the top layer of clothes that no one would notice. Then he pulled off the face mask and gloves before exiting the room and the building, strolling away casually. He was careful not to rush and draw unwanted attention.

He shoved the face mask and gloves into a trash receptacle along the way and paused to study his surroundings. He was alone. No one had seen him. And even if they had, so what? They would just assume he was a maintenance man there to check a leaky toilet.

Perfect. The next time the man opened his suitcase, he wouldn't be able to avoid inhaling the powder. And later, after

Cyrus wrote the reference on the wall, investigators would find a surprise—that is, if they were clever enough to see it.

Would anyone be smart enough to figure out his little puzzle?

Oh, this was so fun.

31

On their way back, Gillian slowed, sensing that Emily couldn't keep up. That was fine; Gillian's legs were aching, and she wondered if they'd gone too far. "Are you okay?"

"I think I just need to sit down for a minute." Emily slumped onto a green bench near the path and rifled through her purse. Sweat dripped down her face. "I know what's wrong with me. I forgot to take my pill this morning."

Gillian's hands tightened around the stroller grips. "Are you okay?"

"Sure, I'll be fine. But would you mind doing me a favor? This is so embarrassing."

"What's wrong?"

Emily held out her hand, revealing a tiny pink pill. She flashed Gillian a pained smile. "With this different schedule, I forgot all about it. Could you get me a glass of water? I'm not sure I can get up."

Gillian stared at her. "Should I call the nurse?"

Emily shook her head. "No, I'll be fine, really. I just need something to drink the pill down with. I don't know how Chuck does it—he can down a whole handful of pills without a drink. I can't do that."

"Okay, I'll be right back." Gillian turned the stroller around.

"It's okay. You can leave Chase here. I'll watch him."

Gillian lingered, uncertain. Emily's face had turned chalky white. Was she going to pass out?

"You go ahead," Emily said. "I'll be fine." *But hurry*, her eyes said.

Gillian left the stroller and jogged toward the suite.

32

Cyrus maneuvered down crowded sidewalks and then little-known pathways at the outskirts of the grounds, far away from the bustle of the crowd and the echo of the protestors. He stopped short. The path, hemmed in by trees, was vacant, except for one unusual sight.

A hunter-green baby stroller sat parked beside one of the benches, where a gray-haired woman in blue jean capris and a white blouse lay on her side, legs curled up, eyes closed, as if taking a nap.

Cyrus approached and peered down at the woman, skin prickling. Color had leached out of her face.

Is she dead?

The steady rise and fall of her chest answered his question.

A whimper drew his gaze toward the stroller and the baby inside. Tiny arms waved in the air. Observant, curious blue eyes met his.

A pulse of recognition danced between nerve endings in his brain. He inhaled sharply. The baby was a spitting image of—

Approaching footfalls jerked his head around. A chunky, red-haired woman rushed toward them, a white Styrofoam cup in hand. "Is she okay?" she called.

He straightened. The woman was talking to him. He found his voice. "Uh, I don't know. I think she might have fallen asleep." *Get out of here now.*

He had a firm rule not to let anyone get a good look at his face. *Too late.* The woman with the cup spanned the distance and crouched at the older woman's side while he stood there stupidly, not knowing what to do. He should leave, but he didn't want to arouse suspicion. If a patron was in distress, fleeing the scene would certainly raise eyebrows.

"Emily?" Concern tinged the woman's voice. "Emily, are you okay?"

He shifted his feet. "Should I call an ambulance?"

Emily's eyes blinked open. The red-haired woman said, "Emily, can you sit up? I've got a cup of water here."

Cyrus clasped Emily's elbows and helped her sit up. She popped a little pink pill into her mouth, accepted the cup, and drank the pill down. Perhaps it was his imagination, but a pinkish hue seemed to return to her cheeks.

Emily took several deep breaths and wiped perspiration off her forehead with a tissue. "Thank you, Gillian. I'll be fine now."

"You sure?" Gillian didn't sound convinced.

"Of course." Emily patted Gillian's hand and forced a smile, clearly embarrassed. "Sorry to give you such a scare. Sometimes I get a spell if I forget to take my pill, but I'll be fine now. Just give me a few more minutes, and we'll be on our way."

Gillian rose and turned toward Cyrus, eyes filled with gratitude. "Thanks so much for your help, um—sorry, I didn't get your name."

"The name's Cyrus, ma'am. And really, I didn't do anything. Just happened to be passing by." Or was that true? Perhaps fate had intended this meeting. He looked at the baby boy again, his pulse quickening. A memory descended without warning.

The children and babies couldn't sleep and were crying, always crying, their unhappy, puckered faces illumined by lanterns since the feds had cut the power, and they had nothing else to use for light. They were up most of the night, trying to calm the children in spite of the maddening noises blaring over loudspeakers outside.

He wished the armed troops outside, the men who'd run over the kids' outdoor toys with their tanks and flashed obscene gestures at the women when they peeked out the windows, would stop the torture and let them be.

A whimper from the baby jerked him out of his dream. Gillian bent and reached for the child, pulling him into her arms. The baby boy looked right at him with those stunning blue eyes. Was it his imagination, or were those small arms reaching for him, too?

He felt a small ping in the center of his chest. He knew he should go, but he could hardly pull himself away. "Such a beautiful child," he said. "Reminds me of my own boy at that age."

"Well, I can tell he sure likes you," Gillian said.

He waited for her to offer to let him hold the tyke. When she didn't, he glanced at his watch. "Well, I gotta go. You ladies have a wonderful day now."

He turned to go.

"Thanks again!" Gillian called.

He glanced back with a wave and got out of there as quickly as possible, though part of him wanted to stay. Stay with the child with whom he'd providentially crossed paths.

But this meeting wasn't over. Not by a long shot.

E very finger on Brianne Hyde's right hand bore a ring diverse from the others, and Marc wondered why. Five rings for five kids? Maybe she played the piano and, like Liberace, wanted to show off her rings. But why every finger?

She'd agreed to meet them in the empty restaurant, where stony-faced workers vacuumed the carpeted floor and wiped crumbs off the round tables like automatons. Tall and thin, with black shoulder-length hair that appeared to be naturally curly, Brianne Hyde seemed agitated.

At one of the round tables, sitting kitty-corner from Marc and Riley, she nursed a cup of coffee, stirring in two packets of sugar, then adding creamer almost as an afterthought. The coffee seemed more like a prop than anything else, something on which to unleash her agitation while they talked. Later, after all the fanfare, Marc couldn't recall her drinking a single drop.

Okay, so maybe she's a little nervous.

Marc was thrilled to have Riley here. Riley knew things about interrogations and body language Marc had no clue about. Riley told Brianne he wanted to record the interview. Was that okay? She nodded.

Something in Brianne's face hinted Hispanic ancestry. Her dark chocolate eyes darted around the room as if she feared they were being watched.

"Danger?" Riley said when she used this word to describe being locked in the bathroom. "You felt like you were in danger?"

Brianne's eyes blinked in surprise as if he were a little slow and just needed more time. "Oh, yeah. I thought somebody was out to kill me. I mean, the door was locked, and I couldn't get out."

Her fear of being murdered seemed unfounded, and Marc tried to wrap his mind around it. "But a maintenance man came in plenty of time to let you out."

"Yeah, sure. But the feeling of being trapped, of not being able to get out—" She pressed palms down on the table as if seeking balance during an earthquake. "And the drain was clogged or something, and the room was slowly filling with blood."

She lowered her voice, her gaze flicking between the two men. "I guess it wasn't really blood, but I had no way of knowing that at the time. It sure smelled like it. Freaked me out. I thought I was going to drown in blood."

The irrationality of her words bewildered Marc. At the rate of flow, many hours would have needed to pass before the blood filled the room—if that was even possible. The floors must have drains. Though the experience had undoubtedly been unusual, she'd never been in any real danger.

Freaky, unsettling, and messy? Yes. Life-threatening? No.

Riley scribbled something and passed the notepad to Marc. "Illogical." Marc passed the notepad back and gave Riley a nod.

Riley asked, "It didn't feel like a prank to you?"

"A prank?" She shook her head with conviction. "Not on your life. It seemed more like a ... like a violation."

"Against you personally?"

"Uh-huh."

"What makes you say that?"

Her bejeweled hand flew to the chest of her teal blouse. "Well, *I* was the one locked in, remember. Why was *I* singled out? Why not Tessa?"

"Tessa?" Marc asked.

"Tessa McCormack. One of the other secretaries."

Marc wrote down her name on his notepad. That was another fly in the ointment—the too-long suspect list was growing longer by the day. How would they ever sort through all
these people?

"Tessa was with me in the bathroom just before it happened.
The whole nightmare began right after she walked out."

"Did Tessa join you in the bathroom"—Riley cocked his
head—"or was she already in there before you went in?" He jaw
worked vigorously, probably on another stick of Juicy Fruit.

"She was already in there. I thought I was alone, but she was
in one of the stalls and surprised me. Is that important?"

"It could be." Riley leaned back in his chair and rubbed his
bottom lip with his thumb. "How well do you know Tessa?"

"Oh, we're like best buds."

"Could she have locked you in on purpose?"

"You think she might have been part of this whole thing?"
When she realized he wasn't joking, her eyes hardened. "No
way! Tessa wouldn't have been involved in something like this."

"Why do you say that?"

"I can't say she's never pulled a prank on me, but something
like this? No way. Like I said, this was way more than a prank."

"So what exactly *did* happen? Do you mind describing the
event for us?"

She sighed. "I already told the sheriff—"

"I know," Riley said, "but it would be helpful if we could hear
the account from you—in your own words—if you don't mind."

After leaking another impatient sigh, she described the
event, initially saying nothing they didn't already know. "I had
this overwhelming sense of dread that we were all participating
in something wicked, that God couldn't possibly be pleased—
I mean, due to the parallel Bible." She chuckled nervously and
shot a quick glance at both of them as if gauging their reactions.
"I guess that sounds pretty silly, huh?"

Marc shook his head. *Not silly at all.*

"How long have you known Jared Russo?" Riley asked.

She gave a small, one-shouldered shrug. "Oh, I don't know. A few years. Ever since Generation Life hired me."

"Did you know him well?"

"No. He was just one of the guys on the committee. Sometimes I gave him messages when his wife called, or I got him a Mountain Dew, his favorite, but that was about it. I mostly assist Dr. Colbert."

"You and Jared never crossed paths, maybe years ago before the committee?" Riley asked.

Confusion clouded her eyes. "No. I'd never set eyes on Jared until two or three years ago because of the committee, as I've said."

"Can you think of anything that might have connected you two other than work?"

Marc discerned only honesty in her eyes when she said no.

Riley turned silent, so Marc decided to make the next move. "Brianne, can you think of anyone who might want to hurt you?"

She shook her head no. Her trembling hand shoved stray bangs behind her ear. "I heard Jared was murdered by a poison frog. You think whoever killed him was coming after me, too. That's what you're saying, right?"

Her eyes flared in panic, and Marc tried to calm her down. "Not necessarily. There's honestly no reason to think anybody was trying to kill you. The blood wasn't real, and there wasn't anyone else in the room who could have hurt you."

Marc wondered why she'd left out an important detail in her retelling. "When you were in the bathroom, did you notice anything unusual written on the wall?"

Her eyes were a study in ignorance. "I don't know what you mean."

Marc's pulse picked up speed. "You mean, you don't know?"

"Know what?"

Marc glanced at Riley, who nodded. Marc told her about the Bible reference the sheriff had found written on the wall. When he described what the Bible verse said, she lifted a hand to cover her gaping mouth.

"But that doesn't make sense," she said. "The reference wasn't written on the wall when I was in there. I'm sure of it."

Marc's nerves buzzed. Had someone written the reference on the wall *after* Brianne left the room? "Do you think you might have just missed it?"

"No, of course not. I'm sure. But I can't say I'm surprised."

"Why do you say that?" Riley asked.

The subtle movement of something like guilt slithered across her face. Her gaze dropped to the mug of coffee she was forever stirring but never drinking. "I know it sounds weird, but a sense of dread came over me just before the water turned to blood. Like God was going to judge us because of"—she swallowed hard—"because of the project the committee's working on. And just before I turned on the water to wash my hands, I heard the protestors chanting through the window. Their voices gave me the creeps."

"The bathroom window," Marc said. "Was it open or closed?"

"The place is air-conditioned, so I'm pretty sure the window was closed. Is that important?"

"Maybe."

Marc's mind raced. The hallway beyond the bathroom had been crammed with people, who'd been drawn to the spot by Brianne's hysterical yelling and pounding on the door. Anyone could have locked her in the bathroom and then mingled with the crowd as it gathered outside.

But who had written the Bible reference on the wall? And how?

Perhaps the same person who locked Brianne in the bathroom had raced outside, entered the bathroom through the window after the maintenance man let Brianne out, wrote the

Bible reference on the wall, and then exited the same way he'd come in. But when would he have done so?

Perhaps the maintenance man who unlocked the door for Brianne had kept everyone out of the room until the sheriff arrived; after all, the place was all bloody and would have looked like a crime scene. Perhaps using the shield of being precautious and not wanting anyone to contaminate the scene, he'd unwittingly or knowingly given the perpetrator the time he needed alone in the room. In that case, two men were working together. Or was it possible one man could have done all that himself?

Marc locked eyes with Riley, an unspoken message passing between them. They needed to check that window for possible evidence.

But why would anyone go to so much trouble? Just to write the reference on the wall?

Perhaps the killer's plague compulsion would lead to his undoing.

34

Cyrus stumbled toward the cabin. Inside, he collapsed in the rocking chair and cradled his face in his hands, taking deep breaths to clear his head.

From his pocket, he pulled out the stack of photos he took with him wherever he went. Red-faced Alex shortly after birth. A grinning, pixie-faced Alex on his Big Wheels. Alex strumming his guitar and pretending he was Eric Clapton. Alex holding up his diploma with a relieved smile at his high school graduation. Alex all spiffy in his uniform shortly before being deployed to Iraq.

Cyrus paused at the dog-eared baby photo and took it all in: the blue eyes; the wispy, blond hair; the tiny nose and mouth. A sob broke out, and he struggled for control, a trembling hand pressed to his mouth. His body rocked back and forth. Back and forth.

Just seeing a baby who so closely resembled his lost son at that age almost pushed him over the brink. But with another deep breath, he knew he couldn't let the baby distract him—not when he had so much to do.

As he shoved the photos away, the thought slammed into him that his son had returned, that this encounter was a sign from the spirits. Of course, the baby belonged to someone else and couldn't possibly be his son. And yet ... perhaps this was another sign that his mission was correct and ordained by fate.

As he strolled away from the cabin, he was unable to shake the image of the baby's face from his mind. Something was special about this child, something that deserved further investigation. Sammy could help. Sammy could keep an eye out for the baby, keep him out of harm's way.

He needed another look. And soon.

He knew the name of the boy's mother. Shouldn't be too difficult to track him down.

He could hardly wait.

PART 2

BURIED IN THE PAST

"The past is but the beginning of a beginning,
and all that is and has been
is but the twilight of the dawn."
—H. G. Wells,
"The Discovery of the Future"

"We cannot escape history."
—Abraham Lincoln,
message to Congress, December 1, 1862

35

Emily Riley swam like Serena Williams swung a tennis racket.

Gillian stood in the shallow end of the pool with Chase in her arms, cool water swishing around her knees. She watched in amazement as Emily completed lap after lap as if there was no tiring her out. And to think that not half an hour ago the woman had been on the brink of passing out because she'd forgotten to take her pill for high blood pressure.

Gillian held Chase close, glad to have him in her arms where he was safe. She couldn't shake the uneasy feeling that had swept over her when she'd found the maintenance man hovering over Chase's stroller. The encounter had been harmless enough, she supposed, but the vibes the staff member gave off didn't sit right. Perhaps that odd scar on his face and neck had unnerved her. Or was it something else?

She bit her lip. *Come on, you really need to get over this paranoia.*

Her cell phone rang, and she checked it. Riley had sent her a message. He'd e-mailed her a list of the Bible translation committee members and wondered whether she and Emily could do some online sleuthing for him. Perhaps they could search for the members' names and look for anything suspicious—anything that could possibly tie them to the murder.

When Emily was finished, they changed their clothes and headed to the lodge lobby to use one of the computers. The task soon turned tedious. After an hour of searching names and exploring related websites, Gillian didn't find much to work with—which depressed her because the sooner the killer was caught, the sooner they could all go home.

And boy, am I ready to go home!

She was glad for the mental activity, though. It helped get her mind off Gabriel and the memories his presence stirred. Did he really think she would call him back?

But then Marc's words from the night before came back to her like a summer memory. *If you can't let the hurt go and release him of the offense, then yes, you need to confront him about how he hurt you. That's what the Bible says is the next step to take. And now that I see how upset you are, I think that's what you need to do.*

Chase's giggle drew her attention to where he lay in Emily Riley's arms, his little blue eyes fixed on blue jays flitting outside the window while Emily spoke to him in baby talk. Emily was such a dear!

Gillian pushed back the chair and stood. She rolled her head, her neck stiff from sitting at the computer so long.

"Anything useful?" Emily asked.

"Not really. A whole lot of academic degrees I don't even know how to abbreviate. Hey, after I do a feeding and diaper change, how about we find that playground I saw on the map? I can't stand being cooped up inside on such a fine day."

The playground offered plenty of swings, a merry-go-round, and a jungle gym with an orange slide. Shade trees lined a wood-chipped walking trail, which Gillian and Emily explored while taking turns pushing Chase, who conked out thanks to the rhythm of the rolling stroller.

They'd walked maybe half a mile when they rounded a corner, and Gillian stiffened. Gabriel Jacobi was strolling across the playground toward them.

Gillian chided herself for not accepting the inevitability of bumping into him again. Besides, she hadn't responded to the message at the front desk or the note he'd slid under her door. Had he intentionally sought her out?

Her mouth turned dry, and she rubbed her hands, which were instantly clammy, on her jeans as he closed the distance. She'd had time to prepare herself for this inevitable encounter and hoped to maintain better composure this time. Besides, if anyone should be on the hot seat, it should be Gabriel. He had a lot of explaining to do.

Gabriel sported a classic wrestler's build—short and stocky with a thick chest and neck. He carried a physique many men envied because he didn't even need to work out to look good. All the girls in high school had gone crazy over him—she worst of all. The only trace that time had passed was his graying sideburns and receding hair at his temples.

He wore nickel loafers, navy chinos, and a baby-blue golf shirt, open at the collar—as if he'd just stepped out of a Macy's catalog. Even after all these years, he still strove to look his best. She wondered if he was still a fanatic for soccer and Kentucky horse racing.

"What a surprise to see you here." She ignored the strange flutter in her chest. "How did you find us? This is a big place."

Gabriel shrugged. "It wasn't too hard. Most mothers with babies usually end up at the playground at some time or another. You weren't here earlier, but I decided to try again."

"Emily, this is Gabriel Jacobi. He's"—Gillian's mind groped in the fog—"an old friend from long ago that I never expected to see again."

Emily smiled and said she was happy to meet him. Gabriel, all charm and ease as always, returned the greeting with aplomb.

"I take it you're here for the translation committee meeting," Emily said.

"In a manner of speaking. I'm here with the protestors."

Understanding danced behind her eyes. "Oh, I see."

Gabriel asked Gillian, "Do you mind if we talk alone?"

Gillian glanced at Emily uncertainly. She could only guess what the woman must be thinking right now.

Emily's smile never faltered. "I'll just find a bench and sit with Chase for a spell. You two probably want to catch up on old times, and my legs could use some rest."

Gillian forced a shaky smile. "Catching up on old times" was hardly how she would have described this awkward meeting.

36

Marc led Riley into the lodge and down familiar corridors until they reached the women's bathroom, where the plague of blood had terrified Brianne Hyde. The corridor outside the bathroom was oddly empty. They needed to examine the window without attracting unwanted attention, but he wasn't exactly sure how.

"Got any bright ideas?" he whispered to Riley.

Riley tried the doorknob to the janitor's closet and found it unlocked. Inside the shadowy space were a mop and bucket, various cleaning supplies, and an "out of order" sign.

Riley grabbed the sign and hung it on the restroom door. He knocked on the door. "Anybody in here?"

There was no answer.

Riley said, "Now we need to be quick before maintenance really does show up."

"Or somebody calls the sheriff about suspicious activity."

They stepped inside. Marc took in the upscale bathroom—in particular, the sinks where the plague of blood had occurred and the now-clean wall where the killer had written the reference—before following Riley to the window.

Sure enough, once unlocked, the fogged window opened easily. But could it be opened from the outside if left unlocked? While Marc remained behind to keep watch, Riley went to check. Thirty seconds later, his bulky shape loomed outside the fogged glass. He slid the window open.

"That was easy," he said.

"So you think our guy had help from someone inside?"

"Yeah. And come see what I found out here under the window."

Marc left the bathroom and returned the sign to the closet before anybody was the wiser. Then he joined Riley outside. Both stood to the side of the window and studied the ground directly beneath.

"Bingo!" Riley said.

There it was, the clear imprint of a man's hiking boot. Rain hadn't fallen in weeks, nor was it in the forecast. There was no fear of evidence being washed away.

"That must be the print of the killer," Marc said. "He must have left it when he accessed the bathroom to write the reference on the wall."

"Not so fast. Whoever washes the exterior windows could have left the print too."

"Oh, yeah. I didn't think of that."

They'd lingered outside the bathroom long enough. As they strolled away, Riley said, "The print could still be strong physical evidence, though. A CSI tech could make a cast of the shoe print and match it to any suspects."

"So where do you recommend we go from here?"

Riley scratched the back of his neck. "I think it's best that I remain incognito for now. You've already got the sheriff on your side, right? Tell him what you found. I bet he'd be interested."

37

After the interview, Brianne returned to the suite she shared with Tessa McCormack and found her roommate in bed, the covers pulled up to her chin. Her pretty face lacked its usual application of makeup. In fact, she looked terrible: eyes bloodshot, hair askew.

"Whoa! What's up with you?"

Tessa rolled over so she faced the wall. "I think I'm sick."

"You think?" Brianne sat on the edge of the bed. Unable to dismiss her mothering instincts, she reached for Tessa's forehead.

But Tessa pulled away. "Can't you tell when somebody's trying to rest?"

"I just wanted to check to see if you have a fever."

"I think I'm old enough to know when I'm sick, okay?" Tessa swiveled her head and shot Brianne a look that would have made anybody think twice.

Brianne rose and stepped away from the bed, giving Tessa space. This wasn't like the effervescent, sanguine Tessa she knew, but she let her have her own way. She didn't hide her sigh at Tessa's childishness. "Where do you feel bad? Should I call the nurse?"

"Just leave me alone. I'll be fine."

Wow, snarky tone of voice too. What's going on?

Tessa seemed more upset than sick. What had happened to set her off? Brianne knew her friend had a volatile temperament in addition to a checkered past. Perhaps she'd spilled Dr. Colbert's coffee, and he'd gotten mad at her. Or maybe he'd given her an assignment, and her work hadn't been up to his high standards.

Brianne tried a softer tone. "Tessa, what's wrong? You know you can always talk to me."

No reply from the bed. Tessa was ignoring her now.

Okay, fine. Let her rest. But Dr. Colbert would demand to know where she was, and he wouldn't be happy when he found out she was in bed. Serious illness demanding hospital time was the only excuse that would satisfy him.

After Brianne left the room, Tessa's cell phone trilled. She groped for it. "Hello?" Moments later, anger steeled her voice. "*What did you give me?*"

38

Just looking at the contours of the face she'd memorized during the most devastating crush of her life transported Gillian back to that lonely apartment and the overwhelming sense that he wasn't coming back. That he'd abandoned her. Abandoned *her*.

Gabriel broke the silence. "I'm sorry, Gillian, for what I did to you all those years ago."

There, he'd apologized again, but somehow it didn't feel like enough. Was he really sorry? If she hadn't bumped into him in the parking lot yesterday, would he really be saying these words?

He touched her arm. She didn't want to look at him, but she faced him anyhow.

"I was living a lie." His face seemed sincere. "I thought I was a believer because I walked an aisle and said a prayer. I thought it was enough, but it wasn't. Everything was an act—the church, the Christian school. Everything."

"It was an act for me, too," she replied. He held her gaze a split second too long. She glanced away.

"I must have hurt you so bad."

She took a deep, ragged breath. "Why did you leave me alone in that apartment, wondering where you were?"

He shrugged. "I was a fool. I'm sorry."

"Saying you're sorry isn't good enough—I want some answers." Now he was the one to glance away when she studied his face. "Do you have any idea how long I waited? Do you have any idea how much that hurt?"

He fixed his eyes on the playground equipment as if he couldn't look at her—or wouldn't. There was no redeeming explanation for what he'd done, and they both knew it.

She glared at him, her anger simmering. "You were just running out to Pizza Hut, you said. So what happened? Why didn't you come back?"

He rubbed a hand across his lean, handsome face, the heaviness of the years and unresolved conflict seemingly weighing him down. "Remember, you just told me you were pregnant. I was shell shocked."

Of course she remembered. All of it. From the yellow, triangle-pattern linoleum kitchen floor to the constantly clogging bathroom sink. She remembered the pallor that had leached into his face when she'd told him he would be a father in eight months.

Even now she could see herself standing before him excitedly, the pregnancy test still in her hand. She'd been overjoyed almost to the point of giddiness. He would marry her now—he would have to. And marrying this man was all she cared about during those days.

And she knew why. Her dad had never been close and intimate, had never shown her much affection. So she'd grown up man hungry, and Gabriel had fit the description of every ideal she'd constructed in her mind of the perfect man who would want her and love her. The fact that he'd seemingly desired her as much as she wanted him had made her dizzy, off kilter, not in any sensible state to think rationally about the choices she made.

But his reaction that day when she broke the news hadn't been what she'd expected. He'd sunk into a kitchen chair with numb eyes and raked a hand through his hair before dashing into the bathroom and throwing up. He'd always seemed so put together; it had taken a while for her to see the real person hiding beneath the polished veneer. As fragile and flawed as the next guy.

"I guess I freaked out," he said. "I wasn't ready to be a father or a husband. The realization of what I'd done to you—to us ... I was scared and ashamed."

"So you got in your car and drove away." Her voice wobbled. "You just left me there, knowing I was waiting for you. You didn't even say good-bye. It was a cold, selfish, and childish thing to do."

His eyes locked onto hers. "That's because I *was* a child. We both were, if you recall."

"But I was the one who had to be the adult. I was the one who had to go back home and face the consequences while you went slinking off like a coward somewhere."

He winced and glanced away. "I'm not proud of what I did."

"Then why'd you do it?"

An inadequate shrug only underlined the senselessness of his choices. "I'd grown up watching my parents run from their problems. You remember my dad."

She certainly did. She'd met his dad at one of Gabriel's soccer games. The man had seemed cold and aloof. She'd never felt like she was good enough for him.

"He never faced his problems," Gabriel said. "When things became strained between him and his boss, he just resigned and found a job somewhere else."

"But I'm not talking about your dad here. I'm talking about you. Take responsibility for your own actions."

His spread his hands. "I am, Gillian. I sought you out today, remember? I'm just trying to help you understand why I did what I did. I'm not saying what I did was right." He must have realized that he'd raised his voice because he lowered it now. "I'd seen the pattern of not facing problems all my life. I chose to follow in my dad's footsteps. I thought if I got far enough away—"

"You could at least have told me how you felt. We could have talked."

Confusion glinted in his eyes. "But talking wouldn't have changed anything. It wouldn't have changed the fact that you were pregnant and I was to blame."

He was to blame? Who cares who was to blame? "I think we were both at fault."

They were both guilty, but he'd left her alone—alone to return home and take the blame. Alone to face her pregnancy, all the while still loving him and not knowing whether he was dead or alive. Alone to be expelled from school and endure the countless whispers behind her back.

Sweat trickled down one cheek, but Gabriel didn't bother wiping it away. He gestured to a park bench facing several children on the jungle gym. She sat but kept plenty of space between them.

"When I had the miscarriage," she said, "I thought for sure you'd come see me."

He stared off into space. "I wasn't even in the area at the time. After the news of your pregnancy became public, my parents told me not to bother coming home."

"You mean, they turned you away?"

He nodded. "So with what little money I had—which wasn't much, if you recall—I flew to Alaska."

"Alaska?" It was amazing that she was hearing these details for the first time.

"I thought if I ran far enough away, I wouldn't have to deal with my problems. Alaska was about as far away as I could think of. I lived with my Uncle Bo, a real loner, at his cabin way back in the woods. No Internet or TV. Not even a phone."

His words made sense. "Your parents told my aunt that they didn't know where you were." But she hadn't believed them;

she'd assumed they were lying and just wanted to keep a wall between the two of them.

"That was true—for a while. I made Uncle Bo promise not to tell them where I was."

"But you stayed in touch with them?"

He nodded. "At first they just hung up on me—at least my dad did. My mom started taking my calls early, before my dad woke up, but she wouldn't tell me much. She told me what my dad believed—that you were the one to blame, that you'd tempted me and were out to destroy my life."

Gillian winced, again amazed that she was hearing this for the first time. His dad, the consummate businessman, had cared about only one thing: Gabriel's following in his footsteps and making boatloads of money. *Wow, he hated me that much?* She supposed it must have been a real blow when Gabriel took a ministry job instead.

Gabriel spewed a mirthless chuckle. "So you see, I abandoned you, but then my family abandoned me. Sweet justice, huh? I know what you're thinking—that I got a taste of my own medicine."

She didn't answer, but that's exactly what she'd been thinking.

"So what did I do? I turned my back on everything I knew—or at least I thought I did. But I couldn't get away from God."

Words from Psalm 139 edged into recall. *Where can I go from your Spirit? Or where can I flee from your presence? If I ascend into heaven, you are there; if I make my bed in hell, behold, you are there.*

He looked at her. "I've never been so depressed or alone in all my life. But then God got a hold of me, Gillian. I turned to Christ, but it was real this time. I didn't just repeat a magical prayer. I confessed my sin and repented and asked God to forgive me. I asked Jesus to save me from my sins, and he did. He set me free."

Gillian wasn't sure what to believe. Had God really gotten ahold of Gabriel's heart? She allowed herself a small nod, but her hands, her chest—she was trembling.

"But not a word from you, Gabriel," she said. "Not a word for all these years. If God changed your heart as you say, why didn't you contact me to explain? Why didn't you check on me later after everything had blown over?"

"I should have—I don't have any excuses. But I don't recall you trying to reach me either. I never received any word from you."

She stared at him, stunned. "But I sent you lots of letters and postcards. They never came back as undeliverable."

"But remember, I wasn't living at home. I was in Alaska—"

"And I didn't know it." The realization slammed into her.

"Do you honestly think my parents would have forwarded your mail to me? Mail from the girl my dad thought was out to destroy their son's life?"

She blinked. "You mean, your parents—"

"They must have thrown your letters away. They never passed them on to me."

His words made sense. When she'd finally called in response to her unanswered letters, his mom had told her Gabriel wasn't available to answer the phone, but she'd suspected Gabriel's mom was lying to keep the two of them apart. She'd never considered that she'd been telling the truth all along.

"Okay, but later, after Alaska, after God got a hold of your heart, why didn't you try to contact me then? You must have known I was hurt after the way you abandoned me."

He hesitated. "By the time my parents saw a change in my life and allowed me to return home, you were attending Bible college. Then I heard you were engaged to some ex-pro basketball player named Marc Thayer."

She felt a small ripple in her chest.

He sighed. "To seek you out then would have seemed like a desperate effort to win you back. I stayed away and decided that what had happened between us was buried somewhere in the past. Forgetting was no longer an option. I *had* to forget you—for your good and mine. You were getting married, and I had no right to insert myself into your life again."

Gillian bit her lip. Even up to the last few weeks before her wedding to Marc, she'd struggled to dismiss her feelings for Gabriel after choosing to let him go. She had once given herself completely to him, body and soul. He had been hard to dismiss, but during marriage counseling she'd chosen to forget him just as he'd apparently chosen to forget her. They'd both gone their separate ways, and she'd committed herself to Marc and tried to forgive and forget Gabriel.

But not everything could be forgotten, no matter how many years had passed.

He sniffed. "I made up my mind to forget you, but I couldn't. Even after all these years, I've never been able to completely get you off my mind. After all, you were the mother of our baby, though only for a little while."

Tears stung Gillian's eyes. Even after all this time, the memories were too fresh, too visceral. Right now, amnesia would have been a blessing.

"And now that we've unexpectedly crossed paths..." His words trailed off. "I realized this meeting was inevitable, and your response in the parking lot made it clear."

She blushed and glanced away, hating to remember how she'd behaved.

"I knew I needed to ask you to forgive me," he said. "Sorry if I've seemed like a stalker, but I needed to hunt you down and put all this to rest."

"And I wasn't being very cooperative, was I?"

His nose was running. She found a tissue in her purse and handed it to him. She pulled out another and dabbed her eyes.

He sounded tentative. "So, now that we've talked, will you forgive me?"

She caught his gaze, held it. "Of course I forgive you—and I really mean that."

"Thank you." He seemed to straighten, as if a burden had been physically removed. "There's no point in dwelling on what might have been. God led us down separate paths. You're married with a daughter and an adopted son. I'm married with five kids."

Five kids? She stared at him, not sure why she was so surprised.

He gave her a smile, the first in a long while. "I always told you I wanted a big family, the laughter of children filling the house. Remember?"

She nodded, and a shudder rippled through her. They might have been *her* children, the very children she'd struggled so hard to conceive. She mentally shook her head, repulsed by the direction her illogical thoughts were taking her. It wasn't right to think of her and Gabriel in that context.

"Even though all these years have passed between us"— Gabriel's eyes met hers—"I can't say that my feelings for you have changed. In fact, seeing you again..."

A sudden barrage of long-dormant emotions made her suddenly feel off kilter and vulnerable in a way she'd never dreamed. Now that she knew the truth, he wasn't nearly the villain she'd thought him to be for all those years. What if things had worked out between them? What if he hadn't driven away? Could they still have had a future together?

But he *had* driven away, and she was married and committed to Marc now. She loved Marc. There was no point in letting her emotions play "what-if" now. Her romance with Gabriel had died long ago, but his words sounded like he wasn't over her, even after all these years. If that was so, this conversation was fraught with new dangers they had no right to explore.

She stood. "I've gotta go."

He reached for her arm. "Gillian, don't—"

She jerked away. The hurt in his eyes couldn't be helped. "It doesn't matter what we once felt for each other or what you may think you feel for me now. We've made our choices, Gabriel. For the sake of God and those we made vows to, we must live with them."

"Sorry, I said too much. I'm not saying—"

"Look, I'm glad we talked. But right now I think we both need some distance, okay?" She stumbled away, not looking back.

39

Half an hour after his meeting with Brianne Hyde, Marc was sweating under the glare of the hot afternoon sun. He faked a jump shot, blew past his opponents, and went in for a layup—all net. The other men, many of whom sported bellies that begged the question of their delivery dates, stared at him in amazement.

They'd asked him to show a few of his moves, and he'd been happy to oblige. But now he wondered if he should return to his suite soon. Something beyond admiration glinted in their eyes, and he hated to be accused of being a show-off. Besides, Riley had said he would meet him at the suite after his talk with Micah Coombs.

Marc asked somebody to sub for him and left the court, pausing behind the sideline, hands on his knees, to catch his breath. He surveyed the men as they played—grunting, cheering, laughing—and was struck by a disturbing revelation. One of their own had been murdered, but no one seemed even remotely upset.

Their apathy didn't sit right in his gut, but perhaps he was being overly critical. Not everybody grieved in the same way. Perhaps some of them had grieved too much, and the pickup game was a way to get their minds off Jared's premature death.

Marc took a seat at a green park-style bench and, feeling overheated, dumped his water bottle over his sweaty head, his tank top sticking to his drenched chest like second skin. The cool blast pushed his internal temperature gauge down a few notches, and the breeze felt a tad more refreshing than it had only moments before.

Vernon, one of the few players who seemed to know what he was doing on the court, took a break and slumped on the bench beside Marc. The gentle breeze sent a whiff of half-spent deodorant in Marc's direction.

"Amazing!" Vernon exclaimed. "That's a mean layup you've got there. You're like a freight train—nobody's gonna get in your way. How tall are you anyhow?"

Marc felt his breath catching up to him. "Six-five."

Vernon whistled. "So what made you leave professional ball—if you don't mind my asking?"

Marc couldn't help the internal eye roll. People were forever asking him this question. Their vocal inflections usually betrayed bafflement that anyone could be so stupid as to make it to professional basketball status and then walk away.

"God had other plans," he said. "I know it's hard to tell, but I hurt my right knee pretty bad in a car accident during my first season with the Bulls. My team doctors advised me not to return to the court in any official capacity. Said my knee would never bear up under that kind of wear and tear again."

"Oh, man. Sorry to hear that."

"I still have problems with the knee from time to time if I'm on my feet too much. So anyhow, I had to give it up—my dream of playing professional ball, I mean. But, you know, that car accident was the best thing that ever happened to me."

"How so?"

"I sank into depression, but a nurse at the hospital told me about Jesus and what he did on the cross for me. God worked in my heart, and I turned to him."

"Wow, that's awesome! But I can tell from your face that not everything was peaches and cream after that."

Marc hung his head. "Playing professional ball wasn't just *my* dream. It was my dad's, too. He couldn't accept that I was turning my back on it. Then he heard I'd become religious and pretty much turned his back on me at that point. But it didn't really matter. I'd already made up my mind, and not just because of my knee."

"What do you mean?"

Marc smiled. "God was calling me to do something else with my life, but I didn't know what it was at first. I spent the summer after the accident at my Uncle Jed's ranch out in Oregon. He loves Jesus like you wouldn't believe. Got me up early every morning, prayed with me, taught me the Bible. That was the summer God called me to preach."

"That's cool."

Except now my dad doesn't even respond to baby pictures. Marc blew out a sigh, trying to cast his cares on the Lord.

"That explains it then."

"Explains what?"

"Jared told me all about it—your love for Western stuff. Cowboy music. Gene Autry. Tumbleweed."

Marc laughed. "You discovered my secret. There's a lot to be said about being out on the open range away from city lights and all those distractions. Something about hearing God's still, small voice."

Enough about him. Marc cleared his voice. "So how did a nice guy like you end up in a dangerous place like this?"

Vernon chuckled. "I guess it all started for me in the military. That's where I met Christ. Fought in the first Gulf War, too. 2nd Platoon, Alpha Company, 1st Battalion, from the 10th Special Forces Group. So did Jared."

"Is that where the two of you met?"

"Yeah. In fact, we were in the same operational detachment. You knew him in Bible college, right? So you may remember him serving in the National Guard at the time."

Memories descended of Marc dropping by Jared's dorm room and seeing him all spiffy in his fatigues just before another weekend trip he called "drill." They'd joked that women were always more attracted to men in military uniforms, so Jared shouldn't give up hope. Though a Hebrew brain, he'd been an absolute worrywart when it came to romantic pursuits.

Vernon said, "One weekend each month seemed like a small price to pay to cover tuition."

"And then after college, Jared joined the US Army, right?"

"Yep, Army Special Forces, like me." Vernon's chin quaked. "I still can't believe he's gone."

"He meant a lot to you too, huh?"

"Jared and I were like those two best buddies described in the Bible. If I was David, I guess Jared was my Jonathan—or maybe it was the other way around." He wiped his eyes and paused as if deeply entrenched in recall. "I can't tell you how many times Jared dropped everything he was doing just to help me. He was amazing."

Marc steered the conversation back to basic facts. "So you guys were both in the Army Special Forces?"

Vernon straightened out of his slouch. "Yep. By then we were both pretty high-ranking officers and had comfy desk jobs to match. But when things started warming up in the Gulf, we both headed off to Iraq. Seemed like the right thing to do."

Marc vaguely remembered Jared being off the radar for a while, but he'd forgotten why. "So how did you both end up here? We're a long way from Iraq."

"After the war, Dr. Colbert, our commanding officer during the war, called me and Jared. He was looking for good linguists, and that was our field. You know what they say—it's who you know."

"But what does your linguistics training in the military have to do with being on the translation committee?"

"Remember, Jared and I were already studying Hebrew and Greek in Bible college. Most soldiers in the Special Forces are required to undergo language training. We were both trained linguists and studied Arabic at the Defense Language Institute in Monterey, California, where you can learn just about any major language in the world."

He pursed his lips. "Of course, the 'hot' language right now is Arabic, which is in the same language family as Hebrew and shares many similarities. You'd be surprised. After the war, both Jared and I went to seminary and continued our study of the ancient languages. Knowing Arabic because of the military helped us learn Hebrew much more quickly and gave us a distinct edge over our classmates."

Two men fought for the ball. Marc turned but didn't really see. Like Vernon, Jared had served under Dr. Colbert during the Gulf War. Was there a connection between his military experience and his murder?

40

From the cover of foliage, Cyrus brought the high-powered binoculars into focus on the tall, gray-blond man in the tank top. He was chatting with Vernon Brannon, and the two appeared to be engaged in more than hoop chitchat.

What if Vernon was remembering something important? What if he was making connections and sharing more than was prudent?

Who was that tall man anyhow? He'd found Jared's body, but he wasn't part of the committee. So what was he doing here?

He needed to find out. So far, the man was an unknown variable, and unknowns made Cyrus uneasy. Almost as uneasy as weak links like Quinn Caruthers.

Cyrus checked his watch and felt his pulse quicken. Questions about the tall man needed to wait. It was almost time for his next move, and he had an inconvenience—another weak link—to take care of first.

41

Gillian stumbled off to another part of the park, not really caring where Gabriel had gone off to. She fished her cell phone out of her purse with trembling hands.

Praise God for speed dial. Her eyes were too blurry to punch in the numbers.

One ring. Two rings. A familiar voice picked up.

"Gillian?"

"Hey, Mom."

"This is an odd time for you to call." They usually talked on Monday mornings.

"I'm sorry. I—"

"Something's wrong. You've been crying, haven't you?"

Gillian sank to a park bench and let the dam break. "Oh, Mom. You wouldn't believe—"

"Gillian, what is it? You're scaring me. Is everyone okay? The baby? Marc?"

"Everyone's ... fine." Gillian swallowed hard and struggled to hold the tears back so she could talk. "I saw someone today. You'll never guess who, Mom."

"Gabriel Jacobi?"

Gillian gasped, and her mind shifted gears from grief to surprise. "How did you know?"

"I don't know. Somehow I just knew."

It was true. Sometimes her mom knew things when there was no logical reason for her to possess such knowledge. Even on the night the Magician Murderer had almost strangled her and Crystal, Gillian's mom had been up most of the night, unable to sleep, certain something was wrong. The phone line had been cut at Whistler's Point, and she'd had no way to reach her daughter for assurance that everyone was all right.

"I can only imagine how you must be feeling right now. Are you okay?"

Gillian felt like a little girl again. She'd tripped and skinned her knee on the sidewalk, and now she longed for her mom to hold her close while sobs tore through her. If only her mom could be here right now.

"No, Mom, I'm not okay."

42

What have I done? This wasn't supposed to happen.

Tessa McCormack rolled onto her side under the covers, goose bumps peppering her arms. One moment she was hot, the next she was cold. But she hardly cared about the chills. She was more concerned about the dizziness, the shakiness, and the steel fingers playfully squeezing her stomach as if about to crush it.

The man called Cyrus had asked her to lock the bathroom door behind her before the plague of blood. *Just a little harmless prank*, he'd said with a wink. *Nothing for you to be concerned about.*

But now she *was* concerned.

Although Brianne hadn't been harmed, Jared Russo was dead, and a poisonous frog was to blame. It didn't take a genius to realize that the two plagues were connected. Somebody would start asking questions and discover her involvement, but she hadn't wanted anything to do with murder.

Just a little harmless prank, he'd said. *And you'll be paid handsomely.*

But how had he learned about her past? How had he known to dangle before her the one thing that would tempt her? Who was this guy anyhow? What did she really know about him?

Even in the half-light she could discern the needle tracks covering her arms; she often hid them by wearing long sleeves, which sometimes provoked unwanted questions. They were scars of a life God had delivered her from—or so she'd thought. She genuinely repented at one time, even admitted herself to counseling, a support group, a rehab clinic. Yet the craving was always there, and she knew she would never be completely free this side of heaven. She was enslaved in a body that hungered for what her spirit knew was wrong.

Voices from years ago were back, accusing whispers echoing in her mind.

A druggie—that's what you are, Tessa. Nothing but a crackhead.

But Dr. Colbert, who had hired her years ago and known about her seedy past, hadn't seemed concerned. *God extends mercy to all of us, Tessa. Do you think you're the only one who's ever made mistakes? I know I've made my share. Mistakes that would surprise you if only you knew.*

But some mistakes could be turned away from and left behind, like memories tossed into the bottomless pit of the past, never to see the light of day. Some mistakes could even be surgically removed, though they left a swarm of emotional scars. But others … others clung to you with tentacles that probed beyond muscle and sinew. Latched onto the soul. Sucked the life away.

And that's exactly what the drugs did. They drained her bank account, made her beat her kids, drove her spouse to file divorce papers, took her kids away from her because she was unfit.

You're a loser, Tessa. Might as well just face it and move on. You're a woulda-shoulda-has been.

She truly wanted to say no, yet her body hungered to return to the bliss, to the state that numbed the pain of her father's fists and curses. Of the long line of lovers who had sweet-talked her, used her, and then cast her aside like yesterday's trash.

That's why part of her always longed to return to the euphoria. To numb the pain.

You'll be paid handsomely, he'd said and handed her a plastic bag of crystal meth. Somehow he'd known her vulnerable spot and had pressed for all he was worth. He'd promised to be discreet, sworn that her participation was only part of a prank. But when Jared had died and she'd called Cyrus in outrage, concerned about her involvement, his message had changed.

He would keep supplying her, but only if she kept her mouth shut.

But they'll find out, she'd protested. *They'll find out that I locked the bathroom door.*

Not if you keep your mouth shut, he'd promised. *Trust me—they don't know anything. And there's no way they can prove you had anything to do with this.*

Now, shaking her head, she knew Cyrus couldn't be trusted. His last payment hadn't given her the fix she'd anticipated. In fact, she'd been feeling increasingly ill with a sickness that ate away at her from the inside out. That's why she'd begun calling him every half hour and leaving stern voice messages, demanding that he deliver what he'd promised and reverse whatever he'd done to her.

If you don't, I'll tell. Tell everything.

Then again, to tell on him meant ratting on herself. It meant confessing that she'd accepted the drugs. *A druggie—that's what you are, Tessa. Nothing but a wasted crackhead.*

That she'd yielded to temptation, though in her heart she wanted to do the right thing.

That she'd locked the bathroom door, trapping Brianne inside.

That she was connected to a murderer's sick master plan.

Dear God, what have I gotten myself into?

43

Cell phone to his ear, Cyrus listened to Tessa McCormack's threatening voice mail and deleted it with a snarl. He mentally chided himself for involving an outsider. It had been a mistake—a hard lesson learned—in a plan that couldn't afford mistakes. One little slipup, and the whole house of cards could collapse.

And now he had to adjust his plans because of it, but not overly so. He'd known all along he would need to eliminate her, but now more so than ever. He'd even added a special ingredient to her last injection to make what was about to happen look like something else.

It was time to remove an annoyance that could become a serious problem if he didn't deal with it now. Or should he wait? He needed an answer, and he needed it now.

Only one way to know for sure. He slackened the leather pouch and cast the Urim and Thummim onto the ground. The stones danced across the dirt and settled.

He pushed a button on his disposable cell phone, one he would discard later, and waited for the familiar voice to pick up.

The voice was there, the man ever faithful, like his personal grunt. His own Igor. "Cyrus?"

"The schedule has changed. Release them."

"But it wasn't supposed to happen now. You said—"

"Change in plans. Release them *now*."

Game time.

O n days like today, Lacey missed Toledo.

She stood at the kitchen counter, wondering if she and her family would have been better off back at the trailer court, where her father had rescued them a couple of years ago. She'd been a checker at Walmart, Quinn had been co-owner of an auto repair shop, and Sammy had been relegated to daycare.

Come live with me, her father had said after her mom's passing from multiple sclerosis. *Your lives will be so much better, and then I won't have to clunk around in this big ol' place all by myself.*

Times had been lean, certainly, and they'd rarely had money for little more than the basics, but at least in Toledo they'd been happy. As co-owner of the repair shop, Quinn had enjoyed a level of control over his life, but now he felt like her dad was always in control. Quinn's attitude of late was making her wonder how long this favor of her dad's—this providing jobs for her and Quinn at the resort—would last.

When Quinn was unhappy, all of them were unhappy.

Sudden cries from Sammy made her heart turn over. Lacey darted into the living room to see what was wrong.

Sammy sat on the living room floor again, his hand banging a brown crayon down on the sketch pad as if he were a marionette puppet, as if someone else were controlling his arm. Grunts and gasps spat out of his small, thin-lipped mouth.

He had these fits every once in a while, and usually it had something to do with drawing something with his crayons. But why was he so driven? If only she could understand him better.

She studied his sketch pad and saw only brown dots. Big dots. Small dots.

He grabbed a tan-colored crayon and began hammering it down as well, as if desperate.

"Sammy, what is it? What's wrong?"

No response. Just little clicking sounds with his tongue.

She bit her lip. What was he trying to say? She hated to guess what he was depicting because she was usually wrong, and being off the mark only heightened his frustration. She grabbed the Picture Exchange Communication book and slid it toward him, but he ignored it.

Sometimes she could recognize what his creations represented, but not today. She thought back to the last time he'd behaved this way. Large, green blobs had covered a sea of blue. Her guesses had almost driven him into a tantrum, so she stayed silent this time. But still, she longed to understand him probably as much as he longed to be understood.

What strange events had been unfolding lately! Sammy had repeatedly been getting out of the backyard while she was napping. She had to find a better way to contain him; otherwise he might wander off and hurt himself. And what was with the canaries?

Sammy had apparently released two of them—Gertrude being her favorite—though she'd given him strict instructions never to handle the birds.

Now, to add to her problems, Quinn said a man at the resort had been killed by a poisonous frog. In fact, his whole body had been found covered by green...

Green.

She stopped, frozen in place by a mind-numbing possibility. No, it wasn't possible. Or was it?

She hustled to Sammy's bedroom in search of his drawings. Five pages later, she found it: his sketch of the green shapes on the sea of blue. That was from yesterday, when she'd tried to guess the object of his passion.

But she had to know for sure, no matter how silly it seemed.

She thrust the drawing in front of Sammy's face. He rarely made eye contact or focused on her long enough to hear a question, but this time he paused from his work.

"Frogs, Sammy? Is that what these green things are?" She slid the Picture Exchange Communication book toward him.

He quickly pointed to the "yes" card before turning back to his sketch pad.

A hand flew to her mouth, her body rigid. No, it wasn't possible. It had to be a coincidence. How could Sammy know—

She stepped back to study his new drawing. The confusion took shape if she studied it from a distance. In fact, the longer she looked, the more convinced she became that the dots resembled a swarm of bugs.

Her cell phone rang, making her body jerk. She fished the phone out of her pocket and answered. The voice at the other end made her stiffen. "I thought I told you not to call me here," she said.

"Sorry," the man said. "I don't mean to place you in an awkward situation, but I'd like to see Sammy again."

"Do you have any idea how hard it was to arrange that last visit without my husband knowing? And now you want to see him again? Maybe if I better understood what you think this is going to accomplish—"

"Please. Just one more time."

She bit her lip. "I'll think about it and call you. But don't call me here again, okay? Good-bye." She hung up.

45

Marc swiped the electronic key card and entered the suite he'd intended to enjoy with Gillian. The place was lifeless, like a cocoon lacking a caterpillar. He checked his phone. No messages from Gillian—or from his dad, either.

In the empty bedroom, he eyed the whirlpool. Why not? But he needed to hustle. He had no idea when Riley would return from his meeting with Micah Coombs. He wanted to be ready for him, and he was hardly presentable at the moment.

Already he could feel the aches and pains stealing over him like some injected poison slowly leaching its way through his bloodstream and into his muscles. His right knee was especially aching. If he felt sore right now, he knew he would be feeling a lot worse tomorrow. But the massaging hot jets and the steamy water did the trick, and he lingered, eyes closed, submitting his achy muscles to the steady, steamy drum. Riley could just wait.

Afterward, he got dressed and headed to the bathroom to comb his hair. Blankets of steam had fogged the waist-to-ceiling mirror, and he grabbed a hand towel to clear some space. He flicked on the wall fan.

Cool air blew and circulated in the steamy room. But something else came pouring into the room from the vent, as if he'd disturbed a bee hive.

Bugs.

They were suddenly everywhere: whirring, darting at his face, and swarming around his body. Hundreds of them. No, thousands of them, judging by how many the vent was vomiting out.

Marc stepped away, stunned.

Just when he'd least expected it.

The third plague.

46

Somewhere between reality and la-la land, a distant buzzing drew closer. A flutter of tiny wings brushed Tessa's checks and caressed her forehead. Something landed in her hair and crawled around as if seeking lunch.

Was she dreaming? Hallucinations were common symptoms of meth, if the injection had indeed been meth. How many times had she scratched her arms until they bled, certain little bugs were crawling just beneath her skin?

A tiny, razor-sharp needle jabbed her neck. She slapped at whatever it was and felt something wet under her fingers.

Tessa's eyes flew open. She sat up, breath catching in her throat.

A dark cloud of swarming bugs clogged the middle of the suite, buzzing in one massive insect chorus. The swarm was so thick she could barely see the door at the other end of the room, and even more bugs were pouring in through the heating duct near the floor.

She rubbed her eyes and gave her head a small jerk. The swarm was still there—she wasn't hallucinating.

She pulled the covers over her head, but some bugs had joined her in the darkness and made a beeline for her blood. They crawled across her exposed arms and legs and delivered a bite surprisingly bigger than their size. Not just one little bite, which she might have hardly noticed, but dozens of tiny pricks. The cumulative effect was like one massive needle jab.

She thrust the covers away, but that act was like opening the prison gates. Gnats sought out her ears and mouth while mosquitoes went after her exposed arms—wherever they smelled the blood rushing through tiny capillaries just beneath her skin. Repulsed, she jerked her head from side to side, hands batting and squashing. But she was grossly outnumbered.

Panic needled her to full awareness. She had to get out of here!

47

It was apparently the north woods' biannual convention of gnats, and the invitations had designated Marc's suite as the location. Not just gnats, he realized. Mosquitoes too. He recognized their dangle-leg formation and their whiny buzz.

A great cloud descended on him as if smelling his blood and deciding to have him for lunch.

One problem: He had no desire to be eaten.

He backed up until the bathroom counter slammed into the backs of his thighs. He flailed hands in front of his face but still inhaled several gnats. He choked, gagged, and spat them out, gasping for air.

He grabbed a hand towel and stuffed it into the vent opening, trying to prevent more bugs from flooding the room. But it was an exercise in futility. Too many bugs were roiling in the room now. He could slap away for hours, but while he was busy fighting them, others would be biting him—and they were.

Tiny pinpricks along his neck, arms, and legs registered in too many places to count. Bugs danced around his dead, found landing strips on his bare arms and feet, and darted into his eyes and ears with their whiny buzzes. Mosquitoes smirked at the thin barrier of his polo shirt and drank his blood right through it.

He swung his head from left to right so the bugs couldn't land on his face. Mashed dozens under his hands, but still they came, undeterred.

The foolishness of fighting so many dawned on him, and he darted toward the door. Blinded by gnats, he stumbled out of the bathroom, crossed the bedroom, and hustled toward the living room.

There's no reason to panic, he told himself. They were just gnats and mosquitoes, right? What was preventing him from walking right out of here? Besides, bug bites weren't dangerous unless the mosquitoes, historical disease carriers, were hosts for something deadly like the West Nile virus or bubonic plague.

But if that was the case, he was dead already.

He swallowed hard and slapped away in a panic, shirt clinging to his sweaty chest. Stinging gnats and biting mosquitoes came after him like angry kamikazes. He darted across the suite like a blind man, barked his shin against the coffee table, and cried out in pain.

Gotta get out of here.

This was the same way Jared had died. Just a trigger of a different kind.

He squinted through the whining swarm, searched every corner of the room. He'd never seen so many bugs in one place. Was someone else here—someone to finish the job?

No, he was alone.

Sweat dripped down his forehead, stung his eyes. The door. Where was the door?

More needles danced along his legs and neck as he followed the wall and stumbled toward the door. He twisted the knob, swung the door open, and barreled into the corridor.

The bugs were there too. Yells echoed everywhere. People rushed down the corridor in a panic. They bumped into him blindly as they hurtled past.

The truth smacked into him. This was no isolated attack.

Someone grabbed his arm. He squinted through the thrumming cloud.

Riley.

His hand tightened around Marc's arm and yanked him away. Toward the main entrance and merciful deliverance beyond.

48

I've gotta get out of here!
Tessa flung the blankets aside and somehow swung herself out of bed and onto wobbly legs. Where had her strength gone?

All the while, little varmints were feasting on her back, her neck, her biceps. It was like someone was running a sewing machine across her body, the needle whirring. In and out. In and out. She cried out more in surprise than in pain.

Unable to support her own weight due to her sickness, she crashed, providing a banquet for whatever she didn't swat in time. She tried batting the bugs away, but her hands mostly slapped air. They cleverly maneuvered away from harm as if she were a plaything, then dive-bombed her again.

She eyed the door but feared she lacked the strength to cross the room and get out. With her hands over her face to keep the gnats out, her eyes peered at the window through splayed fingers. If she couldn't get out, maybe she could entice the bugs to leave. Didn't they prefer the outdoors?

She ignored the feast in progress, clawed her way to her feet in a panic, and groped for the wall. She reached for the window blinds. They crashed down on her bare feet.

She cried out, her gaping mouth a sudden haven, and gnats swarmed in. Her hands flew to her face, and she spat the gnats out in disgust, fingers crushing handfuls of them.

She retched and thrust her mouth into the crook between forearm and bicep. All the while, mosquitoes were needle-stinging her in too many places to count. She gasped and tried to stave off a new wave of panic.

God, please help me!

Gasping, she squinted past darting gnats for the latch, but the room was air-conditioned, the window's sash snug around the appliance. From all appearances the window hadn't been opened in quite a while. But there had to be a way—

Behind her the suite door flew open. It slammed against the far wall above the drone of the whirring chorus. She whirled and thought at first she must be hallucinating.

Cyrus?

He crossed the room toward her as if in slow motion, like something from a movie. A calm, amused smile stretched slowly across his face. She blinked.

She *had* to be hallucinating.

He wasn't slapping at bugs. In fact, the bugs darted away from him as if he were repelling them, as if he were the opposite pole of a magnet. As if he were lord of the insects, and they fled his presence in reverent fear. Not a single mosquito molested him. In fact, as he drew within feet of her, the bugs mercifully fled her presence too.

Her eyes widened. Who was this guy? He was recreating the plagues, and now the bugs were obeying him, too?

In his right hand he held a syringe, his wordless message clear, his eyes compassionate.

You'll be paid handsomely.

She eyed the syringe in anticipation. He'd come to keep his promise after all.

Already fire peppered her skin where the bugs had feasted, but this one little bite would make it all go away. Take all the pain and memories away. What was one more sting among hundreds of others?

Voices bounced around in her head, berating and condemning. *You'll never amount to anything. Look how you've wasted your life. You're nothing but a druggie.*

Tessa ignored the voices. She reached for the syringe, but he batted her hand away. Not angrily. Just to show that she didn't need to do the deed herself. He would do this simple act of kindness for her because he cared. Because he understood.

Understood the need.

She turned her face away and offered her scarred arm willingly.

49

Brianne Hyde was on her way out of the building with several whimpering secretaries when she remembered.

Where was Tessa? Had she gotten out?

She'd left Tessa sick in bed. Tessa might need help.

Brianne told her colleagues to press on without her and sprinted back to her suite, all the while slapping exposed skin and ducking her head to keep the bugs out of her face. They seemed even worse near their suite.

The door was ajar, and Brianne hustled inside.

Tessa huddled in a corner under the air-conditioner, legs pulled to her chest. She faced the far wall.

A cold ache started at the base of Brianne's neck and slid down her spine. Why was Tessa huddled in the corner like that? Why wasn't she fleeing like everyone else?

"Tessa! Tessa, are you okay?"

There was no answer.

Something deep inside Brianne started to give way. She knelt beside Tessa and grabbed her cold arm before seeing the innumerable bug bites dimpling her skin.

The gentle touch toppled Tessa onto her back, revealing her face.

Brianne Hyde screamed.

50

From the vantage point of the bluff, Cyrus sat astride a brown mustang, reins clutched in his hands. He sat tall and straight, allowing the euphoria of success to wash over him like a drug. Perhaps it was something like the rush Tessa had expected, but she'd experienced something else entirely.

Could that be the slight twinge of guilt stirring in his gut? He dismissed the emotion as if swatting a fly. The Tessas of this world deserved to be put out of their misery—all of them—and he was more than happy to do what he could to decrease their population.

People still poured out of the lodge. They emptied the building like a bunch of ants in a rainstorm. A smile tugged at his lips, and he allowed the amusement to reach his face. Just this time.

So far everything had fallen into place and gone exactly as he'd planned. There was so much more yet to come, but he was already two steps ahead.

He regretted involving the secretary. She could have easily sabotaged everything, but that was one mistake he had no desire to repeat. He would retain one more person here—his subservient grunt—and Sammy, but that was it.

He focused on the confused mob below, bitter that they at least could flee their enemies. He remembered being stuck inside a wood-frame structure while his enemies injected tear gas into the building. Sure, he and his comrades could have fled, but where would they have gone? Into the waiting arms of the

FBI and the ATF? The same men who'd shot down one of their comrades like a dog and left his body hanging on a fence for days afterward so the coyotes could eat his flesh?

He shook his head. *Never, ever again.*

Those exiting the building had brought this trouble on themselves. God had been merciful, but even his mercy had its limits. Now he, Cyrus, was an avenger, a sort of Moses, who would bring the judgment God required because they refused to see.

One man in particular would feel the full brunt of his judgment.

His mind ran over the next step, and his hands tightened around the reins. The resort would be closed for a day or two, giving him plenty of inside access.

The mustang whickered impatiently. It was time to move, and the horse seemed to sense it, too. Cyrus had watched long enough. The resort was empty now, like a lifeless shell. The sun beat down hard on Cyrus; his back was damp with sweat.

He dismounted the horse and peered deeply into Blaze's gentle brown eyes, rubbing the white stripe along his muzzle. Of all the horses at the stable groomed for horseback riding, Blaze was his favorite.

He couldn't help feeling sad when he contemplated the next difficult but necessary step.

"You understand, don't you, Blaze?" he said in a gentle, soothing voice. "Sometimes one must make the ultimate sacrifice for the good of all."

In fact, wasn't that what his son had done—giving his life for the masses? In the end, though, he'd been so unappreciated. So unremembered. But by the time he was through, everyone would remember, wouldn't they?

Unblinking amber eyes regarded him with unspoken sadness, as if the horse understood and calmly acquiesced.

"You will forgive me, won't you, Blaze?"

51

Gillian knocked on the hotel room door and waited. Movements rustled inside. The door opened, and Emily Riley's face appeared beyond the crack. She opened the door wide to let Gillian pass.

"How was your bath? Are you feeling better now?"

"Yes, much better. Thank you."

Gillian averted her eyes from Emily's in embarrassment. After leaving Gabriel in the park and calling her mom, she'd found Emily and cried for a solid half hour. But Emily was a saint. She hadn't probed, hadn't pressed her for an explanation. Nevertheless, Gillian hadn't been able to avoid spilling it all out.

So Emily knew everything now. Everything about her marred past. Everything about the wound that felt as raw as if Gabriel had abandoned her only yesterday. Now she regretted that she'd told Emily so much. She felt vulnerable and exposed.

Gillian brushed past Emily to check on Chase, a folder in her hand. Her son was asleep on the bed's comforter, arms upraised as if in surrender, head turned to one side, eyes closed and cheeks rosy. His tiny chest rose and fell—a picture of peace Gillian found herself envying. Oh, if only she could return to infancy, when life had been so simple! What did a baby know of first love and abandonment?

Gillian took the chair by the bed and longed for a cup of tea. Perhaps she could slip down to the lobby, where the tea selection was better, and see if she could finagle a couple bags of Earl

Grey. Then again, they would need to think about supper soon, and she could always order some tea then.

Emily sat on the edge of the bed, eyes inquisitive. Beside her lay a biography of Amelia Earhart, which she'd apparently been reading.

Gillian handed her the manila folder. "You wanted to see samples of my work. I printed a few things from my website."

"Thank you." Emily accepted the folder and perused its contents, a smile on her face. "Wow, your calligraphy is amazing. I do so admire creative people like you. I don't have a creative bone in my body."

"But you swam in the Olympics, right? I would call that creative."

"Creative?" Emily cocked her head. "No, it was pure adrenaline. I hardly slept a wink the night before. How I even medaled is beyond me. God must have been in it, I guess."

"Thanks for watching Chase for me," Gillian said.

"You're very welcome. He's such an easy baby." She paused. "Any word from Marc?"

Gillian shook her head, relieved to talk about something other than the Gabriel problem. She hadn't seen or heard anything from Marc since he and Riley left to interview Brianne Hyde after lunch. She'd left him a voice mail, but he hadn't called back yet, and she had so much to tell him.

It was strange that he hadn't called her back. They needed to talk about their drive to Detroit on Saturday to attend Jared's funeral on Sunday afternoon.

"Have you heard from Riley?"

"He called earlier after his meeting with Micah Coombs and passed on some interesting information. Of course, Micah says he has no idea who would have wanted to murder Jared Russo."

"Any other news?"

"Yeah. Remember the invoice linking Micah to the purchase of the poisonous frog? It was credit card fraud, pure and simple. Chuck also checked into the key card system to see if anyone could have gotten an extra key to Jared's room. The resort security is terrible. Just about anybody could have done it. One more thing—the toxicology report came back. Jared definitely died of poisoning from the frog."

Gillian shook her head, overwhelmed by the pointlessness of it all. "Marc told me the amount of poison in Jared's body was enough to kill ten men."

"I believe that's what they call 'overkill.'"

Gillian had forgotten that Emily had been married to a homicide detective for who knew how many years and certainly knew the lingo. "So it sounds like we're dealing with a crime of passion and not a bunch of pranks after all."

"But isn't that the way life is sometimes? Things are rarely as they appear at first glance."

Gillian's mind drifted, startled by a new line of thought. Had her crossing paths with Gabriel Jacobi really been as coincidental as it seemed? Had Gabriel known Jared Russo? Perhaps. Could Gabriel have given Jared the idea of inviting Marc and her to the resort? Had Gabriel intended this meeting all along?

Her mind took another leap, this one making her pulse quicken. Was Gabriel somehow involved in the plagues? He was Micah Coombs' assistant, after all. Perhaps Micah was being blamed when Gabriel was really the culprit.

Emily said, "The scenario reminds me of *The A.B.C. Murders* by Agatha Christie. Have you ever read it?"

Jostled out of her thoughts, Gillian shook her head and realized she needed to pay better attention.

"See, someone starts killing people based on the alphabet. The first victim's name starts with *A*. The second starts with *B*—you get the picture. So the killer appears to be a serial killer who's going after random people based on the next letter in the alphabet, right?"

Emily paused, eyes blinking. "But in the end it's all a ruse. The killer has a motive to kill a certain person—I think it was the man with the name beginning with the letter *C*. To put police off the scent, he killed two strangers to make the murders appear to be committed by a serial killer following the alphabet. You see what I mean? Things aren't always as they seem."

"So you think the plagues—"

"I think they're a smoke screen. I don't think the murder has anything to do with these plagues."

"Then what's going on here?"

Again, that amazing blue glowed from her eyes. "Hatred and murder. They often go hand in hand, don't they? Perhaps that's why in the Gospels Jesus said that hating one's brother was essentially the same thing as murder. Clearly somebody hated Jared Russo enough to want him dead."

"Or, like in *The A.B.C. Murders*, Jared's death is intended to distract investigators from the real target."

Emily's eyes locked onto Gillian's. "Let's hope not. If that's true, then somebody else is going to die very soon."

Emily jerked in surprise when her cell phone trilled. She grabbed it off the nightstand. "Hello?" Alarm filled her eyes. "Oh, my goodness! Are you kidding?"

Something important had happened—Gillian could feel it. She stared at Emily, waiting for news. Fear writhed like an eel in her tummy. "Is it Marc? Is he okay?"

"Hold on a second, Chuck." Emily covered the mouthpiece with her hand, face ashen. "There's been a bug attack."

"A bug attack?"

"Yeah, and Marc's at the hospital?"

Her chest tightened. "What?"

"They're just checking him over to make sure he's okay." Sadness drowned her eyes. "Something else has happened too. Someone else is dead."

52

That Saturday, Marc and Gillian traveled to Detroit for Jared's funeral while the Rileys remained behind to do some sleuthing on their own. During the drive, Marc described the bug attack in detail. In turn, Gillian told Marc about her talk with Gabriel Jacobi, sharing every important, painful detail she could recall—including Gabriel's confession that he still had feelings for her.

She waited for Marc to ask her if she still had feelings for Gabriel as well, but he mercifully remained silent, and she was glad. What would she have said? It was true that during his confession her resentment had fizzled away, and just for a moment she remembered what she once felt for him.

Finally, Marc said, "Well, that explains why Gabriel never tried to make contact all those years. You had no idea he was in Alaska, did you?"

She shook her head.

"Do you feel a little better now that you two talked?"

She nodded, though the conversation itself had been one of the most difficult ones she could remember. She was still struggling to come to terms with what Gabriel had said. His explanation seemed almost too neat, too convenient. Then, at the end, had he been flirting with her or simply revealing more than he should have? She didn't have any answers, but she'd agreed to forgive him.

Now you just need to let it all go.

But her mind wouldn't. Now that they'd talked and he'd said he was sorry, where did they go from here? Could they have a friendship now? But if feelings could be revived and make either vulnerable, was the renewed relationship even wise?

Afterward, they lapsed into silence, each burdened by the strange events of the last few days.

They checked into their hotel that evening, and Gillian slept fitfully. Once, she woke with the unsettling sense that someone else was in the room, looking for the baby—a common nightmare lately. She flicked on the bedside lamp, but nothing was amiss. Chase was fast asleep in the crib beside her, just as she'd left him.

The next day was unusual for a Sunday. They attended morning worship at First Baptist, Jared's church, and went to his funeral after lunch. The cemetery was sprawling, the weather scalding. Marc served as a pallbearer. Mourners waited patiently in the heat to pay their last respects to Melissa Russo and her three kids.

Gillian had barely known Melissa, Jared's wife, in college, but Melissa's eyes sparkled with recognition when she saw Marc. She thanked them for coming, and Marc assured her he was doing all he could to work with law enforcement and bring Jared's killer to justice. She just nodded, eyes and nose red against a pale, drawn face.

Later, they got into the Tahoe with plans to take a nap at the hotel and drive back to Ishpeming the next day. As they drove, Gillian studied Marc's face.

She'd smothered his face with Benadryl to take away the itching, but the best remedy for the small, red bug bites dappling his cheeks and other parts of his body was time to heal. Thankfully, the blood tests had come back negative. No traces of West Nile virus or anything else deadly had appeared in his bloodstream. Apparently Tessa had been the killer's only target.

Marc wasn't typically one to cry, but his red-rimmed eyes were a sign that he carried more grief than he was letting on. That had always been Marc's way—to keep what was troubling him locked away deep inside, sometimes to his detriment.

Even at the funeral of their twin babies, Marc had been stoic, apparently reserving his tears for when he could have a good cry in private, as if his masculinity were too vulnerable for him to be seen shedding public tears. For a while, Gillian had misjudged him, assuming he didn't care about the loss of their twins as much as she did. What a fool she'd been. But that was all in the past now.

She bit her lip. Sometimes that look on Marc's face made a wave of fear ripple through her. When Marc internalized fear or anxiety, rage sometimes took its place. God had been working on this particular area of weakness, but Marc's temper still raised its ugly head sometimes, and she didn't like being around him when it did.

As they drove, he grabbed her hand and wove his fingers into hers. She wanted—selfishly, she realized—to be back at that romantic suite Jared had reserved for them. Just the two of them, snuggling in the whirlpool.

A semitruck crawled into the lane in front of them. Marc switched lanes to pass.

Her mind drifted back to the cemetery, to the countless headstones. To the dreams that had been cut short, like her dreams for her dead babies—especially her twins, the only ones she'd held in her arms.

She shook herself mentally, not wanting her mind to wander down that painful path. Yet sometimes she couldn't help playing the "what-if" game, wondering how her life would have changed if Meredith and Blaine, her twins, had survived. In the midst of the terrible twos, they would have endlessly questioned everything.

On days like today she found herself reverting to the terrible twos as well. She wanted to know why all of this was happening. *Why, God? Why?*

"Are you okay?" Marc asked.

"Sure, I'm fine. How about you?"

"I'm okay."

She heard his lie and looked at him closely. "Really?"

"Okay, I'm not okay."

"What are you then?"

He kept his eyes on the road and tightened his jaw, muscles bunching.

"Come on, Marc. Talk to me." Communication had always been a problem. Just when she thought they were making progress, one or both of them took a step backward and clammed up.

He swiveled red-rimmed eyes toward her and sighed. "Okay, I'm angry."

"Righteous anger has its place."

"I think God's angry, too, whenever people play judge and prey on the innocent."

"So that's what you think's going on here?"

He nodded.

"But what do you know about Jared? Really? A lot could have happened since the last time you saw him. He could have made enemies."

He looked at her with a small blink of surprise. "We're innocent until proven guilty, right? Jared is innocent until the evidence tells us otherwise."

"I'm just saying, he could have done something to tick somebody off. There must be a motive."

Marc shook his head dismissively. "Knowing Jared the way I do, I don't believe he brought this on himself. Even if he did, nobody but God has the right to play judge—at least not this kind of judge. Nobody has the right to just take a life like this."

And not just *one* life, Gillian thought. Tessa, one of the secretaries, had been found dead after the third plague. So far, while waiting on toxicology reports, all anyone could conclude was that the countless bug bites covering her body had caused her death somehow, but Marc wasn't so sure.

A poisonous frog had taken Jared's life, yes, but toxicology reports had revealed another substance in his bloodstream. Some type of paralyzing sedative had upset his stomach and rendered him incapable of fighting his killer. Now Tessa was dead, too, but perhaps her death wasn't what it looked like either. What had Emily said about things not being as they initially appeared? Although hundreds of bug bites could have made her sick, perhaps a bite of another kind had sealed her fate.

"I have to do this for Jared." An edge of resolve hardened Marc's voice.

"You have to?"

He nodded, and that stubborn set of his jaw was as determined as ever.

"Don't you think you're heaping a little too much responsibility on one person's shoulders?"

He looked at her. "Gill, you don't understand. When I met Jared, I was a new believer. I was like"—he grappled for the right simile—"like a colt learning how to stand. I was falling down over and over again, making one mistake after another. But Jared was always there to pick me up."

He sighed. "If Jared hadn't been there for me, I seriously wonder where I'd be today. Maybe I would have given up on the Christian life, decided it was too tough. Maybe I would have stopped turning my back on all the things that wanted to cling to me."

His penetrating gaze sometimes made her want to look away. "God used Jared to save me from myself. If I hadn't had that lifeline then, I don't know where I'd be today. Jared gave so much of himself to me when he was alive. How can I not give of myself to him now that he's dead? At least until we catch whoever did this."

He blew air out of ballooned cheeks. "I'm going to find whoever did this to Jared, Gill."

She didn't challenge him. This dead-set determination was what had inspired him during his teen years to work hard enough on the basketball court to make it to the NBA. Regardless of the obstacle, he hadn't let up until he achieved his dream. She heard the same determination in his voice now and knew better than to stand in his way. Perhaps a little more of that determination was what they needed to crack this case wide open.

"I'm going to find whoever killed him." He nodded. "I won't rest until I do."

53

Hours away in Detroit. Another hotel. More quiet corridors and Cyrus' magical key to access any room he desired. If only every door in life would open to him as easily.

They were all at the funeral, and he had the perfect opportunity to prowl. He found the correct room number and slid the analytic converter into the key card reader. The red light turned green, and he crept inside.

His eyes roved over the dark room, and at first he wondered if he had the right one. The place was immaculate, the bed made, almost as if no one had slept here the night before. Then he spotted a suitcase and a baby crib.

The baby. His scalp tightened.

He crossed the room and peered down at the small space where the baby had slept last night. Unable to stop himself, he reached past a red plastic toy for the small blue blanket that lay folded in the corner.

He brought the blanket to his face and drank in the aroma of the child mingled with the scent of baby lotion. Wow, even the smell was the same! Unbidden tears sprang to his eyes, burned his throat.

Part of him wanted to wait for the right opportunity and then take this boy. Just grab him and flee before anyone was the wiser. But wisdom told him he couldn't let anyone—not even a baby—derail him from his carefully laid plans.

But maybe ... just maybe there was another opportunity here, after he'd done what he came here to do. Perhaps he could—

Someone knocked on the door. He whirled, the blanket still in his hands.

"Housekeeping!" The voice was a woman's. She had a slight Hispanic accent.

In three quick strides he darted into the black hole of the open bathroom door. The door mechanism clicked unlocked in response to her key card.

54

Dr. Matthew Colbert balled his hands into fists so tightly, he felt like he could break his fingers in two. He stood beside Jared Russo's coffin on a mat of artificial turf bordering the gaping hole and wished he could cry. Wished for some way to release the pent-up anger and sadness building inside him like a summer storm.

Jared had been one of the best fathers and husbands. One of the best soldiers on the battlefield. One of the best Hebrew translators. And now one of the best was dead.

How could anyone ever hope to replace him? Why had someone snuffed out his life like this?

Vernon Brannon, ever faithful and poised in his navy, double-breasted suit, stood at his side, a hand on his shoulder. He said he was working with the sheriff to track down Jared's killer. They wouldn't stop looking until they found whoever was responsible. Then Vernon turned his head and coughed a deep chest rattle before excusing himself.

Colbert heard but didn't really listen. One death was enough, but now they had two. Tessa was gone as well. Another funeral for another day.

Too much death. Too much heartache. God, what's going on here? Where are you in all this?

If he turned around right now, he wouldn't be able to avoid the grief-stricken eyes of Tessa's mother, Sandra, and her condemnation was the last thing he could handle right now. He'd promised to watch out for her little girl, to give her a chance to make a clean start after the system had turned its back on her long ago. But now her sweet girl, who had lugged baggage the size of Mount Everest but made big strides for God, was gone. Memories of her mischievous smile and hard-edged sarcasm nearly rent his heart in two.

The sheriff attributed her death to a possible allergic reaction to the hundreds of bug bites covering her body. Vernon didn't believe it, and neither did he. Her death eerily resembled Jared's murder. In Jared's case, somebody had used a poisonous frog the way someone might use a gun. Perhaps someone had also used the gnats and mosquitoes to kill Tessa, if such a thing were possible. Pending toxicology reports would tell them for sure.

If she'd been murdered, who would have done something so bizarre? The person would have to be a little crazy. Maybe that's why nothing made sense—logic wasn't part of the equation.

His mind turned to the Gulf War and important strategy meetings he'd attended. He understood war and how to win it, but this was something beyond military strategy. Perhaps that's why he felt helpless in the situation—he didn't know how to fix the problem, and he'd been a fixer all his life. By not understanding the battle, how could he possibly win the war?

A familiar flutter around his heart made him grope in his pocket with his stubby fingers for the small pill he'd brought along just in case. He popped it into his mouth, slid it under his tongue, and waited for the tightness to pass.

It did. But the anger didn't.

It was still there, and it seemed more raw, more fierce, than it had been only moments before. Along with the anger came the nagging suspicion of what was really taking place here. Of who was executing these ridiculous plagues. Of why Jared and Tessa were dead. And of why more innocents might die if they didn't avert a sick madman's endgame.

But what *was* the endgame? All these plagues were heading somewhere, weren't they? Perhaps their destination held the key.

A subconscious impression descended on him, a sensation that he was being watched—and not by friendly eyes.

He turned slowly, not wishing to cause alarm, eyes sifting through the crowd. He mentally checked off familiar faces and searched for the one that didn't belong. No, he knew these people. He looked past the crowd of mourners and scanned the row of parked cars, certain somebody was hiding and watching. Perhaps with binoculars.

Whoever was responsible was here—he could feel it.

Or perhaps he was just suffering another episode of paranoia, which sometimes descended on him suddenly like the heart attack he feared would come someday when he least expected it. Some of his war comrades had returned home with Gulf War syndrome; he'd returned with something else—these odd episodes of paranoia.

Time was running out, and he had to do something before more people were hurt or killed. But what could he do? Halt the parallel Bible project and send everyone home? Reschedule the meeting for another place at another time? That might prevent more deaths, but would it help the police get to the bottom of what was going on here? And wasn't stopping the project what the killer wanted? No, he wouldn't allow the project to be thwarted that easily.

His mind wandered down corridors of a history he didn't enjoy exploring. Of a wife in the ground, as Jared would be soon. He went even further back to choices and indiscretions he couldn't undo.

His fingers tightened into fists when he thought about King David in 2 Samuel 12. Of the prophet Nathan's condemning words.

You are the man!

Could the product of a mistake long ago be part of what was going on here? Could the ulterior motive really be that personal and directed so clearly at him? If so, someone else was in danger too.

Sometimes the past refused to stay dead, but perhaps that was the illusion. Perhaps it had never been dead to begin with.

A hand on his shoulder startled him. He turned. Vernon Brannon's eyes were enigmatic.

"Yes, what is it?"

"Got a call from Sheriff Griswold."

Colbert's heart picked up pace. "What's happened?"

"Coombs has been arrested."

"Why?"

"The sheriff found the empty containers where the gnats and mosquitoes were stored. The bar codes led him to an organic supply company in Houston. Micah ordered the bugs."

Colbert lowered his voice. "How do you know somebody didn't just use his credit card like last time?"

"He signed upon delivery. We've got his signature."

55

"I checked the suitcase twice," Marc said. "Nothing valuable appears to be missing."

"Yeah, I checked it too. Whoever it was didn't take anything." Gillian held Chase close and glanced around the hotel room, unable to shake off the unnerving feeling of having been violated. She looked forward to leaving tomorrow and putting as many miles between them and this town as possible.

A sheriff's deputy had just left. He'd taken their statements after they returned from the funeral and received word that a man had been observed fleeing their room. The cleaning lady said a man hiding in the bathroom had darted past her, run down the hallway, and disappeared. Unfortunately, she hadn't gotten a good look at his face, though she remembered blue jeans, a gray T-shirt, and a navy baseball cap.

Gillian sat on the edge of the bed and pressed Chase's head against her left shoulder. She bit her lip, gaze wandering around the room, certain the answer still lay here somewhere.

Why was he here? What was he looking for?

There was no evidence of the lock being forced or the intruder gaining entry through the balcony window. Key card access was unlikely, so how had he entered the room? None of it made sense.

Marc gave her shoulder a gentle squeeze. "Hey, you okay?"

"I'm fine, but do we have to stay here tonight?"

"Maybe we should find another hotel."

"I was thinking the same thing." She sighed. "Marc, am I just overreacting?"

"No, I don't think so. I've already got my stuff together. I'll go get the Tahoe and bring it around front."

"Give me about 10 minutes. I just need to change Chase's diaper and double-check that I have everything."

He disappeared out the door.

She lay Chase on his back in the middle of the bed and removed his diaper. She crossed the room to grab his bag, which she'd left on the floor beside the crib. As she rose, her eyes landed on the red toy on his mattress. She froze.

His blue blanket. It was gone.

She'd carefully folded the blanket before they left for the funeral and left it in the middle of the mattress—she was sure of it.

The cleaning lady said she hadn't touched anything after the man fled the scene. Logically, the intruder would have searched their suitcase for valuables, but nothing had been disturbed. So why had the man taken the blanket?

The flesh crawled at the nape of her neck.

She scooped Chase into her arms and clung to him, brushing her lips against his forehead, the scent of baby powder strong in her nostrils. Deep in her heart had always lingered the secret fear that someone, someday, somewhere would come after her child. Was some sick person obsessed with Chase?

After the diaper change, she grabbed her things, took one last look around the room, and hustled toward the door. She wouldn't be pacified until they were far away from this place.

56

"Call my wife right away! And then I want you to get on the phone with Randall O'Keefe and tell him what's going on. And don't forget to activate the prayer chain."

Gabriel Jacobi paused on the sidewalk and scribbled down his boss's final instructions. Two deputies led Micah Coombs to the waiting patrol car, his hands in cuffs. Gabriel could only watch in disbelief and shake his head.

Arrested? How could this be happening? And here they were, all packed and ready to leave the resort—and boy, was he ready to go.

He'd done everything he needed to do here. He'd even made his peace with Gillian Thayer—at least he'd said what needed to be said, maybe even more than he needed to. Whether she took his words to heart and moved on was up to her now. More than anything, he just wanted to go home, but he seemed trapped here for some reason. As if God had other plans.

Somebody had framed Micah, and Gabriel wanted to know who. It all had something to do with these bizarre plagues. Somebody needed to put a stop to them, and maybe that somebody needed to be him. Solve the crime, clear Micah's name, and then he could go home, right?

Gabriel returned to his hotel suite and pulled out his cell phone to call Celia. He'd been planning to see her in 10 hours, but now he wondered how much longer he would be trapped in this godforsaken place. Away from his wife and kids.

Her sweet voice picked up, and the news tumbled out of him. He did little to hide his frustration.

"Oh, you poor dear," she replied sympathetically.

"Look, I gotta go. I need to see if I can post bond tomorrow and spring Micah out of jail. I just wanted you to know what's going on."

Disappointment seeped out of her voice. "I sure was looking forward to seeing you. How much longer do you think it'll be? The kids are all asking for you."

"Not much longer, I hope. But I've got a few loose ends to tie up here." *Well, maybe more than a few.*

"You be careful, okay? It sounds like a dangerous place, and I'd rather you not stay there any longer than necessary."

Funny that she would say that. He hadn't even told her about potential dangers, not wanting to worry her. Did he know what he was getting himself into?

57

Driving back to Ishpeming consumed Monday. On Tuesday morning, after breakfast at the hotel restaurant with the ladies, Marc pushed through the glass doors and entered the resort lodge with Riley only a step behind. It was amazing how quickly the cleaning crew had removed any traces of the bugs. Less than 48 hours ago, a swarm of gnats and mosquitoes had feasted on him. Even now he could feel those bites calling out to him—in spite of Gillian's TLC and more Benadryl cream at the hotel last night.

Riley said, "We'll talk to the lead investigator later—"

"—that would be Sheriff Miles Griswold—"

"—but I want to take a look at your suite first. I want you to show me where those bugs came in."

Even in a situation probably more bizarre than anything Riley had tackled before, the retired detective didn't break stride, though he did occasionally pause to wipe his nose on a tissue. Over the weekend, he'd started experiencing cold symptoms, and he confessed that he wasn't feeling quite like himself today.

A note was taped to Marc's suite door. A message, written in feminine cursive, asked him to come to the front desk, where a piece of mail was waiting for him.

Questions flailed in his mind as to who would mail him something at the resort. He decided to check later and swiped his key card, swinging the suite door open.

Marc blinked. The place was immaculate, and the faint scent of deodorizer wafted in the air. For a split second the bug attack felt like something conjured from his imagination.

"Okay, now where were you when the bugs came at you?" Riley asked.

Marc ushered Riley to the bathroom. The gray, vertical-slatted air vent on the wall wasn't anything unusual—in fact, it was one of those things people tended to overlook.

"It happened just after I used the whirlpool on Friday afternoon." Marc gestured to the vent. "That's where they came from. Probably thousands of them."

Riley had come prepared and pulled out a screwdriver, working the screws until the external panel slid off, all the while chomping on a fresh wad of Juicy Fruit.

Ducking his head, Riley peered into the silver ductwork. It headed into the wall and disappeared into a void around the bend. The duct opening was clean.

"Well, whoever cleaned your suite did a great job," Riley said, "but I'm pretty sure he didn't clean in here." Riley thrust his full arm into the wall.

"Bingo!" He removed his arm, hand overflowing with dead bugs. Marc draped a tissue on the counter, and Riley unloaded the bugs onto it, sorting through them with a pen.

Riley coughed into the sleeve of his shirt. He cleared his throat. "Gnats and mosquitoes—that's all I'm seeing here. But I'm no entomologist, and there could be more here than meets the eye." He brushed the bugs into a small plastic bag and sealed it closed with a twist tie.

"What are you going to do with them?"

"Send them to a forensic entomologist friend for testing. Another buddy's gonna analyze some of that fake blood from several of the scenes, too. I'm sure the sheriff's already doing that, but it can't hurt to get a second opinion, right?"

"What are you expecting to find?"

Riley shrugged, jaw working on his gum. "Anything unusual, I guess." He eyed the dead heap in the plastic bag. "They look rather yummy, don't they?"

"Yummy" wasn't the first word Marc had in mind. "Ferocious" and "blood-thirsty" would have been more accurate. If for some reason he'd been unable to flee the building during the attack, would he have died as Tessa apparently had? Overcome by bug bites? It seemed like a stretch that bug bites alone could have killed her, unless the bugs had been carrying some kind of disease. But he'd been bitten numerous times, and his blood test had come back clean.

Riley used his screwdriver to return the cover to its proper place. "That's definitely where the bugs came from."

"But how did they get in there?"

"Simple. Somebody must have put them in the ventilation system, and that tells me something right away." He studied Marc with knowing eyes. "The killer somehow had access. Come on. Nothing else to see here, but hopefully the sheriff can tell us more. Time we joined forces."

58

Emily's thin body sliced through the pool as she finished one lap after another under the glowing morning sun. Gillian watched in amazement. The older woman's pace never lagged. Gillian wondered how many more laps before she would finish. This was no Olympic-sized pool, Emily had told her, so she needed to do three to four times her normal laps to get even close to a full workout. Thankfully, few other swimmers braved the water this time in the morning, and the few kids who splashed in the shallow end gave Emily a wide berth.

Gillian rose, weary of watching from the lounge chair. Besides, she hated to linger too long. What if Gabriel dropped by again? She'd asked him for space, but what if he didn't honor her wishes?

She'd repeatedly rehearsed their conversation with conflicted emotions. His revelations definitely cast him in a more positive light, but she wasn't sure how she was supposed to feel about him now. If she'd known the true circumstances of his abandonment years ago, would she still have married Marc? She repeated to herself what Marc had told her numerous times—*there are no "what-ifs" in God's plan.*

She pulled on a T-shirt and sweatpants over her swimsuit and decided to go on a stroll with Chase, who'd splashed and giggled with her in the shallow end for a good half hour. Though he loved the water, he'd turned crabby—a nap was needed—and few things put him out quite like the gentle lull of the stroller.

She gripped the stroller handle and headed down the sidewalk toward the lake. When she reached the bend where the path headed into the trees toward the mine monument, the ground thundered beneath her feet. An animal snort from the trees jerked her around.

A gray horse leaped through the foliage some 20 feet away. On its back, a ponytailed teen girl clutched the reins as if hanging on for dear life, a terrified look on her face. The horse was obviously out of control: neighing, snorting, rearing, churning the air with its front hooves while the girl somehow held on.

Gillian bounded onto the grass with the stroller, trying to flee the disaster path. The horse rocketed toward them. The rider bounced up and down as if she were straddling the back of a bucking bronco.

Gillian hovered over the stroller, putting herself between the horse and Chase. Just when a collision seemed imminent, the horse lurched to a stop as if slamming on the brakes. The girl flew off the saddle and landed in a heap near Gillian's feet.

Gillian rushed over and helped the black-haired girl sit up; she pushed herself up on her elbows with a groan.

"Are you okay?" Gillian asked.

The girl gave her head a little shake as if waking herself from a dream. "I'm not sure. Something doesn't feel right." She reached toward her right ankle and winced.

"Jessie, are you okay?" A husky, brown-haired man rushed to her side. Gillian gathered from his tan jersey that he was a staff member from the stables. "What happened?" he asked. "You were doing great."

Jessie shook her head. "I'm not sure. I think a bee must have stung him. All of a sudden, he just started going crazy."

The staff member glanced at Gillian. "Thanks for your help."

"No problem." Gillian rose and backed away. The girl appeared to be in capable hands now. Nearby, as if aloof, the horse lowered its head and munched contentedly on the long grass.

Gillian turned toward Chase's stroller and froze, wide eyed.

The stroller was gone.

59

The hallway was crowded with stern-faced deputies coming and going. Information from a passing deputy led Marc and Riley to the right suite, where the sheriff had set up a sort of makeshift headquarters. His living room was his office, and a coffee table served as his desk.

The sheriff glanced up at the sound of their approach and rose from the couch where he'd been looking through some paperwork. His eyes were bloodshot, as if he hadn't been sleeping well. Hands on his hips, he asked, "Somethin' I can do for you gentlemen?"

"Sheriff Griswold, you remember me, right? Marc Thayer. I found Jared Russo's body."

The sheriff pumped Marc's hand. "Of course. You reported findin' that footprint outside the women's bathroom. Very clever of you."

"I hope the tip was helpful."

"Sure was. We've eliminated the cleanin' crew. Now we just need the right shoe to match the plaster cast we made of the print."

Marc motioned to Riley. "I'd like you to meet retired homicide detective Sergeant Chuck Riley of the Cincinnati Police Department."

Griswold shook Riley's hand, and the two men stared each other down for a beat. "Nice to meet you," he said to Riley. "As you can tell, things are a bit crazy around here with two mysterious deaths on our hands, so if you don't mind—"

"Actually, that's the reason we dropped by," Riley said. "Do you mind if we talk?"

The sheriff's left cheek twitched. "Like I said, I've got a lot on my plate right now, and I'm not sure—"

"Just for a few minutes," Riley said. "Then we'll get out of your hair. I promise."

With forced politeness, the sheriff offered the two men a seat on the couch across from him and asked a deputy to close the door so they could talk in private. Up close and personal, Marc couldn't shake the impression that someone had deliberately spray-painted that gray patch over the sheriff's left ear. He tried not to stare at it.

The sheriff leaned forward and locked his fingers together in front of him. "Okay, so what's up?" His gaze bounced between the two men.

"I won't bore you with a long speech about my credentials." Riley leaned back and rested his sneakered right ankle on his left knee. "Since I'm in your neck of the woods, I wondered if there's something I could do to help—in an unofficial capacity, of course."

The sheriff shook his head, but Riley lifted a hand. "Now hear me out. I know how this looks—me showing up here all of a sudden—but I'm honestly not here to interfere with your investigation. You're the man. You're in charge."

"I'm glad we're clear on that point. But what *are* you doin' here?"

"I invited him," Marc said.

Griswold swiveled puzzled eyes toward Marc.

"Remember what I told you during my interview?" Marc asked. "Jared was my best friend in college, and he invited me and my wife here as a sort of reunion. I want to help catch whoever killed him."

Griswold leaned back and folded hairy, muscular arms across his thick chest. "If you have new information to share, we're eager to hear it. Otherwise we'd prefer that you leave the investigation in the hands of law enforcement."

"But see, that's where Riley enters the picture," Marc said. "He and I were involved in an investigation once before."

"Ever heard of the Magician Murders?" Riley asked. "It was all over the national news a few years back."

"Sure. Who hasn't?" Griswold's gaze locked onto Marc. "Oh, I get it. So that was *your* wife and daughter the sicko almost strangled, huh? Tough luck."

Marc remained silent. Actually luck had nothing to do with it, but this wasn't the time to argue.

Riley said, "The Thayers—Marc and his wife—helped me catch the killer."

Griswold stifled a yawn. "I see. A couple amateur sleuths, huh? No offense, but we don't need any Hardy Boys or Nancy Drews around here."

"I totally agree," Marc said. "That's why I thought Riley's experience might be helpful."

Griswold shot poison darts at Marc with his eyes. "No, you thought maybe my team and I couldn't handle the job on our own."

Riley leaned forward and offered the sheriff a placating smile. "Look, everybody needs a little help from time to time. Admit it, you've never seen a case this bizarre before."

Griswold spread his meaty hands. "Okay, I admit it."

"I haven't either," Riley said. "I just want to help Marc find whoever killed his friend."

Marc let passion swell in his voice. "I owe it to Jared to do all I can to find his killer, and I won't rest until I do."

"All we want is a chance, sheriff," Riley said. "A chance to help."

Griswold took a deep breath, chest rising, and let it out through his nose, as if letting off some steam. "And what makes you think you'd actually be a help rather than a hindrance?"

"Riley knows a ton about homicide and behavioral profiling," Marc said.

"Share investigation details with me," Riley said, "and I can help create a profile of the perp."

Griswold shook his head. "Sorry, guys, but it's out of the question. I appreciate your zeal and all, but it simply ain't goin' to—"

Just then, an out-of-breath deputy burst into the suite and hustled to the couch. He didn't look a day over 18. Before the deputy could say a word, Griswold lurched to his feet, face reddening. "How many times have I told you—"

"Sorry, but it's an emergency. Just got word from the stable. One of the horses died last night, and several others are sick. The local vet's on his way. I thought you'd want to know."

60

"Somebody, help me!" Gillian cried. "My baby's gone!"

Her heart felt like it might beat out of her chest. She fought a wave of panic as she raced up the hill, gasping and sweating. Her gaze darted across the grounds, searching but not finding.

Oh, God, please. Help me find him. He has to be here. He has to be.

"My baby! Has anybody seen my baby?"

She sprinted down the sidewalk. Campers turned and parted in her wake, probably wondering what was wrong with this woman. How could they even hope to understand? Hadn't she always harbored this private fear—that somebody would snatch her baby? And now it was happening. *It was really happening.*

Her mind raced. Who would take him? Had the man who broke into their hotel room in Detroit followed them here?

She neared the pool. Emily rose from a lounge chair in alarm, gray hair matted to the sides of her head, eyes concerned. "Gillian, what's wrong?"

"Chase." She could hardly breathe, her voice trembling. "Someone ... took ... Chase."

Emily's fingers curled around her arms. "When did this happen?"

"Just—just—a few minutes ago." Her legs began to buckle, but she locked her knees into place. Tears flushed her eyes to overflowing. She dragged a sleeve across her face—she couldn't see, and she needed to. She needed to find him.

"We'll find Chase." Determination steeled Emily's voice. "Do you understand?"

Find him? How can she be so sure?

Emily's eyes flared, the grip on her arms even tighter. "Gillian, pull yourself together. We need to start looking, and I need your help."

Gillian stared at her, not knowing what to do. Dread tempted her to give up, to accept that only the worst could be the logical explanation. She closed her eyes, and a film played on the backs of her eyelids. Some snaggletoothed, bearded madman with Charles Manson eyes was pushing the stroller toward the parking lot and an awaiting car.

"The parking lot!" Gillian gasped. "We've got to search the parking lot before he gets away."

"He?" Emily's voice was strident, fingers like talons around Gillian's arm. "Did you see someone take him?"

"No—I—" She sucked in a breath. Tried to collect herself. She didn't know what she was saying.

"I'll go look," Emily said. "You search the sidewalks here. Some mother might have confused her stroller with yours and pushed him away by mistake."

Gillian nodded to herself because Emily was already gone, racing away with a white towel pulled around her like a cape—like she was superwoman, off to save the world. She would have to—Gillian didn't know how much help she could be.

Fear wound around her like a boa constrictor, as if trying to compress her lungs so she couldn't breathe. Was she having a nervous breakdown? Air shuttled through her lungs—she couldn't get enough of it. She paused, hands on her knees, and just tried to breathe. But just that simple act seemed almost like too much to handle.

Pull yourself together. God will help you do this.

What were those verses from Psalm 34 she and Marc had committed to memory last spring? She tried to remember, fought a mental block. Then a still, small voice seemed to whisper the verses in her ear: *I sought the Lord, and he heard me, and delivered me from all my fears.*

She stumbled away from the pool. *Yes, God. Deliver me from my fears. Please, God.* Her head turned every which way, eyes probing. Chase's name was on her lips as tears swamped her eyes. They blinded her so she couldn't see the pedestrians she kept bumping into. She muttered apologies, hoping people would forgive her.

This poor man cried out, and the Lord heard him, and saved him out of all his troubles.

Perhaps Emily was right. Perhaps another mother had confused Gillian's stroller for hers. This might be a simple mistake. The idea was at least a thread of hope to cling to.

The angel of the Lord encamps all around those who fear him, and delivers them.

She followed the sidewalk, chest heaving, the acrid aroma of her own sweat in her nostrils. *Deliver me. Yes, God, please ... please deliver me.*

Where was she going? She stopped, realizing she didn't have a clue. *Come on, think.*

Most mothers with strollers congregated near the playground, so she headed that direction. She raced over the hill, then froze when she neared the swings.

Something broke inside her at the sight of the hunter-green stroller. She lunged forward. Her lungs ached as she gasped for air, a reminder of how out of shape she'd let herself become.

She raced toward Chase's stroller—or at least a stroller that resembled his. It had to be the right one—it had to be. The stroller was angled away so she couldn't see inside. She couldn't be sure.

A blond-haired boy lingered near the stroller, staring inside. He was flapping his hands in a strange way. As she approached, he said something odd. "H–h–high 86. L–l–low 67."

She ignored the boy, eyes flying to the sleeping baby inside.
Chase.

It *was* him. He was okay.

Her heart leapt. She scooped him up into her arms, eyes flying to his small, peaceful face and the tangle of tiny blue veins crisscrossing his temples. She knew the pattern by heart, this God-given fingerprint of her child.

He lay so still in her arms. He was fast asleep, or—

Her arms tightened around him. Was he … ?

A small sigh escaped those tiny rosebud lips, turning her relieved knees to jelly. He was okay.

She sank onto a nearby bench, relief swelling inside her like a balloon getting too much air and about to burst. It popped in a storm of gratitude and fresh tears. She rocked Chase back and forth, back and forth.

Thank you, Jesus. Thank you.

Oh, magnify the Lord *with me, and let us exalt his name together.*

Heavy footsteps pounded the pavement.

"Sammy!" a woman called in an angry voice. "Sammy, you stay right there."

Gillian turned as a familiar woman marched toward the playground, hands balled into fists.

The woman swept past her and the stroller and grabbed the cowering, blond-haired boy by the arm. She gave him a jerk, almost knocking him off his feet.

61

S ick horses.

Marc glanced at Riley, caught his gaze, and held it.

Griswold rubbed weary eyes with the palms of his hands and turned his wrath on the deputy. "Why are you botherin' me with somethin' like this? What does this have to do with our investigation, huh? So some horses are sick. Big deal!"

The deputy lifted his chin. "With all respect, sir, you said to report anything that seemed out of the ordinary. The man in charge of the stable said they've never had a horse suddenly up and die like this."

Griswold waved his hand as if batting a fly out of his face. "Okay, fine, you told me. Now don't interrupt me like this again unless it's important." He muttered a few obscene words under his breath as the deputy departed. Then he returned to his seat and threw his head back. "Oh, this place has turned into a regular circus. Now we've got sick horses on our hands."

Riley cleared his throat. "Uh, Sheriff, I think I know what might be going on here." He glanced to Marc. "Are you thinking what I'm thinking?"

Marc nodded. "The next plague should be flies."

"For some reason, the perp has gone straight to the diseased livestock," Riley said. "But why?"

Marc shrugged. "I don't know. Maybe staying in Bible order is too predictable for him now. Maybe he's mixing things up to make the investigation more difficult."

"If that's the case, he's not as compulsive as I'd thought, which means I need to tweak his behavioral profile." Riley's eyes sparkled with new insight. "Maybe he's got something special planned for the flies later."

"Whoa, guys! Hold on here." Griswold chuckled. "You honestly think this guy's gettin' his playbook from a Sunday school lesson?"

Before Marc or Riley could answer, the suite door flew open again, and another deputy—this one balding and overweight—stormed in. Before Griswold could chew him out, the man stammered, "Somebody just called an—an ambulance. One of the translation committee members is—is sick."

"Sick?" Griswold lurched to his feet. "Must be pretty serious if they called an ambulance. What are his symptoms?"

"Shortness of breath, chills, and—and severe chest pains."

Marc and Riley exchanged glances again.

"Okay, I'll check it out," Griswold said. "Thanks for lettin' me know."

With a nod, the deputy turned and left.

"It's happening again, isn't it? Another plague." Griswold shook his head at their pregnant silence, not needing an answer. "So this seriously has somethin' to do with the plagues of Egypt?"

"Familiar with them?" Marc asked.

"It's been a few years since Sunday school, so I might need a refresher. The first plague was blood—I remember that much."

"The second one, on Thursday, was frogs," Marc said. "And Jared Russo died."

Griswold nodded. "Right. Then Friday was the third plague—bugs—and Tessa McCormack died."

"Gnats and mosquitoes, to be precise," Riley said. "In fact, I've got a sample in my pocket if you care to see it."

Griswold rolled his eyes. "Uh, no thanks. I've got a pickup truck full of 'em, so I think I'm good."

"The fourth plague should have been flies," Riley said, "but a dead horse sounds like the fifth plague, the diseased livestock."

Disbelief clouded the sheriff's eyes. "I don't know my Bible like you do, and that's what I need right now—somebody who understands what's goin' on." He pointed his chin toward the doorway. "Mind if we talk while we walk? It looks like I'll need your help after all." He paused to aim a half-cocked hand at them. "Just don't interfere with anything I'm doin'. Got it?"

They nodded.

As they followed the sheriff down familiar hallways, Riley said, "I'm new in town and just catching up. Marc tells me Jared was killed by a golden poison dart frog."

Griswold halted mid-step and nailed Marc with his eyes. "Now how on earth did you know that? We haven't even re-leased that detail to the media."

Marc flushed under the sheriff's level gaze. "Vernon Brannon told me."

"Ah, Vernon!" The sheriff chuckled as he resumed walking. "He likes playing detective too. Vernon shouldn't have shared those details with you. On second thought, maybe you didn't need Vernon to know so much."

Marc sputtered. "What? You don't think—"

The sheriff held up a hand. "Look, Marc, I'm just teasin'. I checked out your arrival time on Thursday, and there's no way you could have killed Jared. Besides, would I be acceptin' your help in the investigation if you were on my suspect list?"

"So who is on your suspect list?" Riley asked.

The sheriff's face was grim. "Pretty much everybody, though we've narrowed our sights on Micah Coombs right now."

"Why do you think it's him?" Marc asked.

The sheriff told them about finding Micah's signature on the biological containers storing the mosquitoes and gnats. "A forensic handwritin' expert is taking a look at his signature right now to see if it's legit. If it is, we might be able to wrap up this case pretty quickly, though I must confess that Micah's knowledge and background don't seem to match the type of person we're lookin' for. Our killer is somebody who knows his drugs and poisons."

"And amphibians," Riley added.

They left the building and headed outdoors, where the sun beat down with amazing heat for a July morning in the Upper Peninsula. Griswold seemed to know where he was going, so they followed him. He said, "This guy knows his poison frogs—I'll give him that much."

"And he must know a lot about bugs, too," Marc said. "Didn't Tessa die from bug bites?"

The sheriff shook his head. "Dyin' from mosquito and gnat bites would be a rare event but not impossible, and it certainly *looks like* bug bites killed her. But events in this case are rarely as they seem."

"What do you mean?" Riley asked.

"Like Jared, the toxicology report reveals she had somethin' in her blood."

"Some kind of poison?" Riley asked.

The sheriff pulled up on the gravel path through the trees and faced them with enigmatic eyes. "Either of you familiar with methamphetamine?"

"Crystal meth?" Marc asked.

The sheriff nodded. "Tessa apparently died from an overdose. Judgin' by the needle tracks all over her arm, we're pretty sure she'd been a user for years. According to those closest to her, she'd been drug free for a while, but somethin' must have set her off, and she nosedived. Got too much of a good thing, if you know what I mean."

"So it was an accident?" Marc asked.

"Or maybe a suicide?" Riley suggested.

"No, I don't think so. Guess what was scrawled on the wall of her suite?"

"Let me guess," Riley said. "A certain Bible reference from the book of Revelation."

The sheriff nodded, a look of knowing dread twisting his face. "Her death appears to be like Jared's, part of some sick master plan." He sighed. "Come on, let's see what the vet has to say about these sick horses."

At the end of the trail lay a corral, a growing crowd of gawking onlookers, and a vet who had tragedy written all over his face. A tall, almost-too-thin man in a faded gray shirt, blue jeans, and cowboy boots, he removed his blue face mask and motioned the sheriff, Marc, and Riley toward a small, red barn. He led them to one stall in particular, where a dead, brown mustang named Blaze lay unmoving on the hay.

The sheriff and vet apparently knew each other. "So what are we lookin' at here, Stan?" Griswold asked.

"Wish I knew." Concern etched Stan's leathery face. "Some of the other horses are sick too, and I'm wondering if it's the same thing. No way to know what they've got until I do an autopsy, if that's what you want."

"It is."

"How soon?"

"As soon as you can arrange it. Some strange things are goin' on here. You've probably heard."

The vet looked at Griswold as if he'd sprouted wings. "Who hasn't? It's all over the local TV and in the papers."

"So what's your best guess so far?" Griswold asked.

Stan shrugged. "I'd rather not say until I know more. Horses can get sick from any number of things—poor feed, stagnant water source, old age. But Blaze was only five years old and one of the healthiest of the bunch, and he gets good feed. Doesn't make much sense to me."

The futility in the man's eyes underlined a fact Marc already knew: Little in this situation made sense. What the vet was really saying was that nothing natural could account for the horse's death. Something unnatural, therefore, was at the root of the problem.

After more chitchat that contributed little to providing more answers, Stan promised to be in touch. The sheriff led the way back to the lodge on the same winding gravel path. They reached the main entryway just as two EMTs pushed a stretcher toward an idling ambulance.

A man lay on the stretcher, an oxygen mask over his face.

Marc's chest tightened. It was Vernon Brannon.

62

"Sammy! Where have you been? You took that stroller, didn't you?" Each word was like a rage-filled jab, the woman's hand like a vice around the boy's arm.

Gillian hated to see anyone take her wrath out on a small child and wished the woman would just calm down.

Sammy just lowered his head and flicked fingers in front of his face. "You took that stroller, didn't you?" he said as if mimicking her.

The woman wouldn't let up. "Answer me! I know you did it. I saw you pushing that stroller down the sidewalk."

Sammy made clicking sounds with his tongue. At first Gillian wondered if he was mocking her, then she realized something wasn't quite right about the boy.

"It's okay," Gillian said to the woman's back. "No harm done." Chase was safe, though she wondered what had prompted the boy to push the stroller away. Had he intended the act as a practical joke?

But the woman wasn't finished with her tirade, her voice almost hysterical. "What am I supposed to do with you, huh? You can't go running off with other people's babies. Don't you know that's kidnapping? Somebody might call the police, and then they'd lock you up. Is that what you want?"

The boy didn't answer. He looked ready to bolt, squint-ed eyes straying everywhere except to the woman's face. The woman turned to Gillian, embarrassed. "I'm sorry. Please for-give him. He doesn't even know what he's doing half the time."

"It's okay, really." Gillian remembered the woman's name. "Lacey Caruthers, right? We met at the old mine memorial."

Lacey nodded, hands on her hips, but her scowl was still aimed at the boy. He turned and started trudging away across the playground, pausing only to aim furtive glances in Lacey's direction.

"Yeah, that's right, Sammy!" she called to him. "Go wander off so I can't find you. That's what you're good at."

Gillian's heart ached to hear any mother speak to her son that way. "It's okay, Lacey. I'm sure he didn't mean any harm."

Lacey watched Sammy go and shook her head, her wrath seeming to dwindle away. "He's done this before. He sees a cry-ing baby and wants to comfort the poor child. He means well, but he doesn't think. He doesn't realize that you can't just wan-der off with somebody's baby stroller."

Lacey glanced at Gillian with undisguised frustration. "I'm at wits' end with that boy. He's autistic—did I tell you that?"

Gillian shook her head. She didn't know anything about au-tism, but she knew something about how a mother should love her son.

Lacey crossed to the bench and collapsed next to Gillian, freckled arms folded, a sullen gaze fixed on the playground equipment. "Everything seemed fine at the beginning. The pregnancy, the delivery—everything was normal. He sat with-out my help at six months and walked on his first birthday. But then my mother noticed that he preferred being by himself. He didn't seem interested in other people. Seemed withdrawn."

Gillian tried to lighten the mood. "Well, not all kids develop the same way."

Lacey bit at a hangnail. "But this was something else. He was in his own little world and wasn't communicating. At three he'd lead me to the kitchen sink but never once ask for a glass of water. I guess he would have thirsted to death if I hadn't made the logical leap."

Her chuckle was sarcastic. "Other things were weird too. When I left him with a babysitter, he didn't seem sad to see me go. If he fell down and hurt himself, he didn't run to me for a hug. Most of the time he just wanted to line up colored building blocks—three red ones and then three green ones. Only in that order, over and over again. And heaven help you if you messed up his color pattern. He'd have terrible tantrums, and I'd pray and ask God to show me what I was doing wrong."

Lacey paused for a breath. "At four he finally said a complete sentence. I was thrilled, but I'm not sure if he's spoken a complete sentence since—unless you count his repeating things back to me. He rarely answers direct questions in his own words."

Gillian didn't know anything about childhood developmental problems—Crystal had been well ahead of most kids her age—and she didn't know what to say. But perhaps Lacey wasn't expecting answers; maybe she just needed somebody to talk to. Just needed to vent.

"At least Sammy understands compassion." Gillian didn't recall Chase crying, but maybe the girl on the horse had distracted her. "He heard Chase crying and wanted to comfort him, right?"

Lacey met her eyes with hazel orbs Gillian felt could pierce her soul. "Or maybe he just likes the feel of pushing something down the sidewalk. There's no real way of knowing. It's just another question for my rather long list. Why does he like to watch the Weather Channel for hours on end? Why does he like to draw so much? I have no idea. He may not look you in the eye, but he can ride his bike down a sidewalk full of people and not hit a single person. How can anyone explain that?"

She sniffed. "And I hate taking him to playgrounds because other moms just don't understand. They can be so—so judgmental. If they'd just extend a little mercy..."

A moment of silence followed.

Lacey let out a nervous chuckle. "Sorry to unload on you. Sometimes when I get frustrated, I give long speeches to strangers. But I guess that beats talking to a tree, right?"

What about her husband? Why doesn't she feel like she can talk to him? "You don't have to apologize," Gillian said. "My baby's safe—that's the important thing. Like I said, no harm done, regardless of your son's intentions." She studied Lacey's oval face, her high cheek bones, her ruddy cheeks. She could be a pretty woman if she worked on her appearance a little more. An eyebrow pencil could fill in that scar.

Gillian continued. "Sometimes God has a purpose in mind for things we can't understand at first." She was thinking of her unexpected meeting with Gabriel, but the words applied to Lacey's parenting challenges too. "Maybe God has special plans for Sammy you don't even know about yet."

"His ways sure are mysterious. I confess I can't figure God out most of the time." Lacey abruptly changed the subject. "And how has your stay at the resort been?"

Gillian bit the inside of her cheek. "I wish I could say we're having a wonderful time, but I'm afraid these bizarre murders have disrupted our plans."

"I'm sorry to hear that."

Someone called Gillian's name. She turned.

Emily!

The woman strode toward them, arms hanging limply at her sides, hair askew, face weary. The white towel was wrapped around her waist. "Oh, there you are. I searched the entire parking lot, but I didn't see—" She spotted the stroller, and a look of chagrin crept across her face. "Oh, I see you found him."

Gillian rose and faced her. "I'm so sorry, Emily. I found Chase, then bumped into Lacey here and got distracted. You remember Lacey—we met her before."

"Of course." Emily smoothed back her hair. "Hello."

"Please forgive me," Gillian said. "I should have looked for you sooner."

Emily crossed to the bench and plopped down next to Gillian, sandwiching her in the middle. She patted Gillian's leg. "Don't worry about it. As long as Chase is safe—that's what's important. Oh, it feels good to sit here, but I'm afraid we can't stay long."

"What's up?" Gillian asked.

"Chuck called. He's not feeling well at all. Thinks he might have caught a bad cold."

"Oh, that's too bad," Gillian said.

"I don't suppose you've got any cold medicine with you."

"No, but I've got some back at the hotel."

"Ladies, I've got everything you need," Lacey said. "Just follow me over to my place. That'll save you a trip across town."

"Are you sure?" Gillian asked. "We'd hate to be an inconvenience to you."

"No inconvenience." Lacey shook her head. "Actually, I get a little lonely clunking around in that big ol' place by myself. My dad's in Key West right now—he's always vacationing, it seems—and Quinn's off fixing something or other. It's usually just me and Sammy. Lots of people come and go from this place, but I rarely get to visit with any of them. It's really no trouble, and I won't take no for an answer."

"Honestly, you don't need to worry about the medicine," Gillian said, "but we'd be happy to visit with you."

Lacey rose. "It's all settled then. I'll serve you lunch, and we can talk more."

The thought of a cold drink sure sounded nice right now. Gillian felt exhausted. Then she thought of Marc. She should call him and let him know about what happened with Chase and Sammy. She faced Lacey. "You live in that big, white house across the lake, right?"

Lacey nodded.

"There's something about big, old houses that have always fascinated me. I've been wanting to see the inside of your place ever since we arrived."

Lacey grinned. "Well, then, there you go—it was destiny that we meet. Now you've found your chance."

63

Marc rushed toward Vernon, but Riley grabbed his arm, held him back. "Don't get too close. If what he's got is lethal enough to kill a horse, I'd hate to think what it could do to one of us."

Marc felt cold all over. "Assuming it's the same thing—"

"Oh, it's the same thing, all right. Only it's affecting humans, too. Remember, this guy's calculated. So far, nothing's happened by accident." His lingering look caught Marc's undivided attention. "Nothing."

The sheriff's words from moments ago taunted Marc. *It looks like part of some sick master plan.* But what was the plan? Without understanding it, how could they ever hope to stop it?

The ambulance pulled away. Marc watched until it veered out of sight, a sucking sensation in his chest. The sheriff said he would be in touch, and they exchanged cell numbers. Then he strolled away, a grim look plastered on his face.

Marc glanced around in a daze. First Jared. Then Tessa. Was Vernon to be the next victim? He felt so powerless and wished he knew what to do. Until they knew otherwise, it appeared that another plague had struck, and they needed to put a stop to them. Once and for all.

"Hey, you don't look so good," Riley said.

"I guess I'm a little shell-shocked. I can't believe something like this could happen to Vernon. I'm not sure what to do. Should I go to the hospital and check on him?"

"The sheriff promised to keep us up to speed, and I think you'd do more good here. Why don't we grab some coffee at the restaurant and discuss our game plan?"

"Sounds good to me." Yes, do something proactive—at least that was something he could do.

In the lobby Marc remembered the message on his suite door and asked the receptionist for the mail that had arrived for him. She disappeared into a backroom and returned with a letter-sized, white envelope. He frowned at his name, typed on the front, care of the Sabbath Resort and Conference Center. Oddly, the envelope bore no return address.

At the Backwoods Grille, where a few patrons were enjoying a late breakfast, they filled tall cups with a dark roast Colombian brew and decided to enjoy the beverages in Marc's suite, where they could talk in privacy.

Along the way, Riley called Emily and shared the good news that the sheriff had welcomed their help. Then he broke the sad news about Vernon Brannon and asked her to pray. Emily related the scare over Sammy's disappearance and assured Marc through Riley that everything was fine now. It was a simple misunderstanding. They agreed to meet after lunch, then Riley hung up.

On the way, Riley had another coughing fit. His cold was getting worse, but apparently Emily had plans to get him some medicine.

When they reached the suite, Marc headed to the living room with the letter while Riley busied himself in the kitchen. "Care for some microwave popcorn?" he called, referring to the complimentary bag lying unused on the counter.

Marc smirked. Did the man's appetite ever let up? "No thanks, but help yourself."

While Riley studied the directions—microwave popcorn was apparently a novelty to him—Marc reclined on the couch and opened the mysterious piece of mail.

Inside, to his surprise, lay a piece of pink stationery, folded into thirds. As he opened it, he recognized Gillian's penmanship—he would have known it anywhere. Even her perfect cursive, almost as beautiful as her calligraphy, was pretty enough to be framed. She often left him love notes in his briefcase or in his sock drawer. But why would Gillian mail him a note...

The top left corner of the page had been torn away. Just below the tear were the words "Dearest Gabriel."

Gabriel Jacobi? But why would someone mail this letter to him?

Marc's gaze bounced around the page. Words and phrases leapt out at him like accusing voices. "Love of my life." "Want to see you so bad." "Spend our lives together." "Can hardly wait for you to see the baby."

Can hardly wait for you to see the baby?

Marc stared at the stationery, mind racing. Although the letter wasn't intended for his eyes, he couldn't help himself. He began at the beginning and read every sickening word, stomach roiling at Gillian's sickly sweet words of devotion to another man. Every declaration of love was like a kick in the gut. Certainly they didn't have a perfect marriage, but he'd had no indication that anything was wrong to this level.

Sickened, he cast the letter on the coffee table. A tide of betrayal eddied through him, threatening to drown him. He leaned forward, elbows on his knees, and just stared at the letter.

How could this be true? Gillian had seemed genuinely shaken to see Gabriel again—there was no way she'd faked those tears. Unless ... unless she'd been lying to him from the beginning. But was that possible?

He couldn't stand where his thoughts were taking him. This letter suggested that she and Gabriel had planned to meet at the resort. Worse, it hinted that an ongoing romantic relationship existed between them.

A wave of heat washed over Marc. He balled fists, wanting to pummel Gabriel Jacobi until his face was hamburger.

"Marc, is everything okay?" Riley had crossed the suite and was peering down at him. In the background rose the hum of the microwave and the muted snaps of popping corn.

No, things are definitely not okay.

Marc didn't look up. The letter had nothing to do with Riley, and Marc couldn't bear repeating what he'd discovered ... or feared. "I think you better go for a while."

"Bad news?"

"Yeah, you could say that."

"Anything I can do?"

"No, I don't think so." Marc lifted his stunned eyes, certain that his look telegraphed enough. "I just need to be alone for a while. Sorry, I wish I could say more, but—"

"Okay, no problem." Riley backed toward the kitchen.

"Don't forget your popcorn."

The microwave beeped, and Riley grabbed his snack before heading to the door. He turned. "Give me a call later, okay?"

Marc didn't respond. The door clicked shut, and he sighed. He needed time to sort this out on his own. As tears stung his eyes, he rose and paced, hardly able to breathe. *God, where are you in all this?*

Who had mailed this letter to him? And why?

Marc crossed to the coffee table, snatched up the envelope, and studied the postmark. There was no return address, but the letter had been mailed last Friday from Tucson, Arizona.

Tucson? Did he even know anyone there? Even if he did, who would have known he was at the resort other than local acquaintances and family members?

Gabriel knew. But if he was responsible, how had he mailed the letter from Tucson? Maybe someone had mailed the letter for him. But why?

Perhaps he wanted Marc to know the truth. Maybe he wanted to cause a rift in their marriage.

Well, he succeeded.

Marc sucked in a deep breath and let it trickle out as his mind spun over the myriad ways to handle this crisis. He couldn't delay this—he had to be sure. Just as he pulled out his phone to call Gillian, a knock reverberated on the suite door. Marc opened it to see Riley's stunned face.

"Sorry to bother you, Marc, but everybody on the premises has been asked to report to the auditorium immediately. Something big has happened. Come on."

64

"Wow. This place is beautiful."

Gillian did a full turn in the immense living room, taking in the pricey furnishings crowding every corner. Emily Riley settled in a high-backed chair, her eyes carefully studying each antique in turn. She occasionally remarked on a certain piece of furniture, but her appraisal didn't seem as glowing as Gillian's.

Lacey wondered if they were just being polite. Her father had chosen most of the British colonial antiques with little input from her mother shortly before her final days. Buying things had always been his way to handle stress. The antiques definitely wouldn't have been her first choice.

Over iced glasses of root beer and tuna fish sandwiches, they chatted about the weather, about the calligraphy business Gillian had put on hold for the baby, about the odd deaths no one seemed to understand, and about the sheriff's snail pace at finding whoever was responsible.

In the corner, it was evident the prodigal had come home. Oblivious to company, Sammy sat drawing at the coffee table, his arm moving as if controlled by some wireless device, or like some type of automatic writing.

Lacey stiffened. Automatic writing—wasn't that a type of writing controlled by spirits?

She stood and crossed to the picture window, peering out at the lake with a shiver. She thought about all those dead men buried under hundreds of gallons of water and tons of dirt, sand, and rock. Perhaps their spirits had been as trapped as their bodies. Perhaps they longed to speak and at last had found a way.

She shook her head. She'd dabbled in the occult years ago, but God had saved her from that. She was free of those notions now.

Gillian ventured closer to Sammy and peeked over his shoulder. "What are you drawing there, Sammy?"

Lacey opened her mouth to warn Gillian not to touch him but held her peace. Let Gillian find out for herself. Lacey drew closer to see for herself, her blood running cold when she saw what Sammy had drawn on the sketch pad.

Dozens of horses sprawled on a green pasture. Brown horses, black horses, tan horses with brown, flowing manes. A full moon starkly glowed out of a midnight sky, and on a distant ridge a man on horseback peered down into the valley as if surveying his handiwork.

"Great job, Sammy!" Gillian said. "Those horses look so realistic."

Emily drew closer to see. "Just beautiful."

But something about the horses didn't sit right in Lacey's gut. "Sammy, honey, are those horses ... um, sleeping?"

Of course, Sammy didn't answer. As he drew, blond bangs swung from side to side like a closed stage curtain. If only he would open the curtain and let her inside. She knew he must long to be understood, and she so greatly wanted to understand.

"Are the horses sick?" Gillian asked.

Again, no response from Sammy. He might as well have been alone in the room.

Lacey backed away, a knot in her gut. Were the horses dead? She wanted to know, but, afraid to verbalize the unspoken, she remained silent. Somehow she already knew the answer and turned away, wanting to leave the room.

She had the perfect excuse. When she offered more root beer, both ladies accepted. Now she went to the kitchen for more, hands shaking. She leaned against the counter and let out a deep sigh, trying to collect herself.

What if Sammy could predict the future, as she'd feared?

She found more root beer in the pantry and headed to the freezer for more ice. A heavy footfall sounded behind her, and she whirled with a start, almost colliding with Quinn.

He was tall, big, and round—sort of like a cuddly teddy bear. The thick, brown goatee laced with silver only added to the impression. He was eating an extra sandwich.

"I see we've got some company." His deep bass voice didn't sound pleased.

She bit her lip and realized she should have asked him first. He liked to be consulted for just about everything, even something as minor as inviting friends over for sandwiches and a glass of root beer. Besides, root beer was his favorite, and she'd raided his private stash. She could always replenish it later.

He eyed the doorway to the living room. "I hope they don't stay too long."

Her mouth stiffened. And what if they did? She was here alone each day with Sammy. What was wrong with her having a few friends over once in a while? But she didn't say any of those things.

"Is something wrong?" he asked.

She forced a smile. "No ... nothing."

Was her anxiety that obvious? Should she tell Quinn about Sammy's drawings? But what exactly would she tell him? And if she did, would he even believe her? As he'd done so many times before, he would probably tell her she was batty, entertaining strange fantasies in that superstitious mind of hers.

He chuckled. "You sure you're okay? You look like you've seen a ghost."

Funny, his choice of words. She changed the topic. "So where are you off to?"

He rolled his eyes in an exaggerated manner. "Where do you think? His royal highness e-mailed me a list of tasks to do while he's working on his tan on a beach somewhere. He rang the bell, and his personal slave must make haste."

Her tone was reproving. "Quinn—"

"Well, that's how he makes me feel. Oh, don't worry. I'm just being open with you. When his lordship calls, I always smile and do everything he tells me—like a total weenie."

"Remember, Daddy has allowed us to live here with him—"

"As if I needed reminding—"

"—and pays the bills."

"And provides special therapy for Sammy. And gives us more money than we know what to do with. Yeah, I know, Lace. But sometimes I wonder if there are more important things."

She raised an eyebrow and waited for him to go on.

"Like freedom," he said. "Like being able to do with my life what *I* want to do instead of being at somebody else's beck and call 24-7."

She touched his arm gently. "Quinn, Daddy doesn't think of you as—"

"Well, it's going to change, Lace." Fire blazed in his voice.

"What do you mean?" She searched his heavily masculine features—the bushy brows, the goatee, the strong chin.

He bit his lip as if he'd said too much. "I'm just saying that eventually we'll leave this place and strike out on our own."

"But how will we ever afford—"

"You just leave that to me. I've been making plans."

"Plans?"

He glanced at his watch. "Sorry, gotta go. We'll have to continue this conversation some other time. I shouldn't keep his royal highness waiting."

She watched his fleeing back, annoyance prickling inside her. *How convenient. Run away just when the conversation got interesting.* But what did his words mean? How could they ever afford to move away and buy their own house now? Thanks to Daddy's generosity, they'd paid off their credit card debt, but their credit score was abysmal. They would need time to build it back up again.

She snorted. Quinn and his secrets. What did she really understand about the man she'd married a dozen years ago? Certainly his job at the resort kept him busy, but sometimes he was gone most of the night, crawling into bed long after she'd fallen asleep. Then some mornings he was up long before dawn, his side of the bed cold.

Could her dad or the resort really be keeping him this busy? Or was something else pulling him away? Another woman perhaps?

No, that couldn't be it. Quinn was truly devoted to her—she was sure about that—but something was filling his extra hours. What could it be?

Lacey carried another bottle of root beer and a bowl of ice cubes to the living room, where Emily and Gillian waited. "Sorry it took me so long," she said. "I bumped into my husband."

The sound of Sammy's crayon on the sketch pad drew Lacey's attention away from Quinn's cryptic words and back to her son. She crossed to the coffee table, set the drink and ice down, and sat on the edge of the couch, glancing down to see his work in progress. He'd begun working on a fresh page.

Now a man lay on the green pasture. A man who appeared to be dead.

Fine hairs rose on the back of her neck. She lifted a hand to her mouth and nibbled on a hangnail, trying to come to terms with what was going on here.

Was it possible that Sammy could really predict the future? Could this be an added benefit to his autism? He'd been right about the frogs and the bugs. Now the sight of horses—and a man—lying in a green pasture made her mouth turn dry, her hands shake.

If a terrible event was going to happen, shouldn't she say something? Perhaps the next event could be avoided. Or maybe she was already too late.

Then another possible explanation rattled her. Could Sammy somehow be part of the bizarre deaths at the resort? That would explain how he knew so much about what was going to happen before it did. No, it wasn't possible. Or was it? Lately, Sammy had developed the habit of running off, but what did he know about killing? No, she wouldn't allow herself to entertain such a preposterous idea.

But the horses. The only horses Sammy had seen were those kept at the stable. Were they really dying? She at least needed to know that much.

Gillian and Emily accepted more root beer and drank it down. Then they thanked Lacey for the refreshments and said they needed to go.

She ushered them to the front door, glad they'd cut the visit short. She thanked them for coming and said she hoped Riley would get better in no time. She gave Gillian her cell phone number and asked her to call her if she could be of help somehow.

"Hopefully I'll be seeing you around again soon," she called. They waved good-bye.

She rushed to the kitchen, grabbed her cell phone, and called Sheriff Griswold. One ring. Two rings. Then she hung up as new fears descended on her like birds of carrion.

Was telling Sheriff Griswold about Sammy's drawings the right decision? If Sammy knew what was going to happen before it did, wouldn't she be getting him in trouble? Would the sheriff arrest Sammy? Could social workers take him away from her?

Icy fear froze her chest, and she hugged herself, waiting for the chill to pass.

It finally did. But her questions remained. Then she knew what she must do.

With the phone still in hand, she called a different number.

Sammy had always loved the horses at the stable, especially Blaze, the brown mustang. At first fearful, he'd felt at ease after his second visit. Maybe she would pretend she was scheduling a ride for him later that day. When a voice picked up, the words tumbled out her, and she thought she sounded convincing.

But then her world came crashing down, her hand shaking. She tried to keep her voice steady after hearing the heart-stopping news. She thanked the receptionist and hung up.

No way! How could it be true? What's going on?

She crossed to the great room and paused in the doorway, eyes on Sammy, who was still focused on his work. For the first time, she began to fear her own son.

65

Men in space suits. That was the first thought that crossed Marc's mind.

They filed onto the auditorium's stage—all four of them—like a scene from *The Right Stuff*. They looked like they were exploring an unknown planet somewhere at the outer reaches of space. Except this wasn't space. It was Ishpeming, Michigan.

Without explanation, everyone had been herded into the auditorium—Marc and Riley, translation committee members, a gaggle of female secretaries, various vacationers, and a mob of kids and adult workers who had come for a week of camp, hardly expecting their fun to be interrupted this way.

What's going on? Marc swallowed hard, deciding not to think about Gillian's letter—at least not now.

The apparent leader of the spacemen stepped forward to the microphone in his puffy, white hazmat suit. He breathed with a distinctive in-and-out wheeze that reminded Marc of Darth Vader. Marc's skin crawled at the realization that the leader and his companions were sealed off from the air in the room.

Something's wrong with the air.

The leader lifted suited arms to quiet the crowd and spoke through some type of helmet microphone that made his voice sound tinny and synthetic. "I'm sorry if we've alarmed you. My name is Steve Yarrow, and we're here from the Centers for Disease Control and Prevention."

The CDC was based in Atlanta. Marc and Riley exchanged knowing looks. That didn't sound good.

Only Steve's eyes were visible past the white hood and plastic visor. "As you may have heard, one of the horses at the stable died last night. We've determined that it died from inhalation anthrax."

A two-by-four to the side of the head couldn't have jolted Marc more. The last he'd heard of anthrax was shortly after the 9/11 attacks, when there had been an anthrax letter scare. Between September and November of 2001, 22 people had mysteriously been exposed to anthrax. Five of them had died.

"As many of you already know," Steve said, "anthrax is a disease caused by a bacterium that primarily affects herbivores." Their puzzled faces must have registered. "Oh, sorry. Herbivores are animals that eat grass and other plants—like sheep, horses, or cows."

The scientist paused as if preparing to share even more disturbing news. "As many of you know, one of the translation committee members, Vernon Brannon, was rushed to the hospital this morning. We've confirmed that he somehow contracted anthrax, and I'm sorry to report that he passed away just a little while ago."

Gasps this time. Deep, heart-rending sobs rose from the secretaries.

Marc's mouth went slack. He stared at Steve Yarrow, barely comprehending what was happening. *But Vernon attended the funeral in Detroit on Sunday. He seemed fine then. How is this possible?*

Marc sucked in a deep breath, filling his lungs. The agenda was obvious. Jared Russo had been poisoned by a toxic frog. Tessa McCormack had been killed by an overdose of crystal meth. Now Vernon Brannon was dead from anthrax. In all three deaths, a drug or poison was the common denominator. Marc had laughed off the seemingly absurd notion that terrorists were behind the plagues, but he again wondered if his dismissal had been premature.

Could they be experiencing isolated bioterrorist attacks at the hand of Islamic jihadists?

"Because Vernon was among you when he became sick," Steve went on with a calm that sliced through the bundle of nerves in the room, "we have every reason to believe that some, if not all, of you have been exposed as well. Anthrax's poisonous spores can be breathed into the lungs or absorbed by the skin."

Hence the space suits. Hence the dread each time Marc inhaled a breath, as if anthrax spores were dancing in the air like invisible invaders with a menacing agenda.

Steve didn't sugarcoat the facts. Like fire ants, anthrax ate away at someone's insides, shutting down organs—lungs, liver, and heart—until they died.

The bad news was that from what they knew, Vernon had died from inhalation anthrax, as opposed to the milder cutaneous or skin anthrax. The spores were odorless, tasteless, and virtually undetectable. If someone breathed the spores, he or she wouldn't even know it. Symptoms included fatigue, fever, cough, difficulty breathing, nausea, violent vomiting, painful joints, and headaches.

The good news was that anthrax was treatable with antibiotics. An oral antibiotic called ciprofloxacin had been found to be particularly effective. Everyone would be herded to two outdoor decontamination tents—one for the men and one for the women. Each person would be tested with a nasal swab. They would then strip down, take a shower with soap and water, and dress in provided coveralls while their clothes would be sterilized in boiling water.

"There's no reason to panic," Steve said in a measured tone. "You will then be relocated to an unused wing of the resort while CDC personnel search the facility for the source of the anthrax—that's called 'environmental sampling'—followed by steam sterilization. Then you'll be kept under observation. If any of you show signs of anthrax poisoning, we'll treat you with antibiotics. For obvious reasons, you won't be able to leave until we clear you of the anthrax."

Steve answered the question on everyone's mind. "Anthrax is not passed person to person; therefore, quarantine of the entire resort is unnecessary. Horses, however, are different. Anthrax is known to spread from horse to horse—so the horses will be vaccinated and watched, and the stable quarantined."

Marc swallowed hard. Had he been poisoned by the anthrax but didn't know it yet? He'd spent time with Vernon and been in many of the same places. How could this be happening? He'd played basketball with Vernon just a few days ago.

Everyone was talking at once—from teen campers to weekend retreaters to translation committee members. Their blanched faces told Marc they were as stunned as he was.

Steve Yarrow raised his hands for silence and apologized for the inconvenience. Then he dismissed them, reminding them that CDC personnel would meet them as they left the building to direct them to the proper locations. As they headed out of the auditorium and down the hallway, Marc again wondered who would have done this. And why.

Jared was dead. Tessa was dead. Now Vernon was dead, too.

What did they have in common other than the committee?

Marc glanced at Riley. He was pale and perspiring as he accepted a call on his cell phone. Was his cold getting that much worse?

Moments later Riley hung up. "I just spoke to Sheriff Griswold. Guess what the CDC found written on the wall in Vernon's suite?"

"A certain Bible reference?"

Riley nodded. "They're thinking the anthrax is probably in his room too." He lifted a hand to his mouth and coughed a deep, lung-wracking hack.

Riley waved off Marc's probing glance. He was the type who got irritated if anybody babied him. "Don't worry. I'll be fine."

A wave of fear swept over Marc. "You don't look fine."

"Well, to be honest, I thought it was just a cold, but now I'm wondering." He paused. "Marc, if something happens to me—"

"What are you saying?"

"Just that if I'm out of commission for some reason, you'll need to finish this investigation on your own."

On my own? Marc's chest tightened. "What could possibly happen to you? I'm sure it's just a cold."

"Right now, I'm not sure what to think. I just know I've been feeling weak and nauseous for a few days now. And now that Vernon's gone—"

"But I've been almost everywhere you have, and I'm fine."

"I know. It doesn't make much sense, does it? But I can't help wondering—"

Riley swayed on his feet and reached for the wall. Marc grabbed Riley's arm as he started to go down. A secretary gasped, and a few male committee members rushed to Marc's side and helped lower Riley to his back. His face turned sickly pale.

Within seconds, white-clad health workers wearing face masks pushed Marc away and swarmed around Riley. They lifted him onto a wheeled gurney.

"Do not worry," a foreign-looking woman with large, black eyes told Riley. "This is just precaution. You be okay." She turned to Marc, the mask unable to hide the apprehension in her eyes. "We take good care of him."

As she wheeled him away, Riley lifted a hand in a feeble wave of farewell.

Marc swallowed hard and stared. Would he ever see his friend alive again?

66

Dip delicately, careful not to drip. Press the nib to parchment. Shape the marriage of ink to paper into a letter. A letter that molds a word. A word that conveys a sentence. A sentence that says something important about the world we live in.

How Gillian missed her flower garden! Her home studio was her favorite place for being creative and productive, her burgeoning garden just beyond her window. She would sit, cozy, at her angled table while sunlight streamed in, solo piano music wafting from her small stereo, the glimpse of radiant blooms out of the corner of her eyes. It was the place where she was most at peace.

But for now, since she couldn't be comfortable at her home studio, her hotel room desk would have to do. And instead of typical solo piano, a boys' choir serenaded her through her earbuds. They were singing a sacred song by Thomas Tallis. Their high, angelic voices seemed to pierce the very vault of heaven.

Gillian bent over an angled piece of parchment paper, a new creation, and did what her fingers had been aching to do for days—to grip her fountain pen with the medium nib and script something new in calligraphy. And now that Chase was safe and she'd pushed away thought of everything wrong in the world, she could work in peace. After all, calm hands made her work possible.

Besides, the activity would get her mind off Gabriel and these bizarre murders—at least for a while. Emily had retreated to her room, saying something about needing an afternoon nap; the search for Chase had worn her out.

It was the perfect opportunity for Gillian to get out her pens and paper. She wasn't going to let this opportunity go to waste.

She began scripting Celtic lettering, working on the opening words from Thomas Paine's series of pamphlets *The American Crisis*: "These are the times that try men's souls."

No, the times that try my *soul.*

She closed her eyes, let those high boyish voices clear out any remaining cobwebs from the dark, neglected corners of her mind.

She couldn't forget what a basket case she'd been when Chase had gone missing. The potential loss had reduced her to a blathering, unstable idiot. It had almost incapacitated her. She'd feared the worst and concluded that some deranged stranger had whisked him away.

But why, God? Why had her mind leapt to that conclusion? Why couldn't she have responded in maturity and remembered that all things truly do work together for good to those who love God? Why hadn't she leaned on the Everlasting Arms?

She nibbled on her bottom lip. *God, what is up with me anyhow? Why do I lean on you one minute and distrust you the next? Why do I have such fickle faith? Why—*

Her cell phone vibrated in her pocket, startling her. She checked the caller ID and pulled out her earbuds, setting them aside. Was something wrong? The men were supposed to meet them at the hotel sometime after lunch, but they hadn't shown up.

"Marc."

"Hey, Gill."

"Is everything okay?"

"No, everything's not okay."

"What's happened?"

"Have you watched the news this afternoon?"

"No."

"Then you don't know."

"Know what?"

The news of the anthrax and Vernon Brannon's death poured out of him in every depressing, mind-numbing detail.

The room tilted, and she struggled for equilibrium. "Oh, no!"

"Wait. It gets worse." He told her about Riley's illness. Marc didn't sound quite like himself, his voice heavy with defeat and fatigue.

Her hands turned cold, each finger an icicle. Just when she'd thought things couldn't possibly get any worse, they had. A horrifying thought coalesced in her mind. The killer had claimed Vernon Brannon and gone after Riley too. Now Marc was in danger. In fact, maybe it was too late.

A sick feeling wormed through her gut. She rose, hands shaking. "Marc, get out of there! Get out of there now!"

"Gill, I can't just walk out. I'm under observation, at least until morning, to see if I show any of the symptoms of the anthrax."

Just the word "anthrax" sent abject fear slicing through her. She eyed her bag across the room through tear-stung eyes. "Then I'm coming to you." Chase was asleep, but maybe Emily wouldn't mind—

"You're doing no such thing. You've got Chase and his safety to think about. The best thing you can do right now is sit tight and hope things improve by morning."

Sit tight? How could he honestly expect her to do that?

He seemed to read her mind. "I know it's hard, but just do as I say. Besides, it's a circus here. Investigators need to locate the source of the anthrax and isolate it. Then they need to be sure the place is clean before they let anybody else enter from the outside. Even if you came, they wouldn't let you in."

Gears shifted in her head, the truth dawning. He was trapped at the resort with a sick killer, and she was powerless to help him. She couldn't even give him a hug, and he sure sounded like he needed one right now.

"What can I do? Surely there's something I can do to help."

"You can, but first I want you to sit down. Take a deep breath. Remember Psalm 34."

She sat on the edge of the bed, knees weak. He'd reminded her of the psalm countless times over the last few months whenever she got keyed up—which was frequently—and favorite snippets flooded her mind.

This poor man cried out, and the LORD heard him, and saved him out of all his troubles.

"Gill, everything will be okay. God's in control, right?"

"Yeah." She took a deep breath, let it out.

"You believe that—you really do?"

"Yes." *The righteous cry out, and the LORD hears, and delivers them out of all their troubles.*

"Look, just because I'm being kept here right now doesn't mean I've got anthrax or will even get it."

"Okay."

"After I hang up, I want you to go find Emily and stay with her. I'm not sure if she even knows about Riley yet, so I need you to break the news."

No, Emily couldn't possibly know. If she did, she certainly wouldn't be napping right now. Emily would be devastated by this news and would need someone like Gillian to lean on. "Okay, I'll take care of it."

"Things are pretty chaotic here, and the notification might have slipped through the cracks. An ambulance took Riley to Marquette General Hospital. You can find directions online. Please take her there. She'll want to be near him."

"Of course."

Marc paused for a breath. "I already called my parents and told them I'm okay, but your parents might be worried if they've watched the news. Could you call them? And the church too? Let them know I'm okay."

Due to Jared's funeral and the murder investigation, the church had granted their extended stay. "Sure."

An awkward silence followed. She wondered if Marc had something else he needed to say. Finally, "Gillian, you do love me, don't you?"

What an odd question. "Of course I love you, Marc."

"You're committed to me and to our marriage, right?"

She swallowed. Why was he asking her these questions? Did he fear that the anthrax contamination was worse than he'd said—that he might be dead by morning? Did he suspect that this might be their last conversation and sought affirmation of her love?

"Of course I love you, Marc. What's going on? Why are you asking me these questions?"

His voice sounded throaty, not like himself at all. "When you saw Gabriel here, were you really surprised to see him?"

"Of course I was surprised. I already told you that. What are you trying to say?"

He didn't answer her. "Find the computer in the lobby and check your e-mail. I sent you something you need to see."

"Okay." Why these cryptic questions? Why the accusation in his voice?

"Just look it over, and we can talk later." Shrill, annoyed voices intruded in the background. "I've gotta go. I already took my shower. Now I'm sitting here in a silly hospital gown while they boil my clothes. Just about time for my shots."

Gillian rubbed her forehead. *Goodness. What's he going through?* "I'm sorry. I wish there was something I could do."

A man's voice called Marc's name. "I gotta go, Gill. Whatever happens, just remember that I love you ... no matter what."

No matter what.

What was he trying to say? Was he referring to his possible fate because of the anthrax ... or to something else?

She opened her mouth, head spinning. "Marc."

A click.

"Marc?"

No reply. The line was dead.

Anxiety wrapped its arms around her and held on tight. Would Marc and Riley follow in the footsteps of Vernon Brannon and be dead by morning? How could this be happening?

67

Numbers. Numbers. Numbers.

That's partly how his master plan had begun. Ever since his childhood, he'd been fascinated with all things numerical. Add in his fascination with the Bible and its many numbers, and he'd found a winning combination.

He'd always been especially fascinated with the number 10, one of the perfect numbers in the Bible. It represented the perfection of divine order. And he certainly liked perfection.

Ten.

The number of generations from God to Noah.

The number of commandments in the Ten Commandments.

The number of clauses in the Lord's Prayer.

The number of times Old Testament fires fell from heaven.

And then the one that meant the most to him: the number of plagues that descended on Egypt.

The plagues were especially appropriate given who he was going after. He couldn't help wondering if the man was finally putting two and two together. Or, in this case, five and five.

Cyrus sat in the quiet solitude of the cabin, his ferret climbing on his shoulders. He watched the around-the-clock news coverage about the anthrax and rejoiced in his success. Through carefully planted listening devices and tiny cameras, he could hear and see every important location inside the resort. Hear every gasp of surprise. See every current of dread ripple across their faces.

They were terrified. And that made him happy.

But bringing terror was only a small part of his master plan, and he was nearing the end now. The final act. Would anyone be smart enough to see him coming?

He brought the blue blanket—the baby's blanket he had stolen from the hotel—to his nose and drank deeply of the boy's scent. Not long now, and he would see the baby boy again.

68

What was this mysterious e-mail all about? And why was Marc so concerned that she see it? And what was up with these odd questions and the strange sound in Marc's voice?

Gillian grabbed Chase's carrier and hurried down to the hotel lobby computer. She needed to tell Emily about Chuck and make a few important phone calls, but first she needed to know what was wrong.

At the computer she opened the Internet browser and logged into her e-mail account. About a dozen e-mails were waiting for her. She ignored all of them except the top one titled "Letter" from Marc.

She clicked on it. Two graphics were attached at the bottom. One appeared to be an envelope and the other the letter itself. She clicked on the attached letter graphic to enlarge it.

A letter on pink stationery filled her screen, unraveling from top to bottom.

Her breath caught in her throat. It was *her* handwriting, which hadn't changed much over the years. Then she realized.

Heat trickled down her spine. Her cheeks warmed.

All those desperate letters and postcards she'd mailed to Gabriel Jacobi years ago—this was one of them. She stared at it and wondered where it had come from. And why would someone mail it to Marc here and now?

She skimmed the words, a gasp of incredulity rushing from her lips. It was totally inappropriate for Marc to see this letter now. She'd written it long before she met him, long before God had done his work in her heart and transformed her into his new creation.

She remembered now. She'd written the letter shortly after Gabriel ditched her. She'd been living in denial, certain that her repeated declarations of love—and the letter oozed with them—would win him back. She remembered the pain, the agony, each day when he didn't reply, but she hadn't known then what she did now: Her plan hadn't worked for the simple reason that Gabriel had never seen the letters.

Her gaze slid across intemperate words, down the lines of sickly sentiments never meant for Marc's eyes. Her palm turned slick on the mouse. The further she progressed, the more her stomach clenched.

The person who wrote this letter was a selfish, depraved young woman she had no desire to remember. Whoever had written this letter might as well have been someone else—not her. Praise God, she was no longer the same person. Jesus had broken the chains.

But why would someone mail this embarrassing letter to Marc now? And why had Marc sounded so funny on the phone and questioned her devotion to him? Naturally the letter would have irritated him, but she'd written it so long ago. Surely he understood—

Her eyes flicked back to the top corner where she always dated her letters. Why was the corner missing?

Wait a minute.

She swallowed hard and read the letter again, this time struck not so much by what the letter contained but by what was missing. Realization dawned. What was missing were references to date the letter. Even the statement about the baby—"Can hardly wait for you to see the baby"—could refer either to Chase or to the baby she had miscarried.

Without the corner date, Marc couldn't know the letter had been written years ago.

He doesn't realize it's an old letter.

Tears bit her eyes. Marc had been too much of a gentleman to accuse her directly, but he'd counseled people for years and knew the power of questions. She knew him well enough to know what that sound in his voice meant.

It meant he was beyond irritated. He felt betrayed and hurt—and it was all her fault. If only she hadn't written those silly letters so many years ago, but she'd always been better at saying in writing what she couldn't say face-to-face. She'd always feared those letters would come back to haunt her, and now her fears were realized.

Maybe Marc suspected that she'd lied to him about bumping into Gabriel at the resort. If so, he probably wondered if she and Gabriel had arranged this meeting all along.

He wonders if I'm having an affair with Gabriel now.

She couldn't bear this misunderstanding continuing a second longer. Couldn't stand the thought of what Marc must be thinking of her right now. She pulled out her cell phone and hit his speed dial number with a trembling hand.

God, how could this have happened?

While the phone rang, she wiped her eyes and logged out of her account, not wanting to see the blasted letter again. She closed the browser. Pushed away from the computer, hands ice cold.

He picked up. "Gillian?"

"Marc, I—" She swallowed hard. Why not get right to the point? "I read the letter."

"Good. I'm glad." His voice sounded shaky. "So ... are you going to tell me what's going on?"

He *was* fearing the worst, just like she'd done almost two years ago when she'd mistakenly suspected he was having an affair with one of his counselees. The tables were turned this time. Cruel irony.

"Nothing's going on," she said.

"I find that very hard to believe."

Okay, he was more than a little upset. "Marc, you don't understand. That letter—it was never meant for your eyes." Her face burned when she remembered some of the more embarrassing entries.

Rage throttled his voice. "No kidding. So you love him that much, huh?"

"You don't understand. It's an old letter I mailed to Gabriel years ago—long before I became a believer."

Stunned silence tempered the tension. "What?"

She reminded him of the love letters and postcards she'd mailed to Gabriel the summer after he abandoned her. "I always dated those letters in the upper left-hand corner. But if you notice, the corner's been torn away. And there's nothing else in the letter to date it."

He sighed and let a few seconds pass before he spoke again. "I get it now—somebody wanted me to think it was a recent letter. Oh brother! Maybe Gabriel wants you back."

He was still angry. She couldn't blame him, really. "No, I don't think so. He said he was sorry and was sincere—I'm sure of it."

"Well, maybe he's a good actor. Maybe he's not the person you think he is."

She wondered the same thing. Gabriel had insisted that he never received her letters, but maybe he'd lied. But why? To save face? To present himself in a more favorable light?

She recalled their awkward parting and his confession that he still had feelings for her, even after all these years. It wasn't the wisest thing for him to say. He could have made a mistake and expressed more than he should have, or perhaps he'd intended those words as a flirtation.

Or an invitation.

Maybe he *did* want her back.

Maybe he's not the person you think he is.

Was it possible? Was he intentionally trying to create a rift in their marriage so he could lure her back? Would he really walk away from his own marriage and his five kids to rekindle their old flame? Had he been holding a torch for her all those years?

But if he wanted to reunite, why not just say so? Get it out in the open? Why use an old letter in such an odd way?

"I don't know, Marc. Gabriel never tried to contact me all those years. And when we bumped into each other here, he was just as surprised as I was—I'm sure of it." *Or maybe I'm just gullible.*

"There's something else," Marc said. "Did you notice the postmark? The letter was mailed from Tucson, Arizona, with no return address."

"I didn't even look at the envelope." Her mind flailed with this new revelation. "But if Gabriel's here, how did he mail the letter from Tucson?"

"Maybe he had help."

"But why? It doesn't make any sense."

"It does if he wants to cause problems between us, if he wants to take you back."

But I'm not here for the taking. She sighed. "I find that very hard to believe. You don't know Gabriel like I do. He's certainly not perfect, but I don't think he would have done something as underhanded as this."

Unless he wants me back.

She took a breath. "And even you said that God could have changed him, remember?"

"Okay, but if Gabriel didn't send the letter, what other explanation could there be? Who else would have done this?"

"I don't know. It doesn't make sense." Surely whoever mailed the letter would have realized they would discover the truth in time. Yet the letter *had* stirred things up between them, if only for a few hours.

She rubbed her throbbing forehead between her thumb and forefinger. Gabriel had suggested that perhaps his parents had intercepted her letters, so the letters would have been in their possession—that is, if they still had them after all these years. She'd hoped that somebody would have tossed them out or burned them by now. If only she hadn't mailed those stupid things.

"Either way, you've gotta believe me, Marc," she said. "There's nothing going on between me and Gabriel. Honest. When I saw him on Thursday, that was the first time there's been any contact since he walked out of my life all those years ago."

A long pause passed. He sighed, and his voice sounded more tired—or more relieved—than it had in a long time. "I believe you. I'm sorry for thinking the worst. Can you forgive me?"

"Of course I forgive you. I can see how the letter looked like something else."

Another sigh. "I feel like an idiot. I—"

"Don't worry about it, okay? Look, I gotta go. I haven't told Emily about Chuck yet. We can talk more later. I'll call you."

"Okay." A pause. "I love you, Gill. You know that, right?"

"Of course. I love you too."

"I really mean it."

"I know you do. So do I."

They kissed through the speakers and hung up.

She grabbed Chase's carrier and headed upstairs, mind churning with questions she had no answers for, at least not now. She needed to forget about the letter for now and switch gears. She knocked on Emily's door and waited, her mind flying to the most immediate crisis.

Both of their husbands were in jeopardy. With anthrax threatening their lives, would she even sleep a wink tonight? Her mind leaped to a more important question.

Would Marc even be alive by morning?

69

"Is it true?" Gillian asked. "They found the anthrax in Vernon's suitcase?"

"Yeah," Marc said.

"I'm so glad you're okay. So the CDC folks just let you go?"

Marc pulled Gillian into a tight embrace. "Yeah. There was no reason not to. They checked out my blood, and there was no evidence of the anthrax. So I was free to go."

Marc had missed her so badly last night. Now that they were together, he let the embrace linger as long as possible. But now people in the hospital lobby were beginning to stare.

They pulled apart, and he crouched beside Chase's carrier. He scooped his son into his arms, brushed his lips across his soft, warm head, smelling his baby lotion. "I called Brad Tornelli." He was one of the deacons at church. "Told him I'd be gone for at least a few more days."

Gillian nodded. They were supposed to be back home by now, but it couldn't be helped. Somebody would need to fill the pulpit in his absence.

"So how's Riley?" he asked. "Any word?"

"I got here just before you did. The last I heard from Emily, he at least made it through the night."

"Well, let's go then. Is Emily waiting for us?"

"Yeah, third floor. Room 316." She held back.

"Well, aren't you coming?"

Her eyebrows tented. "Marc, Riley has anthrax. Do you really think I'm gonna take Chase into his room?"

"But I already told you, anthrax isn't contagious."

"Maybe it isn't, but what if the doctors are wrong? I'd rather not take the risk."

Marc knew her well enough by now to know when she was immovable. Perhaps she even had a point, but they would get nowhere by arguing about it now. "Okay, then I'll head up and be back for you later."

He handed Chase to her and turned to go.

"Marc, about the letter..."

He turned back. She swallowed hard, eyes ashamed. "I'm sorry you had to see it. You know it was never meant for your eyes. I wrote it so long ago—"

"I know. And I'm sorry for assuming the worst. I should have trusted you better than that." He hugged her again. "Will you forgive me?"

"It's already forgiven and forgotten."

70

Nobody ever looks his best when lying in a hospital bed.

Marc recalled that not long ago he'd lain, shot by a disturbed counselee, where Chuck Riley lay now. He leaned against the wall of the small room and peered down at his dear friend, who looked far from well.

Riley wore a skimpy, pastel-green hospital gown. Typically, hospital patients at least appeared to be resting, but Riley looked like he'd run 10 miles and had 10 more to go. Beads of sweat dripped off his forehead, and he gasped for air every few seconds as if unable to catch his breath. What remained of his Friar Tuck fringe of white hair was plastered to the sides of his pale, wrinkly head at several unflattering angles.

Ever faithful at his side, Emily wiped perspiration off his forehead and explained that these were all natural symptoms of the anthrax. The bacterium was affecting Riley's breathing with symptoms similar to pneumonia.

From a wheeled machine came a steady beep and digital numbers displaying Riley's pulse and blood pressure. A tube running from somewhere under the covers to a transparent container on the wall drained the excess fluid out of his lungs. An IV line hooked to the back of Riley's left hand administered 400 milligrams of ciprofloxacin hydrochloride every 12 hours.

Marc was familiar with the drug. He'd taken a shot of it that morning—just in case—after a restless night in a dorm-style room with two translation committee members.

Emily rose and asked Marc if he could stay with Riley for a while. "I want to go downstairs and say hello to Gillian. You know, she could have at least come up to the waiting room on this floor."

Marc nodded. "Yeah, well... " He didn't want to go into it.

"I guess it's better to be overprotective than negligent. I'll be back in a bit." She lowered her voice, eyes apprehensive. "Have a nurse page me if—you know—if he gets worse."

Emily left, and Marc scooted her chair closer to the bed. Riley's mahogany-brown eyes flicked open.

"Sorry, I didn't mean to wake you."

"I wasn't sleeping." Riley's gaze roamed around the room as if seeing it for the first time. "It's okay, you can say it—I look horrible." He wheezed and struggled to catch his next breath.

"Well, I wasn't going to say it, but since you already did..."

A hint of mirth teased the corners of Riley's mouth. "You think you're so funny, don't you?"

"Not really. Sometimes humor helps, but I guess there's nothing funny about this."

After every few words Riley paused for a quick breath. "You don't think so, huh? I think this is ... hilarious. Here I am lying on my back, unable to do anything about the"—he drew in a breath with apparent difficulty—"the sicko who killed Vernon Brannon and may still kill me if I don't recover from this."

"You'll be fine." Marc pumped encouragement into words that felt far from certain. "You'll pull through this."

Riley turned his face away from Marc and coughed a deep chest rattle, a fist to his mouth. He motioned to a cup on the wheeled table. Marc grabbed the ice-filled cup and guided the straw to Riley's lips so his friend could take a sip.

Satisfied, Riley rested his head back, eyes closed, as if his strength were depleted and he just needed to rest. "I've been coughing like that all night. Sure wish I could stop."

Marc returned the cup to its place. "You really ought to sleep. I'll leave you alone and go find the ladies."

"Don't be silly. I don't want to be left alone, especially when we've got"—he sucked in some air—"important matters to discuss."

Riley coughed again, but his lungs sounded clearer this time. "I heard back from that FBI forensics expert I told you about just before the CDC called us to the auditorium. I didn't have a chance to tell you. You aren't going to believe"—another snatch of air—"what he told me."

Marc waited.

"Are you familiar with pheromones?"

Something Marc had seen on TV triggered a nod. "Yeah. Aren't they natural chemicals that make bugs and animals behave in certain ways, like mate or attack? They can attract or repel, too, right?"

Riley snatched another breath, eyes weary. "That's right. Manufacturers are even putting it in some perfumes now, so women can literally attract men."

Marc hadn't heard about this advancement, but he wasn't surprised.

"The sheriff had Jared Russo's clothes tested. Remember those frogs you saw crawling all over his back? Well, they were there for a reason."

"Pheromones?"

Riley nodded. "Pheromones were also detected in Tessa McCormack's bloodstream, which she secreted in her sweat. It explains why the bugs went after her so aggressively."

Marc shook his head. *Why they ate her alive.*

"Pheromones were also detected in towels after the mosquito and gnat attack. There's a reason why the bugs went after you in the bathroom."

"Pheromones really do that?"

"Oh yeah. I learned something else that'll blow you away—about the Bible reference scrawled in fake blood on the walls." Riley paused for a breath. "The sheriff's techs didn't go far enough."

"What do you mean?"

"They assumed the fake blood at each plague site was the same, but they should have conducted an independent test each time." He paused, wheezing. "I overnighted separate samples from Tessa's room and Vernon's room to a friend at the FBI lab for analysis. He called me this morning."

Riley's eyes, manifesting renewed strength, nailed Marc to his seat. "Marc, the Bible reference written on Tessa's wall was fake blood, pure and simple. But the Bible reference on Vernon's wall was different."

"Different? How so?"

"Real blood was mixed with the fake blood."

Marc's jaw went slack. "*What?* How is that even possible? Are you sure?"

"I'm not, but my friend at the FBI is."

"Why would the killer mix in real blood? And whose blood is it?"

Riley gestured to the wheeled table bearing the cup of ice water. "I don't know. There's a piece of paper with a phone number. Call Mitch. He'll tell you more."

Marc grabbed the piece of paper, mind in a daze. "Special agent Mitch Reed?"

"Mitch and I go way back. He's a terrific friend and a fellow believer—you can trust him." He struggled for the next breath. "He'll tell you what you need to know so you can take the next step."

The next step? Did Riley seriously expect him to pick up the investigation on his own? "But why can't the FBI get involved?"

"This thing hasn't crossed state lines. It needs to be investigated on a local level first." Riley must have read Marc's mind. "Marc, it has to be you."

"What about Griswold?"

"A well-meaning, sincere man, but he's frankly out of his depth."

"Did you tell him about the blood?"

A weak nod and another gasp for air. Riley really needed to rest. Marc felt bad for taxing him, but he needed more.

"He wouldn't listen," Riley said. "In fact, he lost his temper and told me—well, I'll spare you his delightfully obscene reply."

"But this is a big break!"

"Of course it is, and he knows it. And when he settles down, humbles himself, and realizes he needs to step things up"—he gasped for air—"he might actually do something about it. But we can't waste any more time waiting on him, not when more people could die."

Riley pressed his hands down on the bed, elbows locked, and raised his chest higher so he could breathe more easily. Marc wondered if he should push the button and call the nurse. Marc touched Riley's arm to help, but Riley waved him off.

"I'll be okay." Riley wiped his mouth with the back of a hand that flopped like a dying fish.

"You really ought to rest."

"I will, but let me just say this first. In case something happens to me."

"Riley—"

"Marc, I'm suffering from inhalation anthrax, the worst kind, okay?" They locked eyes. "I'm no dummy. I could take a turn for the worse anytime. I don't want what I know to die with me, so just listen for a minute."

Marc wasn't about to argue, but the topic filled him with dread.

Riley coughed to clear his lungs. Then he shook his head, a small, regretful turn from side to side. "I've been a fool. We haven't been looking at these plagues in the right way."

"What do you mean?"

He strained for his next breath. "We've obsessed over each one without thinking about the final destination. But look at their progression, Marc. They've been getting steadily worse, as if they're building up to something."

"Okay, but where do you think they're headed?"

"The tenth plague, of course. It's so simple, but that's why it's so hard to see. None of this plagues business has been about the Qur'an or Muslim jihadists or the protestors." He swallowed, Adam's apple bobbing, and grabbed another breath. "It's always been about the plagues of Egypt, Marc. Remember hearing that Bible story in Sunday school when you were a kid? Like a good suspense story, you wanted to know what was going to happen next, right?"

Marc nodded.

"So tell me—what's the climax of the story?"

Marc wondered if this was a trick question. "Pharaoh sets the Jewish people free."

"No, that's the denouement."

"The denouement?"

Riley chuckled. "Ask Gillian to explain later—she's the literary person in your family." He paused for another cough and cleared his throat. "The denouement is the final outcome, the result of the climax. But what's the climax of the plagues, Marc? What's the final act that turns Pharaoh's heart? What type of tragedy would turn any parent's heart?"

"The death of a son."

Riley swallowed hard, eyes misty.

Marc thought he was about to cry and wondered why.

"Exactly. But not just any son—Pharaoh's firstborn son, the heir to the throne." Riley wiped his eyes and tried to clear his throat. "Sorry, I lost a son once long ago, and I never know when the emotion's going to hit me. Don't let me distract you."

Marc had never heard about Riley's loss but agreed this wasn't the time. "Okay, so Pharaoh's son died."

"You were expecting more, weren't you? There *is* more." Riley lifted a finger. "I'm going to ask three important but simple questions for you to think about, but then I really must rest." He paused to catch a breath—breathing seemed to be getting more difficult again. "Find the answers, and you just might solve this case and save some lives."

Marc waited.

Riley leveled his gaze at Marc, eyes burning with new energy. "Take a hard look at what's happened and ask yourself this. First, who is Pharaoh? Second, who is Pharaoh's son? And third, who's been playing God?"

Marc's mind was like a clam shell at Hilton Head in South Carolina, a favorite vacation spot. Riley's questions were steaming the clam open. He didn't need to write the questions down.

"The answer to the first question is pretty obvious, don't you think?"

Dr. Colbert. If anybody's Pharaoh around here, it's gotta be him. "But why hasn't the killer gone after Dr. Colbert himself?"

"I don't know, but remember the plagues of Egypt, Marc. Look at the pattern. Did God go after Pharaoh himself? No, first he tried to open Pharaoh's eyes by inflicting suffering on those around him."

Riley's eyes softened, and he seemed to be breathing more easily now. "We have such a skewed idea of who God is, don't we? We picture him as a chubby grandpa who spoils his grandkids and lets them get away with mischief while he looks the other way. God's all about love and forgiveness, certainly, but don't forget his anger and judgment. Don't forget what he does to those who stand in his way—how far he'll push them before they submit and bow the knee. When the suffering of his people didn't turn Pharaoh's heart, God decided to go closer to home. He went after Pharaoh's son."

Marc nodded with sudden realization. "Pharaoh didn't have a change of heart until the plagues affected him personally."

"But isn't that what it takes sometimes? Personal pain to help us see and change?"

Marc thought about Gillian's abandonment and her revived hurt from so many years ago. "So you think Dr. Colbert is the key. He knows what's going on and could stop the murders somehow?"

"That's my hunch." Riley's face firmed with new resolve. "I would talk to him right away if I were you. I suspect he's keeping secrets he's apparently willing to let others die for."

Marc realized he was wasting precious time. *Okay, find Dr. Colbert. But then what?*

Riley said, "Discovering the identity of Colbert's son isn't going to be easy, especially if Colbert doesn't want to talk."

"Gillian investigated the committee members online. Colbert doesn't have a son. He's only got one daughter living in Cleveland."

Riley gasped for breath again. "Maybe he's been a father figure to someone. Maybe this fatherhood is figurative—I can't say for sure. But call Mitch Reed, Marc. He'll help you. And if you get stumped, you can always come back, and I'll do what I can to help—that is, if I'm still conscious at that point."

Riley's words opened a new channel of anxiety in Marc's heart. *God, he's going to be okay, isn't he?*

71

E *nough is enough.*

Sheriff Miles Griswold finished the phone call with the FBI contact and clicked off with a curse. He rose from the chair in his makeshift office, strapped his gun holster around his waist, and tried to calm himself. He made himself pause and suck in several cleansing breaths.

He wasn't about to let a retired homicide detective from Cincinnati or even the FBI steal his show. First, the credit card fraud involved in the purchase of the poisonous frog. Next, Micah's forged signature on the bug containers. Now, real blood—not to mention the identity of whom the blood belonged to and a potential scenario that blew his mind.

Why hadn't his own techs made those discoveries? As soon as they'd seen the fake blood, they'd assumed the rest was fake too. What imbeciles!

It was time for him to take action before somebody else did. This was *his* investigation, after all. He could do this, but first he needed to be smart. To think ahead. To see beyond the smoke and mirrors of what was taking place here.

Misdirection. That's all they'd been—these silly plagues. Except there was nothing silly about murder. Several people were dead, and more would die unless he put a stop to this party right now. People were looking to him to show leadership. Now Sergeant Riley was in critical care, his health still in jeopardy. The only bright light was that since Riley was out of commission, he now had the opportunity to show his mettle.

But he needed to be careful. Investigators on this case had a habit of either getting sick or turning up dead.

A knock sounded on his door. He glanced up as Deputy Moyers, his skinny, bald-headed assistant, rushed in, out of breath. He had a stack of papers in his hand.

"As you requested," Moyers said, "this is a listing of all patrons at the resort since the first plague."

He'd given the order for everyone to remain at the resort until the investigation was completed, even though many were more than ready to leave town. Everyone was a suspect until he or she was ruled out.

Griswold accepted the papers. "Good work. Start interviewing them."

"*All* of them?"

"Yes, all of them." He eyes drilled into Moyers. "Got a problem with that?"

"No, sir."

"Then don't question me."

"Sorry, sir."

"Send the other men out in two groups: one group to search the unoccupied rooms for traces of our perp, the second group to search the rest of the rooms."

Disbelief clouded the deputy's eyes.

"Get search warrants. Get going. *Now.*"

"We'll need more men."

"Call 'em in then—all of them. This is an emergency. CNN, Fox News—everybody's here coverin' this story. It's time for some results."

The deputy nodded. "Do you plan to supervise?"

Griswold sucked in a breath through his nose. "No, you do it. I've got another lead to check out." *Time to put an end to this sideshow.*

"Yes, sir." Moyers headed out, the door slamming closed behind him.

Griswold stood tall, straightening his back. He ran a hand through his hair and thought things over.

He'd been blind to the obvious, but the plagues had occurred so quickly in succession, each one an investigative nightmare, that he'd been left bewildered and confused. But perhaps that had been the perp's intent all along. Give them another plague to deal with while he was two steps ahead. Bury them in investigative questions so they couldn't see the obvious.

Now he had new photographic evidence just back from the lab, evidence nobody else had seen yet. During the plague of blood, the killer had written the Bible reference on the bathroom wall *after* the maintenance man had unlocked the door and let Brianne out. Marc Thayer had tipped him off to the footprints outside the bathroom window that suggested the killer had entered the room that way. But the only footprints on the bloody bathroom floor belonged to Brianne Hyde. If the killer had entered through the window, his tracks would have been all over the bloody floor too. But they weren't.

The killer had used the most logical way to enter the bathroom, write the reference on the wall, and exit. He'd used the bathroom door.

Who had unlocked the door for Brianne? Quinn Caruthers, the director of maintenance. Perhaps he'd done crowd control and called the police while the second man slipped into the room, locked the door, wrote the Bible reference on the wall, and exited the way he came in.

But he'd personally interviewed the stocky, goateed man twice, and Quinn had seemed as genuinely baffled by the plagues as the next guy. Griswold knew when a man was lying during an interview—body language gave away so many people. Caruthers was either innocent or the best liar he'd ever seen.

His alibis had checked out, too. Maybe Caruthers wasn't personally responsible, but maybe he knew who was.

Which left him wondering if somebody else was involved, as the FBI contact suggested. A second man. An unknown variable lurking in the shadows. Maybe he was even watching Griswold right now.

He studied the corners of the room and the sprinkler system gadget hanging from a ceiling tile. Bugs and tiny surveillance cameras?

Oh, brother. Nobody except a character in a movie could be so untraceable and invincible.

Sheriff Griswold drew in a deep breath, crossed the suite, and opened the door. He stormed down the corridor, almost running into Gabriel Jacobi, Micah Coombs' sidekick.

"Sheriff, a word, if you don't mind."

"Not now." Griswold brushed past him. He didn't have time for this.

Jacobi kept pace. "Micah's wondering how much longer you plan to hold him. His signature was clearly forged—everybody knows that now. Somebody else is responsible."

"Sorry, Coombs is stayin' put until we're through with him. Besides, if somethin' else happens while he's locked away, that'll eliminate him as a suspect for sure."

"But the anthrax—that happened while he was in jail. Which means he couldn't have planted it."

Griswold stopped and faced Jacobi. "He could have planted the anthrax ahead of time. Several days need to pass after exposure before symptoms become noticeable. Sorry, Coombs is stayin' put until I give the say so."

Jacobi lifted his hands in desperation. "Then tell me what I can do. Anything I can do to help? I want to help clear Micah's name."

"Sorry, a Boy Scout would only be a hindrance right now."

"Please, let me—"

Griswold pushed past him. "There's nothin' you can do, so stay out of my way!"

72

Persistent drums pounded away in his head, and no medication provided any relief. Eyes closed, Dr. Matthew Colbert lay on his back in his suite with a cold compress on his head, a bevy of secretaries fawning over him and murmuring in concerned tones.

It was true. He loved his secretaries because he loved women. Especially women who ran at his every beck and call at all hours. Though even their best, most determined efforts weren't good enough this time. The headache simply wasn't going away—figuratively or literally.

He thankfully had shown no signs of cutaneous or inhalation anthrax, so the CDC crew had let him retreat to his suite. For that he was thankful, but the problem still wasn't going away. A man was sick, and predicting his ultimate fate was tricky at best. Worst of all, Vernon Brannon was dead.

How could it be?

The man had consoled him at Jared's funeral on Sunday, always poised and in control no matter what cold winds blew. He was his Rock of Gibraltar. But now even *he* was gone, another victim to this madman, and now Colbert felt as if his last pillar of support had been wrenched away. In fact, he felt alone with this business, alone and clueless. And the only logical step beyond praying to a God who seemed as distant as Saturn appeared to be to take a sleeping pill and make it all go away.

So he told his secretaries to go—all their activity wasn't helping in the least anyhow—so he could sleep. Sleep would make it all go away, at least for a while.

Then he was sleeping and dreaming. Dreaming he was throwing a football to a boy in a golden meadow where tall wheat rose against a clear, blue sky. The throw was a perfect spiral—so unlike him—and the boy dove to catch the ball. The son who could have been his but belonged to someone else now.

If he could do it over again, would he have chosen a different path?

He rolled from one side to the other. Then he flipped onto his ample belly and pressed his face into the pillow.

It's my fault. I let him go, but at least he's still alive and giving joy to someone else.

Does he ever think of me? Does he even realize who I am?

He woke with a start, tears or sweat stinging his eyes. The fog burned away, and he wondered what had awoken him. He glanced at his watch and groaned. Only 20 minutes had passed.

A knock banged on his door.

He got up, shirt sticking to his sweaty chest. Perspiration dripped down his forehead. He was burning up. Maybe he needed one of his heart pills.

Another knock. More insistent this time.

Don't tell me somebody else is dead. Please, God.

Which plague would it be this time? He'd lost track, but what did it matter now that the killer had skipped the flies? How could they possibly know what to expect next?

He crossed the suite, head still pounding. It was probably just another secretary with yet another tonic and a promise that it would be the answer to all his problems. It would somehow bring back the committee members, including Brianne, who had fled into the night, though the sheriff had asked them to stay put for the investigation. Thanks to the anthrax scare, the meetings were over, and the project had come to a grinding halt.

Would the parallel Bible ever see the light of day? Wasn't this what the killer had wanted all along—to stop the project?

He staggered to the door, opened it without thinking. "Yes?"

A man stood on the other side, a member of the maintenance staff he'd seen around. Short, stocky. Gray-blue eyes. Gray, balding head. Ugly scars wound down one side of his face to his neck. Anger registered in his features.

"Do you know who I am?" the man asked.

"No."

"Yes, you do."

Colbert blinked. "I'm sorry, but I don't—"

"My son. He died because of you."

The man slammed his fist into Colbert's nose. Colbert stumbled backward, hands flying to his face. He fell flat on his back, the fall knocking the wind right out of him. His lungs instinctively sucked in more air.

Before he could even think about getting back up, the man pounced on him like a panther, pummeling his fists into Colbert's stomach.

Agonizing pain exploded in his abdomen. Colbert gasped and tried to block the blows with his arms, but the man was like a rabid wild animal. Gasping, groaning, whimpering with malice-filled rage as each frenzied blow hit its mark.

Another fist to his face, and Colbert's head snapped to his right, his nose breaking with an audible *crack*. Blood poured onto the carpet. Thoughts like random bursts of light flashed through his sleeping-pill-numbed brain.

Alex Turrow's father.

No.

The man stood and kicked Colbert in the ribs. Pain mushroomed in his side, making his headache feel more like a tickle.

Colbert cried out in agony and pled for mercy, begging Alex Turrow's father to stop.

He was going too far. Cyrus realized it, but he couldn't seem to make himself stop. He, who had always prided himself on his self-control, had gone berserk. Gasping and sweating, he somehow ended the barrage, though the feral part of his nature didn't want to stop.

Wanted to keep going. Wanted to beat the man's face to a bloody pulp. Wanted to wipe any trace of this man's existence from the face of the earth.

But this wasn't the way. Dying was too good for this man—too easy a way out. Cyrus wanted Colbert to live so he could experience just a sliver of the painful loss he'd endured over the years.

Colbert hadn't fought back as Cyrus expected, and the victory felt hollow somehow. This passivity made his plans easier to execute, but what was victory without struggle?

Fuming, Cyrus pulled out a syringe and jabbed it into the side of Colbert's neck.

The man dove into a lake of blissful unconsciousness, which irritated Cyrus. He didn't want anything to deaden the pain he'd planned for the good doctor.

Cyrus pulled out a new, prepaid cell phone. He dialed the number.

The voice picked up. "Yes?"

"Bring the ambulance. Colbert's suite. It's time."

Cyrus unzipped the maintenance jumper and revealed the paramedic uniform concealed beneath.

73

Marc let Riley sleep and took the elevator to the main downstairs waiting room while questions flailed in his mind. He found Gillian and Emily just as a white-coated doctor strolled away. Chase was asleep in his stroller, and on the corner TV a blond, female reporter was describing a new suicide bombing in Iraq. More violence at the hands of Islamic jihadists.

Emily held a tissue to her face and was crying, Gillian's arm around her. The two women looked up in surprise when they realized Marc was standing there.

"Hey, what's going on?" he asked.

Gillian's eyes were heavy with concern. "The doctor just gave us a report after another CT scan. Riley's condition is much worse than they thought."

There was a sucking sensation in Marc's gut. "But I just talked to him. Other than some breathing problems, I'd say he's doing pretty well."

"The drugs have been masking the symptoms. He's getting worse." Emily's voice struggled to stay afloat in the maelstrom of her tears. "They might have to do an operation to relieve the pressure in his lungs."

Marc recalled an article he'd read. Historically, people this sick with inhalation anthrax didn't survive. If Riley recovered, he would number in a tiny percentile—not that cases of inhalation anthrax survival were numerous to begin with.

Emily hunched her bony shoulders and sobbed. Gillian pulled the woman into her arms, her worried eyes flicking to Marc's face with a clear message. *What else can I do but hold her?*

Marc swiped a hand across his face and wondered how the situation could possibly get any worse—and now he had this new, heavy burden thrust on his shoulders. Riley was counting on *him* to fix what was broken. He needed supernatural help for what lay ahead—they all did.

He took a seat on the other side of Emily, sandwiching her between him and Gillian. Without explanation he put an arm around her tiny frame and prayed aloud. God knew what they needed, and they needed him above all else during both good times and bad. Song lyrics teased the fuzzy corridors of recall: "Lord, I need you when the sea of life is calm. O Lord, I need you when the wind is blowing strong."

Marc tuned the waiting room out and prayed for supernatural healing for Riley, for supernatural strength and wisdom for him and the police to catch the man responsible. When he finished, guilt clobbered him that he hadn't called on the Almighty sooner. After all, what did that familiar verse say?

Greater is he who is in us than he who is in the world.

Emily thanked Marc, and her tears dissipated as if supernatural strength were flowing into her veins. Marc's eyes strayed to her wedding ring, and his throat tightened. More than a husband would be lost if Riley didn't pull through. In many ways, Riley had been like a father to him.

God, please don't take him. You can change things. You can heal him. Let it be done, I pray, according to your will.

Marc left Gillian behind to console Emily and retreated down deserted corridors, raking fingers through his hair. He needed to get away, to clear his head. He had to do something to make these plagues stop here and now. Riley was out of commission, so he would have to do it.

But what am I supposed to do? God, please show me. I'm not adequate for this.

He blew out a sigh. Then he pulled out his phone and called special agent Mitch Reed.

74

The loud knock reverberating through the front door made Lacey's heart pound. The knock repeated, more persistent this time, and Lacey wondered what could possibly be so pressing this early on a Wednesday morning.

"I'm coming!" She peered through the peephole before opening the door. One hand subconsciously smoothed back her brown hair. "Good morning, Sheriff Griswold."

He looked all dapper in his black sheriff's uniform, a silver badge shining from his broad chest. "Sorry, Lace. Am I too early? I should have called first."

"No, this is fine. Come on in." She opened the door wide and motioned him in.

The slim man, known for his running and health obsessions, didn't even look at her. His gaze took a trip around the foyer and tried to see past obstructing doorways to other parts of the house.

Is he looking for someone? Lacey wondered what he expected to find. "You look like a man on a mission."

He finally looked at her. "Got a ton to do today and wanted an early start."

"Too much going on, if you ask me, with all these strange deaths." She forced a chuckle, trying to be lighthearted. "I sleep with a baseball bat next to my bed. The thought that somebody's out prowling around and killing people creeps me out. Any idea who could be responsible yet?"

"I'm getting closer. Is Quinn around?"

"No, he's already off tackling the next project—a plumbing problem, I think."

"Is your dad around?"

"Nope. I'm afraid he's out of the country right now."

He seemed distracted but focused long enough to look at her again. "Years ago, before your dad left the movie business, he helped produce blockbusters like *Raiders of the Lost Ark*, right?"

"Yes, that's right."

"I was thinking. He must have had suppliers for all those snakes."

"Well, sure, I suppose—though I'm pretty sure a lot of them were fakes." She'd been only a preteen living in California at the time. She had few memories of her dad before his conversion because all he'd cared about then was making movies and getting rich. Thankfully, his relationship with God had changed everything, and he'd walked away from the industry, though not without a pocketful of cash.

"He would've had access to large quantities of other things too"—his husky voice lingered in the morning stillness—"like mosquitoes and flies."

"Of course." She tensed. "Wait. You don't think—"

"That your dad is involved in these plagues somehow?" He reeled toward her, a knowing look plastered on his face. "Don't mind me, Lace. I'm just checkin' out all options. I wouldn't be a very good sheriff if I didn't, right?"

He pulled out a piece of paper, folded into quarters, from his chest pocket and handed it to her.

She took the paper. "What's this?"

"A copy of an invoice for a shipment of gnats and mosquitoes."

She studied the invoice. Gnats and mosquitoes had played a part in the death of that poor secretary at the resort, though official word was that she'd died of a drug overdose, hadn't she? It was all so confusing.

"As you can see, the invoice has Micah Coombs' signature on it, but a forensic handwriting expert doesn't believe Micah wrote it."

Micah Coombs. He'd brought all those protestors, right? She studied the sheriff, unsure why he was showing the invoice to her.

The sheriff pointed to an address in the upper left-hand corner. "I'd like to know if that's one of the biological supply companies your father used years ago."

"I could call him if you want."

"No, I can do that, but I need his phone number."

"Sure. I can give it to you before you leave."

He headed toward the kitchen, leaving her standing there, eyes fixed on the invoice. She followed him, unsettled by the strangeness of his wandering around their house without explanation. If there was something else he needed, why didn't he just come out with it?

Sammy sat at the granite bar eating a bowl of cereal. The blond hair draping his forehead was getting in his eyes, reminding her that it was time for another haircut—an experience neither of them looked forward to. To Sammy's right lay a sketch pad, where he was drawing something. The problem was, he could usually focus on only one thing at a time, so his cereal was getting soggy.

Sheriff Griswold paused at Sammy's back and ruffled the boy's blond hair. Sammy sprang back as if attacked and shot a venomous look at the sheriff.

Griswold backed away, hands raised. "Sorry, buddy. Just wanted to say hello. I take it you're not a mornin' person, huh?"

"Sometimes Sammy doesn't like being touched." Lacey's voice sounded more snarky than she intended. How many times had she told people, including the sheriff, about Sammy's aversion to being touched? Why didn't anybody listen?

She glanced at the kitchen table and hoped the sheriff wouldn't notice the book or the pile of sketch pads.

"So what are you drawin' there, Sammy?" He glanced at the sketch pad without getting too close.

Back in his own world again, Sammy didn't seem to hear the sheriff, but that didn't deter Griswold. He peered over Sammy's shoulder, a forefinger pressed to his lips, a thoughtful look on his face. Meanwhile, Sammy made clucking sounds with his tongue.

Lacey stepped closer, dreading to look. What if Sammy's drawing was another plague prediction? What if the sheriff recognized it and put two and two together? But Sammy couldn't be responsible for the plagues—she knew that now. He'd been with her most of the time—except when she fell asleep and he wandered off to parts unknown.

Thankfully, Sammy's drawing was only the rough profile of a man's face.

"Is that your daddy, Sammy?" Griswold frowned. "Doesn't much look like him."

Sammy, of course, didn't respond.

Icy fear stroked the skin between Lacey's shoulder blades. If the profile reminded her of anyone, it was Griswold, but the sheriff apparently didn't see the resemblance. He wandered over to the kitchen table, and she realized it was too late to intervene.

Griswold picked up the book Lacey had hoped he wouldn't see. He aimed a sideways glance at her, eyebrows raised. "The plagues of Egypt?"

Her nervous laugh sounded hollow in the room. "Just a picture book Quinn's been reading to Sammy before bed."

The sheriff thumbed through its pages. "Interestin' bedtime reading. Rather coincidental, wouldn't you say, given what's been goin' on lately?"

She folded her arms. "What exactly are you implying, sheriff?"

He paused to study several pages. "Oh, nothing. But seein' a book like this at this particular time—well, it's a little coincidental. That's all."

Actually, the book had dispelled many of her fears. If Quinn had been reading Sammy a book about the Egyptian plagues, perhaps that's why Sammy had been drawing the frogs, bugs, and dead horses. But even so, the timing of Sammy's drawings was still uncanny. Sometimes they'd occurred immediately *before* a plague, as if he'd somehow known the killer's schedule. But how was that possible?

The sheriff returned the book to its place and picked up the sketch pads, glancing through them with interest. She stiffened, knowing she would need to explain. But then, just as quickly, he flashed Lacey a smile, all subtext gone.

"Creative fellow, isn't he?" He returned the sketch pads.

"Yes, he is." She relaxed. The sheriff hadn't apparently seen the connection between Sammy's drawings and the plagues.

"Is drawin' how he spends most of his time?"

"Yeah, I can't seem to get him to stop. He even prefers drawing over watching cartoons."

The sheriff aimed a concerned look at her. "Well, don't discourage him. Could keep him out of trouble when he gets older. I've always believed it's important for kids to develop an interest. You never know—he could be the next Van Gogh." Griswold checked his watch. "Well, I gotta go, Lace. Could I get your dad's phone number?"

"Sure." She crossed to the counter, scribbled the number down on a notepad, and handed it to him.

"And if Quinn drops by, let him know I'd like to see him too. Ask him to give me a call when it's convenient."

She swallowed past her dry throat. "Is something wrong?"

He perched his hands on his hips. "Somethin's always wrong in my line of work. I wouldn't be doin' my job very well if I didn't check out every possibility, right?"

"You think Quinn or my dad is involved somehow?"

He held up both hands. "Now, I didn't say that, did I? Let's just say there are a few questions I'm hopin' they can clear up for me, that's all." He turned and headed toward the front door.

Lacey rushed after him. "Would you like some coffee or—or something to take with you?" Then she remembered that the health nut didn't drink coffee. "I just made some pumpkin muffins. They're organic and probably still warm."

"No, that won't be necessary, but thanks for the kind offer." Griswold paused at the open door and glanced back at her. "One more thing."

She tensed.

"I'd look into formal art classes for that boy if I were you. I think he shows some real talent."

Her shoulders relaxed. "I agree."

"Great job on those horses." He flashed her a wry grin. "He draws them better than my teenagers do."

Then with a wave he was gone. Through the window, Lacey watched him get into his cruiser and speed away, her tension vanishing.

What on earth was that all about? And here it wasn't even 9:00 a.m. yet. Had he been looking for something in particular? If so, what had he found?

The fact that her dad had connections to suppliers of snakes and bugs? That couldn't be any grand revelation.

The fact that Quinn had been reading a picture book about the plagues of Egypt to Sammy? Well, that *was* odd, but it didn't necessarily mean anything, either.

She returned to the kitchen to warm her coffee and leaned against the counter. Sammy was still bent over the sketch pad, deep in concentration. She stepped closer to clear his bowl of soggy cereal.

In the drawing little circles dotted the man's profile. Sammy was coloring in each circle a mean red.

Anxiety gnawed at Lacey's gut. Acne? Chicken pox? Bug bites? She didn't know what else those circles could be.

Sammy had added more definition to the profile, and the resemblance to Griswold was more striking now than it had been only moments before.

This was different than the usual sketches of bugs and horses. Was something bad going to happen to the sheriff? If something bad was going to happen, shouldn't she try to prevent it?

"Sammy?"

He didn't look at her.

"*Sammy*, what's that on the man's face?"

No acknowledgement. Not even a clue that he heard her.

She grabbed his chin and jerked his face toward her. His eyes widened in surprise. She'd never forced him like this before, but she couldn't help it, not when the sheriff could be in danger.

"Sammy, talk to me! What are those red things on that man's face? Is something wrong with him?"

His lips parted. He flapped his hands. "Sick—man—sick."

"What man, Sammy?"

He pointed to the door Griswold had just closed behind him. "Sick."

75

"**M**arc, please let Riley know he's in our prayers here—will you do that?"

"Of course. I'll let him know."

"Did Riley tell you about the real blood we found?"

"Yes. That's pretty amazing."

Special agent Mitch Reed seemed like a competent, caring professional, his tenor voice warm and friendly. Thanks to Riley's preliminary groundwork, he'd anticipated Marc's call and didn't waste time on pleasantries.

"Our techs used a solution that changes color when it comes into contact with hemoglobin or peroxidase in blood. The solution changed color."

"How much real blood was necessary for you to find it?"

"Not very much—about 14 milliliters or a tablespoon."

"Okay, so if you've got real blood, then you've got somebody's DNA, right?"

"Better. When we ran the DNA profile through our database, we got a hit. The blood belongs to a deceased soldier in the armed forces named Alexander Turrow. He was killed in 1991 during the Gulf War."

Marc's pulse spiked. *"What?"*

"The government has been collecting DNA profiles of all military personnel since the first Gulf War. The collection helps with the identification of remains. For reasons I can't explain, Alexander's profile was on file, too."

Why the soldier's DNA was on file didn't interest Marc in the least; his mind couldn't shake another amazing fact. Alexander Turrow had been dead and buried for more than 20 years. "How could somebody even *have* the guy's blood?"

"That's not really so strange if you think about it," Mitch said. "If Alexander agreed to donate some of his organs after death, whoever harvested them in 1991 would have had access to his blood, too. Maybe Alexander donated blood to the Red Cross sometime before his death. Sometimes folks also have blood drawn and stored if they're anticipating surgery and doctors want extra blood on hand in case they need it later. That avoids the need for a blood transfusion from a perfect stranger. I'm sure you've heard cases of the HIV virus being passed on that way."

"Unfortunately, yes."

"So Alexander's blood could have been frozen and stored. In fact, it's possible for blood to be frozen up to 10 years and still be viable."

"But his blood is certainly past its expiration date. If the blood's too old to be usable for medical purposes, can you think of any other reason why someone would keep a supply of it?"

"At this point, I'd only be guessing."

Marc paced and blew out a sigh. "Okay, so you found real blood, and you even know who it belongs to. Any idea why somebody would mix Alexander's blood with the fake blood?"

"It isn't unusual for some psychopaths to play games with the police. My guess is that the killer's sending a message and wondering if we're clever enough to figure out what it is."

"What message?"

"I'm not sure, but here's one theory to consider. I take it you're familiar with Old Testament history?"

"Of course."

"To avert the final Egyptian plague—the death of their first-born—the children of Israel painted their doorposts with blood shed from an innocent lamb, a picture of Jesus Christ in the New Testament. That's how they avoided judgment from the angel of death."

"Okay. So to the killer, maybe the blood on the walls represents his innocent lamb?"

"Maybe that's the intended message—that Alexander Turrow's the innocent sacrificial lamb."

Interesting. "Any idea what else the killer could be saying?"

"Find out what happened to Alexander Turrow, and I bet you'll have a pretty good idea."

"You mean, you don't know?"

Mitch's voice sounded deflated. "Nope. That's the big mystery, I'm afraid. The details of his death are sealed."

"Sealed?"

"Classified by the War Department. But I've got a contact in Congress who's on top of this case. Hopefully he'll uncover something and get back to me soon."

Marc passed a hand over his eyes. "I'm not sure I understand. Why would those details be classified?"

"Oh, for any number of reasons. Alexander could have been killed while on a secret mission the government wants to keep hush-hush. Covert activity isn't unusual during wartime, and there could be certain details we don't want our enemies to know. It's like showing your hand during a game of poker—I'm sure you understand."

"But if Alexander died more than 20 years ago, why would the details of his death still be classified? Whatever happened to the Freedom of Information Act?"

Mitch chuckled. "I'm afraid that wouldn't apply here. Knowing how the military conducts its covert missions is still considered classified intelligence. Keeping certain information secret is all in the interest of national security and the protection of our soldiers abroad. It's really not so unusual for the details of a mission to be kept classified."

Dead ends. Always dead ends. Marc ambled toward the waiting room so he could share this amazing revelation with Gillian. "Okay, so we know the soldier's name, and we know he died during the Gulf War. But that doesn't give me much to work with."

"Wait. I haven't even gotten to the best part yet. I've got a pretty good idea who your killer might be. The soldier's father is Austin Turrow, a retired biochemist."

A biochemist.

The fake blood, the pheromones, the drugs in Jared's bloodstream, the crystal meth that killed Tessa, the anthrax that killed Vernon.

An alarm went off in Marc's head. "Tell me more about this guy."

"Turrow's been a pain in the side of the US government for years. He's a paranoid, outspoken activist determined to cause trouble. A few years back, he was all over Capitol Hill, making a real stink about his son's death, convinced the government was guilty of a cover-up and pleading with Congress to open a formal investigation."

"So what was the reception?"

"Nobody gave him much of a hearing, though his name made it into a few newspapers. Run an online search for his name, and you'll see what I mean. And even though nobody gave him much attention, that doesn't mean there couldn't be a grain of truth in what he was saying. Remember, our government *is* very good at covering its tracks."

Mitch paused. "Either way, Austin was marginalized, and the media painted him as some sort of madman out for attention. Of course, he didn't help matters any. He was quoted as saying that he wanted to dismantle the entire US government brick by brick, and if nobody was willing to help him, he'd do it all by himself."

"That sounds like a threat."

"More like a promise. Oh yeah, you can be sure the CIA have had their eyes all over this guy."

Okay, so Turrow didn't like the government. What was so unusual about that? Marc wasn't unsure what any of this had to do with the murders at the resort.

"Austin has good reason to be a little paranoid," Mitch added. "How much do you know about the siege at Waco?"

The question was like a curve ball out of left field. "Oh, just the basics, I guess. Some cult leader—I can't remember his name—was holed up with his followers in some compound in Texas, right?"

"It was spring 1993 in Waco, Texas, and their leader was David Koresh. He claimed to be a prophet of Jesus Christ and was the leader of the Branch Davidians, an extremist offshoot of the Seventh-day Adventists."

"The name rings a bell."

"The government wanted Koresh to surrender due to a firearms violation, which later turned out to be false. However, he *did* have quite the harem of underage girls, even though the girls were consenting. Thankfully, relations with underage girls is still considered statutory rape. That was the legitimate gripe the feds had with Koresh when they asked him to surrender."

"But Koresh and most of his followers refused to come out, right?"

"Yeah. They were really big into the book of Revelation and the seven seals. They thought it was the end of the world and that the government was the antichrist. The harder the government pushed, the more stubborn they became. They believed they were supposed to defend themselves—with force, if necessary—and even give their lives until Jesus Christ returned and delivered them."

"Didn't the government send in tanks?"

"Yeah, they punched holes in the walls and injected tear gas into the buildings. The FBI thought the tear gas would encourage the Davidians to come out."

"But it didn't work."

"No, Marc. We at the FBI were horrified. There were children, even babies, in there. We thought for sure parental instinct would kick in, that they'd surrender to protect their children."

Marc stopped and peered out a window. "Wasn't there a fire?"

"Even to this day, nobody's exactly sure how it started. Either way, only nine of Koresh's followers walked away from the flames. Seventy-four people died, unless you include the two unborn babies."

"I do. And Koresh died from the fire, too?"

"No, he died from a single gunshot wound to his forehead before the flames reached him. In case you didn't know, that's an unusual place to shoot yourself if you intend to commit suicide. It looks like somebody—we don't know who—put him out of his misery before the flames reached him. In fact, several victims died the same way."

Marc shook his head and resumed walking. "Okay, but what does Waco have to do with Austin Turrow?"

"Austin was one of the nine survivors, Marc."

Marc's mind raced.

"He saw the assault happen right before his eyes. During the fire he must have heard the screams of those trapped inside. Later, he wrote a book about his experience and traveled across the country, making speeches about how our government killed innocent people."

"Well, using tanks and tear gas does seem a little over the top, don't you think?"

"I'm not here to debate who was right or wrong at Waco. I'm just trying to give you some context to better understand where this guy's coming from. Understanding his background might help us see what he's doing and why."

The psychological profile. Riley's game. But now Riley was out of commission. "So if you think Austin Turrow's our killer, couldn't somebody pick him up for questioning?"

"There's one problem. A few weeks ago he disappeared from his private compound near San Antonio, Texas. Now nobody knows where Turrow is, not even his ex-wife."

"And you think he's here?"

"I'm almost positive he is. Think about it. Who else would have the combined biochemical expertise and knowledge of the Bible, specifically the book of Revelation?"

The Bible reference on the walls. The bizarre interpretation of the book of Revelation.

Marc reached for the wall, leaned against it.

"Do you better understand who you're dealing with?"

"Yeah."

"I already called the sheriff there and shared the same information. If you're working with him on this, I'd be very careful about approaching Turrow. In fact, I told the sheriff to get as many men to help as he can. Remember how paranoid and dedicated Koresh and his followers were?"

"Yeah."

"Turrow was an ardent follower. In fact, he's got a nickname. His closest friends call him Cyrus."

"Is that important?"

"The transliteration of the Hebrew name Cyrus is 'Koresh.' David Koresh thought of himself as a modern-day Cyrus the Great, who delivered the Jews from Babylon. Maybe Turrow sees himself as Koresh's successor. If Turrow's got a beef with somebody that's religiously motivated, there's no telling what he might do or how far he might go."

Marc pinched the bridge of his nose.

"There's something else about the blood, Marc, something you might have already figured out on your own. If Austin Turrow's responsible, he told us loud and clear that he's connected to these deaths. That tells me something else: He doesn't plan to walk away."

He's going to finish his plans and kill himself.

Marc's mind spun as he wandered back to the waiting room. If Turrow was responsible, he must see himself as God, as the person in charge of the plagues and the murders, able to control each move in this sick game.

Which brought him back to Riley's questions. If Colbert was Pharaoh, what was his connection to Turrow? Colbert had a military background and had served in the Gulf War. Was there some connection between him and Turrow's son, Alexander? And what did any of this have to do with Colbert's son? He needed to find out.

"Marc, are you still there?"

Just as Marc opened his mouth to apologize for letting his mind wander, somebody grabbed his arm. He turned and faced Gillian's stunned expression.

"Hold on a sec, Mitch." He lowered the phone and turned to her, covering the mouthpiece with his other hand. "What is it?"

"Lacey just called me with surprising news. Dr. Colbert must have the anthrax too. Paramedics just took him away by ambulance."

The doctor discussing Riley's condition with Emily whirled toward them, face puzzled. "Excuse me? What did you just say?"

Gillian repeated what Lacey had told her.

The doctor checked his clipboard, face bemused. "Something's not right here. If we had another anthrax victim, I'd be the first to know. Hold on." He stepped away, pulled out a cell phone, dialed, and talked to someone in quiet tones.

Moments later, he hung up and faced them, eyes bewildered. "I don't know who your friend is or what's wrong with him, but he can't have anthrax or be coming to this hospital."

Marc's expression froze. "What do you mean?"

"We keep meticulous records here. If paramedics picked him up for anthrax poisoning and took him away by ambulance, they didn't come from this hospital."

Marc stared at him. "But this is the only hospital within hours."

"I'm sorry, but there must be some mistake." The doctor turned and walked away.

PART 3

LORD OF THE FLIES

"If you prick us, do we not bleed?
If you tickle us, do we not laugh?
If you poison us, do we not die?
And if you wrong us, shall we not revenge?"
—William Shakespeare,
The Merchant of Venice, act 3, scene 1

76

"Sheriff Griswold could be in danger," Lacey said, "but I can't reach him on his cell to warn him. Got any idea where he is?"

Cell phone to his ear, Quinn rolled his eyes at Lacey's frantic jabber. He didn't have time for this. "Wait. Hold on, Lace. You aren't making sense. Calm down and start at the beginning. What's this all about?"

Quinn twisted the steering wheel and directed the ambulance away from the main housing wing. He fixed his eyes on Cyrus in his rearview mirror. Cyrus was in the back, watching Colbert just in case the man woke up. Not everything was going according to plan, and Cyrus was furious. They couldn't afford any more mistakes, and Lacey was turning into another one.

She described the sheriff's odd visit and said he'd been looking for her dad and Quinn. Then she told him about Sammy's portrait of the sheriff and the red spots on his face. Some of his past drawings had seemed strangely prophetic, she said.

Prophetic? What's she talking about?

Quinn's hands tightened around the steering wheel as if to choke it. He couldn't believe this game had gone on as long as it had. Worse, Cyrus had been manipulating him for his own agenda since day one—ever since Quinn had spilled his discovery in the old mine. If only he could find a way out of this maze, but so far he didn't see any clear exit.

After the second death—the overdosed secretary—Quinn had known that only Cyrus could be responsible and that he must be lying. When Quinn confronted him, Cyrus had finally told him about his evil plans. But now his hands were tied.

Cyrus had pretended to be Sammy's special friend and had been using him as a pawn too. Cyrus said that Quinn would do what he ordered, or something bad would happen to Sammy.

But Cyrus had made a fatal mistake about Sammy's autism. He'd assumed that Sammy didn't have the communication skills to share his secret, but he'd forgotten about Sammy's love for drawing, that sometimes pictures said more than words. Now, because of Sammy's drawings, Lacey was getting smart to what was going on.

I gotta put a stop to this. If Lacey kept digging, she would discover his involvement, too. But then again, maybe that was the only way Cyrus could be stopped. He was willing to go to prison if the truth could spare Sammy's life. But how could he tell Lacey anything important with Cyrus listening in?

"Lace, those pictures don't mean anything," he said. "You know I've been reading that picture book about the plagues of Egypt to Sammy. He's just been drawing pictures like the ones in the book. You know how he likes to copy things."

"But this picture's different. The man in the drawing is the sheriff—I'm sure of it—and something's wrong with his face. I'm afraid something bad is going to happen to him."

"Lace, that's crazy. You know how you let your imagination go a little wild sometimes."

Cyrus' eyes nailed him through the mirror; he'd heard enough to know what was going on. His unspoken look meant he was counting on Quinn to smooth things over, to put Lacey's mind at ease—in other words, to lie.

But Quinn was weary of the deception.

He hated being used and realized how expendable he was in this situation. As soon as Cyrus finished using him for what he wanted, what would he do to him? Toss him aside like a dirty rag? Quinn had kept Lacey out of the know for her own safety. He didn't want Cyrus to have any reason to go after her too. Sometimes ignorance truly was bliss.

"But what if I'm right about this?" she asked. "Couldn't you at least try to track the sheriff down? Make sure he's okay?"

"Why don't you try calling the sheriff yourself?"

"I already tried. Nobody knows where he is right now. He must be over there somewhere, looking for you. Couldn't you do this little errand for me?

"I can't. I'm a little busy right now."

"Where are you? What are you doing?"

"That's not important. Look, I'll do what I can."

"Thanks, Quinn. That makes me feel a lot better. Let me know what you find out, okay?"

"Of course. Bye."

After Quinn hung up, Cyrus said, "Colbert can wait. Now we've got another problem to deal with, for Pete's sake."

In the mirror, Quinn watched Cyrus cast those weird little rocks on the floor. It creeped him out how Cyrus consulted the spirit world for guidance. Were demonic forces somehow guiding Cyrus' every move? He certainly wasn't consulting God.

Why did I ever get involved with this man?

Cyrus glanced up. "I've been playing games with the sheriff long enough. He's gotta be here somewhere. Find him."

77

Marc listened to the dial tone and waited ... waited. His call went to the sheriff's voice mail.

"Sheriff Griswold, this is Marc Thayer. Something strange is going on. My wife learned that Dr. Colbert was taken away by ambulance, but get this—the hospital didn't send the ambulance or the paramedics. It's critical that you call me as soon as possible."

He hoped the sheriff would call him back soon. Unanswered questions were like an itchy rash he couldn't help scratching. Why would someone pretend to be paramedics and whisk Dr. Colbert away?

Was Turrow involved? If so, he wasn't working alone. More than one paramedic had been observed.

Marc sighed, not missing the significance of this development. Now he had no way to ask Dr. Colbert about Riley's hunch that he represented Pharaoh in the plagues scenario. But he had another lead that could perhaps take him to the same destination.

Marc told Gillian about his call with Mitch Reed and the revelations about the blood and Austin Turrow. Her eyes widened in disbelief.

He said he would be right back and found an available computer in the hospital lobby. Searching for Austin Turrow's name produced several hits. About a dozen news articles popped up, detailing the angry father's tirade in Washington, DC. Mitch

Reed's backstory was confirmed by their headlines: "Slain sol-dier's father requests congressional investigation." "Turrow pleads with lawmakers to open investigation." "Details of sol-dier's mysterious death sealed by War Department."

Marc clicked on a *Washington Post* article at random. Out of the page of words glared Austin Turrow's angry face in full color.

A prick of recognition stilled him. He'd seen this man be-fore—he was sure of it. Turrow was somewhere at the resort. Who else would have used his son's blood?

He's playing a twisted god, and his son, Alex, is the innocent lamb.

Marc grabbed his phone and hit redial. He sighed when the call went to the sheriff's voice mail again.

Where is he? Why isn't he picking up?

78

If you want a job done right, sometimes you just gotta do it yourself.

How many times had his father said those words to him? Sheriff Griswold had lost count.

The cruiser's tires spat dirt and gravel as he steered out of the Caruthers' driveway. He eyed the bottle of Excedrin in his middle console, grabbed it, and popped a pill, washing it down with a hot splash of organic herbal tea from his thermos. He would pay good money right now to make his splitting headache go away.

There was probably only one true remedy—he needed to catch his perp, and he wasn't wasting another minute.

The book about the plagues of Egypt at Lacey's had sealed it for him. He'd never believed in coincidences, so why start now? Quinn supposedly had alibis for the murders, but now he doubted their accuracy. Quinn was somehow connected to these murders, and he wanted to know how.

He checked his cell and listened to the voicemails from Marc Thayer, his forehead wrinkling. So now he had another reason to pursue Quinn. Perhaps he had something to do with this alleged abduction of Dr. Colbert.

He left a voice mail for Deputy Moyers to bring him up to speed. Then he put his cell on voice mail, not wanting to be disturbed, and called dispatch using his police radio.

"920, Marquette County."

"Marquette County, go ahead 920."

"Put out a stop and hold on a red Chevy pickup. Owner operator, last name of Caruthers. Charles Adam Robert Union Tom Henry Edward Robert Sam. No further."

"10–4, 920. Proceed with caution."

"10–4, Marquette County."

The resort resembled a ghost town. The protestors had packed up and gone home. It was apparently even too early for the press. But then he supposed that the anthrax had scared most folks away, though he'd specifically requested that they stay. Apparently only he, the diehards, and a killer remained.

He cruised the few paved roads crisscrossing the plush grounds, head swiveling, eyes searching for Quinn's red pickup. When he didn't see it, he ventured onto back roads that wound around the outskirts of the property, dust billowing behind him. He passed a 20-foot-high brush pile, a tangle of sticks and browning heaps of lawn trimmings. Still no pickup.

If Quinn's so busy, where is he?

According to Lacey, Quinn was fixing a plumbing problem somewhere. If that was true, his pickup should be parked at one of the buildings. But it wasn't.

He slammed his hand down hard on the steering wheel and cursed.

Where are you hidin', Quinn? I don't have time for this.

His higher-ups had called him the night before and made it clear that if he couldn't handle this case, he needed to say so pronto so they could appoint somebody who could. These deaths were too high profile now for small-town tactics, and the entire department's reputation was on the line.

He needed to step up his game or get sidelined. But he wasn't about to let that happen—not after working so hard and climbing the ladder for so many years to get this job.

His temples were still pounding when the cruiser ascended a gravel road lined with scrubby pines. The cruiser crested the hill, and Griswold touched the brakes. Just over the rise, a red pickup—Quinn's pickup—was parked outside a chain-link fence surrounding a white igloo-looking building. A sign on the fence declared, "WASTE TREATMENT FACILITY. AUTHORIZED PERSONNEL ONLY."

Well, I'm about as authorized as you can get.

To his right, a man-made rectangular pool was sunk into the earth, surrounded by a grassy berm and another chain-link fence. The cesspool was filled with stagnant-looking muck, its contents best left to the imagination.

Griswold slowed to a stop beside the treatment plant's chain-link fence and turned off the ignition. His engine died, then ticked.

He scanned his surroundings through the windows. The fact that Quinn's pickup was parked here didn't necessarily mean the man was inside the facility. He could be checking something outdoors—perhaps a problem with the pipes leading to the cesspool.

But Griswold saw no signs of life. Not even ubiquitous deer munching on prairie grass could be found.

He opened his door and stepped out. An instant heat-wave slammed into him, as if God had left his oven door open. Something else assaulted him: the foul stench drifting from the cesspool. He raised an arm over his face and breathed through his sleeve until the wind shifted direction and the stink pursued somebody else's olfactory nerves.

Hands on his hips, he looked around.

Come on, Quinn, where are you?

He expected the man to emerge from the pines edging the other side of the fence to his right, but he saw no one. To his left beyond the cesspool stretched a fallow field of what remained of a corn crop somebody had harvested years ago. He could see for miles, and nobody was out there. Just a lot of weeds and ruts from ATV joyriders.

The sun beat down on him as if he were a tiny fly under a magnifying glass. His back and underarms prickled with sweat. High above, an eagle circled for a kill, dark wings sharp against the blue sky.

He eyed the single gate to the six-foot-high chain-link fence encircling the treatment facility and strode toward it. The open padlock hanging on a loose chain did little to deter him from opening the squeaky gate and stepping inside the fence.

Gravel crunched underfoot as he headed toward the single gray door atop three cement steps. The door led into a white circular building that resembled a flattened igloo, or maybe a flying saucer.

He smirked. *Looks like something from* The X-Files. *Must be where they produce the alien virus.*

Right hand on the holster of his Glock, he knocked on the door with his left. "Quinn Caruthers?"

There was no response.

"Quinn, are you in there? This is the sheriff. I need to talk to you."

Again, nothing. Just the rustle of the breeze through nearby pines.

He eyed the door, hesitating. He didn't have a warrant, but he could enter if he had good reason to think Quinn, the suspect, was here and possibly had Dr. Colbert as a hostage. He had to find out.

He reached for the knob and found the door unlocked. Slowly, he opened the door, noting the blackness beyond.

Something exploded in his face. He lurched backward, hands upraised.

He forgot the three steps behind him and tripped down them, toppling onto his back with a gasp. He struck the back of his head on the gravel.

He hardly noticed the pain of his head because of his burning face. It was as if a hundred bees were stinging his cheeks, nose, and eyelids.

He howled. His hands flew to his face to mash the bees or whatever was causing such torment. Tears leaked out of his eyes.

Beyond the pain, he was vaguely aware of blue sky above and a stranger hovering. A man peered down at him, silhouetted by the sun.

It wasn't Quinn Caruthers. It was a blue-eyed man he'd never seen before. The man bore a gray crew cut and wore a white mask over his nose and mouth. He clutched a small, silver aerosol can in his hand.

He sprayed my face!

Griswold gasped and groaned, bent and unbent his legs. The white-hot burning was pure misery.

He tried wiping off whatever was burning his face but only succeeded in transferring some of the acid to his hands. Now his fingers were on fire too.

He didn't want to look. He was afraid he would see his skin bubbling away.

Gasps fueled by panic and pain shuttled through his lungs. Surely God never intended such torture.

"What did you do to me?" he cried.

Through his mask, the man with the crew cut said, "Only what justice demands. How does it feel to burn alive?"

"My face!" Griswold shouted. "*Please*! Help me. Make it stop!"

"Now you know how the children of Waco felt. Your government burned them alive, and nobody lifted a finger to stop it."

What was the man muttering about? Griswold remembered the FBI agent's call. Was this Austin Turrow, the Waco survivor?

Griswold remembered his gun and reached for it. But the man's booted foot clamped down on his fingers, grinding them into gravel. Griswold howled and jerked his hands away.

"*Please*," he gasped. "Please—help me."

Tears dripping down his cheeks only gave the sensation of a knife tip digging into his face and tracing a path down to his chin. Along with being burned alive, he was now being flayed.

The man crouched to his haunches, peered down at him as if fascinated. But he didn't lift a finger to help. "Hurts bad, doesn't it? Sort of like the eternal fires of hell."

"Yes. Please. Help me!"

The man pulled out a syringe, the needle long, amber fluid shiny in the sunlight. "I can make the pain go away if you really want me to. I can extend mercy nobody ever gave the children of Waco."

"Please. Just make it stop."

The man smiled with his eyes. "I can make the pain go away—forever—if that's what you really want."

Forever?

A drop of the amber fluid dripped onto Griswold's cheek. He jerked his head away, tried to focus. What was the man saying?

"You'd never feel pain again."

Death or pain? What an outlandish choice. Who was this madman?

The syringe hovered close to Griswold's face. "I ended David Koresh's suffering, and I can end yours too, if you want. Just say the word."

Thankfully, Griswold passed out.

79

Back in the waiting room, Marc showed Gillian one of the printed news stories bearing a high-resolution photo of Austin Turrow. "Does this guy look familiar to you?"

Gillian studied the photo, her forehead furrowed. "I'm not sure. Wait a minute. Yes, I remember now. The day Emily needed her pill, I went to get her a drink. When I came back, a man was there with her and Chase. I think this might be the same guy."

"I think I might have seen him too."

"Why do you ask?"

"I think it's Austin Turrow. I think he's here."

"What?" Her face was stricken.

"But two people are involved, which explains why Quinn Caruthers had alibis. Turrow could be pulling the strings while everybody's focused on Quinn."

Marc's phone blurted its cowboy ringtone. He stepped away from the ladies to answer it. It was Deputy Moyers.

"Thanks for calling me back," Marc said. "I've been trying to reach the sheriff, but his cell isn't responding. Any idea where he is?"

"I'm afraid he won't be taking any calls for a while. He and his patrol car were found a little while ago near the resort's waste treatment facility. The sheriff's hurt pretty bad."

Marc's breath caught in his throat. "Is he okay?"

"No, he's not okay, but he's alive. Looks like some kind of nasty chemical burn on his face."

"What happened?"

"No idea. Maybe when the sheriff wakes up, he'll tell us."

"He's still unconscious?"

"Yeah, and he's got these strange red bumps all over his face and hands. I know it sounds crazy, but the doctor says it sorta looks like biological warfare."

Marc didn't need a doctor's diagnosis to know what was going on, but he didn't know if Moyers did, so he filled him in.

Moyers was already up to speed. "So you think this could be the plague of boils?"

"That's next on the list. Our perp's been following the biblical order pretty closely, though he skipped the flies for some reason."

"This is bizarre."

The fact that the sheriff was out of commission sobered Marc. Whenever investigators got too close to the killer, something bad happened to them. Now he and Moyers walked in the shoes of those who were either sick or dead. They needed to watch their backs.

"There's something else you need to know—unless you've already heard." Marc told him about Dr. Colbert's apparent abduction.

"Well, things have been a bit chaotic at the hospital since this anthrax business hit the fan. Maybe something slipped through the cracks. Maybe the doctor simply wasn't informed about another anthrax case."

"I'm at the hospital now. I checked. There's no record that Dr. Colbert was ever admitted here. So if paramedics took him away by ambulance, what happened to him? Where did he go?"

Moyers' frustration ebbed over the connection. "I better look into this. Seems pretty far-fetched to me that somebody would abduct Colbert. I mean, what's the point? To hijack this project the translation committee's working on? From what I understand, the committee disbanded because of the anthrax."

"Maybe there's another reason."

Moyers cleared his throat. "Okay, what else have you got? You said something about new information from the FBI. Your contact may have spoken to the sheriff, but he didn't share the information with me."

Marc passed on everything Mitch Reed had told him. Moyers didn't seem as surprised as Marc had anticipated.

"I looked up Turrow's picture on the Internet," Marc said. "My wife and I think we might have seen him at the resort. If what Mitch Reed says about the blood is true, Turrow is probably here somewhere."

"Okay, we'll hunt down his photo and send out an APB. Maybe when the sheriff wakes up he can tell us who attacked him. Until then, we can certainly start looking for Turrow. If he's here, we'll find him."

The confidence in Moyers' voice made Marc wonder about the deputy's naïveté, especially considering what Mitch Reed had told him about Austin Turrow. The Waco survivor was a dangerous radical who wanted to dismantle the US government brick by brick. Timothy McVeigh had been so fueled by hatred because of the FBI standoff at Waco that he'd bombed the Alfred P. Murrah Federal Building in Oklahoma City on April 19, 1995, the Waco disaster's second anniversary. More than 160 people, including children, had died as a result of the blast.

If Turrow was anything like McVeigh, they had much to fear.

The police had also been looking for the killer for days. Did Moyers really think they would find Turrow so easily if he was, in fact, responsible? So far the killer had used only unconventional methods and had evaded all classic means of detection. Doubtless his lair would be unconventional too.

Marc asked, "So what do you know about the sheriff's last movements?"

"He dropped by to see Lacey Caruthers this morning and was looking for her dad and Quinn, her husband."

Lacey Caruthers. Gillian had mentioned meeting the woman at the mine disaster memorial and later having lunch at her house across the lake.

"His last radio transmission confirms he was in pursuit of Quinn," Moyers said, "but then something must have happened. I'm wondering if he and Quinn had some kind of altercation. Tire tracks at the treatment facility where we found the sheriff are consistent with Quinn's truck. But until the sheriff talks, there's no way of knowing for sure if Quinn was involved."

"But you could pick him up and ask a few questions," Marc suggested.

"We would, except there's another problem. Quinn has disappeared too."

"What?"

"Yeah, nobody knows where he is, not even his wife. I'm wondering if he was involved, and maybe now he's on the run."

"Any leads on where Quinn could be?"

"Lacey reached him on her cell earlier and told him the sheriff was looking for him. For whatever reason, he wouldn't tell her where he was. She's tried calling him nonstop ever since, but he hasn't picked up."

She warned him. Maybe she's part of this game too.

Moyers sighed. "I need to go. I appreciate everything you've done to help, Marc. Until we know otherwise, I'm thinking Turrow's our man, or else he and Quinn are working together. Either way, we'll find them."

"Is there anything I can do to help?" Marc asked.

"I don't think so. I'm sure my men can handle things from here, but I'll be in touch."

The dismissive tone was obvious. Moyers clearly didn't want his further involvement, perhaps out of concern for his safety. But he'd never enjoyed being sidelined during a basketball game, and he certainly didn't enjoy it now. At the same time he understood Moyers' reluctance. After all, he was no cop. But how could he take a backseat now that he was on the cusp of finding Jared and Vernon's killer and Riley's poisoner?

Marc said good-bye, terminated the call, and returned to the waiting room, where Gillian and Emily hadn't budged. Their heads were bowed, hands clasped as if in prayer.

Marc felt too restless to sit, his mind buried under an avalanche of questions. So he paced and let his mind dig away at the problem.

Did Lacey know about the possible link between her husband and Austin Turrow? If she did, maybe she even knew how to reach Turrow. But Deputy Moyers was no dummy. Certainly he would ask her those questions, right?

Marc paced some more. *You've done all you can. You just need to sit tight and let the police do their jobs.*

But he couldn't get Lacey's possible knowledge off his mind. After the sheriff's conversation with Lacey, he'd reported that he was in pursuit of Quinn. Why had he been after Quinn? Had Lacey shared something important?

Marc noticed that the ladies had finished praying. He approached Gillian and touched her arm gently.

"You know Lacey Caruthers, right?"

"Sure."

"I need to talk to her about the investigation. Since you're a familiar face, would you mind coming along?"

Gillian's eyes were uncertain. She glanced at Emily.

"I'll be fine," Emily said. She seemed to have more strength in her eyes now than she'd had earlier. Perhaps the prayers had helped, or the doctor had shared encouraging news. "You go ahead and help your husband. I'll look after Chase while you're gone."

"You're sure?"

"Absolutely."

"It shouldn't take long," Marc told Emily. "Feel free to head to lunch without us. We'll grab a bite on the way."

Gillian stood and peered into his eyes. "Marc, is this really necessary? I'm scared about what's happening at the resort. The killer's still at large, and nobody knows where he is."

Maybe his mind wouldn't let go of these questions because God wouldn't let him. For whatever reason, he needed to talk to Lacey. "I need to do this, and I need your help."

"What's this all about?"

"I'll fill you in on the way."

80

She was alone, and the house was quiet. Too quiet.

Another knock on the door almost sent her through the roof, her nerves frayed.

Lacey stormed through the kitchen toward the front door, clutching her cell phone. Why would somebody stop by now, when she was waiting for Quinn to call her back? And of course, on top of everything else, Sammy had wandered off again, probably putting himself in danger.

She nibbled at a hangnail. Sometimes she didn't know why she even bothered trying to be a mother. Somehow she'd missed the memo.

Another knock on the door.

When she glanced out the side window, she glimpsed a tall man she hadn't seen before. At his side stood Gillian Thayer.

Oh, that must be her husband.

Tension eased out of her shoulders. Maybe they'd heard the news that Quinn was missing and had come to cheer her up. She opened the door and tried to be cheerful, but she hardly wanted company right now.

"Hey, Gillian. Good to see you. This is an unexpected surprise."

"Unexpected is right," Gillian said. "Sorry to just drop by like this, but it's important. Lacey, this is my husband, Marc."

Lacey held out her hand, and Marc's hand swallowed hers. "Nice to meet you," she said.

Goodness, he *was* tall. And good-looking, too.

"We heard about your husband's disappearance," Marc said. "We know you've got a lot on your mind right now, so we won't take much of your time. I was just wondering... " He handed her a piece of paper. "Have you seen the man in this photo before?"

She recognized the face—it wasn't a very good likeness—and handed the paper back. "Sure, that's Austin Turrow, an old-time hunting buddy of my husband's. My boy, Sammy, calls him Uncle Austin because he's taken a real liking to him. Why do you ask?"

Marc and Gillian exchanged surprised glances. Marc asked, "Do you have any idea how I could reach him?"

She cocked her head, temples pounding. "Do you mind telling me what this is all about?"

Gillian offered an apologetic smile. "It's a rather long story. Do you mind if we come in?"

Lacey led them to the living room, invited them to sit on the couch, and offered them packaged chocolate chip cookies. It was all she had handy, and she couldn't trust her current presence of mind to hunt down much else. Thankfully, they'd just eaten and declined—said they couldn't stay long.

She took down two framed photos from the fireplace mantle and handed them to Marc. One was a portrait of her, Quinn, and Sammy with Christmas decorations in the background. She remembered that they'd been late and rushed, as usual, on that day.

In the other photo, Quinn squatted in the woods next to a deer he'd shot. A blue-eyed man with a gray crew cut stood at his side, a rifle in his hand. Both men wore camouflage. Only Quinn was smiling.

"That's my husband"—Lacey pointed—"in case you happen to see him."

"And the other man?" Marc asked.

"Austin Turrow."

Marc asked, "Lacey, how much do you know about the mysterious deaths at the resort?"

She stiffened, remembering Sammy's pictures and Quinn's dismissive words. "Not a whole lot. Just that some crazy person's been killing folks in some pretty bizarre ways. Now this morning I hear that the sheriff's hurt, and my husband has disappeared. That's why I keep this phone handy. I keep hoping he'll call me back."

She felt herself tearing up again and hated to be having a meltdown in front of them. "The police haven't exactly come out and said it, but I'm pretty sure they think Quinn's responsible for what happened to the sheriff. But that's just crazy. Quinn would never have done something like that."

"I'm pretty sure it wasn't your husband," Marc said. "The sheriff has new evidence that links Austin Turrow to the deaths at the resort."

She'd heard this before but couldn't believe it. "But Austin's such a nice man—how could he be responsible?"

"DNA's a pretty solid link."

"DNA?"

"It's a long story, and so far the evidence is only circumstantial. That's why the sheriff wants to talk to Austin. Do you know where he is?"

She glanced at her watch. "He should be at the resort right now. My husband offered him a summer position on the maintenance staff."

Marc shook his head. "I called HR on the way over here. There's no record of an employee by the name of Austin Turrow."

"Oh, that's right." Why was her mind so frequently on the blink? "Sometimes he goes by the name Cyrus."

Marc's expression froze. "Could you excuse me for a minute? I need to make a phone call." He pulled out a fancy cell phone and stepped into the hall.

Lacey glanced at Gillian, who gave her a reassuring smile, but she felt far from reassured. In fact, she felt nauseous. Quinn and Austin were buddies. If Austin was responsible, could Quinn somehow be involved too? Was that why he was missing? He had certainly sounded funny during their last phone call.

"You'll get through this." Gillian patted her hand. "When they find Turrow, they'll clear your husband—I'm sure of it."

Lacey hoped she was right. She glanced at her watch again. "Oh, I need to go."

"What's wrong?"

Lacey sighed. "Sammy's run off again, but he's never been gone this long before. I'm worried he might have gotten hurt."

"He's developed quite a habit of running away."

She rose. "Sorry, but I've gotta go look for him. I already called the police, but their plates are too full with the investigation to be of any assistance right now."

"Marc and I can help look. Where did you last see Sammy?"

"He was in here drawing, but I unfortunately fell asleep on the couch again. Now that Quinn's gone, I'm afraid for Sammy, too. I sure could use your help looking for him, if you don't mind."

Marc returned. "Turrow's missing from work, but Deputy Moyers is already trying to track him down."

Gillian filled him in about Sammy.

"Okay, let's go," he said. "If we look for him together, I'm sure we'll find him."

81

Dr. Colbert.

Quinn.

Turrow.

And now Sammy.

Were all these disappearances coincidental? Could they possibly be linked somehow?

Denim shorts. Orange T-shirt.

The boy shouldn't be too difficult to find.

While Lacey and Gillian drove off to the resort to look there, Marc headed on foot toward North Lake, one of Sammy's favorite hangouts. Lacey said that Sammy loved to throw rocks into the lake, but he was too afraid of the water to actually go in. Still, Marc strolled along the shore with a fearful twist in his gut that he might find Sammy's floating body. Thankfully, he saw no one in the lake. Nothing to make him suspect the worst.

As he neared the woods, a burst of orange flashed in the foliage.

"Sammy?" Marc called.

The boy raced into the trees, and Marc regretted calling out. What had Lacey told him? He wasn't supposed to yell the boy's name, but he'd acted on impulse and driven the boy farther away. Sammy didn't know him, and Sammy was terrified of people he didn't know.

Smart move. So now I need to find him, but if I get too close, he'll just run away from me because I'm a stranger.

Marc shook his head. Lacey needed a searcher the boy knew and was comfortable with. How was the search on his end possibly going to work?

But then he remembered something that quickened his step. Sammy not only knew Austin Turrow, they were on friendly terms. If Turrow was at the resort somewhere, perhaps Sammy could lead him straight to the man.

Marc picked up his pace. Trampled brush revealed where the boy had left a path. He plunged into the woods in pursuit, ferns and honeysuckle up to his waist. Far ahead, thanks to a dip in the terrain, he spotted Sammy about 50 yards away. His orange T-shirt shone like neon against the browns and greens of trees and foliage.

Every dozen feet or so, Sammy glanced back to see if he was being followed. Each time he saw Marc, he picked up his pace, and Marc had to hustle so he wouldn't lose the boy. The combination of exercise and heat made Marc pull up, panting, and brush sweat from his forehead.

This wasn't working. Maybe if Sammy no longer thought he was being pursued, he would slow down.

Marc darted behind the nearest pine and waited a full minute, chest heaving. He stole a peek. Sure enough, Sammy tromped through the thicket with a sense of purpose, but he was no longer running. Where was he going?

Five minutes later, after Marc had darted from tree to tree to avoid detection, Sammy seemed to disappear into thin air. Marc crouched at the edge of woods that made way for a clearing and a dip in the terrain. He stole a closer look, and his pulse quickened.

A dirt road wound down a hill toward a black, truck-sized hole in the earth, and Sammy was nowhere to be seen. A large pile of brush and grass clippings lay in front of the hole as if someone had unsuccessfully tried to hide it.

A black hole? No, more like a tunnel. But a tunnel to where? And why?

And where was Sammy?

Marc used his shirtsleeve to brushed sweat out of his eyes. The tunnel wasn't far from the Barnes-Hecker Mine memorial. He remembered what Gillian had told him about the old mine. It had been sealed shut since the 1926 disaster, but perhaps somebody had found another way inside.

But if so, why? Why would someone venture into a tomb where so many men still lay buried? Could the tunnel lead him to Turrow's lair? If so, it explained why the police hadn't yet tracked him down. What a great hiding place. Who would have thought he would be hiding underground in an old, forsaken mine?

Marc waited in the brush and wondered whether Sammy might show up, but he didn't. A mosquito buzzed near his ear and landed on his arm. He brushed it away.

He fished his phone out of his pocket, pleased to see he still had service, and called Deputy Moyers to report his discovery. But no one picked up, and the call went to voice mail. "Deputy Moyers, hey, this is Marc Thayer. I wanted to call and let you know about something I just found in the woods."

Marc froze. About a hundred feet away, a man emerged from the brush on the other side of the clearing. Was it Turrow? Marc couldn't be sure from this distance.

He crouched lower in the brush to avoid being seen, his senses on high alert. He couldn't continue the call without being heard, so he closed the phone and hoped the stranger hadn't detected him.

So far, so good. The brown-haired man in jeans and a short-sleeved, navy-plaid shirt abandoned the tree line and stepped tentatively into the clearing. He took a few steps toward the tunnel, then stopped. Glanced around, as if lost. He appeared to have made the same discovery as Marc, his head swiveling from left to right as if searching, as if wondering if he was alone or being observed.

Marc wondered who the man was. He didn't appear to be armed, though he clutched something in his right hand. A black flashlight.

He'd come prepared.

Marc's legs cramped. He shifted his weight and realized too late that he hadn't put his phone away. It slipped from his fingers and dropped to the forest floor, making a racket in the brush. He cringed.

The stranger's head snapped toward the sound. His eyes roved the brush and widened when he spotted Marc.

Marc knew he'd been discovered. Should he run? Was the stranger friend or foe? He resembled neither Austin Turrow nor Quinn Caruthers, but perhaps he was a third accomplice.

Marc didn't have a gun or anything else to use for defense. The man, however, still clutched the flashlight, which he could use either for light or to bash somebody over the head.

Somewhere in the distance, a crow cawed. The men eyeballed each other across the clearing. Marc knew somebody needed to break the stalemate but decided not to step into the clearing as the stranger had. Such a move didn't seem wise considering that they didn't know who might emerge from the tunnel at any moment.

Marc motioned to the stranger to join him. Until he knew otherwise, he would treat him as a friend. He retrieved his phone and slid it into his pocket.

The stranger backed into the brush and skirted the tree line. He came within two feet of Marc and crouched, eyes wary. "Who are you?"

"I should be asking you the same question." Marc studied the stranger.

His brown hair was thick and well styled, a whisper of gray at his sideburns. Usually pretty good at remembering faces,

Marc didn't recall seeing this guy around the resort. Who was he, and what was he doing out here in the woods?

"So what's going on here?" the stranger asked. "Where does this tunnel lead to?"

"You tell me. You're the one who came with the flashlight."

The flashlight showed intent. The man wasn't necessarily seeing the tunnel for the first time. His ignorance could be a ruse.

"I discovered this place, oh, maybe 20 minutes ago." The stranger kept his baritone voice low. "The tunnel opening was hidden behind that pile of brush, so I moved some of it away for a better look. Then I went back for a flashlight."

Likely story. "So what are you doing here?"

The stranger met Marc's gaze. "What are *you* doing here?"

Marc realized they could linger in the brush all day if neither extended some trust. Sammy could have wandered into that tunnel and be in danger right now. They didn't have time for this. "Okay, I'll go first. I'm trying to find a boy named Sammy Caruthers."

"The autistic kid. Yeah, I know who he is."

"I told his mom I would help find him and tracked him here. I think he might've gone into the tunnel."

"I know he did. I saw him."

"You did?"

"Yeah."

Marc sighed. He was in the right place, then. "So what are *you* doing here?"

"I'm trying to find whoever's responsible for the murders at the resort. Earlier I overheard some of the sheriff's men talking about Quinn Caruthers, so a while ago, I followed him to this general area. When I took a closer look, I found the tunnel."

Another investigator? Why didn't Marc know who he was? "I've been investigating the murders too. Are you with the sheriff?"

"No, I'm just"—the man hesitated—"just a concerned citizen who wants to know if this tunnel has something to do with the murders."

"Me too."

The man chuckled. "Well, since we both appear to be here for the same reason"—he extended his hand—"I'm Gabriel Jacobi. Nice to meet you."

82

The revelation of the man's identity was like a burst of fire igniting along Marc's nerves. He tried to mask his surprise and a certain level of distaste behind a cordial smile but was certain he failed. The guy certainly had him beat in the looks department, and he felt a tinge of jealously when he remembered this man had been Gillian's first love.

He didn't even want to look at Gabriel. Hadn't he mailed one of Gillian's old love letters to him? Wasn't he trying to cause problems in his marriage?

He had no choice but to shake Gabriel's hand, but then he dropped the bombshell. "I'm Marc Thayer, Gillian's husband."

Gabriel glanced away with a wince as if stung. "No kidding. Isn't it funny how God orchestrates things sometimes?"

You have no idea.

Gabriel hung his head, and his uncertain gaze flicked back to Marc's face. "I'm being sincere when I say it's nice to finally meet you, though I doubt the feeling's mutual."

Marc fumed. Was that supposed to be sort of a half confession? So Gabriel was feeling guilty about what he'd done?

Marc bit back his anger. "That was a nice touch—sending me one of Gillian's old love letters to you so I'd think the two of you were still involved. Yeah, that showed real class."

Gabriel's eyes widened. "What old love letter?"

The man deserved an Oscar. Marc glowered at him. "You're honestly gonna act like you don't know what I'm talking—"

"But it's the truth."

Marc's internal thermometer shot up several degrees. "The truth? You tell my wife you're sorry for hurting her years ago, and then you send me one of those old letters and try to make me think—"

"I don't know what you're talking about." Gabriel rose and started to back away. "Maybe this wasn't such a good idea."

He turned to go, but Marc rose and grabbed the back of his shirt to stop him. "Hey, don't turn your back on me!"

Gabriel whirled around and knocked Marc's arm away. "Don't touch me!"

Marc's temper flared. He readied a fist, but something held him back. Perhaps it was the look on Gabriel's face that indicated he didn't have a clue what was going on. Could Gabriel honestly not know the reason why he was so ticked?

"Look, I don't know what this is all about." Gabriel was breathing hard. He gripped the flashlight as if prepared to use it for defense if need be. "What happened between your wife and me was a long time ago. I said my piece, and she said hers. It's over, okay? It was over a long time ago."

Marc dug into his pocket and pulled out the letter in question. He thrust the pink stationery at Gabriel's face. "Okay, then how do you explain this? Somebody anonymously mailed it to me here at the resort."

Gabriel grabbed the letter and flushed as his eyes skimmed the words. "I've never seen this letter before."

Yeah, right. This guy never did anything wrong, did he? Marc's thermometer inched up a few more degrees. "You're gonna tell me—"

"It's the truth." Sincerity glistened in Gabriel's eyes. "I never saw the letters. Your wife mailed them to me, thinking I was living with my parents. But I was gone, and my parents—"

A boy's cry rent the summer air. It sounded like it was coming from the tunnel.

Gabriel whirled toward the tunnel entrance. "What was that?"

Marc's heart pounded. "I'm not sure."

"It could be Sammy."

Marc glanced at his watch and wondered how long he'd been wasting precious time. "Look, I don't know what's going on with this letter business, but we'll have to sort it out later. If Sammy's in the tunnel, I need to go after him. Do you mind if I borrow your flashlight?"

"You mean, you want me to stay here?"

Marc nodded. "It could be dangerous in there. I don't know what I might find. If I don't come back with Sammy in 10 minutes, then go for help."

Gabriel shook his head. "Not on your life. If anybody goes, we go together." He held up the flashlight. "Besides, you need this, and maybe I don't feel like giving it away and staying behind."

Marc gritted his teeth. Why was Gabriel being so difficult? He couldn't help loathing the man, but now it looked like they would have to work together whether he wanted to or not.

Gabriel shrugged. "It's up to you. Sammy could be in danger. Aren't we wasting time?"

Marc nodded. He had no choice. *Okay, Gillian forgave the man, but that doesn't mean I have to like him.*

The men rose, abandoned the tree line, and stepped tentatively toward the tunnel opening. Marc shook his head. So he and Gabriel were forced to be partners for the time being. God certainly had a sense of humor. He tried to push aside his dislike for Gabriel and focus on Sammy. Why had the kid gone into the tunnel anyway?

Marc let Gabriel take the lead since he had the flashlight.

"Got a gun?" Gabriel asked.

"No. You?"

"Nope."

The sun blazed on the back of Marc's neck. "So maybe this isn't so smart. A flashlight doesn't work so well in a gun fight."

"But there isn't time to get a gun. Sammy could be hurt. Maybe we should call the police."

"I already tried. Besides, I know for a fact that their hands are pretty full right now, and this tunnel could lead nowhere."

The tunnel loomed before them now, a yawning opening into blackness. Marc swallowed hard, buoyed by a familiar tinge of adrenaline. Ever since he'd been trapped in car wreckage years ago, he suffered a phobia of closed-in spaces: elevators, closets, a hay maze at a church harvest party, tunnels burrowing into the earth.

But now he needed to make an exception. He took a deep breath, perhaps his last relaxed one in a while.

Gabriel pointed. "Hey, those must be Sammy's tracks. Look at the shoe size."

"Yeah." Marc noted another pair of tracks. He couldn't be sure, but they resembled the tracks he and Riley had found outside the women's bathroom. Was Turrow waiting somewhere inside?

An alarming possibility jolted him. Was this a trick to lure them inside? If so, it was the perfect trap. But Sammy could be in danger, so they had no choice.

As they entered the tunnel, Gabriel flicked on his flashlight. The temperature dropped several degrees, but Marc was sweating. His chest tightened, and each breath became more difficult.

Gabriel's flashlight beam raked across wooden timbers to their left and right; they supported a low ceiling that appeared to be composed of rough-hewn rock. The timbers looked new.

So it wasn't an old tunnel. Somebody had positioned the timbers recently. But who?

See the timbers, Marc told himself. *They hold up the ceiling. It's safe here. There's no reason to feel this way.* But trying to reason his phobia away seemed like an exercise in futility.

Their footsteps echoed eerily as they found just enough room to walk side by side, the rocky floor sloping downhill. Gooseflesh broke out on Marc's arms, and a damp, moldy smell assaulted his nostrils. Somewhere in the distance water dripped.

Like it or not, he was stuck with Gabriel, and there was no point in giving him the silent treatment. He tried to make conversation to get his mind off their close quarters. "Any idea why this tunnel's here?"

"Beats me. I didn't see anything at the resort about underground accommodations. Did you?"

Marc wondered what Gabriel knew about the old mine and filled him in as they walked. In turn, Gabriel shared what he knew about the murders, and they compared notes. Gabriel knew enough to be a snoop, but Marc prided himself in being much further ahead in the game.

Shadows draped over them, giving the impression of walking down a long, dark corridor. Marc glanced back. The tunnel opening was only a pinprick of ambient light now.

A sudden wave of claustrophobia nearly drowned him. He staggered and reached for the rocky wall, unable to draw a deep breath.

Gabriel slowed. "You okay?"

"Sure. I'm fine." He sucked in a shallow breath and forced himself forward, yielding to his pride. He wasn't fine, but he wasn't about to let Gabriel see his weakness. He would show Gabriel that he was a much finer pick for Gillian than Gabriel had ever been.

"Hey, I don't see Sammy's tracks anymore," Gabriel said.

The floor was compacted rocks and pebbles now. Grayish, red chunks of rock lay strewn everywhere. Was that what iron ore looked like?

Gabriel put a hand to his mouth to call the boy's name, but Marc stopped him.

"He'll run if he doesn't know you."

"Does he know you?"

"No."

"Then how are we going to get this kid to come with us?"

"Good question." It was definitely a complication Marc hadn't planned on.

The tunnel forked, and they had to choose.

"We both lean right politically, so let's go right," Marc said. "We can always backtrack if we come to a dead end."

The farther they walked and the deeper they descended, the cooler the tunnel became. But Marc sweated as he battled little panic attacks, tried to get a deep breath, and thought about how the ceiling could crush him like a bug. He wiped sweat off his forehead and smeared it on his jeans, hoping Gabriel wouldn't notice.

The farther they ventured, the more distant the outside world became. What if they somehow got stuck down here? And where was Sammy? Certainly they should have found some trace of him by now.

New anxieties descended. What if they stumbled across Turrow? They had only one flashlight to use as a weapon. The more Marc thought about their risky exploration, the more he realized the foolishness of their search. He should have told Deputy Moyers about this place, but now it was too late to go back. Maybe...

He pulled out his phone and frowned. No service.

Perhaps the boy wasn't far ahead, and they could lead him back to his mother. Then he could call Moyers and let him take on the tunnels with his men.

"Just for the record," Gabriel said, "I had no idea you and Gillian were going to be at the resort."

Great. Gabriel had to open his mouth and remind him why he disliked him so much. "Does that really matter now?"

"I guess not. I just didn't want you to think I'd planned to hurt her again."

"I don't think you could hurt her more than you already have."

"Look, I told her I was sorry."

Marc couldn't hold back his snarky tone. "And I suppose that makes it all go away?"

"I didn't say that. I just—"

"Let's just drop it, okay? This isn't helping anything. Let's just find the kid and get out of here."

Something scraped across the tunnel floor behind them. A footstep? Marc stopped, pulse revving, and glanced back. But he saw only blackness and heard only silence.

"Thought I heard something," Marc said. "Probably just my mind playing tricks on me."

After another 50 yards, and Gabriel said, "Hey, look."

His beam revealed a large opening of some kind in the tunnel wall, a sort of carved-out room. In one corner lay various supplies stacked together: jugs of water, kerosene, kerosene lanterns, shovels, several sleeping bags, two folding metal chairs.

"Looks like some kind of hangout," Marc said.

"Sammy's hangout?"

"I doubt it. How could he have gotten all this stuff down here?"

In the opposite corner sat several stacked cardboard boxes. They approached the stack, and a faint buzzing sound emanated from whatever was concealed inside. The words "biological supply" were stamped on the side of the top box.

"Hey, what do you think's in here?" Gabriel wedged the flashlight in one armpit and opened the box flaps.

Marc reached out to stop him. "I don't think—"

"Ouch!" Gabriel leaped forward and arched his back as if in pain, trying to reach his hands back. "Hey, something just stung me. Take a look."

Marc grabbed the flashlight, eyes widening. A small black dart protruded from Gabriel's back. Marc pulled it out, mind racing.

"What is it?" Gabriel asked in a panicky voice. "What did you find?"

Before Marc could process the questions, something hissed past his ear and clattered off the tunnel wall. He dropped the dart and whirled.

With the flashlight he probed the tunnel behind them. He couldn't see or hear anyone, but somebody was there just out of sight. Somebody had to be. A shiver traveled down his spine.

"Oh man!" Gabriel moaned and reached for the tunnel wall. He sank to his knees. "I don't feel so good."

Two vague shapes with bobbing flashlight beams rushed Marc out of the darkness. A fist connected with his stomach, and he doubled over in pain. When he looked up, Austin Turrow's angry face leered out of the shadows.

Marc aimed a fist at the man's gut, but Turrow was swifter and darted away. His booted foot caught Marc in the chest.

Marc tumbled backward, slammed into the buzzing boxes. The box on top toppled off the stack.

Turrow cursed.

The room swarmed with buzzing bugs. Fluttering. Capering. Darting into Marc's eyes.

Marc squinted and turned his head; he didn't see the fist aimed at his nose. He reeled backward, hands flying to his bleeding, stinging face. Turrow grabbed him from behind, put him in a headlock with one arm.

Marc struggled to break free. Something red hot pierced his neck. Was Turrow injecting something into him?

Marc's mind flew to Tessa. *Death by an overdose.*

No!

Marc's legs turned to jelly. He stumbled and thrust out his hands to break his fall. He waited for the pain, but it never came. In fact, he felt nothing. It was as if someone had pulled a plug, and everything just ...

... stopped.

83

"Thank you for calling."

"I'll be in touch if anything develops," Deputy Moyers said.

Gillian hung up and paced the waiting room on weary legs. She'd spent the whole night here, waiting for word about Marc. But still nobody knew where he was.

Too restless to sit, she crossed to the window and peered out at the first rays of morning piercing the brooding sky, her finger tracing calligraphy letters on the glass. Fear soured in her stomach. What was it—Thursday? Where was Marc? Why hadn't he called?

Just after lunch yesterday they'd split up and helped Lacey look for Sammy. Now, not only was Sammy missing; Marc had apparently vanished too. He'd left a cryptic voice mail on Moyers' phone about finding something odd in the woods, but then the call had abruptly cut off. Now when she tried calling Marc, she only got his voice mail.

God, what's going on? What am I supposed to do?

So many were missing—Dr. Colbert, Quinn, Marc, the suspect Turrow, even Sammy. Was it coincidental that they were all gone at the same time?

God, how can five people just disappear into thin air? Where did they go?

Emily joined her at the window, her face weary as if she needed to sleep but knew she wouldn't catch a wink. "No word on where he could be, huh?"

Gillian shook her head.

Both of their husbands were in jeopardy now. Riley's condition hadn't improved; in fact, it had only gotten worse. The surgery to drain his lungs had been successful, but the doctors weren't giving Emily any guarantee that he would pull through. The brutal truth was that the next 24 hours would determine whether he would live or die. This fact, however, didn't seem to distress Emily.

"God knows what he's doing," she said, as if reading Gillian's thoughts. "Remember, he doesn't want us to be anxious about anything. I know"—her smile met Gillian's sigh—"that's easier said than done. But it can't be impossible. Otherwise God wouldn't have told us to do it."

Gillian glanced at Chase, who slept in his stroller, and envied the peace emanating from his face. Beyond God, at least she wasn't totally alone; she had her son, God's good gift. "I know he's good and in control, but I can't stand the waiting. I wish there was something I could do."

"But sometimes waiting is all he expects of us. Waiting and praying."

Guilt chafed her. They'd invited the Rileys here to help with this investigation, and now Chuck was apparently dying from anthrax. In some ways his peril was her fault, but how could they have known what would happen?

Gillian stilled her restless hands. She reached for her purse. "Do you mind watching Chase for a while?"

"Where are you going?"

She passed a hand over her eyes. "I don't know, but I can't stand sitting here anymore. Maybe I'll go for a walk."

"But it's still pretty dark out."

She didn't need a second mother right now. "I'll be fine."

"Okay. But before you go, do you mind spending some time with me in prayer?" Emily's voice wobbled. Perhaps she was struggling more than Gillian realized.

Gillian felt stung. Marc could still show up, but Riley might not last the day. How selfish of her to run off and make herself feel better when Emily clearly needed her comfort and support right now.

She dropped her purse and joined Emily. Neither cared about who might walk into the deserted waiting room and see them. They clasped hands, and Gillian partnered in the older woman's tearful plea to the heavens.

When they were finished, Emily wiped her eyes. "None of this seems real. Two weeks ago, I never would have guessed this could happen."

"He might still pull through."

"But he might not, too, and I need to be prepared for the worst. I guess being prepared is better than being taken by surprise, like when our son was killed." Emily met her surprised glance and held it. "Chuck never told you?"

Gillian shook her head.

"It was a long time ago, and Nathaniel was only 10." Emily swallowed hard. Peered down at her arthritic fingers, knobby and bent. "I remember that day like it was only yesterday."

"You don't need to tell me if you don't want to."

"It's okay. It actually helps me to talk about it."

Emily sighed. "Nathaniel was so excited about riding the Fourth of July church float that afternoon that I could hardly get him to finish his lunch." She chuckled.

"So what happened?"

Emily sighed again. "At the same moment he reached for a balloon that was floating away, the float went over the bumpy railroad tracks. Just when somebody realized Nathaniel had fallen off, the float went over a bigger bump." Her lips stiffened, her gaze cutting back to Gillian's face. "Except it wasn't a bump. And just like that, Nathaniel was in glory." She shook her head. "It all happened so fast."

Gillian's throat tightened. "I'm so sorry. I can't imagine how terrible that must have been like for you."

Emily smiled at the floor, eyes swimming. "The Lord gives, and the Lord takes away. Blessed be the name of the Lord. He makes no mistakes." She met Gillian's eyes. "I understand you've lost your share of children too, so you understand how that kind of loss feels."

Gillian's cell phone vibrated. She didn't want to be rude, but it could be good news about the missing men. She excused herself and grabbed her cell out of her purse. It was Lacey. That's right, she'd called Lacey earlier to give her an update on Riley's condition.

"Gillian, I've been up all night, and I don't think I can stand it anymore. I'm here all alone, and there's still no word from Deputy Moyers about where Quinn could be."

All alone? "You mean Sammy still hasn't come home?"

"No, and he's never been gone this long before. I'm worried sick."

"I'm sorry, Lacey, but I'm not sure there's anything I can do."

"I'm gonna go out of my mind if I have to stay in this big ol' place alone another night. I was wondering—would it be too much to ask you to stay here with me tonight? Just until the sheriff finds our husbands. Emily can come too."

"I wouldn't want to be an inconvenience."

"No inconvenience. Believe me, I've got more guest rooms than I know what to do with."

Gillian struggled with the idea. She barely even knew Lacey, but at least now they had something in common—both of their husbands were missing. Yet Sammy had run off with Chase's stroller. Was staying at her house really the best decision? "But we don't know how long the wait could be. It could be days."

"That's fine. You can stay however long it takes, and I'll make sure Sammy stays away from the baby." She sighed. "Would you at least think about it?"

Gillian had dreaded charging another day at the hotel to her credit card. Perhaps this was an answer to prayer. And Lacey had extended the hand of friendship by inviting them over for lunch. Why not return the gesture? "Okay, I'll let you know. Who knows what might happen today. Let's pray that I won't need to join you. Pray that our husbands will come home."

84

Either darkness had swallowed the whole world—an impossible plague for anyone to recreate—or Marc had gone blind. Darkness reigned supreme in this dank, motionless subterranean world. Not the faintest glimmer of light or hope shone anywhere. Not the faintest breeze touched his face.

The thick darkness was suffocating, and he struggled not to panic. Long, deep breaths steadied his nerves. At least it was a wide-open space and not close quarters with a rocky ceiling only inches above his head.

Water dripped somewhere in the distance, and something overhead squeaked. Bats?

He'd awoken to a drug-induced headache, the darkness so thick that he could almost feel it on his skin like a heavy, stifling blanket. Except this wasn't a blanket to keep him warm, and he longed for such a blanket. The humid air was cool enough to make him uncomfortable in his short-sleeved shirt.

Marc lay on his side on moist, rocky ground, his whole body aching like one big bruise—and that didn't begin to describe the woozy feeling in his head. Thankfully, his nose wasn't broken, but the throb was intense. He probed the sore spot on his neck where Turrow had injected something into his bloodstream and winced. But hey, at least he was alive.

He hoped the trip into the tunnel was only a bad dream, but the harsh reality was that he was probably a mile or so underground, and most likely nobody knew where he was. If only he'd told Deputy Moyers where he was going—then he would have at least some hope that help was on its way.

Gillian knew he was gone by now but probably had no idea where to look. What was going through her mind? Almost two years ago he'd barely survived the bullet of an unbalanced counselee. She probably feared he wouldn't be so fortunate this time.

Something moved in the darkness, and his heart pounded.

"Marc?"

Gabriel. Although the man didn't exactly engender tender feelings, Marc was glad he wasn't alone in this place. "Yeah."

"You're alive!"

"You are too."

"But there's somebody next to me I'm not so sure about."

"Don't move. I'm coming toward you."

Marc rolled onto his hands and knees, temples pounding. The floor undulated beneath him. He edged forward on the mostly level surface, the ridges in the rock hurting his knees. Unable to see anything, all he could do was inch toward the sound of Gabriel's voice. He touched an arm.

"You found me." Gabriel gripped Marc's arm. "Where do you think we are?"

"Judging by the echo of our voices, I'd say a pretty big cavern."

"Does your head ache as bad as mine does?"

"Like the worst hangover? Yeah. That was quite the cocktail Turrow gave us."

"How'd we get here?"

"Turrow and the other man carried us, I guess."

"Other man?"

"Don't you remember? Two of them came at us out of the dark just as you were passing out. Do you still have your flashlight?"

"No."

"Hey, I've still got my cell phone. I can't believe Turrow didn't take it. Do you have yours?"

"Yeah."

Marc fished the phone out of his pocket and opened it, the display light blinding him for a second. It was amazing how even a small light could seem bright in the right circumstances. "Rats, no reception."

"That's probably why Turrow didn't bother taking the phones. He knew they wouldn't do us any good down here."

"But what about GPS?" Marc's phone illumined Gabriel's face in a glowing, Halloween haunt sort of way. "Couldn't somebody track us?"

"Only if our phones have GPS—not all of them do. Even then, the signal would have to penetrate the rock overhead, which isn't likely. I have no idea how deep underground we are."

"You say there's somebody beside you?"

"Yeah. I think he might be dead."

Marc investigated the rocky floor beyond Gabriel and found a hiking boot. He shone his light up the man's leg until he came to his hand, which was so white it could have been modeled in wax. Marc touched the hand—it felt unnaturally cold—and drew back. The man's middle was wet with something. Was that blood? He could administer CPR if needed, but if the man's injuries were extensive, he was no substitute for a doctor.

He illumined the man's face; he appeared to be unconscious. "It's Quinn Caruthers."

"You sure?"

"Yeah, but don't ask me what he's doing here."

An unfamiliar male voice penetrated the darkness. "He's still alive, in case you're wondering."

Marc whirled to his left, gasping. Was it Turrow? "Who are you?"

"Matthew Colbert."

The white-haired man in the cafeteria. The chairman of the translation committee. Marc had finally found the elusive Dr. Colbert, but now he wondered if that was such a good thing.

First Gabriel. Then Quinn. Now Colbert. What did it mean—this meeting in the dark?

"Welcome to the plague of darkness, my friends." Dr. Colbert chuckled like someone on the brink of losing his mind. "You missed the plague of hail a while ago."

"Plague of hail?"

"Turrow told me he was going to detonate some kind of explosion and seal off the entrance just before he left. I felt the impact a while ago when you were still unconscious."

So now we're trapped. "How long have you been here?" Marc asked.

"Beats me," Colbert said. "Hard to say when it feels like nighttime all the time. I'm sorry you got dragged into this mess, but at least it's nice to have someone to talk to."

Marc checked the time on his phone. It was now Thursday. 5:23 a.m. Dr. Colbert had been abducted sometime Wednesday morning. He and Gabriel had found the tunnel on Wednesday afternoon, so they had been unconscious for quite a while.

His stomach growled. Yesterday's lunch had been his last meal. No wonder he was hungry.

Gabriel decided to contribute to the conversation. "How did we get here?"

Dr. Colbert cleared his throat like he was fighting a cold. "The same way Turrow and Quinn brought me. They carried you over the chasm using a bridge and head-mounted flashlights. Then Turrow shot Quinn—I saw it all. Quinn probably exceeded his limit of usefulness."

So Quinn had been working with Turrow all along. "Tell us about this bridge," Marc said.

"Pretty crude. Just pieces of plywood on top of a ladder."

"A ladder?" Gabriel asked.

Weariness tinged the low timbre of Colbert's radio-quality voice. "Don't get all excited. It's long gone by now, I'm sure. I explored this place while you two were unconscious. About five feet behind you is a sheer drop-off. We're on some sort of cleft between a chasm and a sheer wall of rock. We're not going anywhere, gentlemen, not without some kind of bridge to the other side of the chasm."

Marc wasn't ready to give up. There had to be a way out of here. "A lot of people have been trying to find you."

"You don't say? And who might you be?"

Marc realized he hadn't introduced himself, so he did. Colbert apparently already knew Gabriel and his connection to the protestors.

"Thanks to you and Micah Coombs," he said to Gabriel with distaste, "all those people were here with their lungs and placards."

"It's a free world," Gabriel said in a flippant tone. "Some of us didn't exactly embrace the idea of the Qur'an being merged with God's Holy Word. In all respect, sir, if you'd listened to what we had to say—"

"Look, we don't have time for this." Marc had no patience for infighting. "Any idea why we're here?"

"I know why *I'm* here," Colbert said, "but I can't speak for the rest of you. What's your connection to the plagues?"

Marc described Jared Russo's invitation and the informal investigation he'd begun with Riley after Jared's death.

"Jared was like a son to me." Colbert's voice trembled. "Turrow deserves to burn in the hottest part of hell. He's doing all this to punish me, you know."

"Punish you," Marc said. "Why would he do that?"

"It's a long story. You sure you want to hear it?"

"Why not?" Hopelessness dripped from Gabriel's voice. "From the looks of things, it doesn't look like we're going anywhere anytime soon."

"Very well." Colbert sighed. "During the Gulf War, Turrow's son, Alex, was under my command as part of a secret mission in Iraq, the details of which the government has kept classified for years. But I know what happened and don't mind telling you. It's unlikely we're getting out of here alive anyhow."

His crisp, educated voice echoed across the cavern. "The mission itself failed miserably. Most of my men got away, but Alex and a few other soldiers were captured. I don't want you to have nightmares, so I won't describe how the militants tortured Alex and his comrades before putting them out of their misery."

Marc swallowed hard. "And Turrow blames you?"

"Absolutely."

"But why? Islamic jihadists were responsible."

"I was his son's commander. I was supposed to keep Alex safe from those kinds of monsters, but soldiers die in battle—sometimes in horrible ways. It's just a fact of war." He sighed. "Worse yet, the ill-devised plan came from some higher ups in the War Department, and I was the fall guy when it all went down. Turrow did some digging. He even went to Iraq to investigate and became convinced that negligence on the part of the US military had factored into his son's death."

Colbert coughed a deep, lung-scraping hack. "He raised a ruckus on Capitol Hill and demanded a formal investigation. But when nobody listened, Austin apparently decided to take matters into his own hands and mete out justice as he saw fit. I think the plagues were just his way to make the deaths look like something having to do with the Bible project and the protestors to distract investigators."

Misdirection—just like Riley thought. "How were Jared and Vernon involved?" Marc asked.

"Both were under my command, but they were only following orders. If anybody's at fault for the failed mission, it should be me. I was in charge."

"But it was a poorly devised plan," Marc said. "You said so yourself."

"Yes, but I still have to take responsibility."

"But what about Tessa McCormack?" Marc asked. "And Quinn here, if he doesn't pull through?"

Colbert heaved a resigned sigh. "Collateral damage, I guess, though that doesn't make their deaths any less important. It's probably the same reason you guys are here. Turrow despises investigators. If they get too close, he eliminates them."

That explained why Turrow went after the sheriff. "If you knew Turrow was responsible," Marc said, "why didn't you tell the sheriff or do something yourself to stop him?"

"I didn't realize he was the one pulling the strings, not at first. Like everybody else, I was blind to the truth. I honestly thought Micah Coombs or one of the protestors, like Gabriel here, was to blame."

Marc snorted. "Yeah, right. If you knew him so well, surely you must have seen what he was up to."

"Actually, most of what I know came from Turrow himself after he brought me here. I didn't know so much earlier. Turrow raised Cain on Capitol Hill, and I knew he was an angry father with connections to Waco. But I couldn't fathom that somebody would hatch a plan as elaborate as this one—not until he came to my suite. Then I realized the truth too late to do anything about it."

The facts still weren't adding up in Marc's head. "Okay, but if Turrow is seeking revenge because of his son's death, why are *you* still alive?"

"To understand that you need to understand Turrow's twisted mind. Killing me would have been an act of mercy. He wants me to live and suffer—that's been part of his game all along. He told me so in his ridiculous speech just before he left me here."

"I'm not sure I understand," Gabriel said. "Make you suffer? Why not just kill you?"

Colbert coughed again, another hack of misery. "Look at the pattern. Turrow went after those in my closest circle—Jared, Vernon, Tessa. Even Brianne, the secretary spooked by the plague of blood. They were all special people in my life. But now I'm in the worst position imaginable. I know the truth, but I'm powerless to do anything. The worst kind of torture is knowing something terrible is going to happen to someone you love but being unable to stop it."

"So someone else is in danger?" Gabriel asked.

"Yes. Turrow plans to go after the one person he's had in his sights all along." A sob broke from Colbert's lips. "My son."

85

"Good job, Sammy. You did a great job leading those men into the tunnel just like I asked you to. Oh, and that scream was a nice touch—that really brought them running. Sometimes you surprise even me."

In the cabin near the mine, Sammy sat on an old sofa and nibbled on a cookie, his eyes following Uncle Austin's every move. Uncle Austin always made him feel good when he did what Uncle Austin asked—normally, that is. This time he didn't feel so good because somebody was missing.

"Daddy," Sammy said between bites. He made little grunting sounds.

Uncle Austin turned from the big box that buzzed and smiled at Sammy in a fatherly sort of way. "Oh, didn't I tell you? Your dad's checking something in the north tunnel. We'll see him later."

But Sammy wasn't stupid. He'd heard the big bang and the tunnel caving in. Sometimes Uncle Austin lied. Lied big time.

Sammy finished his cookie and flapped his hands. He glanced at Roberta, his mom's canary, in her cage, her black eyes darting toward him, wings fluttering. The fact that she was fine proved that no poisonous gases lingered in the cabin. But perhaps a poison of another kind mingled in the air. Perhaps she, too, knew that Uncle Austin was lying and was pretending to believe. Just like he was.

Sammy was close to being through with this lying. Meanwhile, he continued to pretend—because he was good at that too—and wondered about his dad. Wondered if Uncle Austin was lying again. Wondered what the true story could be but was too afraid to ask.

"Come here, Sammy. I want you to feel something."

Sammy rose. Uncle Austin grabbed his hand and guided it to the big box. The buzz vibrating through the cardboard made Sammy's eyes widen. It wasn't one vibration but hundreds. What could be inside?

Sammy reached for the flap, but Uncle Austin slapped his hand. Sammy snatched back his smarting fingers.

"Not yet—it isn't the right time." Uncle Austin's enigmatic eyes glittered in the light. "We don't want to let them out too soon. I have special plans for them."

What plans?

"I had plans for the locusts, too, but that didn't work out because *you* let those men go down the wrong tunnel." Uncle Austin scowled at him, gray-blue eyes almost white with anger. "They weren't supposed to go that way and find the locusts. You didn't follow my instructions. That was b-a-a-a-a-d of Sammy."

Sammy cringed. He hated when Uncle Austin made the bleating-sheep sound. Sammy was just a stupid sheep—that's what Uncle Austin told him whenever he made a mistake. Sammy hated when Uncle Austin thrust his angry face so close, when the ugly scar running down his face throbbed red like a traffic light.

Then, as if a valve had been switched, Uncle Austin shrugged and smiled. "It's okay, but don't let it happen again."

But it didn't feel okay, not the way Uncle Austin said it.

"Run along now, Sammy." Uncle Austin mussed his hair and nudged him away as if he didn't want to be bothered. "I've got work to do. Run along now to your mother—she's probably worried. And remember, not a word. This is our little secret, and buddies don't tattle, do they?"

86

During his childhood Sunday school lessons, Marc had tried to imagine what the plague of darkness must have felt like for the Egyptians so long ago. Now, through experience, he knew what it felt like to be embraced by darkness—and the hopelessness it represented—for hours on end, not knowing if he would ever see sunshine again. In fact, this was Turrow's intent, he realized, this plague of darkness.

Or perhaps this was his version of "outer darkness," a term Scripture used to indicate hell. Turrow saw himself as God. He'd created his own version of hell, minus the eternal burning, and tossed them in. Colbert's misery seemed fitting in such a place.

For a long time nobody spoke, and Marc had no idea how many hours slipped by. He prayed, dozed a few times, then woke with a start. Finally, the silence was more than he could take.

"But you don't have a son," Marc said, resuming their earlier conversation. "My wife researched the committee members. You only have a daughter."

"No, I do have a son." Colbert's voice was almost a whisper now. "The son of my shame."

In a tear-filled voice, he told them a story that was familiar almost to the point of cliché only because of its repetition in churches across America. Years ago, when he was a pastor, he committed adultery with his church secretary, and she became pregnant with his child. He sought forgiveness from her, his wife, his congregation, and God before stepping down from pastoral ministry in shame.

He moved with his wife and daughter to an out-of-the-way place where no one would know them or anything about his scandal. He had a military background—had served in the Gulf War—so he reenlisted to support his family. The secretary, a single woman, had wrestled over whether to put the baby boy up for adoption. She'd decided to keep him but chose to keep the father's identity a secret—but that meant she needed Colbert's cooperation. Even to this day the boy didn't know who his biological father was.

But Turrow did. Turrow had done his homework well and found the weak spot in Colbert's past to exploit it for his own ends.

Marc heard the anguish in Colbert's voice and thought of the chasm only feet away. If only Colbert could cast the burden of his guilt into that chasm. Hadn't God done the same for them? Burying their sins in the depths of the deepest sea?

"I'm so ashamed"—Colbert's voice trembled—"but I can't change the past."

"But you've confessed your sin and apologized to the offended parties," Gabriel said. "God has forgiven you because Jesus paid the penalty."

"Yes, but that doesn't make what I did just go away. We can choose to sin, but we can't choose its consequences. All these years I've wondered about that boy. You see, my wife struggled with a chronic illness, and she couldn't have more children. The secretary offered us the child, but my wife was in no condition to help raise an adopted son either."

Marc was struck by the oddness of chatting with someone he couldn't see. "You've regretted not raising your own son."

"Yes. And now the son I've always loved and longed to know—he's the object of Turrow's wrath."

Marc sobered. Pharaoh's firstborn son. Turrow truly was playing God.

Bats fluttered above their heads, their squeaks and chirps filling the silence. Somewhere, water dripped.

"But," Marc began, "I'm still not clear on what your son has to do with any of this. Why would Turrow care about your son? Just to follow the pattern of the tenth Egyptian plague? Is he really that obsessed?"

"That's a question for Turrow, but I have my own theory. He trained under David Koresh for years, and his theology is all messed up. From what I gather, after Waco he explored various religions and even dabbled in the occult. Sort of came up with his own belief system. A dab of this and a dab of that—whatever worked for him."

"Syncretism on steroids, huh?" Gabriel chuckled.

"From what I remember," Colbert continued, "Koresh and his followers were fanatical about the book of Revelation and the seven seals, so Turrow must be too. The curse in chapter 22 must have given him the idea for his elaborate plan—that is, unless he believes God actually sent him to fulfill those verses as his judge. I can't say for sure. Who can understand the mind of a psycho?"

Colbert cleared his throat. "Are either of you familiar with the Old Testament principle of *lex talionis*—'an eye for an eye and a tooth for a tooth'? I think Turrow is driven by this Old Testament system of justice. Such a system demands that my son die for his."

Understanding overwhelmed Marc, as if the blinders had at last come off. "So who is he? Who is your son?"

87

Perhaps if I just wait long enough, this will all be over, Gillian told herself as she drove to Lacey's house that evening. Then she would look back at the event from the distance and safety of recollection rather than from the pain of the moment, as she was doing now. The waiting was almost more than she could bear, but Emily was right. What else could she do now other than wait and pray?

She'd agreed to visit with Lacey for a while but had decided not to spend the night. Lacey had called with news about Sammy's return. She wondered if he might know something about the missing men, and Gillian wondered the same thing.

But the change in location for the evening made her uneasy. What if Marc showed up at the hotel, looking for her? She'd left a message containing her whereabouts with the hotel clerk in case Marc showed up.

As Gillian drove, her cell phone kept ringing, as it had been doing all afternoon, ever since the news story about the disappearances broke on TV. Crystal had called and said she'd requested permission to miss music camp for a few days; she would be there as soon as she could. One of the deacons from church had heard the news and wanted a report on Marc. Next had come a call from her mother.

The fact that Austin Turrow was still at large unnerved her, in light of what Marc had told her. It meant that he could still inflict pain. Had he fled the police, or did he linger somewhere at the resort with more plans up his sleeve?

"It sure was thoughtful of you to invite me over like this." Gillian let her eyes wander around the beautiful living room again. She set Chase's carrier down beside her.

"Thoughtful?" Lacey laughed. "No, it was selfish. I was lonely in this big ol' place and wanted company, even though Sammy's back."

"Is he okay?"

She shrugged. "Something's bothering him for sure, but good luck prying whatever it is out of him. Hey, where's Emily? She was more than welcome."

"She's at the hospital with her husband. She won't leave his side, and I can't really say that I blame her."

Gillian wondered if Lacey was sharing her thought: that she would prefer to be at her husband's side right now, though perhaps not for Emily's reason.

Lacey glanced around the room as if seeing it for the first time. "It's funny how you don't truly appreciate people until they're gone. My mother spent her final weeks in this house, and I nursed her until the end."

Gillian studied Lacey's face, touched by a daughter's love. Her eyes bore only tears wrung from a worry-sick heart. *It must have been difficult watching her mother weaken a little each day, the end as inevitable as the fall of autumn leaves.*

"I loved my mom when she was alive," Lacey said, "but I think I appreciate her more now that she's gone."

Absence makes the heart grow fonder. In many ways Gillian appreciated Marc more now, too.

Lacey went to get the crib so Gillian could put Chase down for a while. Gillian sank to the edge of the bed, gaze straying to unfamiliar furniture and wall hangings. How she longed to be home with all her familiar things and with Marc at her side. What a weekend getaway! Why had they ever decided to come to this place?

She bit her lip, regretting her thoughts. For whatever reason, God had used Jared's invitation and orchestrated events so they would be here. No point fretting about something she couldn't change. Time to look forward.

What was something constructive she could do in light of Marc's disappearance and her being here? She barely thought the question before the answer came to her.

Encourage Lacey.

Minutes later, Gillian settled Chase in the crib, and he sucked on his thumb, ready for a nap. How odd. He always seemed extra tired when she was stressed.

"What time is it?" Lacey glanced at her watch.

"I have no idea." Gillian's internal clock had stopped the moment Marc hadn't returned to the hospital.

"Did you have supper?"

"I don't think I could eat even if I tried."

"How does some iced tea sound? We could sit on the front porch and talk."

"Tea always works for me."

Gillian lingered. Lacey must have sensed her uneasiness at leaving Chase alone in a strange place and suggested that they put him in one of the guest rooms and lock the door. Neither of them wanted Sammy to walk off with the baby again. Just in case, Gillian stationed her baby monitor near Chase and took the receiver along, clipping it to her waist so she would hear if he needed her.

She and Lacey sat on rocking chairs and faced the breathtaking sunset, the weather perfect. The breeze had died, and North Lake lay still, the surface like glass that might shatter at any moment. Gillian wrapped her fingers around a tall, iced glass of black tea that had been perfectly sweetened with a spoonful of honey. Lacey lit a citronella candle to keep the mosquitoes away and stuck the matches in her pocket before returning to her rocker.

Gillian studied Lacey's face and again wondered why she didn't try harder to be attractive for Quinn. Gradually, the story poured out about her early days in California, when her dad had been a big-shot movie producer rubbing shoulders with celebrities like George Lucas and Steven Spielberg. So much of the world there had revolved around external beauty that she rebelled and went the opposite direction. She'd focused on internal beauty—a noble pursuit—but at the negligence of her appearance.

Gillian pursed her lips. *She just needs some encouragement, I bet.*

The conversation turned to the investigation, and they compared notes. Lacey seemed shocked when Gillian told her about Turrow's connection to Waco and possibly to Dr. Colbert. Gillian leaned her head back against the rocker, a question nibbling at her mind.

What had Marc told her about Dr. Colbert? Something about Turrow and the plagues. Something about Dr. Colbert being Pharaoh. Oh, if only she could remember.

Then it was Gillian's turn to be surprised when Lacey told her about Deputy Moyers' most recent call. They had reason to believe another man was also missing—one of the protestors—Gabriel Jacobi.

Gillian's fingers tightened around her glass. She thought Gabriel had left with the other protestors days ago. What was he still doing here? Had he and Marc somehow crossed paths? Was it possible they were both gone for the same reason?

Lacey must have sensed her tension. "You know him?"

Gillian nodded, guarding her words. "He was an old boy-friend—well, more than a boyfriend actually. But it's a period

of my life I don't like to remember, long before I turned to
Christ. I made a lot of mistakes I'm not proud of. Thankfully,
God forgives."

"And you bumped into him here?"

"Yeah, it was just one of those things." Gillian shook her
head. "God has his reasons, I guess."

Lacey sighed. "Sounds just like what I've been going through
lately."

Gillian looked at her. "What do you mean?"

"There's a man at the resort from my past, too—from before
I met Quinn. I wish he hadn't come. He keeps calling me, wanting to see Sammy."

"Sammy? But why would he—?"

"Please, don't tell anyone." She touched Gillian's arm, eyes
pleading. "Quinn doesn't even know the man's identity because
I haven't told him. You see, I have a past I'm not proud of, either."

"So Sammy isn't Quinn's?"

"No, and Quinn knows that. I just never told him the father's
identity. He loved me enough to marry me anyhow, and he's
never asked too many questions, so I've spared him the details." She shook her head, bit her lip. "I'm not sure why I'm
telling you all this. I guess—well, you once loved someone you
thought loved you too, so you know how I feel."

"Used and cast aside? Yeah, I know."

"Lately my mind keeps going back to what happened years
ago. He was married, and we both knew it was wrong." She
hung her head, face reddening. "Like you said, it's not a period
in my life I'm proud of. Having this man at the resort right now
has dredged up the past—and not in a good way, if you know
what I mean."

Gillian nodded. *I certainly do.*

Lacey sighed. "Oh, I might as well tell you, but we need to
keep this between us."

"Of course. I can keep a secret."

"Do you know Dr. Colbert from the translation committee?"

"We haven't met, but I know who he is."

A cry from the house almost made Gillian spill her tea.

Lacey lurched to her feet. "Great! Now, on top of everything else, Sammy decides it's time to have one of his tantrums. As if I didn't already have enough to worry about. I'll be right back." She headed toward the front door.

"Wait, Lacey."

Lacey turned.

"Are you saying Dr. Colbert is Sammy's dad?"

Lacey nodded, eyes heavy with regret.

88

"So Sammy's your son?" Marc said. "But I thought—"

"—what everybody was supposed to think," Dr. Colbert said. "That Sammy belonged to Lacey and Quinn Caruthers. And he does, legally."

Gabriel had grown silent, apparently lost. But Marc was putting the details together. "Oh, I get it now. That's why you chose to have the translation committee meetings here, right? You wanted to see your son after all these years."

"Yes. I arranged a time to see the boy, and Lacey's been more than gracious given the circumstances." He sighed. "But the meeting was rather a disaster, I'm afraid. Lacey tried to warn me about Sammy's autism, but I didn't know what to expect. I don't think Sammy said one word to me the whole time we were together. I'm not sure he even understands who I am, but I still love him. If we just had more time together, maybe he'd warm up to me."

His voice broke. "Now I shudder to think what Turrow's going to do to him. Remember, Turrow's son was tortured before he died. I fear whatever Turrow has planned for Sammy won't be quick and easy. He'll inflict as much pain as possible, and he wants me to suffer with the knowledge of what he's going to do."

Not a sound from Quinn. Marc assumed the man was still unconscious and couldn't hear about Turrow's terrible vendetta that would affect his son. Perhaps not knowing was best.

Marc's mind raced. What had Lacey said about Turrow?

That's Austin Turrow, an old-time hunting buddy of my husband's ... We call him Uncle Austin because Sammy, my boy, has taken a real liking to him.

Rage kindled in Marc's heart. Turrow had manipulated his way into this family for one sole, devious purpose—and the scheme had apparently been a while in the planning.

Turrow had planned to kill Sammy all along. The thought that revenge could lead anyone to take such measures chilled him.

An eye for an eye. A son for a son.

Marc gripped his head in his hands. How would he feel if he knew someone planned to kill Chase? A father would do almost anything to save his son. He knew he would.

Marc's mouth dried. Where was Sammy now? Maybe there was still time to save the boy. There had to be a way out of the mine before the worst took place.

89

Lacey strode into the living room, fists on her hips, and spotted Sammy in the corner. Since his return, he'd refused to eat or draw. He just sat in a dark corner, knees pulled to his chest, and stared out the window with a worried look she'd never seen before. He repetitively twisted the hem of his shirt.

His lips parted. "Daddy. Gone."

Ever since she broke the news about Quinn's disappearance, he kept repeating those words with anguish she'd never before seen from him.

She stopped. Wait a minute. He'd said those words *before* she shared the news about Quinn's disappearance. But how could he have known?

Then she noticed the carpeting. Dirt from his shoes covered the floor, reddish soil unlike anything she'd seen around the yard. Where had Sammy been all this time?

She could handle only so many questions. It was time for some answers.

She crossed the room and crouched before him. "Sammy, where were you last night and today?"

He flapped his hands.

"We looked everywhere. Do you have any idea how worried I was?"

"Daddy. Gone."

He bumped his head against the wall. Then he did it again, only harder this time.

"Sammy, don't. You're going to hurt yourself."

Again, even harder. *Bang.*

"Sammy!"

Bang!

"Sammy, don't!"

BANG!

If she didn't stop him, he would dent the dry wall, not to mention possibly injure himself. She grabbed his arm and wrenched him away from the wall. He screamed and jerked away from her, running from the room.

She raced after him, toward the sound of his feet pattering up the stairs. She hoofed her way up to his bedroom, found him hiding under his covers. His shape rocked back and forth, back and forth.

She reached out, then held back. She kept her voice gentle. "Sammy?"

"Uncle Austin," Sammy said.

She blinked at the mounded shape under the covers. The police had said they thought Austin Turrow was somehow connected to the plagues, but she'd found their charge laughable. Uncle Austin had always been kind to their family, especially to Sammy. A harmless man.

Or was he?

A picture took shape in her mind. Now Uncle Austin was gone, too, along with Quinn. Could the disappearances somehow be connected to him?

The police had asked if she knew where Austin Turrow was. She, of course, hadn't had any idea. They'd wanted to ask Sammy too, but she'd refused access, certain they would only terrify him.

From the blanket came three words.

"Uncle Austin. Lied."

Lacey ripped off the blanket and revealed Sammy's cowering form. Blond hair stuck out in every direction like a springtime dandelion. "What do you mean, Sammy?"

"Lied."

She grabbed another copy of the Picture Exchange Communication book and turned to the yes or no pictures. "Do you know where Uncle Austin is?"

Sammy ignored the book. He bobbed his head as if to the rhythm of a song in his head. "Tunnel."

Her heart flipped. "What tunnel, Sammy? What are you talking about?" The only nearby tunnels she knew of were... No, it wasn't possible. But what other tunnel could he mean?

Sammy gripped the hair on both sides of his head and rocked side to side, moaning with frustration. She feared he might rip out some of his hair if she didn't calm him down, but she had to know.

"Is Uncle Austin in a tunnel?"

More groans of frustration. More rocking. Her heart went out to him. If only she could get past this communication hurdle. Then she remembered.

The drawings.

Sammy *did* know how to communicate, but she was using the wrong language.

She dashed to his desk and grabbed a sketch pad and some colored pencils. She rushed over and set them down on the bed beside him. "Can you draw this tunnel, Sammy? Can you draw where Uncle Austin is?"

Sammy stared at the pencils, anguish etched on his face.

"You love Daddy, don't you?"

He just made grunting sounds.

Lacey prayed for patience. "Sammy, if you love Daddy, can you draw where he is?"

Sammy grabbed the sketch pad and pencils and began drawing as if the challenge were a game. He liked games. His little hand worked, tongue pressed between his lips. The frustration was gone. He was clearly in his element now—he was expressing himself the best way he knew how.

As the drawing neared completion, Lacey drew in a sharp breath. "Sammy, can you take me there?"

He moaned and rolled his head around, eyes squinting and darting everywhere.

She tried to keep the panic out of her voice. "Sammy, can you find Daddy?"

"Sammy. Find. Tunnel."

She raced for her cell phone, grabbed it, and punched the speed dial with shaking hands. His familiar voice picked up.

"Deputy Moyers, this is Lacey Caruthers. Sammy might be able to lead you to those missing men."

90

Marc worked his lips, mouth parched. How long since he'd last had a drink? They would die of thirst long before hunger. He prayed help would arrive in time.

"Quinn's awake." Gabriel's weary voice echoed across the cathedral-sized vastness of the void.

Good, maybe he can tell us how to get out of this place. Marc roused himself and stretched, pushing his shoulders back. He couldn't remember having a worse backache.

For what seemed like a long time they heard only groans and sighs. When they made their presence known, Quinn didn't ask who they were, confirming Colbert's claim that Quinn had been working with Turrow and already knew their identities.

His injuries, however, suggested a shift in the status quo. Turrow had clearly turned on him in the end, or perhaps Quinn had turned on Turrow, and Turrow had defended himself. Either way, Quinn was on their side now, on the side of being against Turrow and trapped down here. But could they trust him?

"We thought you were dead," Marc said.

"I thought I was, too. The bullet must have passed through at just the right angle." Quinn's optimistic tone soured. "Doesn't really matter, guys. We're all going to die anyhow—you realize that, don't you? You have no idea who you're dealing with. Cyrus means for us to slowly waste away from thirst or starvation. If it helps, guys, I just want to say I'm sorry. Sorry that you're stuck down here with me."

Marc didn't know whether he should believe the man. There was a moment of quiet.

Desperation rang from Quinn's voice. "Please, you gotta believe me. I've done a lot of things I'm not proud of, but Turrow left me with no choice. He said he'd push Sammy, my son, into the chasm if I didn't do what he said."

Marc heard the truth in his words, but he was still puzzled. What was Quinn's role in the plagues? And why had he gotten involved to begin with?

"It must be quite a drop," Gabriel said. "How far down does it go?"

"More than fourteen hundred feet," Quinn said. "Deeper than the Empire State Building is tall."

Colbert whistled. "You seem to know an awful lot about this old mine."

"Yeah, why is that?" Marc asked.

Quinn sighed. "I guess I'm cursed with relentless curiosity. After my family and I moved here to live with Lacey's dad, I heard about the old Barnes-Hecker Mine tragedy and became curious. I read everything I could get my hands on. Then I stumbled across an old ventilation shaft in the woods and decided to take a look. A lot of the mine had collapsed, but some tunnels were still accessible."

"But why investigate the mine?" Gabriel asked. "This is a tomb."

"During my research I came across the journal of Rutherford Wills, the only survivor of the mine collapse in 1926. He kept a secret about the mine most of his life and told his wife only days before his death."

Everybody waited for him to go on.

Quinn spewed a mirthless chuckle. "Well, I'd hoped to keep it to myself, but why not tell you guys? We're all going to die down here anyhow."

"What was his secret?" Gabriel asked.

"Just before his escape from the mine, his brakeman, Jack Hanna, said he saw something unusual in the ore. Keep in mind that everybody thought Wills was senile, so nobody took him seriously. I thought he was crazy too until I took a look for myself."

"What did you find?" Marc asked.

Quinn sighed. "Gold. Gentlemen, this place is full of it."

91

"Right, Sammy? Should I turn right?"

Sammy didn't answer, face illumined by the glow of the instrument panel. He didn't say yes, but he didn't say no either.

Lacey was at the wheel with Sammy riding shotgun. In the backseat beside Chase, Gillian prayed Sammy would know his way in the dark and that they would be able to understand him. Deputy Moyers followed in a squad car filled with deputies. He probably wanted to determine whether Sammy's claim was legit before calling in the full force.

Please, God. Please let everyone be okay.

Sammy had indicated that Quinn was here. There was no guarantee that Marc, Dr. Colbert, and Gabriel were in the same location, but Gillian prayed this was so.

"Is this the place, Sammy?" Lacey asked.

Sammy flapped his hands excitedly. Gillian hoped that meant yes.

Skirting the resort was a dirt road that was more like a two-wheeled rut for RTVs; the bumps made Gillian's teeth rattle. They entered a clearing, and Lacey's headlights settled on a large mound of rocks and debris. Sammy moaned.

"What's wrong, Sammy?" Lacey braked to a stop.

They piled out of the SUV. Gillian unclasped Chase's carrier and brought him along. Sammy dashed toward the mound and gripped his head in his hands. "Gone."

Gillian met Lacey's baffled glance. What was he talking about? How could a tunnel just disappear?

Sammy began lifting rocks and tossing them to the ground behind him. Lacey dashed to Sammy's side, with Gillian only a step behind. "Sammy, is Daddy here?"

"Daddy. Tunnel."

Lacey grabbed his arm and pulled him away. The rocks were too large; he could hurt himself trying to lift them.

Gillian's heart sank. She'd expected an obvious mine entrance, but all she saw was a pile of rubble. Was Sammy mistaken? She glanced around in desperation, nose wrinkling. What was that strange smell? It reminded her of fireworks.

Deputies emptied out of the squad car. Its headlights cut a swath of light through the darkness, adding its illumination to the pile of debris. Deputy Moyers ran to Lacey's side.

"I'm sorry," Lacey said. "I don't know what to say. I'm pretty sure Sammy thinks the tunnel's here, but this doesn't look like—"

"Do you smell it?" Deputy Moyers asked another deputy.

"Yeah. Smells like gunpowder."

"More like explosives," said a third cop.

"Smells fresh." Deputy Moyers turned to another cop. "Okay, get on the phone. Find somebody who can get a backhoe out here and start moving these rocks. Somebody else go see what you can find about the Barnes-Hecker Mine. A map of the tunnels is what we're looking for. *Move!*"

He turned to the ladies. "If there was a tunnel entrance here, somebody covered his tracks."

Lacey said, "You mean—"

"Your husbands could be in a tunnel buried under that mound. We won't know for sure until somebody digs this place out. Until we know more, I'd advise you ladies to go home and sit tight. I'll call you when I have news."

Gillian bit her lip. *Yeah, right.* Their husbands could be struggling to survive under their very feet, and he expected them to go home? "I'm staying."

Lacey nodded. "Me too."

"Be my guest." Deputy Moyers pointed to where the dirt road opened to the clearing. "But I'd like you to park back there and stay out of our way. It could be a while before we know anything."

The wait was worse than anyone expected.

An hour later, Gillian rubbed droopy eyes. Sammy had fallen asleep on the backseat next to Chase. Lacey had drifted off too, face buried in her arms stretched across the steering wheel.

A backhoe and several other big pieces of machinery Gillian couldn't even name had finally arrived, but they were barely making a dent in the rubble. Gillian glanced at her watch. It was after 11 o'clock. What were they doing sitting here?

She touched Lacey's arm and woke her. "Come on, there's nothing we can do here. We should take Sammy home and put him to bed. Moyers promised to call when he has news, right?"

Gillian hated to admit it, but they needed to return to Lacey's house and do what Emily had recommended: wait and pray.

92

So close now. So close to achieving my final goal.

Cyrus crouched amid towering pines and waited for darkness to descend and the spirits to confirm the timing of his final act.

The game wasn't any fun if he was the only one with any hope of winning, but apparently the investigators were brainless. He'd left plenty of clues, trying to make the game more competitive, yet here he was with virtually no resistance standing in his way. The culmination of his plan felt too easy.

So be it.

He reached into his pouch for the Urim and Thummim and cast them on the forest floor for confirmation that this was the right moment. The glistening rocks said no, so he hunkered down to wait a while longer.

Foraging deer munched on long grass, not even seeing him. When the breeze shifted, sending his scent their direction, they bounded away, primordial instinct and the fear of man kicking in.

In the clearing below, shining in a green cast through his night-vision goggles, stood a large plantation-style house, its many windows alight. A Tahoe was parked out front. On a night as warm as this one, nobody had thought of lighting a fire in the fireplace.

That was good.

Earlier, Lacey and Gillian had driven off with Sammy, just as he expected. The task of digging out what remained of the mine entrance would distract investigators, providing the diversion he needed. Now the women and the boy were back, and he only needed to wait a while longer until he was sure everyone had gone to bed. Oh, how he loved the element of surprise.

He breathed in deeply through his nose, noting the Christmasy scent of pine trees wafting in the air. In some ways he regretted shattering their quiet evening, but he'd waited too long already. God had called him to mete out judgment on this very night, and there was no turning back now.

He pulled out the photos of his son and sorted through them one last time, eyes moist.

He'd always had a soft spot for kids. That's why, when David Koresh had invited him to live at the Mount Carmel Center near Waco, he had such a hard time saying good-bye to his son. He wanted to take Alex along, but his mother wouldn't allow it. She didn't want the Branch Davidians filling his head with what she called "nonsense."

So the children of Waco latched onto his heart instead, and he held David Koresh's dozen or so children in his arms, those who would make up the house of David and help him rule the world in the latter days. How could he forget their innocent eyes and voices?

Then the tanks and the fire came on April 19, and more than 20 children—children he had held in his arms—perished in such a terrible way. He was sure God had spared him to ensure justice for the children.

He chose to remain at Waco after others fled in the wake of the ATF/FBI raid on February 28. He understood the dangers in staying, but many of the children didn't. They had no choice of their own, staying because their parents had told them to. Their innocent blood was shed, and he knew what Scripture demanded: an eye for an eye.

Afterward, he waited for justice that never came. As usual, the government played cover-up and blamed everyone but themselves. The children were never vindicated, and he pleaded with God, begged him to bring justice. Then one night the spirits told him in a dream that God had appointed him for such a task, but it wasn't yet his time—not until his own child died in Iraq.

The burning alive of Waco's children was bad enough, but then his own child was dead—and once again the US government was responsible. Enough was enough. It was the final straw, and on the day of his son's funeral, a plan began to form in his mind.

He would start with the small fish—Dr. Colbert and his lackeys. Then, if the spirits granted success, he would go after the big fish—all those big shots in the government who were responsible for the deaths of those children.

They would go down, every single one of them.

Nearby, an owl hooted. Cyrus stood, adjusted the backpack, which was heavy with reinforcements, and stretched stiff calf muscles. He checked his watch—almost midnight—and waited a while longer until lights flicked off one by one.

A half hour crawled by before he decided to move. But even then, to be certain, he cast the Urim and Thummim on the forest floor once more. The stones appeared wet in the moonlight. His scalp tightened.

A smile crawled across his face.

He backtracked to the grove and the crate he'd delivered earlier.

He eased closer to the crate, the buzzing loud enough to make his palms sweat, and unclasped the latch. With one quick motion he flung the top off and cast himself to the ground. He could only imagine the size of the swarm as it shot into the night.

93

"That's outrageous!" Colbert cried. "There isn't any gold in Michigan's Upper Peninsula. They only mined iron ore in this region."

"I guess you guys have never heard of the Ropes Mine, a gold mine near Ishpeming, not far from here," Quinn said. "I took a look for myself and proved Rutherford Wills right. I even had what I found tested. Guys, there's millions—maybe even billions—of dollars' worth of gold down here."

Marc scrubbed a hand across his bewildered face. "That's amazing, but I still don't understand. What does Turrow have to do with the gold you discovered in this abandoned mine?"

"I met Turrow during one of his many hunting trips in the area. We became friends, and I made the mistake of trusting him. I told him about the gold and agreed to give him a share of the wealth if he kept my secret and provided financial backing for my enterprise, since he seemed to have unlimited wealth. He agreed, as long as I helped him in turn. He'd learned that Dr. Colbert was coming to the resort. He had an old score to settle, he said, and knew exactly what to do."

"The plagues." Weariness seeped through Colbert's voice.

"At the time, his plan seemed like nothing more than an elaborate prank based on a Bible verse. I agreed to help and let him store his supplies out of sight in the mine."

"How did you think you were going to extract all that gold without anybody knowing?" Colbert asked. "Your secret would have come out eventually."

"Turrow said the plagues would be so realistic that they'd spook everybody away from the resort. When the place went out of business, I planned to approach my father-in-law and offer to take the resort off his hands. I never suspected that Turrow had more than a prank in mind—that is, until Jared Russo died."

"Likely story." Colbert snorted. "You knew what Turrow was up to from the beginning. You're just trying to save face."

"I didn't know he planned to murder anybody. Really, you've gotta believe me."

Marc stared into the darkness, not sure what to believe. What Quinn said rang with truth. What was his motive? Perhaps it had been only simple greed, not murder. Quinn clearly lacked Turrow's personal vendetta.

And if Turrow *had* threatened to kill Sammy if Quinn didn't cooperate, his further involvement made sense too. What would a father do to save his son?

Colbert gasped.

"Look!" Gabriel cried.

From across the chasm bobbed a tiny light—so tiny, in fact, that Marc blinked a few times to ensure his eyes weren't playing tricks on him. He sprang to his feet, heart pounding like a jackhammer. Had someone found them?

94

Gillian kept repeating Psalm 34 to herself, praying for sleep to come but knowing it was hopeless, especially when she was facing a second night without Marc at her side.

I will bless the LORD at all times; his praise shall continually be in my mouth.

Even with Marc gone, Lord, I'm supposed to bless you, she prayed.

She hadn't intended to stay the night, but by the time they'd returned to the house, it had been so late that it seemed pointless to head to the hotel. Lacey had graciously agreed to let her sleep in one of the guest rooms and offered her an extra toothbrush.

Gillian lay on the bed. Lacey had said something was wrong with the air-conditioning, so Gillian had opened the windows wide and plugged in the oscillating fan Lacey had provided. Alert as could be, she stared up at the dark ceiling.

My soul shall make its boast in the LORD; the humble shall hear of it and be glad.

That morning they'd joined hundreds of volunteers combing the woods for the missing men, but they'd come up empty handed. She should have been bone weary after all that tromping through the trees in the heat, but she wasn't. If anything, her senses were on high alert.

Oh, this is madness. How am I supposed to sleep with all this heat and worry?

Were Lacey and Sammy sleeping any better than she was?

The big house creaked in the night stillness. Gillian rose on her elbows and glanced around the room, a ribbon of moonlight draped across the crib. Thankfully, the fan hadn't kept Chase awake. It swiveled in her direction, and she delighted in the man-made breeze.

But just then the fan's hum ceased, and the blades spun to a stop. She got up to check the cord; the fan was still plugged in. What was going on—a power outage?

A glance at the bedside digital clock, hazy in the moonlight, confirmed that the power was out. No digital numbers glowed from its display. The last time she'd checked, it was well past midnight.

Great! Now the heat will be even worse to bear, and I won't be able to blow-dry my hair in the—

Behind her, an odd buzzing sound rushed past the window.

Gillian whirled and listened intently at the screen. The odd sound moved farther away, as if following the line of the house. Then it was gone.

She'd never heard anything like it before. A swarm of bees might have made such a sound, but bees didn't swarm in the woods at night, did they?

Maybe that kind of bug activity wasn't so unusual in the north woods, but a power outage was a problem she needed to investigate. Maybe Lacey knew what was going on.

She got up and checked on Chase. He lay on his back fast asleep, a hand curled over his face.

Nothing wakes you, little man.

He would be fine—she didn't plan to be gone for long. She flicked on the baby monitor and clipped the receiver to the waistband of her pants. Then she retrieved a flashlight from the bureau drawer. Just as she turned it on, something landed on her arm. She slapped at the unseen bug, but it darted away.

One of the biggest horseflies she'd ever seen zigzagged across the room and batted against her door as if it wanted out. She grabbed her Jane Austen novel from the bedside table and crept toward the door. Just as she was about to smack the fly, it swung toward the floor, slid under the door, and was gone.

She faced the door and stilled. A low-vibration hum came from somewhere nearby, inside the house. What could it be?

A knock on her door startled her. She opened the door and faced the dark hallway.

A flashlight half lit Lacey's anxious face. "I heard a strange sound in the living room."

"What is it?"

"I don't know. That's why I came to find you."

Gillian sighed. "I was coming anyhow. The power's out."

"It is?"

"Yeah, something's wrong."

Gillian crept forward, Lacey trailing her.

The house waited in unnatural silence. Not a floorboard creaked. Not a curtain rustled in the breeze seeping through screened windows, which Lacey had opened wide to cool the place.

The hardwood floor felt cool under Gillian's bare feet. She crept forward, her flashlight's steady beam cutting a path across a hallway that would have otherwise been lost in blackness.

She spotted a light switch and toggled it. Nothing.

Her hand bumped into a framed piece of artwork on the wall, and she pulled away just in time. The picture teetered, then stilled.

To her right the kitchen beckoned, and they took a detour. Lacey reached for the wall telephone and put it to her ear. "The phone's dead."

In TV shows, bad guys always cut the phone lines before going after their prey.

Something's wrong here.

They left the kitchen and followed the hallway to the spacious living room. Night sounds met Gillian's ears: frogs, crickets, cicadas. A loon called from the other side of the lake, its sound both beautiful and eerie. A whimper emanated from the baby receiver. Chase was stirring, but Gillian wouldn't be away long.

A strange, new sound made Gillian whirl toward the far wall. The sound reminded her of when she made popcorn, kernels bouncing against the plastic top before tumbling out and filling the bowl.

"Do you hear it?" Lacey asked.

"Yeah."

The odd noise came from the fireplace, as if something was trapped inside. She imagined a trapped chipmunk—but no, it didn't sound like an animal. It sounded more like—

She crouched in front of the fireplace and shone her light on closed glass doors. She opened them wide and peered inside, the aroma of old ashes spilling out. She saw nothing but an empty grate and more ashes. Without thinking, she reached for the flue lever and twisted it.

A buzzing mass rushed at her from the darkness.

95

Legs stiff from crouching, Cyrus rose, grabbed the assault rifle, and moved noiselessly through the trees. He reached the house, pressed his body against the white vinyl siding, and listened.

The house was still silent, but that wouldn't last long. He skirted the side of the house, staying well below the windows to avoid being seen.

He froze. A baby's whimper—he was sure he heard it. Now finding the room in question would be as easy as following the boy's cry.

He found the window and took a deep breath. Held it while he stole a peek.

The baby lay in a crib near the window. Tiny hands flailed in the moonlight.

Cyrus' eyes flicked across the dark room and spotted the empty bed. Where was Gillian Thayer? Perfect timing. She'd left the child unattended, just as he hoped.

The baby whimpered again, and he felt his palms sweating. Memories pounced on him without warning.

Tear gas and flames and crying children. Screaming children. The gas masks wouldn't fit their small faces. The tanks used to insert the tear gas had brought part of the building down, blocking the route to the concrete walk-in cooler. There the trapped mothers rocked the children, soothing them under wet blankets used to shield them from the tear gas. But it wasn't enough—it was never enough—and the screams and tears continued until the fire burned them away ... until they and the children were gone forever.

96

Marc drew in a deep breath. "Hello, is somebody there?" His voice echoed across the cavern—from rock to stone and then back again.

"It's probably only Cyrus," Quinn said in a hopeless voice. "Coming to put us out of our misery. He likes to do that, you know, after he inflicts as much misery as possible."

The faintest reply came from the direction of the light. "Hello?"

"It isn't Turrow," Colbert said.

"It's Deputy Moyers!" Excitement energized Gabriel's voice.

The deputy's call shattered the silence. "Is anybody there?"

He can't see us. Marc fumbled for his cell phone and flipped it open so his little light could shine through the darkness. He lifted it high above his head, a childhood song about "this little light of mine" filling his mind.

"We're over here!" Marc shouted. "Can you see us?"

The reply echoed back. "Yes! Marc, is that you?"

"Yes, it's me."

"Who else is there?"

Marc told him and described Quinn's injuries. "He's hurt really bad."

Gabriel and Colbert were on their feet beside him. The combined light from his and Gabriel's cell phones illumined their relieved faces.

The light drew closer, revealing the shape of Moyers and two more deputies; they were about 30 feet away on the other side of the chasm. Moyers shone a flashlight in their direction. The other deputies had flashlights too. The cavern grew brighter, revealing their home over the many maddening hours. Craggy rocks were everywhere, and a rocky ceiling hung high above their heads.

Marc had no idea how Moyers and his men had gotten here, but it hardly mattered. *Thank you, God!* They were going to get out of this place.

"We need a way across!" he shouted across the chasm. "Do you see a ladder?" Likely Turrow had tossed the ladder into the chasm.

"We brought our own!" Moyers yelled back.

Marc's heart lifted. Strange shadows flickered across the cavern as Moyers and his men wrestled with something in the dark. Moments later, Marc sensed rather than saw something sweep through the darkness and land with a metallic clang at the chasm's edge.

He shuffled forward to see and flipped open his cell phone again. The light was enough to reveal a shiny, aluminum extension ladder spanning the chasm.

Marc felt giddy at the thought of escape. They could leave this place, but what about Quinn? He was in no condition to cross the makeshift bridge.

Colbert must have read Marc's mind. "Don't worry, Quinn. We'll send help back for you."

"You guys go on ahead," Quinn said from the shadows. "I don't much like the idea of crossing that chasm on a small ladder anyhow."

Marc wasn't so sure either. Crossing meant inching across on his hands and knees. If either end of the ladder didn't rest securely on level ground, the whole thing could teeter under their weight and tumble into the chasm. His palms moistened at the thought.

"We should cross one at a time," Gabriel said. "I'll go first, unless we want to flip a coin."

"No, you go ahead," Colbert said.

Yeah, you be the guinea pig. If the ladder shifted and Gabriel fell, wouldn't part of him feel a little glad? Marc tightened his jaw, stunned by his own thoughts. *Jesus, forgive me.*

"Heights have never bothered me." Gabriel got down on hands and knees and began shuffling across the aluminum frame, moving forward in fluid, confident motions. It was a tough act to follow. Marc wondered if he would be as confident when his turn came.

Somewhere in the distance echoed a sound like distant thunder. The ground began to rumble beneath their feet.

"Hold on, Gabriel!" Colbert cried.

Marc ducked for cover.

97

Gillian fell onto her backside and dropped the flashlight in surprise. She instinctively raised her arms to shield her face. Hundreds, if not thousands, of buzzing, whirring, darting insects poured out of the fireplace and into the room.

She cried out and pressed her face into the crook of an arm, eyes squeezed shut. Whatever the bugs were, they were burrowing into her hair, brushing her cheeks, landing on her bare arms. But they weren't biting. At least not yet.

In the darkness she couldn't tell what the bugs were. Didn't care. She just wanted—needed—to get away from them.

She waved her hands in a frenzy before her face, batting them away from her nose and eyes. Several varmints tried to burrow inside her ears, and she smacked them too. She looked for Lacey but couldn't see her in the dark. Simultaneously rising and batting at bugs around her head, Gillian grabbed the flashlight and dashed to the sliding patio doors.

Already there, Lacey shoved one of the doors open and stepped outside. Gillian followed and hoped the largest horseflies she'd ever seen, now illuminated by her flashlight, would follow them outside.

But the flies didn't seem interested. Even the flashlight, which normally attracted bugs, did little to get their attention. *What do they want?*

Gillian recognized the horseflies as the same kind as the one she'd seen in her room, the kind that could bite and cause pain.

If enough attacked their prey at the same time, there was no doubt in her mind that they could kill if they were just plain mad enough.

She heard Chase from the baby receiver; he was crying now. She knew he would be fine—he would just cry himself back to sleep. Unless … unless the flies were going after him, too.

Panic tightened her chest. She had to check on him—she had to be sure he was okay. But how could she get to him with so many flies blocking the way?

The insects darted around the room in one writhing, aimless frenzy. She instinctively stepped back, hoping they wouldn't come after her.

If they did, then what? At least she could run. But where? To the lake?

How on earth did they get in the fireplace? Did something hatch in there?

The roiling swarm drifted across the room and disappeared deeper into the house. It was on the move.

Moments later a child's scream pierced the night.

It was as if an icicle stabbed her chest.

Sammy!

98

Marc cowered against the rock wall with Colbert and Gabriel, who had wisely abandoned the ladder. He blinked into dusty darkness. How long before the unstable mine caved in and pulverized them like chalk?

The whole place shook. Rocks, pebbles, and sand tumbled onto their heads. Along with the shaking came the groan of rocks, some weighing tons, as the seismic disturbance wrenched them out of place and toppled them over.

God, please save us. Please let us see our loved ones again.

When the strange hail tapered off, Marc rushed to the chasm's edge, surprised to see the ladder still in place. But another sight made his breath catch in his throat. A fissure had opened in the cavern wall near Moyers and his men, glimmering in the light of his flashlight. A torrent of water gushed from the fissure and cascaded into the chasm.

"Moyers, are you okay?"

A faint cry echoed over the roar of the gushing water. "Yes, but hurry!"

The sudden flood could erode their place to stand. How long before the water washed them into the chasm?

Marc shouted to the others. "Come on, we've got to get out of here!"

"Oh, no!" Quinn said. "It's just like 1926. Water's gonna flood the tunnels and drown all of us."

History repeats itself. Wasn't the axiom often true?

Marc pushed the thought away. "Gabriel, you first."

Gabriel scrambled onto the ladder and moved quickly. The ladder creaked beneath him but didn't budge.

A minute later Gabriel reached the other side and gave a whoop. Marc ached to cross the ladder and get out of this place, but he turned to Colbert. "You go next. I'll bring up the rear."

Colbert's voice shook. "I don't know if I can do it. Sometimes I get vertigo."

"You're wasting time," Marc said between clenched teeth. "If you want to live, you've got to go now!"

Colbert lowered himself onto the rungs.

"Come on, Dr. Colbert!" Gabriel shouted from the other side. "You can do it!"

Behind Marc, the wall of rock cracked and splintered. He whirled.

Water seeped out, at first a tiny trickle. The trickle widened to a spurting stream. Then a blast exploded out of the rock with the strength of a fire hose, as if a spigot had been opened deep in the earth. The flood drenched his feet and gushed along the cleft where they'd been waiting and praying for help. It obeyed the law of gravity and rushed toward the cliff, pouring into the chasm.

How long before the water overflowed the chasm, washing them all away? If the chasm was deeper than the Empire State Building was tall, they had some time. But how much?

The rock wall disintegrated before Marc's eyes. Something white and elongated emerged from the crumbling dirt and rock. The flood washed the dirt and ore away, revealing a skeleton in a miner's hat—one of the 41 lost miners.

The fissure widened and morphed into a gushing river, pushing the skeleton past Marc, toward the cliff, and into the chasm. More rock crumbled, and something golden glittered in the half-light.

Gold? It hardly mattered now.

Colbert finished his trek. "I made it!" he called. "Hurry, Marc!"

Marc hustled toward the ladder, but the river gushing from the rock wall blasted down in a torrent. Struck the ladder. Wrenched it out of place.

Marc surged forward on glistening, slippery rock. "No!"

99

The dream shattered. Turrow blinked and remembered where he was—back to reality. The assault rifle in his arms. The whimpering baby.

Ever since he'd seen the boy's likeness to his own Alex, he hadn't been able to get the child off his mind. For days he'd been toying with the idea of snatching this baby and keeping him as his own.

Why not?

His son had been cruelly snatched from him, and he could never have him back. He'd secretly obtained some of his blood after his death in Iraq, hoping for advancements in cloning so he could create a new Alex. But when would technological advancements ever make such a dream possible?

Perhaps the plan was pure fantasy, but here was something tangible. He could save this one precious soul, though he'd been unable to save the children of Waco. Could start again. Be a father again. David Koresh had assembled his own house of David through multiple women. Why not a house of Cyrus?

The baby cried, as if calling out to the fatherly instinct flickering in his heart.

Sudden cries from the front of the house, loud through open windows, jerked his head around. A smile played on his lips. Earlier he'd climbed onto the roof and removed the chimney cap, which routinely prevented entry to animals and bugs.

But not this time. The flies would seek an entry point, and the chimney provided the best one in the house.

An eye for an eye.

Colbert's negligence had killed Alex, so Sammy Caruthers would die in his place.

But he didn't just want Sammy to die; he wanted Satan himself, the lord of the flies, to claim the boy. If the flies weren't enough, then he would finish him off himself. After all, mercy killings had always been his specialty—after prolonging as much suffering as possible.

Earlier, when the women had driven off with the boy, he'd stolen into the house—Quinn had given him a key, after all—and poured the pheromones where they would do the most good: on Sammy's clothes and sheets.

The pheromones would drive the flies crazy, push them into attack mode. The boy would provide a veritable feast. In many ways, he wished he could be a fly on the wall so he could watch the spectacle.

The sound of the crying baby roused him. He had time—and what a perfect diversion. He could grab the child, hide him in the woods, and return for him later after he was finished.

He gripped the assault rifle. He needed assurance that Colbert's whelp was dead. Put Sammy out of his misery, if necessary, then take the baby before hightailing out of here. Head south. Cross the border to Mexico. Start a new life with his son, the new Alex.

Yes, he could do this.

He pulled out his bowie knife, slit the window screen, and climbed into the bedroom. Then he flicked off the baby monitor.

100

Lacey raced past Gillian on her way to Sammy's room, and Gillian made a quick decision. She needed to know if Chase was okay and paused in the dark hallway, clutching the baby receiver. It was silent now. Chase must have gone back to sleep. Relief washed over her, and she stuffed the receiver into her pocket before racing after Lacey.

Every scream punctuating the silence slammed her heart into her rib cage. They sped into the dark, buzzing bedroom, rushing toward the little boy on the bed in the dark. He was one writhing mass of flailing arms, kicking feet, and panicked cries for help. A strange, pungent odor filled the room.

Gillian didn't need her flashlight to perceive the mass of swarming flies. The bedroom was like one massive hive, the mother lode of bugs. The surreal, low-vibration gathering of so many flies in one place was unlike anything Gillian had experienced before. Her flesh crawled. Her instincts yelled at her to get out, but Sammy needed their help.

But why had the flies come here? Why were they going after Sammy?

Marc had said something about pheromones. The natural chemicals had attracted the gnats and mosquitoes to Tessa McCormack. Was the same thing going on here?

She wasn't sure if Sammy's cries were out of fear of the flies or because the flies were actually biting him. Then the sight revealed in the beam of her flashlight shoved Gillian's heart into her throat.

The flies covered every inch of Sammy's little body except for his wide, panicked eyes and the small hole of his crying mouth.

"Leave him alone, you monsters!" Lacey yelled.

She batted and smashed flies with her hands, even if that meant slapping Sammy's little body. Gillian joined in, crushing as many flies as she could, bug guts slicking her hands. She moaned, half in desperation, half in revulsion.

The flies must have seen her and Lacey as attackers because they went after them too. Needle-sharp stings on Gillian's arms and neck gave her a taste of what Sammy was enduring. She cried out in pain and surprise but kept on the attack, angry and desperate.

Please, God, help us!

It wasn't working. There were too many flies. As soon as they crushed them, others filled the gap.

"Got any bug spray?" Gillian yelled over the unnerving drone.

"Bathroom!" Lacey shouted back.

Gillian grabbed her flashlight off the floor where she'd dropped it and surged toward the hallway. She wasn't sure where the bathroom was. She guessed and dashed into an open doorway.

Bingo! She ripped open drawers and cabinets. Her panicked hands fumbled over cosmetics, lotions, shampoos. Shaving cream. Baby powder. Hydrogen peroxide. Mouth wash.

She brushed sweat out of her eyes so she could see.

Nothing. There wasn't any bug repellant.

Had whoever sent the flies also removed the bug spray from the house?

She hurtled back to Sammy's room, the drone of swarming flies loud, Sammy and Lacey's cries even louder.

"There isn't any spray!" Gillian yelled.

"Yes, there is!" Lacey cried. "I know there is."

"No, it's gone! Somebody took it."

Think, Gillian. Think.

Pheromones sprayed or poured onto Sammy's pajamas and bedding could be the only reason for the flies' frenzied attack. Was that the pungent odor she was smelling?

"We've gotta get him to the bathroom!" Gillian cried.

"What?" Lacey's voice teetered on the brink of hysteria.

"We need to give him a shower! Now!"

101

Marc slipped on the wet rock, toppled backward, and slammed down hard on his already-aching back. He gasped, struggling to breathe. The torrent of water pushed him toward the cliff and the yawning chasm.

He rolled onto his belly in a panic, grasped at a rocky outcropping midway to the cliff's edge, and held on with both hands. His legs flailed into empty space, his heart shoved somewhere near his ankles.

Next came the scrape of aluminum.

The ladder!

Marc couldn't see, but his mind filled in the gaps. The ladder had toppled into the chasm. It was gone forever. Despair wormed into his gut.

Shouts echoed over the roar of the cascade, but he couldn't tell what the others were saying. It sounded like they were cheering him on. But to what?

He was doomed. Without the ladder he had no way to cross the chasm. He glanced toward the cleft where Quinn had been lying, but the man had vanished.

Had the flood washed him into the chasm? Now it was his turn.

God, please help me!

The ear-splitting, wrenching sound of boulders being crushed and torn apart threatened to deafen him. Something massive and unseen swept through the dark and slammed into the rocky floor only a yard away.

He couldn't tell what it was. Had a gargantuan boulder fallen from the ceiling and now lay at the cliff's edge? Or perhaps it had lodged into the chasm itself. He had no way of knowing.

A voice. Gabriel was yelling at him. What was he saying?

"The rock, Marc!"

What about it?

"Cross over on the rock!"

The rock was really that big? Big enough to bridge the chasm?

Colbert called out, "Hurry, Marc! Hurry!"

Marc gripped the outcropping with tired, shaky hands. His strength was almost gone, but he somehow pulled himself to his knees. The water pummeled him as if from a massive wave pool.

He held onto the rock with his left hand and let go with his right. Reached toward the rocky mass. His fingertips barely brushed it.

Gabriel called, "Let go, Marc! Let go and grab the rock!"

Let go? How could he? The torrent would wash him into the chasm.

"Let go, Marc! Have faith!"

Faith. The substance of things hoped for, the evidence of things unseen.

He knew what faith was all about. He who couldn't see had to trust Gabriel's eyes. But could he trust Gabriel? He had no choice—he had to let go.

102

Gillian wedged the flashlight into her armpit and grabbed Sammy's feet while Lacey latched onto his shoulders. They jerked their faces away from the swarm and lifted him, hustling him toward the doorway. The flies were apparently coming along for the ride.

They carried him to the bathroom and unloaded him in the shower. Lacey turned on the faucet. Warm, cold—it didn't matter.

The water blasted down, strong at first. Then it petered off to a trickle. And stopped.

Gillian stared at the faucet in dismay. The power was out. Now the water was gone too?

Somebody's doing this on purpose. The thought chilled her.

"Where's your main water valve?" Gillian shouted.

"What?"

"Your main water valve. Do you know where it is?"

"You're asking me?" Lacey shook hands in front of her face. "In the basement somewhere, I guess. How am I supposed to know?"

Gillian shook her head. *This is why wives should never let their husbands do all their thinking for them.*

The bathroom echoed with Sammy's pathetic cries. The flies were still eating him alive. Fly bites hurt, but could they kill? She didn't want to find out.

"Come on!" Gillian shouted.

"Where are we going?"

"To the lake." It was the closest water source.

They lifted Sammy and carried him again. Flies swarmed on Gillian's bare arms and legs, but she ignored them. They stumbled down the stairs and through the dark hallway toward the living room and the sliding patio doors.

They set writhing Sammy down on the floor beside the doors, the biting flies seemingly omnipresent. Gillian didn't know how much more of his cries she could take.

God, please make it stop.

Lacey slid the screen door open. Gillian bent, reached for Sammy, and lifted him. He embraced her, legs wrapped around her waist. Her back strained, but she ignored the pain.

Lacey played defense, smacking flies, while Gillian carried the boy through the door, down back steps, across the lawn, and away from the house. Lingering flies bit Sammy's back through his shirt before Lacey could stop them. He cried out.

Gillian tried to shush him and realized they both were crying. "Not much longer, Sammy! Hold on!"

The moon was full. The night sky was as clear as crystal, pinpricked by stars. They passed a cobblestone entertaining area. An outdoor fireplace. Wicker furniture. A stainless steel outdoor grill.

Lacey dashed ahead with her flashlight to light the way. They left the lawn for a winding path bordered by brush and saplings.

Gillian's gaze darted right and left, searching for anything out of place. Whoever had orchestrated this attack might be watching. For some reason he seemed dead set on one thing: Sammy's misery. If he was hunting them, Sammy's cries would tell him exactly where they were.

Panting, Gillian sucked in great gulps of air. Spat out a few stowaway flies and kept going. Pushed herself past the pain. Flies bit her neck, but she ignored them.

She winced, almost out of strength. Sammy was too heavy.

Lacey grabbed his legs.

Better.

The lake. Shining in the moonlight. Fifty feet away. Not far now.

Flies can't go underwater, but we can.

The flies weren't leaving. The writhing, darting mass enveloped them. They were truly in the eye of the storm.

Come on, come on! Gillian moved as quickly as her straining legs could carry her. She gasped for breath, body drenched in sweat. Flies tried to get into her eyes. She jerked her head away from them.

Through small trees the lake sparkled in the moonlight, a most glorious sight. Not far now, and the pathway opened to a small clearing with a fire pit and a dock beyond.

Thirty feet! They were going to make it.

Two feet away, automatic gunfire shredded a sapling into ribbons.

Gillian and Lacey dove off the path, taking Sammy with them.

103

Marc steeled his resolve and let go of the outcropping. He rolled toward the rock, arms outstretched toward its mass as gushing water pummeled his body. He hugged the slab, embracing it as if it were Jesus himself. The relief crashing through him was unlike anything he'd experienced before.

The others cheered, their excited voices faint but discernable over the cascade's roar.

Groaning, wrenching sounds of the cavern's ceiling breaking apart belched from the heart of the earth. The whole place trembled as if from an earthquake.

He didn't have much time.

Marc climbed the rock's craggy side, reached the top, and crawled on hands and knees. Unable to see much through the shadowy haze of flickering flashlight beams diffused by falling pebbles and muck, he listened for the voices. He knew which way to go by their sound.

"Run, Marc!" It was Colbert this time. "Get up and run!"

Run! How can I run? I can't even see.

"Stand up, Marc!" Moyers cried.

Marc rose on trembling legs. His line of sight changed, no longer obscured by the rock itself. Flashlight beams from the other side merged like a shining beacon, illuminating the rugged, massive wedge spanning the chasm.

Now he could see.

Now he could get to the other side.

He would survive because of this rock, this bridge to freedom.

Marc ran.

104

Weeds and brush scraped against Gillian's face. She braced her elbows and lifted her torso, gasping.

On her knees she peeked above the brush and searched the moonlit world for the source of the gunfire. She saw nothing but trees and the dark house hulking in the distance. Night sounds surrounded her, the warm night air humid. She glanced toward the lake and spied the fire pit through the brush, even a few half-burned logs.

Whoever had orchestrated the fly attack was now shooting at them. But who? Turrow?

Who else could it be? But why was he going after Sammy?

"Stay down!" Gillian crouched amid brambles and ferns, wondering what to do. Meanwhile, Sammy kept howling.

"What now?" Lacey slapped at flies.

"I don't know." Gillian's mind raced. "Do you have your cell phone?"

"No."

"Me neither." In all the confusion she'd left it in her room. Thank God she'd also left Chase in the safety of the house. Would he be okay in his crib with her gone so long? The baby monitor remained silent, but maybe she was out of range.

Silence. No more gunfire. If Turrow planned to kill them, what was he waiting for? Maybe he was approaching them now to finish the job.

Another thought bloomed in her mind: Maybe his only intent was to prevent them.

He doesn't want us to reach the lake. He doesn't want Sammy to survive.

Thoughts clicked.

If Colbert was Pharaoh, Sammy was Pharaoh's son.

Turrow, the angel of death, was going after the firstborn son.

The realization took her breath away.

The lake was only a dozen or so yards away now, the gentle lap of its waters caressing her ears. They were so tantalizingly close to help—so close, yet so far away. Should they make a mad dash for the water?

Lacey sounded unhinged. "We've gotta get Sammy into the water. Now. I'm afraid if we don't—" She broke off.

Gillian bit her lip. How many more bites before Sammy's condition turned serious? "The shooter can't possibly see all of us if we stay low. Maybe I can crawl away, swing around from behind, and take him from the rear." The plan sounded ludicrous even as she spoke the words.

"You mean attack him?" Lacey sounded incredulous. "You don't even know where he is."

Not to mention that she didn't have anything to use for defense other than the flashlight.

God, what are we supposed to do? If we go to the lake, Turrow will cut us down—I'm sure of it. But if we stay here, Sammy could die.

"Look, we can't just sit here," Lacey cried. "We've gotta do something."

Gillian glanced at the fire pit, and another idea sparked. "Hey, remember when you lit that candle earlier? You don't still happen to have those matches, do you?"

105

Marc ran.

Colbert, Gabriel, and the others were only yards away, faces expectant. They reached toward him and yelled his name.

The rock bridge beneath Marc trembled and lurched. Marc's eyes widened. The bridge shifted, buckled, began to give way.

No!

His adrenaline rushed. Marc leaped toward their outstretched arms as the bridge and his stomach plunged. He flew toward the ledge but realized too late that he lacked enough momentum to land on his feet.

His body slammed into the rocky edge, arms groping toward Colbert's feet. His hands scrambled for something to hold onto. His fingers clawed, like tines on a rake, toward the brink, fingernails splitting.

He ignored the pain and gripped the cliff's edge with both hands, legs kicking into the void of the chasm, heart bucking in his chest.

Colbert, Gabriel, Moyers—they reached toward him and shouted his name. His straining hands were slipping—he couldn't hold on. His fingers weakened—but just as he lost his hold on the rock, he grabbed someone's wrist with both hands.

He felt himself going down, the fatal plunge. But the arm held him in place. Lifted him.

Marc peered up, eyes stinging with sweat, every muscle in his arms straining.

He clung to Gabriel's arm.

Gabriel groaned and lifted Marc, face reddening with exertion. Colbert and Moyers locked their arms around Gabriel's middle, providing the needed fulcrum.

"Hold on, Marc!" Gabriel shouted. "God help me, I'm not letting go!"

But Gabriel had every right to let go. Marc had misjudged Gabriel, had condemned him in his mind. But Gabriel wasn't letting go; he was doing the right thing, regardless of what Marc thought of him.

Gabriel pulled. Marc felt himself being lifted. Up to the cliff. Over the edge. His chest and then his legs slid onto solid, wet ground. He scrambled to his knees and longed to kiss the ground—kiss all of them. But he had only a second to rest before Colbert and Gabriel grabbed his arms and lifted him to his feet.

The flooded ground began crumbling beneath them. They dashed away from the edge just as it slipped away and plunged into the depths. Moyers led the way with his men and their flashlights. They abandoned the collapsing cavern and ran up the growling tunnel as fast as their feet could carry them.

106

Cyrus leaned against a tree and watched their green, huddled shapes in the brush through his goggles. One larger shape pulled down low and vanished from sight. He searched again. Only two shapes remained. Where had the woman gone?

They thought they were so clever, but they weren't fooling anyone. Maybe she planned the ludicrous—to get a gun from the house and try surprising him from behind. He shook his head. *Nobody could be that stupid.*

Cyrus rose from his cover, pulled on his heavy backpack, and gripped the rifle. He needed to finish this and get out of here before the police arrived.

Time for the final kill.

Adrenaline coursed through his veins. His favorite fix.

He tromped through the brush toward the lake, not caring about the racket he made. He broke from the trees, hands tight around the rifle, and jogged down the path. Twenty feet from where one woman and Sammy cowered in the brush, he pulled up.

One woman had taken a chance and left their cover. She crouched beside the fire pit. What was she doing?

The nerve!

He surged forward.

Flames leaped up.

He held back.

No! He hated fire above all else.

Flames licked up the walls, rippled across the ceiling, and reached for the children of Waco. Their cries of torment from the tear gas rent the air, and the mothers rocked them, whispered that it would all be over soon. He heard their cries and wanted to end their suffering, but the way was blocked. He couldn't get in. He could only save himself through a hole in the wall and burn his face on the way out—

Cyrus snapped back to the moment, felt himself sweating. Fingers absently trailed along the pulsing scar on his neck.

He clenched his teeth and cursed himself for his stupidity. He should have used more attack pheromones in Sammy's bed. Now the fire would help keep the flies away. Sammy might yet survive.

Rage coursed through his veins. No, not on his watch. The boy was going down.

Forget the flies. It had all come down to this. The game was almost over, and he had the final play. They were going down now—all of them. Collateral damage if need be.

He was going to end this once and for all, even if that meant braving the dreaded flames and hunting them down one by one.

He raised the rifle to his shoulder, took aim at the brush where they huddled, and pulled the trigger.

107

It was working! Hope flared in Gillian's heart.

Flames leaped high from the pile of dry kindling and logs. The flies were drawing back.

They'd taken a risk, left their hiding spot, and used the tall brush for cover so they could crawl closer to the fire pit. If they couldn't get to the lake, fire was their second-best option to save Sammy's life. So far, their adversary hadn't responded with any reprisal, but they were far from safe.

The fire made them easier to hunt down, but did they have a choice?

While Gillian searched the underbrush for more twigs, staying low, Lacey sat and cradled Sammy across her lap, as close to the fire as she could get without singeing them both.

Exhausted from the attack, Sammy finally slept, his breathing shallow. Ugly, bloody bites dotted his face and neck. *Will he be okay?* Gillian had no idea.

An occasional horsefly ventured close, risking the fire's heat. But either Lacey shooed it away or the flames consumed it.

Gillian paused and listened. Nothing. Would help come soon? Surely someone had heard the gunfire and reported it to the—

A burst of automatic gunfire broke the silence.

Gillian gasped and fell flat.

Bullets slammed into the small tree near Lacey's head. She flattened herself on the ground, pulling Sammy down beside her.

Another bullet zipped into the brush. Cold fire traced a burning line across Gillian's leg. She yelped.

The gunfire ceased. Gillian groaned.

Lacey rose on her elbows. "Are you okay?"

"I think I've been hit!" Gillian gritted her teeth and wondered if she might pass out. The burning in her leg mushroomed into pure agony.

She was bleeding, but how badly? Had the bullet severed a major artery? She couldn't tell, and she didn't want to turn on her flashlight to find out. Turrow would know for sure where they were. Then again, didn't he know already? Maybe the fire wasn't the wisest—

Another blast of gunfire. Ferns danced.

A half gasp, half moan. Lacey fell on her back.

Gillian's breath caught in her throat. "Lacey," she whispered, voice frantic, "Lacey, are you okay?"

No response. Dread froze her blood in her veins.

She rolled onto her belly and crawled closer on her elbows, dragging her burning leg. She moved too quickly and slowed, lightheaded. Firelight illuminated the growing circle of red on Lacey's side. At least she still appeared to be breathing.

Panic threatened to strangle Gillian. Turrow was done playing games. He meant to kill them all now.

Her eyes flicked from side to side, mind racing. What could she do? Where could she go? The pain in her leg pulsed with every heartbeat.

Nearby, a baby wailed. She froze.

Chase!

She knew his cry anywhere. But she'd left him in the house. *How—*

Three feet away, something passed between her and the flames, blocking the light.

Gillian lay still and closed her eyes. Played dead. But through one eye slit she could see.

A camouflaged man wearing a backpack stood near the fire, a rifle in his hands. Firelight flickered across his face.

Turrow.

When he glanced her direction, she held her breath, kept her body still, and waited for the seconds to crawl by. Perhaps he saw the blood and was drawing conclusions. Assuming the worst.

When she peeked again, Turrow had turned away.

Chase was crying, but she couldn't see him. Where was he?

Rage boiled inside her. Turrow had taken her child, but he wasn't getting away with it, not while she had breath in her lungs. She couldn't just lie here; she had to do something. Besides, both Lacey and Sammy needed medical attention.

Turrow turned to Sammy and crouched low, studying his face. Yes, Colbert's firstborn son appeared to be his main concern. Thankfully, Sammy was asleep. If he were awake, what would he have thought of dear Uncle Austin now?

A small, teary face peeked over the top of Turrow's backpack.

Fear, shock, and rage intertwined in Gillian's heart.

Chase was howling in Turrow's backpack.

How dare he!

Maternal instinct tempted her to confront Turrow now, but such a move would have been reckless. It was all she could do to lie still, pray, and wait for the right moment. But what could she do?

Turrow rose and mumbled something under his breath, the rifle gripped in his hands. "An eye for an eye, a tooth for a tooth."

Sammy. He was going to shoot Sammy.

Gillian tensed. She couldn't let him do this. She had to do something. Now.

Turrow said, "This is for you, Alex, and for the children."

She raised a knee, shifted her weight to her good leg, and pressed her foot to the ground. Summoned what strength she had left.

Turrow lifted the rifle. Aimed it at Sammy.

Now!

In one fluid motion Gillian rose on her good leg, grunting through her pain, and hurtled herself toward Turrow.

The rifle swung her direction. Gunfire spat. Missed.

She tackled his legs. He toppled and dropped the rifle, thrusting his hands forward to break his fall. He rolled away, just missing the flames.

Chase toppled clear of the backpack and the fire, crying. He was only feet away from her.

Gillian pushed herself past the agony in her leg. She rose on one elbow and reached for the dropped rifle beside Sammy, but it was just beyond her fingertips.

Turrow rose and came at her. He pulled out a handgun and pointed it at her head, panting through clenched teeth. "Now you're gonna die."

Gillian braced herself.

108

Something leaped through the fire-dancing shadows. A man tackled Turrow and slammed his arm down on the ground. The gun went off once, twice—stray bullets streaking into the brush. Then the gun went flying.

Gillian gasped. *Dr. Colbert!* Where had he come from?

The men rolled, but the contest would be short lived. Turrow was wiry and strong, while Colbert was overweight and out of shape.

Gillian reached for Chase and pulled him close. His wails split the night.

Turrow kneed Colbert in the groin, and Colbert groaned. Turrow bounded to his feet, anger sizzling in his eyes. He grabbed the rifle, removed the spent magazine, and shoved a new one in.

Fool! She shouldn't have let him have the rifle so easily. They were dead now unless—

Colbert rolled to his feet. He reached for the rifle, and the two men fought for it. The assault rifle spat a *rat-a-tat-tat* into the brush. The gunfire missed Gillian and Chase by a mere foot.

Blood roared in Gillian's ears. *Where did the handgun go?* She searched the brush.

There. Near Lacey. Something silvery in the light. Just inches from her hand. Maybe target shooting with Marc would finally pay off.

Turrow brought the rifle butt back and cracked it against Colbert's jaw. Colbert's head snapped back.

They would all die if she didn't do something.

One arm around the baby, Gillian reached the other for the handgun. Felt its coolness in her hand.

Turrow lifted the rifle, aimed it at Colbert.

Gillian swung the handgun up—it was surprisingly heavy. She pulled the trigger.

The pistol bucked in her hand. Her arm swung wild.

Turrow groaned, dropped the rifle, and clutched a shoulder with reddening fingers. He toppled onto his back three feet from the flames, a stunned expression on his face.

Gillian dropped the gun, hand shaking. *God forgive me— I shot a man.*

Chase's cries rose to a fever pitch.

Turrow writhed. He arched his back and reached bloody hands toward the backpack as if he'd been impaled on something sharp from behind.

Gillian pulled Chase close, stomach heaving as if she might be sick. Thankfully, Chase was no longer in Turrow's backpack. But had something else been crushed by his fall?

Colbert rose and grabbed the rifle, cradling his jaw with one hand while pointing the rifle at Turrow just in case. But Turrow wasn't getting up.

"No!" Turrow's face twisted in agony. "The vials."

He rolled onto his side, wrestled off the backpack, and thrust it away, as if not wanting it anywhere near him. From inside came the tinkle of broken glass. The backpack appeared to be covered in something wet. Blood?

A pungent odor assaulted Gillian's nose. No, it wasn't blood. She recognized the foul stench from Sammy's bed. The backpack must have been filled with more pheromones in glass tubes.

"No!" Turrow said in a raspy voice. "Too much pheromone!"

Colbert backed away, eyes cutting to Gillian. "What's he talking about?"

Turrow turned panicky eyes toward Colbert. "Help me, please! Help me get to the lake. Hurry!"

Colbert's confused eyes met Gillian's gaze, an unspoken message passing between them. Could they really trust Turrow enough to help him? Besides, before they provided help, Turrow needed to be restrained. At least they could call an amb—

A low-frequency vibration filled the night. It was coming from everywhere as if they were surrounded by one mighty, malignant swarm.

Gillian's skin crawled. *No, not again.*

Colbert glanced around uneasily and stepped away from Turrow.

Horseflies burst from the brush and trees, thousands of them massing as one. They sped at Turrow, attacking him where he lay.

Turrow screamed. Apparently, he wasn't close enough to the fire to make a difference. The pheromones were too strong.

Gillian turned her face away and shielded Chase. Between cries, Turrow begged them to help him. But what could she do? She needed to get Chase out of here, but could she even walk?

Horseflies darted around Gillian's face. Panic seized her. The size of the swarm was astonishing. Would it turn on her and Chase too?

More agonizing screams.

To the lake. Gotta get to the lake.

Gillian held onto Chase with one arm and used the other to drag her body toward the lake, pushing with her good foot. The water wasn't far now. Maybe she would make it before the flies finished feeding on Turrow and came after her and Chase.

A hand clamped around her arm and lifted her to her knees. It was Colbert. He hauled Sammy over one shoulder. With the other arm, he slung her free arm around his neck, and she leaned on him and her good leg for support.

Together, they hobbled away from the swarm and toward the safety of the lake.

109

"Gillian. Gillian?"

The voice sounded like Marc, but surely she was dreaming. Wasn't he buried under a pile of rocks somewhere? The rubble stretched for hundreds of miles, and in her dream she was desperately heaving one heavy rock after another, blouse soaked in sweat, fingernails broken. She had to hurry—he was running out of air. He—

"Gillian, can you hear me?"

Gillian blinked through the fog, head woozy, and gauged her surroundings. Bland hospital room. A familiar antiseptic smell. She'd always hated hospitals. Now she was not only in one—she was a patient.

Marc's familiar face came into focus. She wasn't dreaming; he *was* alive. He held her hand, an IV trailing from her inner forearm.

She sighed and worked her lips, mouth pasty. "I'm so glad you're okay. Where have you been? I was worried sick."

He graced her with tender eyes. "I'll explain."

Her head whirled. "Where's Chase?"

"He's here. He's fine."

"I feel really weird."

"You're on pain meds for your leg."

My leg? Everything came back in an avalanche. She and Colbert carrying Sammy and Chase to the lake in spite of her wounded leg. Splashing in the cold water away from the flies, glad to be alive. An ambulance wailing in the distance. Her heart aching for a lost friend.

She tried to sit up, but Marc held her down. "Hey, take it slow."

"But Lacey. Turrow shot her. She—"

"She lost a lot of blood, and they had to do surgery, but she's going to be fine. Sammy's going to be okay too, though he's going to have a few battle scars to show his friends."

His face sobered, his voice thick. "Lacey's gonna need your support. Quinn didn't make it."

She lifted a hand to her face. "Oh, no. What happened?"

He told her. Her heart twisted. Lacey would need her friendship now more than ever. "Turrow?"

Conviction firmed his voice. "Dead." He sighed and touched her face. "Sounds like you had quite the adventure and, as usual, while I was gone." Bandages covered his fingers.

"Marc, what happened to your hands? And why the crutches?"

He gave her the whole story and concluded with how Gabriel had helped save his life.

So the two of them had finally met. She was glad. "Is Gabriel okay?"

"He's on crutches like I am. A lot of rocks fell on us on our way out of the mine. He dropped by earlier to see you, but you were still asleep." He paused. "He's a good man, Gillian. I had my doubts about him at first, but he's more than proved himself. I still don't know what's up with that old letter, but Gabriel couldn't be responsible. You should have seen how he and Dr. Colbert helped me get out of that terrible place."

"Dr. Colbert. Is he okay?"

"Other than dehydration and some bruises and scratches, he's better off than the rest of us."

"Mom?"

Gillian jerked her head around. Someone moved toward her. Blue eyes. Curly blond hair. Chase in her arms.

Delight washed over her. "Crystal!" She must have been patiently awaiting her turn.

Her daughter handed Chase to Marc and hugged her, smelling faintly of her favorite perfume. "I'm so glad you're okay. I came as soon as I could."

"I'm so glad." Gillian cupped a hand to her daughter's face. "Now we'll have time to catch up on your summer."

Marc stood. "Are you ready for a few more visitors?"

Gillian combed fingers through tangled locks. She must look a sight, and she didn't even have a mirror. But what did it matter now?

Emily wore a bigger smile this morning than the one Gillian remembered from a couple of days ago. Riley had pulled through and was going to survive, though he faced a long recovery before he would feel like his old self again. Even then, he could struggle with long-term impairments like chronic cough, fatigue, memory problems, and depression. They would have to wait and see how he responded to treatment, but at least he was alive.

After Emily left, Crystal turned confused eyes toward Gillian. "Okay, I still don't get what happened here. Could somebody just start at the beginning and explain?"

So Marc did, with Gillian interjecting comments here and there. They concluded with Dr. Colbert's secret about his son's identity.

"But why would anybody keep someone a secret like that?" Crystal asked. "I mean, regardless of what happened, Sammy's still his son, right?"

"Sometimes when people make mistakes in life," Marc said, "it seems easier to let the past hide them than to face the consequences and unresolved conflicts. Sometimes that's where those mistakes stay, but not always. Sometimes God has his way of bringing them to light in his time."

Gillian peered into Marc's eyes. He was, of course, referring to Dr. Colbert's adultery and Sammy—the consequence—but she was thinking of Gabriel's abandonment.

She was glad God had brought Gabriel back into her life. Although the emotions weren't easy to deal with, the old conflict, the old sore, had never healed. But knowing more about his situation had made her realize that she'd made mistakes, too. She'd allowed resentment and bitterness to fester in her emotions, even though she'd made a conscious, objective decision to forgive Gabriel. Now she could release him, even though she'd already forgiven him in her heart. She hoped to tell him so.

"And sometimes"—she met Crystal's eyes—"when the past buries those mistakes, the truth gets buried too. Sometimes people spend their whole lives angry with someone because of a past misunderstanding." She shook her head. "God doesn't want us living that way. Believe me, the resentment can eat away at us like a cancer."

Someone knocked on the door, and it opened. Gillian gasped.

A tall, thin man with a full head of white hair lumbered into the room. A short, plump woman with gray-streaked black hair followed him in, her expression tentative.

The man said, "We heard the story on the news and had to come see for ourselves."

"Mom!" Marc's voice cracked. "Dad!"

The elder Thayers crossed the room and embraced the son they hadn't seen or barely spoken to in too many years to count. *Sometimes it takes a near-death experience to draw estranged people together,* Gillian mused. Marc's eyes filled with tears, and Gillian felt her own filling and overflowing. God had done a miracle this day, restoring loved ones she'd thought were lost.

Crystal and Emily retreated to give Ted and Rosemary room to sit and talk and coo over baby Chase, the grandson they were meeting for the first time. In only a moment, the years seemed to vanish away, and Gillian felt like they'd never been apart.

110

Drawing was his way of coping. Hers was immersing herself in the psalms.

Lacey lay in her hospital bed, Bible open on her lap, the truth settling in that she was now alone with her autistic son to raise. Could Quinn really be gone? The thought seemed impossible to comprehend. She kept glancing at the door, expecting him to walk in at any moment.

But it wasn't to be.

History had indeed repeated itself. The old mine that had once been closed because it was too unstable was now too unstable for Quinn's body to be recovered, according to Deputy Moyers. The bodies of 41 men, lost in 1926, had never been reclaimed. Now she supposed there were 42.

Even if the old mine was crammed with gold, she doubted anyone would ever be able to claim it. Then again, maybe the government would get involved and use the gold to help pay off the national debt. One could only hope.

God, how am I going to do this on my own? What's ahead for me now? How are you going to lead us?

She wished she'd told Quinn about Dr. Colbert being Sammy's father. Now Quinn would never know the truth.

In the bed next to her, Sammy was back to his drawing as if nothing had happened to interrupt their lives. The more she realized how Sammy had helped save those people, the more she realized that autism didn't make him any less a child with value.

He did something truly amazing. What other plans did God have in mind for her little guy?

She recalled Sammy's sketch of the man with the red spots on his face. Had Sammy really intended the man in the sketch to be Sheriff Griswold? If so, how had he known what was going to happen before it did?

Perhaps the drawing had been only a coincidence. Maybe, as Quinn had said, Sammy had only been copying the book about the plagues. Maybe, but maybe not. Maybe her son was gifted in more ways than anyone realized.

She glanced down at Sammy's latest creation. The nurse had been kind enough to ferry the drawings back and forth. Sammy had drawn a blue sky with fluffy, white clouds. In the center of the clouds stood a golden house with yellow rays shining from it.

"Is this heaven, Sammy?" she called.

He didn't answer, but she felt like she understood him well enough by now. He didn't seem sad at all. Did he really understand that his father was gone?

Lacey studied the drawing and sighed. *Maybe Quinn has found his gold after all.*

EPILOGUE

—Two weeks later

"Want another s'more, Mom?" Crystal Thayer swung her metal stick away from the bonfire and toward Gillian's face. The black thing clinging to the end bore no resemblance to a marshmallow.

Gillian grimaced. "Uh, no thanks. It's all yours."

"I just know how you *love* 'em charred."

Ryan, Crystal's boyfriend, tall and dark on a lawn chair beside her, snickered.

"You're such a tease." Gillian reached for one of the metal sticks. "Let me show you how it's done, sweetie. You want your marshmallow—"

"—slightly brown on the outside and warm and gooey on the inside. Yeah, I know. Go ahead, Martha Stewart. Show us how it's done."

So Gillian did.

After the lesson, Gillian leaned her head back in the Adirondack chair and relished the heat and glow of the bonfire washing over her. Logs crackled. Tongues of fire licked into the night sky, where stars pulsed and reminded her of God's many promises.

Marc squeezed her hand, and she smiled at him, so glad to have him close and safe. They'd just spent a week together at another resort—this time without interruption. She loved this man and wished she could stay by his side always.

Before her stretched Lake Superior, its gentle waves sparkling under the moonlight. If she'd glanced over her right shoulder, she would have seen the Whistler's Point lighthouse, where she and Marc had served as temporary staff a few years ago. It was always a nice place to visit, and a bonfire on the beach seemed like the perfect way to end an August evening with some friends.

Gillian adjusted her left leg, which was outstretched on a lawn chair, trying to make it more comfortable.

"Still hurts, doesn't it?" Lacey asked.

"Yeah. It's been two weeks! I thought I'd be over this by now."

"Gunshot wounds take time."

"Yeah, and don't I know it. Go ahead, call me a whiner. Your wound probably hurts worse than mine anyhow."

Lacey chuckled. "Only when I breathe."

"Which is always, right? But hey, at least you're alive."

Which was more than she could say for Austin Turrow and Lacey's husband, Quinn.

Gillian bit her lip, regretting the reminder her words must have aroused. She craned her neck and peered into the distance. Sammy and Dr. Colbert had strolled off somewhere and were now out of sight, exploring the rocky shoreline. Father and son together, just the way it was meant to be. Tomorrow, her friend Nicole would give them and Lacey a full tour of the lighthouse.

She glanced at Chase, who had fallen fast asleep in his stroller. She should try to keep him awake so he would sleep better later, but she didn't have the heart to rouse him.

The patter of feet on wet sand jerked Gillian's head around. Dr. Colbert ran toward them. "Hey, Sammy found some weird fossil in the sand. You should all come see."

Marc, Crystal, and Ryan rose to follow him. Marc glanced back. "You coming, Gill?"

"Crutches and sand aren't exactly the best of friends. You go on ahead."

He cast a probing glance. "You okay?"

"Fine. Just thinking—that's all."

She watched them go, saw how her daughter lingered close to Ryan's side, their arms brushing. Sadness swelled in her heart. Crystal wasn't her little girl anymore. In just a few weeks she would be off to college, and no doubt wedding bells were inevitable at some point considering how her relationship with Ryan had blossomed over the last few years. Just not too soon. Crystal needed to finish college first—that was their firm rule.

Dr. Colbert appeared at the fire's edge. "You coming, Lacey?"

"I guess I better. My doctor says I should move around as much as possible. I'll need someone to lean on, though."

"I'd be happy to oblige." He offered her his hand like a gentleman.

They left her alone to face the flames, and she wondered about Lacey's future. Lacey would grieve Quinn's loss for a while, but Dr. Colbert appeared attentive. Maybe there was a future there, but not just yet. Could God take a relationship born in sin and make something beautiful out of it? Could God take her once-immoral relationship with Gabriel and turn it into a godly friendship?

God could do whatever he wanted to, yet she knew what Marc would tell her if she asked. Extending forgiveness to Gabriel didn't necessarily equal a continuing relationship. If they still had feelings for each other, it was best not to leave the door open. They'd made their peace, yet staying in touch probably wasn't the best idea.

Marc had agreed to her idea of inviting Gabriel and his family to join them for the beach party, but Gabriel had politely declined. In his lengthy e-mail, he had again apologized for hurting her and said he hoped she could forgive him someday.

What's done in the past cannot be changed or erased. But God has forgiven us, Gillian, and removed our sins as far as the east is from the west. What's important is moving forward. We've both changed, and now we can move on with our lives, free from the hurts and bitterness of the past.

Thank you for the invitation to the beach party, but I decided to decline for the simple reason that it's just not smart for us to reconnect, considering the relationship we once had and possible risks. I hope you understand. We need to grow in our love for the spouses God has given to us. By the way, Marc's a good man. I'm so glad God gave him to you.

Maybe in time God will help you grow stronger, and you'll learn to think of me as a brother in Christ who's moving forward in spite of past mistakes. We serve a God of second chances, don't we? I hope I'll be in your prayers as much as you'll be in mine. Take care.

At the bottom of the e-mail he'd insisted that he hadn't sent the old love letter to Marc. Of course, that was old news, now that she knew the truth.

When she was in the hospital, Holly, Gabriel's mom, had come to town to visit her injured son. During her visit, she'd dropped by unexpectedly with a certain stack of letters and postcards bound together by a single rubber band. Now, Gillian pulled them out of the bag beside her chair and studied them in the flickering light, remembering their conversation.

Please, take them before my husband causes any more trouble.

You mean—

Gabriel's wife called us. My husband found out you were staying at the resort and mailed that old letter to your husband while he was on a business trip. But don't be too hard on him—I think he had good intentions. He meant to warn Marc so he'd intervene in case Gabriel got any ideas about you. Either way, these letters belong to you. They always have.

Now Gillian pulled out the first thing her fingers touched—an old postcard to Gabriel that Gillian had sent when she was touring Washington, DC, with her parents. She remembered the trip well, the beautiful cherry trees blossoming at the Jefferson Memorial.

She began reading and stopped, emotions reeling. Heat rushed to her face as she reencountered her flirtatious, immature words. She returned the postcard to the stack and made a decision.

She sighed, eyes on the flames, and remembered words from Lewis B. Smedes in *The Art of Forgiving*: "Forgiving does not erase the bitter past. A healed memory is not a deleted memory. Instead, forgiving what we cannot forget creates a new way to remember."

A new way to remember.

What was the point of revisiting an immoral romance that never should have taken place? Why remember the lost, shallow person she had been at the time? God had saved her from that lifestyle and later saved her soul. By God's grace, she was no longer the same person.

That person had died, crucified with Christ.

Old things had passed away, and new things had come.

By God's grace.

In one quick motion Gillian tossed the bundle into the fire, rubber band and all. The flames licked up hungrily, consuming the remnants of a life she had no desire to remember. God no more saw those old sins from her past than she saw those old letters.

Soon they were gone, ashes scattered on the wind. They couldn't hurt her or anyone else ever again.

She closed her tear-filled eyes and leaned her head back, at last feeling at peace. She whispered a prayer of thanks to God for forgiving her for old resentments. She thanked him for her redeemed life. For her husband. For her children.

And, most of all, for being a God who never lets go.

ACKNOWLEDGMENTS

Once again, I relied on the wisdom, encouragement, and advice of so many folks during the researching and writing of this novel. Special thanks to:

My family, who often offered an encouraging word just when I needed it. A special word of gratitude to my wife, Kim, for encouraging me on this unpredictable roller coaster called publishing. Without you I would have given up long ago. Special thanks to my mom, Rhoda Blumer, and my in-laws, Dick and Mary Melzer, for their consistent love and affirmation. Who needs a marketing department when I have you folks to sell my books? Also thanks to my daughters, Laura and Julia, who often came to Daddy's office, bearing encouraging gifts. Your smiles and hugs (and treats) were just what I needed.

My long-suffering beta readers for their gentle and encouraging advice during those important formative stages: Kim Blumer, Art and Deb Brammer, Michael Coley, Philip Crossman, Rick Dobrowolski, Brenda Strohbehn, and Laura and Rick Wright.

Aaron Blumer, Art Brammer, Dave Coats, Rick Dobrowolski, and Curt Lamansky, who helped me better see the theological implications of my story. If I compromised accuracy in any way, it was unintentional and strictly of my own doing.

The following who helped me better understand the sticky and sometimes-confusing issues of adoption: Ruth Christison, Sandy Sperrazza, and Josh and Loraena Tuttle.

Natalie Everson, Kelly Langston, and Susan Lawrence, who shared their knowledge about working with autistic children.

Thomas G. Friggens, author of *No Tears in Heaven: The 1926 Barnes-Hecker Mine Disaster*, who shares my desire to be historically accurate. He kindly looked over my prologue and straightened out a few details related to the true and heartbreaking story I dramatized there.

E. W. Bullinger's fascinating book, *Number in Scripture* (Grand Rapids: Kregel, 1967), which provided fascinating information about the number ten.

Jason Curtman, law enforcement instructor and consultant, who took the time to answer my questions about police procedure in the context of my story.

Matt Reuhl, Doug Burman, and Edward Bolme, for their military advice.

Others who provided general advice and encouragement along the way: Rick Barry, Andrea Boeshaar, Deb Brammer, Mike Dellosso, Susan Donetti, Diana Flegal, Rachelle Gardner, Graham Garrison, Heather Day Gilbert, Patti Lacy, Richard Mabry, Chip MacGregor, Susan Marlow, Beth Murschell, and Chris Solaas. A special thank you to my former literary agent, Terry Burns of Hartline Literary Agency, for his advice and extra effort in seeking a publishing home.

My Kregel friends who, though unable to pick up this project, provided valuable support: Steve Barclift, Dennis Hillman, and Janyre Tromp. Janyre especially went beyond the call of duty in helping me see where my true story lay.

My Kirkdale Press friends for taking a chance: Kyle Fuller, Justin Marr, Bethany Olsen, Ryan Rotz, Abigail Stocker, and Elizabeth Vince. Also many thanks to Jim LePage for his work on the cover design and to Liz Donovan for designing the back cover.

God, the shaper and enabler of dreams. May the Lord receive the glory!